TEMPTING THE *Tight End*

LISA SUZANNE

TEMPTING THE TIGHT END
© LISA SUZANNE 2024

Published in the United States of America by Books by LS, LLC.

ISBN: 978-1-963772-12-8

This book is a work of fiction. Any similarities to real people, living or dead, is purely coincidental. All characters and events in this work are figments of the author's imagination.

Books by Lisa Suzanne

THE NASH BROTHERS
Dating the Defensive Back
Wedding the Wide Receiver

VEGAS ACES
Home Game (Book One)
Long Game (Book Two)
Fair Game (Book Three)
Waiting Game (Book Four)
End Game (Book Five)

VEGAS ACES: THE QUARTERBACK
Traded (Book One)
Tackled (Book Two)
Timeout (Book Three)
Turnover (Book Four)
Touchdown (Book Five)

VEGAS ACES: THE TIGHT END
Tight Spot (Book One)
Tight Hold (Book Two)
Tight Fit (Book Three)
Tight Laced (Book Four)
Tight End (Book Five)

Visit Lisa on Amazon for more titles

Dedication

To the three people who make me smile every day.

Chapter 1: Asher Nash

I Fucking Love Wild, Unpredictable, Spontaneous Asher Nash

I glance up at the scoreboard as the two-minute warning is upon us.

We only have two minutes left, and we're tied. But we don't have the ball.

This is it. The Forty-Niners either force overtime or try to win, and they're not going to give us the chance to beat them.

I'm right. They take it down the field. They run the clock down to three seconds, and if the kicker succeeds in getting the ball through the goal posts, they win. We lose.

My chest is tight as I watch helplessly from my position on the sidelines.

This is it. We've worked our asses off to get to this point, but so have they.

I feel it slipping away.

It's my first full season playing on the Vegas Aces, and it's about to end one game too early.

The ball is snapped to the holder, who spins it so the laces face out. The kicker sprints toward it, plants his foot, swings his other foot, and extends it after making contact with the ball.

The ball sails through the center of the goalposts, giving the Forty-Niners the victory with no time left on the clock to give us a chance.

Desolation fills me. Over the next few days, we'll be told what a great season we had. There's always next year. We worked hard.

All the shit that doesn't give us the win.

It should have been us celebrating on our home turf. Instead, it's them.

I shake my head in disgust. It was a team effort. We made some mistakes, but we played hard. We played to win. We just didn't pull it through.

And now we get a little time off.

Unofficial workouts off-site start next week, but I don't know if I'll go.

I'm not really close with anyone on my team except my brother Grayson, who is probably about to announce his retirement, and my other brother, Lincoln, who's the head coach. I don't have the respect of my teammates because of a stupid lack of judgment I made a year and a half ago that cost me an entire season on the field.

And because of that, even tonight, I think I'll probably head home after the game rather than out with the guys. I'm not really in a party kind of mood tonight, anyway.

I beeline for my bedroom as soon as I'm home so I don't have to face the jeers of my father, who, in a strange twist of fate, is my roommate, and in the morning, I head out before he's up.

I get to the practice facility long before exit interviews begin, and I clean out my locker. I get in one more workout. Most guys start showing up a little before ten, when our team meeting begins, and they look hungover after staying out far too late.

And it's only a few minutes later that I stare at my brother as I try to make sense of his words, but I'm failing.

Lincoln Nash, head coach of the pro football team I play for and my oldest brother, just told the entire team the morning after a season-ending loss that our offensive coordinator took a head coaching position for another team.

The OC is leaving, and he's taking his playbook with him—the playbook we've worked our asses off to memorize and execute this season.

League rules state he couldn't interview until our season was over, and he already took a new job this morning.

He can't rip the plays we've memorized over the last two years from our brains, but he *can* take his plays and move elsewhere.

I'm sure Lincoln is happy. He never got along with our former OC since Mike's plays leaned on the conservative side. Lincoln is a risk-taker on the field, and I grew up worshipping his shadow.

When he scored the head coaching job here in Vegas, he pulled me from Indianapolis to play for his team. But then I did something stupid, got myself suspended for an entire season, and let him down.

I've been back a full year now, though, and still, the chatter hasn't faded.

People think I'm only here because my brother got me here. I intend to prove them wrong, and I will do that by working my ass off to show that I belong here.

One more win and we'd be playing in two weeks at the big game. Instead, we'll be sipping mai tais on a beach somewhere…or something along those lines. I guess we've all got different plans for the offseason.

Mine is to duck out of town for a few weeks, and then…I'm not sure.

But maybe my offseason will include more playbook memorization than I'd been planning since someone new will swoop in with his ideas. Maybe he'll be good enough to lead us past the conference championship game next year. Time will tell.

"It's been an honor being your head coach for a second straight season, and I pledge to all of you here with us today that with Jack and Steve's help, we will find the best replacement for Coach Sharp that we can possibly find," Lincoln says, naming the team owner and the general manager. "We'll find someone that'll help guide us past the conference championship so we can contend for a ring."

My brother's impassioned speech is met with cheers all around as he makes the claim that was in my head.

We might all feel a sense of disappointment in the end of a season, but Linc's great at leaving us with that *there's always next year* feeling. We made it far, and there's no shame or disappointment in that.

I glance around at everyone gathered here. This meeting room won't look the same come July's training camp. The people will change. Moves are yet to be made in the offseason, and apparently the OC was the first.

"You throw any money on this game?" Austin Graham asks me once the meeting's over. He's bitter because he's also a tight end who isn't as good as me, and so he spends more time on the sidelines than on the field, but he likes to think it's because our head coach is related to me rather than the difference in our skill set.

I'm about to open my mouth to defend myself when my other brother, Grayson, walks by. "Fuck off with that shit, Graham." Grayson isn't a fan of Austin, either. I guess he hit on Gray's girl a while back. It's complicated, but I don't need my brother sticking up for me.

"I can handle it," I mutter to Grayson, but the truth is that I was suspended my first season here in Vegas for betting on the outcome of games *for my dad*, and even though I served my punishment, I'm still paying for the sin.

I'm not sure I'll ever live it down, but I intend to make a new name for myself.

I worked hard this season to rise above the gossip and shed the reputation that I walked in here with before last season even got underway, but it looks like it didn't matter since a year and a half after the offense, it's still being thrown in my face.

I guess that means I still have work to do.

I kept my nose clean this season. I ditched the wild, unpredictable nature I've always had and forced my spontaneity into a box. I put my full focus into the season, and now that I have an entire one under my belt with the Aces, I'll work on stepping up into leadership roles wherever I can—provided it doesn't look like my brother is giving me preferential treatment.

Playing for Lincoln was too good to be true. Hindsight tells me that now.

I never should've agreed to come here. Even without the scandal of getting caught betting on games when I was betting for us to win and in no way threw games in either direction, I never had a chance to make a name for myself that wasn't going to be overshadowed by the fact that two of the Nash brothers were on the same team for the first time. Add Grayson into the mix as another Nash brother on the same team, and I don't even get the chance to stand up for myself to assholes like Austin.

Hindsight also tells me that I can't win no matter what I do. If I play like shit, I don't deserve to be here. If I play well, I got lucky.

At least in Indy, I could be a leader without people thinking it's because I have an *in* with the coach. I was never deemed old enough to be a leader back then, but now I'm twenty-eight. I've been playing in the league since I was twenty-two, barring that one season I was forced to sit out.

But nothing I do on that field is ever chalked up to my own skills. It's always because of my goddamn last name.

I can't change my name, though, and I learned that a long time ago. Rather than try to change it, I'll do what I can to live up to it.

And now that the offseason has officially begun, maybe it's time to go back to wild, unpredictable, spontaneous Asher Nash. I fucking love that guy.

Chapter 2: Desiree Dixon

All the Things Vegas Doesn't Have

"When I got to that last page and the rock star was on top of her *in his own brother's bed*, I literally threw the book across the room," Chloe says. "And then I glared at the book and shook my finger at it when I walked by. That'll teach it."

I giggle. "Good thing it was a book and not a TV show."

"And good thing the next book is already out," Addy adds. "I already downloaded it. I'm actually on book three now." She makes a cringy face of apology.

"God, you read fast," Lauren says.

And that's it—the four of us who make up our little book club.

We meet every other week and rotate who's hosting, and this week it happens to be me. We're at the apartment I share with Addy, the girl who has been my roommate and best friend since our freshman year of college, and this week we're talking about the juicy first book in a love triangle trilogy.

"Speaking of being on top of someone in a bed, how are things with Carter?" Chloe asks Lauren.

It always starts with book talk, snacks, and booze, and it inevitably turns to gossip, snacks, and booze. It's one of the things I love most about being one of the Fearless Four.

Lauren laughs at her sister's question. "It's still just physical. He's hot and good with his hands, but I'm pretty sure the connection ends there." She taps her temple as if to say he has nothing up in his head.

"Too bad," Chloe laments. "I was hoping you'd marry him so I could look at him every Thanksgiving dinner."

"He has a brother," Lauren says.

"Single?" Chloe, Addy, and I all ask at the same time.

Lauren nods.

"Dibs!" Chloe yells first, and more laughter makes its way around the room.

"But gay," Lauren finishes.

"Dammit!" Chloe curses, and she grabs another pretzel bite and dips it in the cheese sauce. "I guess I'll just continue to live vicariously through book boyfriends." She glances at me. "Unless Desi's dad can hook us up with some tight ends."

I make a face. "He won't even hook *me* up with one of them." I roll my eyes. "Life's so unfair sometimes." My dad is the tight end coach for the San Diego Storm, and he's also incredibly overprotective of me—which is why I moved in with Addy after graduation three years ago instead of moving back home with my parents.

And it *is* unfair. It's unfair and unfortunate that my dad has access to all these amazing men who I root for on a weekly basis, but they won't so much as *look* at me because he's adamant that no player of his will touch his daughter.

I'm twenty-freaking-five now. I can make my own decisions. But he says I can do better than a football player who's only around half the time. This stems from the fact that the last football player I dated broke my heart, and combined with the fact that I guess he sees things I don't, I try to believe he's overprotective out of a place of love rather than control.

"So unfair," Addy agrees. We both laugh at the ridiculousness of the conversation.

"What about Braden?" I ask Addy.

A little smile graces her lips, but it's Chloe who answers for her. "I saw the two of them walking down the hallway together the other day. I think she's getting somewhere!"

"Shut up," Addy says petulantly, shooting a glare at her colleague at the middle school where they met. Addy has a huge crush on Braden, and they've been flirting with each other for the entire school year, but he has yet to make a move.

"Maybe *you* should make the first move," I suggest to her.

She wrinkles her nose. "That's so not me."

"Step out of your comfort zone. Live a little," I say.

"I'm not like you," she protests. She's more of a stay-in-on-a-weekend-to-read kind of girl, while my preferred way to spend my weekends is either being active outdoors, taking pictures, or partying. Those interests led me toward the career path of party planning, and I've landed the title of junior event planner at one of San Diego's most exclusive venues.

Someday, I'd love to drop the *junior* title. Someday, I'd love to be my own boss and run my own events. But right now, I'm still learning. I love what I do, and I love my friends, and I love my life exactly how it is.

There's only one thing missing, and it's a hot football player. I mean a *man* who's smart and good with his hands. Someone who will sweep me off my feet like those boys we read about in books who don't seem to exist in real life.

I don't need a man to be happy. I have a vibrator that gets the job done, but I wouldn't mind a friend with benefits. Someone who I can turn to at the end of a long day for both sex and conversation without the side of commitment.

It's harder to find than you'd think.

We gossip a little longer, and then Chloe yawns. "Sorry, but I gotta be up and at 'em early tomorrow for a parent meeting before school." She glances at her sister. "You ready?"

We always meet on Wednesdays since I'm usually working weekends, and this upcoming weekend is no different. I have a retirement party on Friday, a wedding on Saturday, and a quinceañera on Sunday.

Lauren stands and stretches. "I have an early day, too. My first client is coming in at nine thirty for a color and cut."

"Nine thirty isn't early," Chloe points out.

"It is when you're planning to spend the night on top of Carter," Lauren says, and we all laugh as we walk to the door to say our goodbyes.

"I need to go finish book three. Sweet dreams," Addy says after she helps me pick up the family room where our appetizers and drinks were left abandoned.

"Enjoy. No spoilers," I warn, and she laughs as she gives me a thumbs-up and heads to bed.

The events over the weekend go off without a hitch—except for the wedding where the priest was twenty minutes late—and I find myself at my weekly Tuesday night dinner with my mom and dad.

"What do you think of Vegas?" my dad asks. He keeps his voice low since we're at a restaurant and anyone could be listening.

"Vegas?" I repeat. "I love the vibe there, but I've never visited. Why do you ask?"

My dad's eyes edge to my mom, and then he lays the truth on me. "They have an OC position open, so I interviewed."

I gasp. "You…you *what*?" My voice is louder than it should be given that we're in a restaurant and he's trying to be quiet.

He presses his lips together and nods. "And it went well, thanks for asking."

Oh, right. Etiquette and all that. I clear my throat. "How well?"

"They offered, and about an hour before dinner, I accepted."

My jaw drops clear to the floor. I am without words.

"Your mother and I are moving to Vegas, and we'd love for you to come, too." He says the words for her, and I guess we've gotten lucky that my dad played for the Storm for years, and when it was time to hang it up, he moved into coaching with the same team. Working in the sports industry means your job could be gone just like that, but we've been in the same area of San Diego for my entire life.

And now, poof. They're moving.

I can't move. My life is here. My friends, my career, my entire livelihood. It's all I've ever known, and I'm making a name for myself in the event planning industry. I can't just take off for Vegas.

I glance at my mom to see what she thinks of all this. She's never been very good at hiding what she's thinking, and she shifts her gaze away from me so I don't catch onto her real thoughts. But he's not letting her speak, and when he does that, it's because they're not in agreement about something.

"Mom, is this what you want?" I ask.

She clears her throat. "It's your father's dream job, honey. Of course it's what I want. And Vegas has palm trees like home but with slot machines, all the food…plus probably thousands of events every weekend. I'm sure you could find something in event planning there."

She's probably right about that, but I don't want to find something there. Vegas doesn't have Addy, Chloe, and Lauren. It doesn't have the beach. It doesn't have the Storm. What, I'm supposed to become an Aces fan because my dad has a job there when I've bled black and silver my entire existence? No fucking way.

If I'm in Vegas, I don't get to sing the Storm's fight song on my home field anymore. It'll be some trendy Vegas song at the Aces stadium instead. Fuck that.

"I'm staying here," I say, and I keep my voice firm and resolute.

My dad nods, and my mom looks disappointed.

"We do hope you'll come visit," my dad says.

"Of course." I'm not sure when they're moving, and I'm not sure when I'll have a break to visit, but I'd love to swing by and check out Vegas.

You know…someday.

Chapter 3: Desiree Dixon

A Mural He Can Point To

"You haven't taken a day off in the last year, Desi. This is your father's first major event, and you should be there," Bea says.

Bea is my boss's secretary, and I know she's right. I also know if Bea is saying it, it's because she's repeating my boss, Angelica.

I sigh. The Vegas Aces announced my father as their new offensive coordinator nearly four months ago, and my parents moved there immediately. They bought a house, and I haven't been out to see it yet. I keep citing work as my reason, but the truth is that I could do my job in my sleep most days. Every event is unique and different, but I'm a *junior* event planner, so everything I do gets approved and overridden by Angelica anyway.

I love my job…most days. But some days—like today—it feels like one frustration after another as I'm on the line for our clients to scream at while Angelica gets to swoop in with *my* solutions as if *she* is the hero here.

I'm tired of that piece of it, and I know if I were working for myself, I wouldn't have those issues. But I'm not, and it's important to me that I learn from an expert in the field so I can build my empire from the ground up rather than throwing money into something I'm still learning.

My dad thinks I should start my own company. My mom agrees. I saw the way they looked around the tiny two-bedroom places Addy and I were looking at when we first graduated from college, but it was all we could afford on our salaries. I'm their only child, and their only wish is to spoil me, which is why they pay the monthly rent at an upscale place right on the water in San Diego.

And that's why I text my mom after Bea convinces me to go.

Me: *My boss gave me tomorrow through Monday off. Can I come visit?*

Mom: *Of course! I'll call up Vicki for the plane ticket.*

Vicki is her travel agent, and an hour later, a first-class plane ticket to Vegas leaving early tomorrow morning appears in my email.

Me: *Thanks, Mom. Can't wait to see you.*

Mom: *Fly safe. I'll arrange for a car service to bring you home.*

Me: *I'm fine with a Lyft.*

Mom: *Just let me do this for you. [smiley face]*

At noon the next day, the car she sent for me pulls up to a gorgeous mansion with palm trees lining the sidewalk leading to the front door. I step out into the dry ninety-eight degrees of mid-June in Vegas, weather I'm not used to back home since we live near the humid beach, and the driver gets my suitcase for me.

I knock on the rather large wooden front door, and my mom opens it a minute later. "Desiree Joy, I've missed you so!" she says, pulling me into a hug.

We've never gone four months without seeing each other. Ever.

But I've also never been twenty-five and living in a different city from my parents, either.

I sigh as she holds me a few extra beats, and then she invites me in.

"Dad's at work. Let me show you around and then we can head to the Shops at Crystals and find you a gown."

"Sounds good. The event is tomorrow?" I ask.

She nods. "The annual Vegas Aces Charity Ball. I booked salon appointments for us this afternoon and tomorrow morning. Dad was able to secure a last-minute ticket for you, but I don't think you'll be at our table."

"It'll be fine. I'll make friends." I'm fairly outgoing most of the time, and I've never been intimidated by football players since I grew up around them.

But I have to be honest here. I don't know many players on the Aces. They're not in our division or our conference, so we don't regularly play against them.

And I kind of like that fact. They won't know me either, unless my dad has a picture of me in his office...which definitely seems like something he'd do. Maybe a full-length mural so he can point to me and tell them to stay away.

But with my dad here now, hopefully I'll get to know some of the players—at least through watching the games from my couch back in San Diego, probably late Sunday nights since I'm usually working on Sundays.

My mom shows me around the seven-bedroom mansion that's just for the two of them, and it's...a lot. Way more than they need, but they love nothing more than to show off their money.

The money didn't come from my dad's playing days. Player contracts weren't worth half of what they are now, and his more recent position as a position coach didn't pay all that much, though the OC position came with more money.

My mother hails from the fortune of the Berkshire line of luxury hotels. In the early 1900s, my mom's grandfather purchased a local hotel in Los Angeles that became one of the most popular hotels around. Over a hundred years later, Berkshire boasts fourteen different brands of hotels and over five thousand locations worldwide.

When I graduated from college, I was offered a position on the executive board. I declined, and my parents were devastated since I'm the sole heiress to the Berkshire fortune.

But I can still be the heiress without being on the board. Hotels don't interest me other than as a place to stay, and it's not like my mom serves on the board any longer, either.

"Who will be at your table?" I ask.

"Oh, the defensive coordinator, head coach, and general manager. Plus their wives." She lifts a shoulder.

"Have you made friends with all these people?"

"A bit with Barb Shanahan," she says. When she sees my quirked brows that definitely tell on me that I have no idea who that is, she clarifies. "The general manager's wife."

"Ah. And the others?"

"We're quite a bit older than the others. The head coach isn't even in his forties yet, though he and his wife are a lovely couple. And the defensive coordinator is great, too. Your father has gotten close with everyone here already, but you know how he is."

I do. He's social, which is where I get that trait, while my mom leans toward the quieter side—likely as a means of protection since as soon as people know who she is, they want every detail about how much money she has in the bank. But my dad makes friends wherever he goes, and I think it's one of the things my mom fell for when she went against her parents' wishes and married the bad boy football player.

Though I'll be honest, my nose scrunches up in disgust every time she calls him that.

I settle into the bedroom my parents chose for me, and then we head toward the CityCenter complex for shopping and pampering.

We return home relaxed after a massage, facial, manicure, and pedicure, and my dad is there waiting for us.

So is the personal chef my mom hired when they moved in here.

I hug my dad and greet the chef, and my dad and I plop onto the couch as we wait for dinner.

"How's it going with the Aces?" I ask.

"It's been great so far. I'm working as a team with the coach and the GM, and the three of us are drafting up the kind of playbook I've always dreamed of."

I laugh.

"What?" he asks.

I shake my head. "No, it's just...we have very different dreams, I guess." Mine tend to be about my book boyfriends swooping in with the ultimate fantasy, not that I'd admit that to my dad.

He narrows his eyes at me. "Let's not go there. I got to test out some of the plays this week with our mandatory minicamp, and it's been everything I was hoping for. The players are receptive, the coaching staff is welcoming...it's been incredible."

"I'm happy for you. But I miss you two and our Tuesday night dinners."

He reaches over and squeezes my knee playfully, and I bat his hand away as he laughs. It's our thing.

"We miss you, too, Desi-doo."

I went through a Scooby Doo phase when I was a kid, and the nickname stuck.

"Are you okay all by yourself back home?" he asks.

I nod. "Of course I'm okay. I've got work plus Addy, Chloe, and Lauren. I'm keeping busy and allowing some time for fun."

He smirks at me. "Not *too* much fun, though, right?"

I roll my eyes. "Of course not." He doesn't need to know what I do in my spare time. My entire life, he's issued cautionary tales about behaving myself, but sometimes I don't *want* to behave.

My mom has the makeup artists and hairstylists over to the house to help us get ready for tonight, and I slide into my gown, a strapless, gold embroidered leaf pattern over sheer tulle that offers peeks of skin. I pair it with strappy stilettos and check myself in the mirror. My red hair is curled into loose waves, and I feel pretty in this dress, like the golden color is a warm complement to my fair skin, bright hair, and green eyes.

I feel *ready*. Ready to meet my dad's players. Ready to party. Ready to let go and have a little fun.

And fun always starts with shots—just maybe not when I'm with Mom and Dad.

My parents are gorgeous in their dressy fits when I walk down to meet them in the foyer, and my dad shakes his head as his eyes fall on me while I descend the staircase. "I don't know if this is such a good idea."

I shrug. "I'm here, and I'm ready, so it's too late to pull the protective dad card now."

He sighs as I reach the bottom step, and he slings an arm around me. "You're too good for them, Desi-Doo." His voice is soft.

"I know, I know. And I promise to behave myself." I cross my fingers behind my back, just in case.

I'm not going to embarrass him or anything, but I'm in Vegas. Sin City. The Entertainment Capital of the World.

What happens here doesn't *have* to stay here, and I plan on having one hell of a good time tonight so I have some stories to bring back home with me.

Chapter 4: Asher Nash

Dirty. Extra Dirty.

I tug at my collar as I give myself a once-over.

Good enough, I guess.

I wouldn't even go to this stupid thing tonight if my brother wasn't one of the chairmen of the event, but since he's not *just* my brother but also my head coach, I kind of *have* to go.

Lincoln will be there with his wife, Jolene. My parents will both be there, along with my brother Grayson and his wife, Ava. It's a family affair, with the exception of my other brother, Spencer, who is in San Diego as he starts his season with a new team.

And so I'm sort of going under protest, which is why I chose threads that would annoy my brothers to no end. It's honestly what motivates me to make the majority of my fashion choices—that and trying to lighten the mood around me. Ever try to have a serious conversation with someone when you're wearing a shirt covered in cat faces? Works *almost* every time.

I kept it more subtle tonight than usual, anyway—at least in terms of animal print. I chose a paisley gold jacket and paired it with a white shirt and sand-colored pants.

My hair is done in my usual *rolled-out-of-bed-this-way* style, though honestly, I spent a good fifteen minutes making it look this good.

I meet my dad in my kitchen. He sort of fell from grace with some scandals over the last few years, and when he and my mom got divorced, he asked if we should live together. I didn't have a great reason to say no since it was around the same time I was suspended.

It's not like my bank account is padded, exactly. I lost an entire year of income during that suspension. I'm not smart and responsible with money like Spencer, and I'm not a natural leader like Lincoln. I'm not the social guy who brings the party with him everywhere he goes like Grayson.

I'm Asher. I'm the youngest and fastest of the four Nash brothers, and I'm the adventurous risk-taker who sometimes makes impulsive decisions but *almost* always comes out on top.

I hate it when people call me Ash Nash, and I hate it even more when people call me Asher Nasher.

I don't mind having a roommate, but having a roommate who's also my dad can get…annoying. He doesn't care who I bring back, but when I walk a woman out of my bedroom in the morning only for her to run into *my dad*, things can get awkward.

So I've taken to finding alternative places to hook up.

It's been a while since the last time I hooked up with somebody, though, and I'm getting restless. I guess I've always been labeled a player, but I've had a front row seat to watch all three of my brothers settle down over the last couple years, and that sort of makes me feel like I'm next.

The problem is, well, I live with my dad.

Not because he's a cockblock but because of other things.

For one, he instilled in all four of his sons that the game of football comes first above all else. He made the *mistake*—his words—of knocking Mom up with Lincoln when they were young, and he didn't like being tied down when he had a game to focus on. Four years later, Grayson came along…so it couldn't have been *all* bad. But still, he made it clear that kids make everything harder, and he seemed to blame Lincoln for that. It's probably why Lincoln waited until he was thirty-six to have his first kid, and that *still* seems far too soon to me.

And for another thing, after forty years of marriage, my parents got divorced.

They were much younger than my current age of twenty-eight when they first met, so maybe they didn't have the best decision-making skills. But that didn't give them the happy ending they were hoping for, and I guess that left their four boys with scars.

It left me with some, anyway.

Maybe it doesn't affect the others the way it does me. Since I'm the youngest, I was around for more of the stage where things started to fall apart. Lincoln's nine years older than me, so he was already playing in the NFL by the time I hit puberty.

And I guess watching it fall apart made me see that commitment really isn't for me.

I think it also made me see that sometimes walking away is easier than dealing with conflict. And that's not the kind of personality trait that does well when it comes to commitment.

I'm not picking sides, but if I were, I'd choose Mom's. My dad can be a dick, but mostly we're a couple of single dudes having a good time. On my dime, usually, but it's a small sacrifice to make given the fact that he's my dad. Is he perfect? No. But has he been there for me through some of the most difficult moments of my life? Yes.

I'd been planning to bring a date with me tonight, but when I looked through my contacts, nobody was calling out to me.

I was somewhere around the Js when I stopped looking.

Jackie, Jada, Jayla, Jasmine, Jess, Jocelyn, Josie, and Juliana were all unique and I'm sure lovely women, but to be honest, I can't recall specifics about a single one of them.

I called Lincoln a few days ago and let him know he could have my plus one ticket back, and I opted to go solo. Maybe I'll find someone there, maybe not.

I don't know what he did with it or if he gave it away, but I guess I'll find out if someone is beside me when we take our seats tonight.

"Ready?" my dad asks. He's wearing a boring black tuxedo, and he gives me a once-over. "The fuck you wearing?"

"It's paisley," I say, glancing down at my jacket. "The invitation said it's a formal event, so I skipped the animal faces tonight. What's wrong with this?"

His brows quirk, but he holds up a hand as he raises his brows and sighs as if he can't figure out where he went wrong with me. "Nothing," he mutters. "Let's go."

I smile as he turns. There's something really satisfying about annoying my father purely with my choice of clothing.

We're photographed on the red carpet as we walk into the star-studded event, and I'm interviewed by my sister-in-law, Jolene, after I walk into the hotel where the event is being held.

"Who are you wearing?" she asks, and I tell her. She asks me a few other questions about who I'm hoping to see tonight, and I give the standard answers about my teammates who are like brothers to me when, in truth, they're not.

Grayson retired, as predicted at the end of last season, so my actual brother isn't my teammate anymore. I can't count the head coach as a teammate, and my real teammates don't really seem to like me all that much, with the exception of a few of the wide receivers I've gotten friendly with.

I'm not sure if it's because I'm the coach's brother or if it's because I was suspended for a year, but either way, I often feel like an outcast. And if you can't be a part of the brotherhood with your own teammates, well, you're pretty much fucked.

But I'm here tonight, and I find Grayson and Ava by the bar when I walk in, which is where I plan to be stationed all night.

I head in that direction, and I greet some teammates along the way with a friendly nod of my head or one of those close-lipped smiles.

Ava gives me a hug, and Grayson slaps me on the back as I nod at the bartender.

"What's on tap?" I ask.

"Stella, Coors Light, Michelob Ultra, Leinenkugel Summer Shandy, and Guinness."

I'm not picky when it comes to beer. Sometimes I like an IPA, sometimes I prefer a lager, and sometimes I'll really throw things off and drink whiskey just for fun.

And as I glance around the room tonight, I can't help but think it's a whiskey kind of night.

"Whiskey," I say, and the bartender nods with a chuckle. "Ice?"

I shake my head and toss a bill into the tip jar. When he sees the denomination of the bill, he pours a little more into the tumbler.

He hands it over with a smile, and I stand chatting with Grayson and Ava for a while until Ava sees some of the other football wives she wants to catch up with.

"What's going on, man?" Grayson asks. "How was mandatory minicamp?"

I roll my shoulders and reach up to massage one that's got a knot in it from a week of training. "Same shit every year. You'd think at some point I'd be smart enough to stop putting my body through it, but it's the addiction to the game. How'd you give it up?"

He laughs and holds his drink in the air toward his wife. "I found a woman I was more addicted to than I was to football."

As he says the words, a woman with long, red hair wearing a gold dress that offers see-through peeks of her skin walks up to the bar. She tosses that long hair behind her shoulder, and I listen, mesmerized, as she orders two drinks: a shot of vodka and a dirty martini, extra dirty.

She picks up the shot of vodka while he makes the martini, and fuck, she's sexy. I watch her as she taps the shot glass on the bar, then tips it up to her lips. She sucks back the liquid, swallows without a flinch, and slams the glass back on the bar without even wiping her mouth.

"You know what I mean?" Grayson says. "Ash? Asher? You with me?"

I clear my throat as I tear my gaze from the woman and force it to my brother. "Huh?"

"Minicamp," he says, as if I have any idea what he's talking about.

"Oh, right." I shake my head a little. "What about it, again?"

He laughs and slaps me on the back. "I was just saying how minicamp is the first impression of what this year's team will look like."

"Yes. Correct." I nod as I try to focus on this conversation. "And it's different without you in there, man." I clap him on the shoulder.

I glance over for one more look at that gorgeous woman again, but she's gone.

I look in front of us to try to spot her again, but the crowd is getting bigger, and it's like she disappeared into thin air.

"Dude, what the fuck is wrong with you? Is your golden jacket too tight?"

"What?"

He sighs.

"Sorry. That woman at the bar a second ago…do you know who she is?"

His brows dip. "What woman?"

"The one with the red hair."

He shakes his head. "Sorry, man. I didn't see her."

I suck in a breath and force myself to pull it together and focus on my conversation with my brother. But the truth of the matter is that I haven't found a woman who grabbed my interest immediately like that in a long, long time. Maybe ever.

It's purely physical. That little peek of her skin under her tit was what snagged my attention. It's been too long since I've had sex.

But tonight…maybe all that can change.

Chapter 5: Desiree Dixon

A Meal, a Drink or Two, a Dance, and Then…

My parents introduced me to the general manager as soon as we walked in, and my mom got involved with a conversation with the wife while my dad chatted up the husband, so I excused myself to the bar.

I start with a shot of vodka since I don't know anybody here, and then I move onto my martini. I head over toward the silent auction tables to browse the items, and I'm reading about a couple's weekend at the Red Rock Resort in Vegas when a woman in a black mermaid dress that's fitted down to her knees walks up beside me.

"So sorry," she says, and she grabs the pen to write down her bid on the auction item.

"Ellie Dalton," I read off the list. "Are you related to the Dalton brothers?"

She nods. "Luke's wife," she says, and she sticks out her hand for me to shake.

"Lovely to meet you. I'm Desi Dixon, the new OC's daughter."

"Oh, right!" she says, and she leans in to give me a hug. "We're so excited to welcome you to the Aces family."

"Thank you," I say. Luke Dalton is a legend. He was a wide receiver for the Aces for a decade, and he's a household name even to families who don't tune into football every weekend.

"I'd heard Coach Dixon had a daughter. Are you sitting with your parents tonight?"

I shake my head. "I was a last-minute addition." I glance at the card I picked up when I walked in that boasts my table number along with the menu for tonight's seven course meal featuring classic French dishes. "Table thirty-one."

She presses her lips together. "Damn, we're at fifty-seven."

"Too bad," I lament.

"So did you move here to Vegas, too?"

I shake my head. "No, I'm visiting for the weekend. I'm still in San Diego."

"Well, look me up when you're in town. Always happy to leave my children at home to meet a new friend for a drink." She winks at me, and I chuckle, though knowing she has kids at home makes me feel like there's a pretty big difference between the two of us.

She's a mom, and I don't even know if I *want* kids—never mind the fact that I don't know a man who I'd want to knock me up with said kids.

"Will do," I say warmly, and I see it before it happens.

She offers me a wide smile as she turns to walk away, and just as she turns, a waiter carrying a tray filled with champagne flutes walks by.

She crashes into him.

The tray drops to the floor, and champagne bounces everywhere, soaking the bottom of Ellie's beautiful black dress. A bit of the liquid splashes in my direction, too, coating my feet with the sticky drink.

"I'm so sorry!" Ellie groans, and she asks the waiter, "Are you okay?"

He nods, apologizing profusely as he bends down to pick up what must be ten glasses of champagne. She turns to me and asks the same question since she doesn't seem to be able to bend down in her dress that's now wet.

"I'm fine," I say, and I move over to help the waiter pick up the mess.

"No, ma'am," he says to me. "We don't want you to cut yourself."

"It's fine," I say, though the second I pick up a piece of glass, sure enough, I cut my pointer finger. "Fuck," I mutter.

It's not bad—no worse than a paper cut, really. I straighten and excuse myself for the bathroom to wash my hands and feet.

Or, I try to.

This is one of those bathrooms with no paper towels and only hand dryers, so I grab some toilet paper and scrub at my feet the best I can as I hold another piece of toilet paper around my finger to get the bleeding to stop.

When I emerge from the bathroom fifteen minutes later, all I can do is hope nobody saw me walk in there, spend fifteen minutes, and walk out looking flushed. I can only imagine what they'd think.

I hear the announcement before I even walk back into the ballroom. "Ladies and gentlemen, please take your seats. Dinner will be served shortly."

My mom and dad are up front at table four, and I swing by to say hi on my way to the bar to grab one more drink before dinner.

I'm not the only one who had that idea, though. The line is ten people deep, and by the time I turn around with my drink in hand, I see the servers clearing plates after the first of the seven-course meal, an amuse-bouche consisting of a cheese puff with truffle butter.

Damn. That sounded good.

I practically run to my table, and I grab the only open seat. I see the cheese puff thing still sitting there, and I slip it into my mouth just as someone comes to clear my plate.

"Perfect timing," I say triumphantly, holding my fist up in the air.

And then I glance around my table.

It appears I'm sitting with a bunch of football players and their spouses. There are ten chairs, and it's a big enough table with enough noise surrounding me that there's no way I can hold a conversation with someone across the table from me. I glance at each couple, and they all smile and wave, and finally I look at the man sitting to my right.

Our eyes connect, and…

Holy shit.

It's *Asher Nash.*

I'm a huge football fanatic, and of course I know the Nash family. Who doesn't? They're household names.

And whoa.

He's *hot.*

Not just, like, *hot,* but steamy, spicy, sexy, book boyfriend material hot.

He's got dark hair that's styled in a trendy sort of lazy way, and his blue eyes seem to hold me hostage. He looks surprised, and my eyes fall to his full lips that are slightly parted and the scruff peppering his strong jawline.

Holy hell. I don't know that I've ever seen a man up close like this that's just so…so…so…gorgeous.

He's wearing an obnoxious paisley gold jacket, and oddly, it's the perfect complement to my dress, as if we planned the coloring even though we didn't. I look around him at the woman on the other side of him, and she's leaning in and kissing the man she's with, so I assume she's not his date. As they part, I see the man she was kissing is Grayson Nash.

I realize my father coaches for an NFL team, but that doesn't mean I'm not a bit starstruck by these men.

Still, I pull it together. I act like I have no idea who he is.

"Oh, uh," I stammer. "Is this seat taken?"

He chuckles. "It is now. I'm Asher."

"Desiree," I say, giving my full name rather than the shortened version everyone calls me by.

I leave out my last name on purpose. I can't tell him that I'm the daughter of his new OC—especially because I'm interested, and there's a very real possibility my father has already warned his players off dating his daughter.

He puts out his hand to shake mine, and as our palms touch and his eyes catch mine, a crackle of something sizzles between us.

He glances down at our joined hands, and he pulls mine up closer to inspect the cut on my finger. "What happened?"

"Champagne tray accident a few minutes ago," I admit, and he chuckles.

He presses his lips to my fingertip, and it's both oddly intimate and extremely hot. "All better." He lets go of my hand and leans in playfully toward me. "Want to play the role of my date tonight?" He jerks his head at the woman next to him. "Everyone at this table is married, and they're pretty much always doing, well, that."

I chuckle even though heat rises up my back. The role of his date? *Hell yes.* "I think it's sweet."

He wrinkles his nose. "I was just sitting here hoping this seat would get taken so I had someone to talk to."

"You've got me now," I say. "And I'm interested in hearing more about what playing the role of your date would entail. Is it talking through dinner?" If it's more of his lips on my fingertips, I'm in.

"Well, the seat you're in was supposed to be for my date, and I gave it up at the last minute since I couldn't really come up with someone I wanted to drag along to this. And now you're sitting here, so it feels like fate."

I roll my eyes. "Are you always this cheesy?"

He laughs. "See? You're already calling me out on my shit. It's like we were meant to be."

I giggle. "Okay, so fate had us written in the stars."

"Right. So we share a meal, maybe a drink or two. Dance the night away, and then…" His eyes are on mine, and his are getting darker and hotter.

Or maybe it's my imagination.

Maybe it's the shot plus the martini and a half.

But I want him to say something else—something that'll take us past a meal, a drink, and dancing.

He wouldn't be that forward, would he? I think I want him to be. I've heard about his reputation, and as sleazy as it sounds, part of me *wants* to be one of the women on the list of women he's been with. He's hot as hell, and my curiosity is piqued. I want to know if the rumors are true.

All of them.

Maybe this is my shot at a friends with benefits thing, or maybe he can be my Vegas hookup. I want to have the kind of Vegas experience that I can use to brag to my friends when I get home. I want the book boyfriend treatment in real life—the hot, bad boy football player with a bit of scruff and navy eyes taking a random woman he meets at a charity event somewhere private where they can bang.

I can tell that beneath that paisley jacket, he's fit and trim. I'd love to snag a peek at the *full* package.

"And then?" I whisper, my eyes never leaving his.

"Your scallops, ma'am," a server says, and I nearly jump out of my seat as he places the dish in front of me.

Shit. Right. Scallops. The second course. I pick at the prosciutto on the side of the scallops, avoiding the shellfish altogether.

"You don't like scallops?" Asher asks, his voice deep and low.

"My dad's allergic, and I saw his reaction once, so I've never tried them. I avoid eating mostly anything that swims." I scrunch up my nose.

"Really? Even shrimp? Fuck, I love shrimp." He licks his lip, and whoa, the dart of his tongue out to wet his bottom lip does something to me.

Something I'm not sure I've felt before. Something *insane*. Paired with the way he utters the word *fuck*, I'm not sure I've ever felt the pulse of need that throbs down low.

All I can think of is that tongue as it moves along my skin, his scruff leaving a delicious burn in its wake.

Well, that and the word *fuck* coming from his mouth while he performs the act of said word on me.

I suck in a deep breath, and I shake my head to answer his question.

He doesn't ask, instead reaching over with his fork and stabbing my scallop. "Speaking of weird allergies, my brother's allergic to mustard." He shoves his fork in his mouth and savors the taste of my scallop.

I wish that was a euphemism for something, but sadly, it is what it is.

"Mustard?" I repeat.

"It's not real common I guess." He shrugs.

"What happens when he eats some?"

"It starts with an itch, but if it's really severe, his mouth swells up and it can get pretty nasty. What was your dad's reaction to scallops?" he asks.

I wrinkle my nose. How did we go from that sexual "and then" insinuation a moment ago to talking about how my dad reacts when he eats shellfish?

And what's worse, I'm not about to admit he had diarrhea for days the last time he ate a scallop.

I clear my throat. "Stomach pain."

Our plates are cleared, and for the third course, we're served cream of wild mushroom soup.

It's Asher's turn to make a face. "Cream of mushroom? No thanks." He pushes his bowl away as if the mere smell is upsetting to him.

"The cream or the mushrooms?" I ask as I dip my spoon into my bowl. I blow on the hot soup before I stick my tongue out to check the temperature, and then I take the spoon into my mouth.

His eyes are on my mouth through the entire process. I'm literally eating a bowl of soup, and he's looking at me like he wishes *he* were my spoon.

And the longer I sit beside him, the more I want to make that particular dream a reality.

Chapter 6: Asher Nash

The Meal, the Dance, More Drinks, and Then…

Jesus Christ, this woman is something else.

Her eyes are this bright shade of green I'm not sure I've ever seen before, and the dress she's wearing is…fuck. It's tickling all the parts of my imagination that want to explore every piece of what's under it, and the way she's looking at me makes me think she's into it, too.

I can tell. I have a sixth sense for these things, I guess, but the way her eyes keep flicking to my lips when we're talking makes me think she wants me to kiss her.

And I can't seem to stop watching her mouth as she does the simplest task, like taking a bite of her soup. She has a sexy way of shoving a spoon into her mouth that very nearly makes me want to try mushrooms, which happen to be my number one most hated food.

Who the fuck picks up a fungus off the ground and thinks *oh hey that looks delicious, I think I'll take a bite*? And how do we know *for sure* the one we're taking a bite of isn't poisonous? It seems like an awfully big gamble for something that tastes like dirt anyway.

Don't get me started on the fact that these are *wild* mushrooms. I have too much to live for to give it all up on a fucking wild mushroom, that's for damn sure.

She finishes her soup, and since I snagged her scallop, I push my bowl over to her. She lifts a shoulder, and then she eats it.

She fucking eats it.

As if she could get any hotter than she already was, she practically licks that goddamn bowl clean, and seeing her go after it makes my cock beg for release—especially when she licks the spoon. If she wants to lick my cock like that...

Thank God I'm sitting and my legs are under the table because I sure as shit wouldn't be able to hide this bulging motherfucker right now.

The fourth course is more fish, which she pushes toward me with a laugh that sounds like a song, and next we're given a sorbet to cleanse the palate, whatever the fuck that means.

The main dish is Steak Diane, which is a filet mignon, and I watch her with a slackened jaw as she cuts into the medium-rare filet and closes her eyes in delight at how delicious it is.

And when she moans?

All bets are off.

There's no way I'm leaving tonight without hearing her moan like that for me.

I drain what's left in my glass of whiskey, and I nod to her empty glass. "Would you like another martini?"

She nods, and her eyes find mine. Those green irises sparkle at me with mischief. "I like it extra dirty."

"Are we still talking about the martini?"

She doesn't laugh the way I think she will. Instead, that sparkle seems to dissipate as heat fires between us. "If we're not, then I like it filthy." She raises a brow as if she's daring me, but I'm not sure what the dare is.

I hold a hand to my chest like I'm having a heart attack because for a second, it feels like I am. My chest races as I suck in a breath and let go of it slowly. She's affecting me, that's for damn sure.

I push my chair back, hopeful that the giant boner in my pants that are a bit too fitted is hidden enough beneath my paisley jacket, and I stand and head over toward the bar, shifting my cock as I walk to try to get it under control.

It doesn't help. Shifting it is only giving it attention, and once I give it a little attention, it simply begs for more until it gets what it wants.

And maybe there's a chance. Maybe the evening will end and Desiree—with her gorgeous green eyes and long, red hair and sexy dress—will be wrapping her legs around me.

A guy can hope, anyway.

I order myself more whiskey and an extra dirty martini for the woman who suddenly feels like my date, and when I return to the table, the chocolate mousse dessert is waiting for me.

I set the drink in front of her, and she holds it up with a thank you.

And then she says, "To whatever happens after that dance you promised me."

"Indeed." I touch my glass to hers, and we each take a drink.

Desiree picks up her spoon and pretends like she's going to take a bite off my own plate, and I pick up my knife as a threat in jest. I'd never actually stab someone's hand for stealing my dessert, but the mousse looks fucking fantastic.

She giggles, and hearing the girlish sound come from someone who is *all* woman makes her all the more interesting. It makes me want to get to know who she is, what she's doing here, why she claimed the ticket I gave to my brother at the last minute…and everything in between.

And that's a strange thought.

Typically, when I hook up with a woman, it's nothing more than a hookup. But Desiree is fascinating. She's tempting. She's gorgeous, and obviously the attraction between us was instant, intense, and insane. Yet the longer we sit together, making each other laugh as we make sexual innuendos, the more I could see myself enjoying functions like this with her as my date.

"So how'd you end up as my plus-one tonight?" I ask.

"I was a late addition, and I guess Coach said there was a ticket available." She shrugs, not really giving me much to work with.

"Are you local?"

She shakes her head. "I assume you are?"

I nod. I don't want to get into the fact that I'm currently living with my father because, well, it's straight up embarrassing. We're renting. I haven't bought a place yet since I wasn't sure how long I'd stick around when I first signed on with the Aces, and my dad was looking for a roommate.

But tonight, I'm not taking this gorgeous woman back to the house I share with Eddie Nash.

No fucking way.

I have a different idea instead.

I finish my mousse and push my plate away. I think about asking her where she's from, but she's being as dodgy about questions as I am, I suppose. Maybe we're more alike than I first realized.

I'm just about ready for that dance, but first, I need to head out to the lobby and see if I can execute my plan for the evening.

I move to a stand. "I'll be back in a minute. Don't go anywhere. You promised me a dance."

Full lips tip up in a smile, and she glances up at me from under her lashes. Her eyes connect with mine, and Jesus Christ. It's the same sort of look I can imagine her giving me but with my cock between those lips.

Fuck.

"I always keep my promises," she says.

I groan as I bolt toward the lobby to find the reception desk so I can book a room at this hotel for tonight.

I don't want a quick fuck in a bathroom stall or out in the garden.

I want to take my time with this one, and I want to wake up with her in my arms tomorrow morning.

Fuck. I just met her. I barely know a thing about her other than her name.

I think I might be in a hell of a lot of trouble.

Chapter 7: Desiree Dixon

Lose Control

I spot my mom as I sit alone, waiting for Asher to return. She's searching through the crowded tables for something, and when I see her, I start to wave.

She rushes over toward me. "Your dad and I need to leave." She rolls her eyes. "He ate the scallop. He wasn't even paying attention, just talking away and eating, and now he's been in the bathroom for the last twenty minutes."

My heart sinks. "Oh, okay." Asher told me not to move, but honestly, what am I doing? I don't even know this guy. He's a player on my dad's team with the reputation of a player.

It's an insane attraction, that's all. That's all it *can* be. My dad would *never* be okay with me dating a player on his new team when he's trying to build his own reputation, and furthermore, not one who was suspended for an entire season for gambling on games.

If that doesn't scream *bad boy who will never touch my daughter*, I don't know what would.

But I don't *want* to leave. It's not like I can do anything for my dad tonight, anyway. He'll be fine in a day or two, and I want to see where this can go tonight. I want to have some Vegas-style fun with someone who has no idea who I am.

But if they're leaving, I should go too. I push my chair back to stand, and that's when she sets her hand on my shoulder.

"You can stay if you want. I bid on a couple of auction items, so if I win, can you grab them?"

"Oh, sure. Of course." I nod. "I'd love to." I try not to sound too eager. *Back it off, Desi.* "Take good care of Dad, okay? I'm not sure how late I'll be."

She sighs. "Okay. Be safe. I'll text you the front door code so you can let yourself in."

"Great," I say. I stand and give her a quick hug, and then she bolts to take care of my dad.

As bad as I feel for my dad, he'll live. And now I'm truly here alone. I won't have my parents over my shoulder watching my every move. I can dance the night away without anyone knowing I'm the new OC's daughter—unless, of course, they pointed me out to everyone at their table, which is a possibility.

And so when Asher returns to the table with a gleam in his eye and another dirty martini—extra dirty, just like I like it—I feel like something shifts. No longer do I feel the need to censor myself, not that I was before. But there's something about having your parents in the same room as you while you're attempting to make a connection with someone that sort of…pops the balloon, I guess.

Well, the balloon is fully inflated, or whatever metaphor we're using, and so is that throbbing between my legs.

He raises both brows quickly at me when he catches me looking at him.

I narrow my eyes at him. "You look like you're up to something."

He twists his lips. "How can someone have just met me and already seem to know me so well?"

"I'd say something cheesy about it being fate, but honestly, your face is giving it all away. What did you do?"

He laughs. "Stick with me long enough, and all will be revealed."

I pick up my drink, and before I tip it to my lips, I ask, "Why does that feel like a dare?"

He lifts a shoulder. "Maybe because it is."

I laugh, and I hold up my glass. "To whatever happens after we dance."

He holds his up, too, and clinks it to mine. His eyes are full of that same mischief. "To having breakfast together tomorrow morning."

His voice is low, flirty, and deep, and I need a sip of my drink to cool the heat between us.

But as we all know, alcohol doesn't exactly cool much of anything. Instead, all it does is add fuel to the flames.

"Come with me," he says, and he pushes to a stand and grabs my hand.

"Where are we going?"

"I bid on a couple auction items. Let's check if I'm still winning."

I nod, and we head over toward the auction tables, which is perfect since it'll give me a chance to see how my mom's bids are doing, too.

He doesn't let go of my hand, instead tightening it as if he's trying to show that we're here together regardless of whether the night started that way.

I can't say I mind that one little bit.

I spot *Sue Dixon* on a spa treatment package, and she bid way over the value price. She could easily go get the spa treatment, but she's trying to pump up the bids since the money goes to a good cause. It's sweet, really.

Asher stops in front of a basket filled with Arizona lottery scratcher tickets and checks the bids. He's still in the lead, and I glance over at him.

"Lottery tickets?" I ask.

"There's no lotto system in Nevada, and my dad will go ape shit over these scratcher things. Usually we either have to drive forty-five minutes to California or over an hour to Arizona to get some."

"That's sweet that you're getting them for your dad," I say. "I'd love to scratch some with you. Maybe together we'll get lucky." I raise a brow.

He blows out a breath as his eyes study me, and then he leans in toward me. "Either way, I think I hit the jackpot tonight." His breath is hot against my ear, and thrills race up my spine at his proximity.

Holy hell.

He smells good—clean and fresh with a hint of manly cedar underneath and something else. Cinnamon, maybe.

He looks good.

He seems invested.

I wasn't expecting all this tonight, yet here we are.

"Damn, some of these are getting high bids," he muses, and he seems like he wants to say something more, but then he hesitates.

I wonder what he was thinking and where he might have been going with those thoughts, but we continue walking and checking the other auction items.

He adds a bid on that weekend at the Red Rock, outbidding my new friend Ellie. When he turns away, though, he doesn't crash into anyone carrying a tray, and instead, he leads me toward the dance floor, his hand still clutching mine.

Some Calvin Harris remix is playing, and we start to move with each other. It's just about over, and the beat eases into the familiar keyboard stabs of "Lose Control" by Teddy Swims.

Asher moves in a little closer to me, reaching one arm around my waist to haul me into him, and I grip onto his upper arms as we start to sway to the song.

I listen to the words and feel like I can relate. I'm losing control more and more every second I'm in this man's presence.

He sings about needing release, and I feel Asher's arm tighten around me as his other hand comes up to palm my face. I lean into his touch and close my eyes as I really feel myself starting to slip.

I don't know a damn thing about him other than his name, that he hates mushrooms, and that his dad likes lotto tickets.

I don't know where he lives. I don't know who his friends are, or if he drinks coffee in the mornings, or even if he's single.

But as I open my eyes, one thing is made very clear.

He wants to fuck me, and that feeling is most definitely mutual.

Chapter 8: Asher Nash

She Doesn't Know Who I Am

The tension between us is palpable. Can I wait until the auction winners are announced to invite her upstairs? I'm not sure.

I'm not sure I've ever felt this strong of a need to tear off someone's clothes before.

She pulls her face back from my palm, her eyes opening as if she just had the same thought. Her eyes are hooded when they move to mine, and she flexes her hands where they land on my biceps as the song comes to an end and Whitney Houston's "I Wanna Dance with Somebody" starts playing.

She clears her throat, but neither of us moves out of the grasp we have on one another.

And then Grayson walks by and flicks my ear, clearly misreading the tension between Desiree and myself.

That fucker.

I turn around, letting go of her as those around us did once the slow song ended and the faster one began, and I offer him a glare.

I know better than to retaliate. He's the tallest and heaviest of the four Nash brothers, perfect for his position as a defensive back, and he's got about three inches and thirty pounds on me.

He grins at me, and he and his wife start to dance.

This woman dancing with me is here at the Vegas Aces annual charity ball, but I can't tell if she knows who I am—or who my brother is. So who the hell is she, and why is she here if she doesn't know the two of us? We're related to the head coach. We hail from the infamous Nash family. Everyone in this room knows who we are.

The reason why doesn't matter. The truth of the matter is that I kind of like that maybe she doesn't know who I am.

I've never looked for something meaningful, but I've also never been with a woman who wasn't vying for my attention because of who I am.

Do I use that status to my advantage? I suppose the answer to that would be yes—in the past, anyway.

And I'm not saying I'm looking for something meaningful now, but everyone around me has changed over the last year or so, and it feels like I'm next in line. I'm due. And maybe this is it. This is the moment of change for me.

I'm not interested in commitment.

Neither was Lincoln, and now he's here with his wife while his stepson and daughter are at home with his in-laws.

Neither was Grayson, who's dancing with his wife as if this is their foreplay.

Neither was Spencer, who managed to find himself drunkenly married in Vegas, and now, well, I'm not really sure what the hell is going on with him now. He's not here tonight, so I assume he's in San Diego training with the Storm, the team that picked him up when he was released from his contract with the Vikings at the end of last season.

I guess that means I'm next.

Settling down isn't for everyone, and maybe it isn't for me.

But as the woman with the green eyes and red hair looks at me with all that need in her eyes, I'm tempted to do things I never would dream of doing.

Fuck it. If I win one of the auctions, someone will let me know.

I grab her hand. "One more drink?"

She nods, and I tug her over toward the bar. I get my whiskey, she gets her extra dirty martini, and we take our drinks outside to the gardens. It's quiet out here, and the night is a beautiful seventy degrees while the dance floor was starting to get a little overheated—not from all the dancing or from the crush of people around us, but from the sizzling undercurrent passing between Desiree and myself.

I blow out a breath as I find an empty bench, and we sit. She raises her drink to me, the third toast we've shared tonight, and I wonder what she'll say this time.

To my surprise, she nods at me to give the toast.

To finding a quiet place to fuck seems inappropriate even though that's the current thought in my mind. Maybe whiskey drives me to drunksville faster than beer does.

My eyes flick down to her dress. "To seeing what those leaves are hiding."

Her jaw drops a little in surprise at my words, but she dishes it right back. "To showing you all the wonders hidden beneath."

Fuck.

I chug the rest of my whiskey and slam the glass on the bench beside me, and then I move to take her glass from her hand. She raises an eyebrow and shakes her head, and then she tips her head back and smoothly finishes down what's left in the glass. She sets her glass beside me and stands, and she reaches to pull me up with her. She doesn't take a step back to allow for more space as I stand. I tower a bit over her since she's maybe four or five inches shorter than me even in her heels, and I reach in to wrap an arm around her waist. I wrap the other one, too, and I haul her in closer to me. A quiet, intimate moment passes between us as she links her arms around my neck.

We might be alone out here, or maybe we're not—but either way, it feels like it's just her and me in this moment as our eyes meet, and the heat that's been smoldering between us since she slid into the chair beside me ignites into something I'm not sure we'll ever fully extinguish.

I lean down closer to her and run my nose along hers, and I hear the soft hitch of her breath at my proximity. I pull back a bit, and her eyes are closed. Her lips are parted, and I've never felt a stronger urge to kiss a woman in my life.

I lean in and softly brush my lips to hers.

I'm rewarded with a quiet moan, and I tighten my arms around her, hauling her as close as I possibly can as I press at the seam of her lips with my tongue. Her lips part, and I feel her tongue as it meets mine, slow and luxurious. There's nothing tentative as her confidence seems to kick in, and Jesus, who the hell is this woman?

Her name is Desiree.

Her dad is allergic to scallops.

She doesn't eat anything that swims, she prefers her martinis filthy, and she isn't local.

She's hot as fuck, her red hair and green eyes are full of temptation, our bodies seem like they were made for each other based on the way we danced before, and she wants to show me what's hidden beneath her leaves.

Oh, and she can fucking *kiss*. Her lips are soft and firm as her tongue moves against mine in a way that makes me want to know how that tongue would feel as it moves along my shaft. She sucks on my tongue for a second, and she bites down softy on my bottom lip—all things I want her to do to my cock.

Fuck.

And that's it. That's all I've learned about her tonight. I don't know what she does for a living, who her family is, who her friends are, where she lives, or anything important about her. And still, there's this inexplicable understanding that makes me feel like there's an unbreakable connection between us—a deep one that's been there for years even though we only met a few hours ago.

Maybe it doesn't matter, and maybe I'm going to take her upstairs and treat her the way I've treated the last string of encounters that ended up meaningless.

But something tells me this one won't be meaningless. Something tells me my life is about to change in ways I haven't begun to even think about yet.

And it all starts with my next words.

I pull back slowly as a haze seems to fall over both of us.

"I have a room here tonight, and I'd love to take you upstairs."

She doesn't miss a beat. "Let's go."

Chapter 9: Desiree Dixon

A Strip on the Strip

He drags me through the ballroom like he's on a mission, and he leads me through the lobby, through the casino, and toward a bank of elevators. It's not a short walk, but he presses the button for the top floor, and if we were alone on this elevator, I have a feeling he'd start his exploration of what's beneath the leaves.

The kiss outside was hot. The man's mouth is talented, and the way he worked my mouth made me want to feel his tongue all over my body. All night and maybe again in the morning if my body can handle the pleasure.

It felt like more than just a kiss.

I wish I could pretend like it was more, but it *can't* be. He's Asher Nash. My dad is his newest coach, and he doesn't even know that about me yet.

I like it that way.

This connection—it's the vodka paired with heat simmering between us. It's lust. That's all it is, and I need to take a step back and remind myself of that.

We're two adults consenting to a fun time together. That's all Asher Nash does. It's what he's known for. He doesn't call women back, nor would I expect him to…which is why I already know I'm not going to leave my number.

He'll see me again, and that's almost a certainty. Once the season begins, I'll attend some home games. I'll sit with my mom while we watch my dad do his thing on the sidelines. We'll cheer for the team—unless it's on the off chance they're playing the Storm. Then I'll be torn on who to cheer for.

We'll see each other again, yes. He just doesn't know it yet.

And I'm not going to spoil the lusty promise of tonight with that particular truth.

Since we're traveling to the top floor, others exit the elevator on our ascent toward the top. We find ourselves alone with fourteen floors yet to travel, and the very millisecond the elevator doors slam shut, he makes his move.

His mouth is immediately dragging along my neck. "Jesus Christ, you taste like heaven." He trails his lips down my neck and toward my collarbone, and I shiver. He backs me into the corner, his hands moving up my torso as he starts his ascent with his tongue back up my neck. His mouth is hot and needy when it meets mine, and his hands are traveling slowly, achingly slowly, up my torso. My nipples tighten and my body aches for him, so much so that I groan in what feels like agony, but all it does is encourage him.

He shifts, and I feel his hard cock as he positions it between us.

It's at that moment that reality slams into me.

Holy shit, I'm going up to Asher Nash's hotel room for sex.

I feel giddy as I revel in this moment. I suppose I have more access to football players than the average woman my age, but it's still a pretty damn exciting thrill to know that he's interested.

I arch into him involuntarily, and a little growl escapes him.

"Christ, Des," he pants, his mouth just below my earlobe. "I can't wait to get to my room and fuck you." The way he drags out the *z* sound in the shortened version of my name nearly makes me come on the spot.

Nobody calls me that. It's Desi or Desiree. Always. Never Des. There's something illicit about it, like I only ever want to hear him call me that in the heat of a moment as the single syllable comes out in a rasped whisper.

I shiver as I feel his tongue beneath my ear, his breath warm against my skin, the sounds sexual and animal at the same time. His mouth moves back to mine, and I twine my fingers into the back of his hair. It's a little long, like he didn't care enough for a fresh cut and a shave, and his shadow of a beard is already burning my mouth.

I don't care.

It's hot as hell. *He* is hot as hell.

And for tonight, he's mine.

I can live in my altered state of reality and pretend like it's more than just for tonight, and I get to go home and brag about my conquest to my best friends, that I bagged one of football's most eligible bachelors during my wild Vegas weekend.

He slams his hips to mine and breaks our kiss again. "I'm so fucking hard for you. Do you feel that?"

"Mm," I moan, my head rolling back and hitting the mirrored wall behind me. His hand moves up to one of my tits, and I arch further toward him.

"Tell me how dripping wet that hot cunt is for me," he demands.

Jesus. His mouth appears to be good for more than just kissing.

"I've never been so wet," I admit honestly. This is the stuff fantasies are made of. Making out with Asher Nash on an elevator on the way to his hotel room while he talks dirty to me? Are you kidding me?

"I can't wait to taste you," he growls, and then the elevator skids to a stop and the doors open. He leads me down the hall toward his room, and when we walk in, I find us in a room overlooking a gorgeous view of Las Vegas Boulevard.

I glance around the room. It's spacious with a bed, a desk, a couch, and a lounge chair overlooking the view, and it looks as if he hasn't even been in here yet.

In fact, I don't see any luggage.

I turn toward him, and he's got heat in his eyes. "Strip."

I glance toward the window. "Yes, that's the Strip."

He doesn't crack a smile as he shakes his head. "Strip with the Strip behind you."

"A strip on the Strip?" I repeat, my smart mouth getting the better of me. "Wait a second, cowboy." I hold up a hand.

"Cowboy?"

I tilt my head and set a hand on my hip. "Did you rent this room for the night...for me?"

He snags his bottom lip between his teeth, and he's caught red-handed. He doesn't seem embarrassed by that fact, though. "What if I did?"

I narrow my eyes at him as I contemplate that. On the one hand...it makes me feel a little cheap. On the other hand...it makes me feel like a million bucks. What a paradox. "I guess I'd feel pretty damn special to be the girl who snagged your interest tonight."

He takes a step toward me, and it's nearly predatory as his navy blue eyes turn black with lust. "You've done more than snag my interest, Desiree."

My full name this time. I swallow hard, suddenly nervous that I won't be enough for him. I'm never insecure, but apparently that's what a star like Asher Nash does to me.

Still, I hold my head high. "Oh?"

"You've commanded my attention this entire night, and my sole focus has been lasered in on you. From the moment I first spotted you at the bar when you walked in, took that shot of vodka, and walked away with your dirty martini, I was fascinated." He takes another step. "And when you sat beside me at the table, as cheesy as that line was, it really did feel like fate stepped in. I kept looking for you, and you showed up as if out of nowhere in the seat reserved for *my date*. If that's not fate at work, I'm not sure what is."

He turns his attention behind me and out the window, and he seems to grapple with his words—as if he wants to say something, maybe make a confession, but he isn't sure he's ready to.

I'm not ready for that, either. I can't get too invested in this guy, but it may be far too late to prevent it.

I can't come up with a snappy remark. I find myself without words, something that rarely happens.

He shakes off wherever his mind went, and he turns back toward me. "And I like to treat my dates to a good time at the end of the night."

"I figured someone like you would be able to offer more than a simple *good time*," I say. It's a challenge, one I'm certain he'll meet head-on.

Before he can, though, I move in closer to him, taking the initiative. I unbutton his jacket and reach in beyond the lapels toward his shoulders to help him shrug it off. He catches it when it falls to his wrists, and he pulls it off and tosses it on the desk beside me.

I reach for his wrists, unbuttoning the cuffs.

"What are you doing?" he asks.

"You said strip. You didn't say which one of us you wanted naked."

He stretches his neck back and groans, and I chuckle as I start to unbutton his starched white shirt, slowly moving down one button at a time. He watches me silently, carefully, the only sound the quiet hitch of his breath as I make my way down toward where the shirt is tucked into his pants.

He grunts when I move toward the bottom, freeing his shirt from its tucked position and finishing the buttons. I reach my hands in, much like I did to his suit jacket a moment ago, but I let my cool hands wander along the planes of his warm skin.

He's toned, firm, and hard everywhere, and I push his shirt off. I allow myself a moment to run my fingertips along the marble ridges that make up his abdomen.

He's a professional athlete, and the hard cuts of muscle on his body showcase the amount of work he puts in.

"God, is this cut from granite?" I ask.

"Steel," he jokes.

I move in closer to him until I feel his erection against my body. Speaking of steel...

He shifts his hips. "You've seen what's beneath the paisley. Time for me to see what's beneath the leaves."

Instead of waiting for my reply, his hand circles my throat, and it's the first time I realize I'm up in a man's hotel room, and nobody knows where I am.

He might play for my dad's team, but he's still a virtual stranger.

I only know about him what the media has portrayed, and that's not much to go on.

I should be scared.

But even though his hand is on my throat and he holds all the control in his hands, I'm not.

There's something in his eyes when they fall on mine that tells me even though he has the reputation he does, he's still a good guy.

He keeps his hand on my throat as he backs me up toward the window, and he holds me there once my back is up against it, his hand never leaving my throat as his other hand moves up to grab one of my tits. He's rough with me, and it's hot.

I'm trapped, and I want him to use me however he wants to.

His mouth collides down to mine, and he finally moves his hand off my throat as he uses it to slide down my torso and around to my ass, which he squeezes firmly. I bring my hands up to lace them around his waist, and he moves so quickly I barely even realize what's happening.

He spins me so I'm facing the view out the window, and he grabs both my wrists in one of his, holding them there behind my back. He reaches around the front of me and pulls the top of my dress down so my tits spill out over the top of it, and he pushes me against the window so the cool glass meets my nipples.

"Show those pretty tits to everyone on the Strip," he mutters close to my ear. "Show them what's fucking mine tonight." His mouth presses to my neck, and the hand that's not still binding my wrists moves down, skating over my hip toward the bottom of my dress.

He bends down and pulls the material at the bottom of the dress up until it's at the height he's satisfied with, and then he yanks my hands to the side as he bumps his cock against my ass with a grunt. At the same time, he slips his fingers down the top of the barely there, nude-colored thong I chose to go with my dress tonight, and he feels the soft, bare mound of my pussy. He moans, then slides his finger between my folds, his breath close to my ear as he feels how wet I am.

"Fuck, that's a dripping wet pussy," he moans.

I grind down on his hand, desperate for relief, desperate for him to slip past the folds and push his finger inside, desperate for friction against my clit, but he keeps teasing me as my tits remain pressed against the window for anyone walking down below to see us.

The chances are slim that we'd actually be spotted. We're way up on the top floor, and the windows are tinted. But still, the exhibitionism of it all is something I didn't know I needed.

It makes me want to find places where he can fuck me, and nobody would ever know.

It makes me want to continue seeing him after this, after I confess to him that I'm his new coach's daughter, but in secret since nobody can ever know.

It makes tonight an illicit secret that I want to keep repeating.

He continues teasing me, my hands still bound behind me as his fingers move everywhere except where I need them to be, his cock slamming against my ass as he tries to find some relief, too, and when I feel like I might combust if he doesn't finger me, I start to beg. "Please, Asher," I whine as I don't even recognize my own voice.

"Please what?" he asks, his voice low and gritty.

"Finger me," I beg.

"Now ask nicely. Say it all together," he demands.

I tug on my wrists, trying to surprise him enough to let go, but he doesn't budge. I move my hands as I try to feel around for him, and he sees what I'm doing. He shifts my hands so they're straight behind me and right where he was thrusting toward me, and he stops to rub his cock on my open palms.

I feel his length against my palm, and *holy shit*, he's *huge*. My mouth waters and my pussy aches as I have the dizzying need to touch him, to taste him, to feel him.

"Please fuck me," I blurt. "Please, I'm begging you, give me some relief."

I meant to say please *finger* me, I think, but I'm so lost in lust that I can't even think straight, let alone make coherent words come out of my mouth.

He dips a finger into my pussy at my words, and I grind down on his hand as I try to grip around his cock on the outside of his pants.

He hisses at the feel of my soaked pussy, but he doesn't back his finger out the way I need him to. I shift upward, trying to get some friction—any friction—but he doesn't move it, instead staying close with me every time I try to move.

I feel the ache pulling even stronger as the need to come becomes my sole focus. I'm trying to figure this guy out. He takes me up here, shoves me against the window, and doesn't finger me even though his finger is *in* me, and I'm not sure what's happening, but I'm crazed with need.

Ohhhh. Some coherency seems to fire in my brain. That's what he's doing.

He's making me as hot as he can for him so he can swoop in with the kind of release I've never experienced before.

I. Am. Here. For. It.

He finally, *finally* pulls his finger back and shoves it back in, and I ride his hand as he starts to get moving, the feeling of release edging its way in.

He won't let it happen yet, though.

He yanks his finger out, and he spins me back around after he lets go of my hands. His mouth is *immediately* on my nipple as he grips my tit in his hand. He's squeezing it as he licks and sucks my nipple, and the feeling is extraordinary. It's pain and pleasure at the same time, and he moves back and forth between each nipple, laving them each with attention as that building need between my legs throbs heavily.

"Tell me what you want," he says. His eyes are black with lust as they meet mine.

"I want you to fuck my mouth first, and then I want you to fuck my cunt. Please."

His lips curl up into a sly smile, and he turns me so he can unzip my dress. He lets it fall to the floor in a pool, and I'm standing in only my thong.

"Fuck," he says, and he reaches down to unbuckle his belt, pop his button, and lower his zipper. He's out of his pants in no time flat, and he's wearing just his boxer briefs, and my eyes zero in on the rather large bulge there.

He reaches in and pulls his cock out, and oh. My. God.

He's huge, hard, and definitely ready. He fists himself, the large purple head disappearing into his fist before he jerks his hand down, and I can see even from here that he's already leaking for me. He's as needy as I am, and he's stroking himself while I watch, trying to give himself some semblance of relief, just like he made me beg for.

I bat his hand out of the way and get down on my knees. I fist him, pumping my hand up and down his long shaft a few times before I take him between my lips.

"Fuck," he mutters, drawing out both the beginning and the end of the word as he starts to pump his hips toward my mouth.

I take him as far back as I can, and I'm not even close to getting the whole length in. I fist him at the base of his cock with one hand and fondle his balls with my other hand, and then I pull back and suck the head of his cock while I move my fist up and down his shaft.

He grunts as I work, and I taste the salt of him on my tongue.

He grabs onto the back of my head, tangling his fingers into my hair. He holds my head steady and shoves his cock in harder, and I feel it at the back of my throat.

"Oh, fuck yes, Des," he grunts. He does the same thing again, and I try to open my throat to allow him to shove in as deeply as he can. "Your mouth is so hot, so perfect." He pulls back, and I suck in a breath as he shoves in again.

He fucks my mouth like I asked him to, but when my dumb mouth requested that, I failed to think about how that meant my own achy need would continue to grow.

I let go of his balls to reach down to try to give myself some relief, but he catches me before I'm able to get anywhere.

He pulls out of my mouth and reaches down under my arms, hauling me up to my feet before he grabs me up and carries me over to the lounge chair by the window. It has flared arms and a tufted back, and he tosses me onto the long part of the chair.

"Put your legs over the arm," he says, and I do as I'm told. He yanks me so my head falls onto the seat and my ass is up over the arm, and he peels my thong off, tossing it aside. He kneels to the floor, pushes my legs apart before setting them on his shoulders, and moves his face down toward my pussy.

He stares at the wet, needy flesh. "Beautiful," he murmurs before lowering his mouth and licking a line through my slit from my pussy up to my clit. I cry out, my hands moving to his head as I thread my fingers into his hair. He slides a long finger into me and moves his mouth to focus on my clit.

One little suckle on my clit is nearly enough to push me straight over the edge, and when he curls his finger up inside me while he sucks a little harder on me, I'm done.

I cry out as the orgasm plows into me. "Oh, God, I'm coming!"

"Say my name while you come," he demands, his heated breath cool on my hot pussy.

"Oh, Asher, Asher, yes, yes, yes," I cry, and he continues the onslaught of pleasure with his finger and his mouth as he helps me ride through the rhythmic pulsing of my body. He keeps going even when the pulsing stops, and my skin prickles with goose bumps as my every sense is heightened. It's as if I have superpowers, clinging on to the silky strands of his hair while I smell his scent and mine comingling in the air around us, the sound of him continuing to suck on me while holding his fingers, two now, steady inside me.

He pulls back a moment or two after my body starts to come down, and he moans. "Fuck, your pussy is pure heaven." He licks through me again, and my hips jerk at the feel of him there when my body has become overly sensitive. "I'll never get enough," he murmurs so quietly that I almost miss it, but that odd superhuman strength allows me to catch it.

I'm not sure I'll ever get enough, either.

Chapter 10: Asher Nash

Something Different and New

Well, I discovered what's beneath the leaves, and let me tell you.

It's an entire world that's my playground for the night.

The way her body pulsed beneath my tongue is something that's going to stick with me for a long time to come.

I'll be thinking of it when I'm handling my solo business, if you catch my drift.

I reposition her so she's lying across the chaise lounge, and I head over toward the pants that we abandoned on the floor across the room.

When I went to the front desk to book the room, I learned they sell condoms in the hotel gift shop. I ran and snagged a couple before I headed back inside toward my date, and I take one, roll it on, and move in behind her on the chair so I'm spooning her. I nestle my cock between her ass cheeks, and Jesus, it's warm and welcoming right there.

She shifts back on me, and I feel like I could come just from the tiny measure of friction. I thrust my hips toward her, and she shifts back in response.

I think about moving down and fucking her from behind, but then I can't see her beautiful face or watch her gorgeous tits as they bounce over me.

And as much as I feel the need to come, I'm not quite ready to give up this nice moment of her quiet afterglow.

Seeing her come…fuck.

I'm still not over it.

I don't know if I'll ever get it out of my head, the way her red hair sort of flew all around her and her face scrunched as she gripped onto my head and held it against her pussy while her legs quivered all around me.

It was hot. Real fucking hot. Maybe the hottest thing I've ever had the pleasure of witnessing, and I've witnessed some things. One-on-ones, threesomes, orgies, strip clubs, sex clubs…you name it, I've probably checked it out at some point, but something about this woman right here has caught my attention in a way nobody else ever has been able to.

And it's only been a few hours.

What a fucking terrifying realization.

I push away the terror, though, because right now, I need to come. I need to hit the release that'll clear my thoughts. That's all it is. I'm horny, too horny—*overly* horny—so I'm thinking things and feeling ways that aren't representative of the truth.

"You okay?" I murmur.

"Mm," she murmurs, and I take that as an affirmative answer even though it sort of sounds like she's halfway to dreamland.

Well, it's time to make some different kinds of dreams come true.

I shift so I'm lying on my back, and then I tug on her shoulder until she turns to face me. I take the opportunity to seat myself more toward the center of the chair, and then I urge her on top of me.

She sits up, straddling my hips, and then she reaches down, fists my cock, and slides her body down onto it.

Holy motherfucking hell.

She's tight as *fuck*, and I'm going to come.

I'm not going to last three goddamn seconds in this sweet cunt that feels like it was made for me.

She claws at my chest as she gains her balance, and she starts to move slowly over me.

Our eyes meet, and something passes between us as we fuck for the first time.

Something different and new, something beautiful and dangerous.

She grabs both my hands and links her fingers through mine, and I hold my arms up to help her keep her balance as she starts to move. I watch her tits as they bounce in front of me, my mouth watering to taste them again, to suck one of them into my mouth and listen to her little moans, but I know feeling her nipple on my lips would push me even faster into my own release.

Fire rolls up my spine, and I know it's going to happen.

I force my gaze to the window. I force myself to concentrate on something else, anything else, to try to stave off the impending climax, but it's useless. She fills my view as she bounces up and down on my cock, her red hair swirling around her like a goddamn halo, and I'm done for.

She's sexy, mysterious, funny, smart, and beautiful, and if only for tonight, she's mine.

"Oh, God, Asher, you feel so good," she moans. "So, so good."

"This tight cunt was made for me," I mutter. It's too intimate a thing to say for a one-night stand, but the feelings pulsing in my chest already tell me this is far more than that. "Tell me how much you love my cock inside you."

"I love it, Asher. I love how your cock feels in my pussy. Fuck me harder," she cries, and I let go of her hands and grip onto her hips at the request. I shove into her from underneath, and her tits start to bounce in earnest.

"Hold onto the armrests," I command, and she does it, giving me the right angle to let go of her hips and still direct our movements from beneath her. I reach up and grab onto her tits, and with the way she's bending over, I can stretch down to get one in my mouth. I grab it, and she cries out as I keep hammering into her from below her. "Tell me how you want me to fuck you," I say around her breast.

"Oh God, oh God, oh God. It's perfect. Don't stop!"

I want to reach down to thumb her clit, but it'll only slow us down, and she just told me not to stop. I slam into her as fast and as hard as I can, keeping her nipple between my lips, and she cries out my name over and over as her pussy starts to contract over me.

It's fucking heaven as my balls draw up. I can't stop it any longer, and I don't want to. "Fuck Des!" I yell.

My body jerks as I hit my climax, and I fill the condom with my come as I continue rocking my hips against hers.

She thrashes wildly over me, her second orgasm hitting her far harder than the first did, and this wild, beautiful woman who caught my attention from the moment I saw her tonight manages to burrow her way into my thoughts and my chest in a way that tells me she's not going to let go anytime soon.

She lifts off me, and my cock is still rock-hard despite the release. It thumps against my stomach, and she settles in beside me, laying sweetly with her head in the crook of my shoulder as we both pant to catch our breath after that pleasure-filled workout.

I lean toward her and breathe her in, and she smells like coconuts. She sort of reminds me of a mermaid—the one with the red hair and big eyes, the scent of the beach overwhelming me. I draw in a deep breath as I try to memorize everything about this moment—everything about this night.

This isn't me, this simp who falls easily under a woman's charms, but Des is different, and I'm not quite ready to let go.

She gets up anyway, presumably to use the restroom as girls do after sex, and she returns a few beats later. She slips into the bed naked since she really doesn't have any other clothing choices, and I use the restroom next, disposing of the condom and cleaning myself up.

I don't have a whole lot of clothing choices myself, so I slip into bed naked beside her. She's already fast asleep, her breath coming in even puffs. I lean over and watch her, and she's gorgeous even at rest. I press a soft kiss to her cheek then wrap my arms around her as sleep calls me under.

Chapter 11: Desiree Dixon

I Left My Number

Ding-ding.
    Was that a ding?
    Where am I?
Two minutes pass, and I hear it again.

Ding-ding.

I roll over. The room is dark, but for the lights flashing in the window, and *ohhh,* right.

I'm in Asher Nash's hotel room, asleep after he made me come.

Twice.

Oh, shit.

I hadn't meant to fall asleep.

I glance at the clock, and it's a little after two in the morning.

Asher is out. He's breathing evenly, and the dinging of my text notification doesn't appear to be bothering him in the slightest.

We drank a lot last night, and I might still be a little tipsy, but not in a bad way. Not in the *I'm-gonna-lose-my-dinner-in-the-bushes* kind of way, anyway.

I glance at the screen and see a text from my mom, which only presses on my guilty conscience more.

Mom: *Would you mind grabbing some more Pepto on your way home? We're all out, and Dad could use some more.*

I sigh. The question presumes I'm coming home tonight, which I really should. I'm staying with them this weekend, and while I'm an adult certainly capable of making her own choices, I also don't particularly want to have to explain myself to them by rolling in wearing the same outfit I wore to the ball last evening.

And I'm certainly not about to fill them in on the fact that I had the steamiest encounter of my life with one of my dad's players.

I text her back.

Me: *Of course. Be on my way soon.*

Mom: *You stay out if you're having fun! Don't want to ruin your good time.*

I glance at Asher. As much as I don't want to leave, it's not like she's ruining my good time. I should go anyway. Neither of us went into this night with expectations, and it's probably better to leave without them, too.

Still, I don't want to leave without at least saying goodbye.

I find my thong and dress, and once those are in place, I strap my stilettos back on, my feet begging me to leave them off.

I head over to the bed and study him, and I lean down and press a soft kiss to his temple.

"Asher?" I ask softly near his ear.

"Mm," he murmurs, and he doesn't open his eyes.

I shake his arm a little. "Asher?" I say a little more loudly.

He doesn't move. His breaths are still even, and it would appear he's a heavy sleeper.

"Asher!" I call, and...nada.

I sigh, not sure what to do for a minute, and then I lean over and give him a hug. "Thanks for a great night. I'll never forget it."

I walk over toward the desk and spot a pad of paper and a pen, and I leave a note behind, praying he'll see it in the morning even though I hadn't planned on leaving my number.

A-

Hope you enjoyed what was beneath the leaves. I know I liked that steel beneath the paisley. Had to run out, but I'm sure I'll see you again soon.

-D

I leave my phone number on the bottom with the words *call me*, and I search around the room to try to find the right place to leave it so he'll see it. Ultimately, I choose the nightstand where his phone is, study him one more time, and let myself out of his room.

I reserve a Lyft while I take the elevator down to the lobby, and I spot a twenty-four-hour gift shop on the way toward the exit. I swing in, grab some Pepto, and head outside, feeling like I'm leaving a piece of myself behind.

And maybe I am. Maybe he took a piece of me that I'll never get back, or maybe I'll see it again sometime down the road.

I get back to my parents' house with the Pepto, and despite the late hour, my mom is awake and waiting for me.

"Dad's been in the bathroom all night, so it's not like I can sleep," she says, rolling her eyes. If she notices that I'm a bit mussed up compared to how I was earlier, she doesn't mention it. "Oh, did I win any of the auction bids?"

Oh, shit. I knew I forgot something.

I scramble to come up with something even though my brain is currently in sleep mode. "You know, I was chatting with someone when they announced it and totally missed hearing the winners. But I'm sure they'll call you if you won. They won't miss collecting payment, right?" I toss the shade off what I was really doing. I mean…we *did* chat at different times throughout the evening, so it's not a lie.

She narrows her eyes at me. "Are you okay?"

I nod. "Just tired."

"Did you have fun?"

"I had the best time. Really. I'm going to go head up to bed now. See you in the morning."

As it turns out, it's nearly afternoon by the time I force myself out of bed. I take a long, steamy shower to help awaken my aching muscles that were twisted and bent in ways I'm not used to, and I head downstairs.

I checked my phone the moment I woke up, but I didn't have anything from him yet. Maybe he's still sleeping, too. We really took it out of each other last night.

I roll my shoulders as I pad into the kitchen in sweatpants and a Storm T-shirt, and my dad is sitting at the table looking both tired and a little green.

"How're you feeling?" I ask.

He nods to the plain toast in front of him. "Regretful that I didn't look at what I was eating," he admits.

I wrinkle my nose. "I'm sorry."

"Did you have a fun time?"

I nod.

"Wish I could've been there."

"How's it going out here so far, Dad?" I ask.

He sips from a steaming cup of tea, and I stand and head over toward the Keurig for a cup of coffee. "I inherited an incredible offense, and I'm excited to get started building on their strengths to grab some Ws this season."

We chat while it brews.

"I have no doubt you'll grab a ton of Ws, Daddy." When my coffee is ready, I take my cup of black coffee and sit beside my dad.

"That smells great." He inclines his head toward my cup, and I shake my head at him.

"No way. Mom would kill me if I gave you coffee when you can barely get a piece of toast down. Where is Mom, by the way?"

"Sleeping. She was up all night for some reason." He shrugs and widens his eyes innocently, and I laugh.

"You're terrible."

"Don't I know it. How are you really doing in San Diego all by your lonesome?" He lifts his toast to take a bite, and he sets it back down without taking it.

"I'm not all by my lonesome," I remind him.

"I know, I know. You have your friends, and they're like family. I hate having you so far. I can't keep an eye on you when you're three hundred fifty miles away." He offers a wry smile.

I refrain from mentioning that he also couldn't keep an eye on me when we were in the same room. "I'm fine, Dad." I nod toward his toast. "And you will be, too, you know. If you avoid the scallops." I raise my brows pointedly, and he laughs.

My mom joins us shortly after, and I can't stop thinking about my dad's words that he can't keep an eye on me.

I've enjoyed the freedom while he's missed the protection, and I feel a little guilty about that. I still managed to have a good time last night even with my parents close, and Vegas doesn't seem so bad, if I'm being honest.

I haven't exactly gotten the full view of Vegas, but seeing the Strip from Asher's hotel room pressed up against that window was pretty damn spectacular. It was also lovely in the background behind me when I was riding on top of him.

I want to see him again.

I check my phone.

No message.

Dammit. I wish we would've thought to trade numbers earlier, but we were too busy drinking and flirting and fucking for it to come up. But it's not like I can ask my dad to procure me Asher Nash's number, so in all honesty…the ball's in his court.

Chapter 12: Asher Nash

She's Gone

I roll over, the intense pressure in my head reminding me why I typically choose any other beverage over straight whiskey, and as I reach to wrap my arm around the woman who seems to have stepped out of my dreams, my arms can't seem to seek her out.

The other side of the bed seems empty, and the sheets feel...cool. As if they've been vacant a while.

"Des?" I say—or I *try* to say it, but my voice comes out all raspy and hoarse.

I swallow, but my mouth is dry, and I clear my throat before I give it another attempt. "Des?"

She must be in the bathroom.

My eyes open slowly to the light coming in through the windows. We never closed the drapes last night, I guess. I squint as I try to adjust to the brightness.

I sit up and rub the sleepiness from my eyes, and when I open them again, I can focus.

That's when I spot my clothes from last night. My jacket is on the desk where we left it, and as I recall, her dress wasn't too far away...but it's not there anymore.

Those strappy shoes that made her legs look like a million bucks are gone, too.

I force myself out of bed. The headache is pounding, but I've been much worse off after a night of drinking than I am now. I thank my genes and my youth for that luck, I guess.

I pad over to the bathroom, poised to knock on the door...but it's open.

And dark.

She's not in there. She's not anywhere in this room at all.

Even her thong is gone. She bolted and didn't even leave me a souvenir.

I take care of my bathroom needs and splash a little water on my face when I exit, and I pad over and sit on the edge of the bed as I reach over toward the nightstand and pick up my phone.

So she just...disappeared.

She's gone, and it's like she was never here at all.

I check my phone, searching for Desiree in there, but I don't recall exchanging numbers. We didn't even take a photo together.

It's almost like I dreamed last night up, and maybe I did. Maybe it was hallucinations from the whiskey, and this Desiree doesn't even exist.

Maybe she went downstairs for coffee or something, but somehow I doubt she went downstairs in last night's ballgown since neither of us had any other clothes with us.

Maybe she went downstairs to find some other clothes. Now *there* is a real possibility.

I lean against the headboard, still stark naked, and I wait in case she's about to return.

I have no idea how long she's been gone, though, and it seems rather delusional that the sheets would be as cold as they are on her side if she just left.

I know I'm a heavy sleeper, but why would she bolt like that?

I guess she just wanted a night with the tight end.

Well, she got it.

I shouldn't be broken up about it. I shouldn't care at all, really. It's not like this was my first one-night stand.

So why do I care?

I draw in a deep breath as I force myself up to gather my clothes. I'll need to walk out of this hotel in my suit from last night, as if it's a badge of honor that I'm walking out in daylight in the same clothes I wore to the party last night.

Today is for nursing hangovers and letting go.

I don't know anyone at that charity ball last night who knows who this woman was. She seemed to be fully disconnected from everyone present. But what are my options here? I could ask Lincoln who she was and track her down through him—if he even has that information.

Or I can take it for what it was—one night with an incredible woman that I will more than likely never see again.

She's the one who left without leaving a number behind. Trying to track her down and call her up out of the blue at this point will make me look like the desperate fuck I am.

No…the ball is in her court. If she wanted to get in touch, she would've figured out a way. Hell, she figured out a way to get a last-minute ticket to a sold-out charity ball, so if she wants to find me again, I have no doubt that she will.

Chapter 13: Desiree Dixon

I Didn't Finish

I head back home on Monday, and I vaguely recall I promised myself I'd finish the book on the plane ahead of Wednesday's book club meeting, but I can't concentrate.

Instead, I think about Asher and our night together.

It hasn't even been forty-eight hours yet, but I'm getting the message loud and clear.

He's not interested enough to call me back.

It's a shot to my ego.

He made me feel special for one night, and it was one night for the books. But as it turns out, he's not much of a book boyfriend if he won't even use the number I left to give me a call.

A tiny thought somewhere in the recesses of my mind wonders if maybe he never got my note. What if he didn't?

Of course he did. I couldn't have left it in a more obvious place, but I think of the millions of times my mom has complained about my dad. *I could leave his keys in his hand, and he'd still ask me where they were.*

If he didn't see my number directly under his phone, he'd find a way to get in touch.

I'm home early enough that I decide to swing by the office—in large part to distract myself from checking my phone every few minutes, as if I'd miss his call when I'm glued to the damn thing.

I have plenty to catch up on when I return, and I stay late. The next day is equally busy, and I remind myself never to leave for a whole weekend again.

Except…I'm starting to feel restless, and I'm not even sure why.

I've had a one-night stand before, and it didn't leave this sort of impression on me. So why did Asher? What was so different about him—about us together—that's pulsing all these new feelings in me?

Being a junior planner isn't my dream, and I have three years of experience under my belt now. Isn't it time to stop chasing paperwork and start actually planning events?

Like the charity event I attended this weekend, for example.

And, of course, my mind turns back to Asher. It's only been a few days at this point. The memory will fade, hopefully sooner than later, because I'm already driving myself crazy with how often he pops uninvited into my thoughts.

I was so wrapped up in him that I didn't take the time to appreciate the event itself, nor did I bother networking in any way whatsoever. Who planned the event? Do they need help for next year? Does a private company plan it, or is it run by the Aces organization?

It could've been a great place to get my foot in the door in Vegas if I'm so inclined to move closer to my parents, but Asher distracted me.

He distracted me so much that I find myself at my Wednesday night book club meeting without having finished the book we're discussing.

"What did you think about the twist in chapter thirty-two?" Addy asks.

Chloe and Lauren give their thoughts, and then they all look at me.

"I didn't get to it," I admit. The eyes already looking at me widen. "I didn't finish."

"You didn't finish?" Addy repeats. "But we *always* finish."

"I know we do, and it's like the *one thing* we can count on in this life, but I had planned to read the rest of it on the plane ride home, and then I was just…" I trail off. They're staring at me with slackened jaws.

"You were just," Chloe prompts.

"Distracted," I finished.

"By what?" Lauren asks.

I draw in a deep breath as I prepare to launch into the story that feels like it started as a fairy tale but ended in a way I didn't really expect given how connected I felt to him.

"Oh shit," Chloe murmurs. "Did you see that deep breath?"

"What happened?" Lauren asks.

"You don't have to say," Addy says a little defensively. "What happens in Vegas stays in Vegas and all that. If you did something that you need to leave there—"

I hold up a hand to interrupt her. "It's fine," I say. "Of course I'll tell you all what happened."

"So something did happen," Chloe says flatly.

"Something big," Lauren agrees.

"Oh my God, stop. I met a guy at the charity ball, and we had a really nice night together, and that's it. It's not like it meant anything."

"It's not like *what* meant anything?" Addy asks. "Wait. Did you have sex with him?"

My cheeks burn, and that's my first mistake—letting them see me sweat.

"Oh shit," Chloe breathes. "Feelings." She shakes her head. "She caught feelings."

"Don't embarrass her about it if she did," Lauren scolds her sister.

"Oh my gosh, you two. If she did, then you sitting here blabbing about it isn't going to make her feel any better." Addy shakes her head, and I know I shouldn't be mortified about this in front of my best friends, yet I am.

He hasn't called.

Why the hell hasn't he called?

And that's when Chloe asks, "Was it a football player?"

Everyone knows who the Nash brothers are. They're football royalty, and Asher is the only remaining eligible one of the four brothers who seem to have been God's favorite when they were born since they're all beautiful, athletic, and smart.

If I can't be honest about my weekend with my best friends, then who can I be honest about it with? I need to talk about it, and these are the people I talk about every life event with, major or minor.

"I guess my dad somehow got a last-minute ticket from somebody who was going to bring a date and decided he wasn't. When I sat in the seat reserved for his date, he threw a line at me about how it must be fate because I was sitting in the spot of his date. We got to talking, which led to flirting, which led to drinking, and—"

"And it led to a hotel room?" Lauren guesses.

"Well, he didn't exactly *have* a hotel room when the night started, but I guess he got one when he thought we were heading in that direction," I admit, and I realize how trashy it sounds when I say it that way. It didn't *feel* trashy at the time, but that may have been the alcohol talking.

"Who?" all three of them say at the same time.

I clear my throat. "Asher Nash."

I'm met with silence, followed by squeals and choruses of *holy shit, oh my God*, and *how big was he?*

All at the same time.

I turn to Chloe, who asked the size question, and I hold out my hands to indicate.

All three women gasp.

"Surely not," Chloe breathes.

"I'm not even doing it justice," I admit.

"And he could use it, too?" Lauren asks.

I nod slowly. "Oh yeah. He knew what he was doing."

"So lucky," Addy breathes.

"So then what? He treated you to breakfast, and you're leaving us for Vegas?" Chloe asks.

"Not quite. My parents had to leave early thanks to my dad's stomach issues, and my mom texted me at like two a.m. that they were out of Pepto. I didn't particularly want to explain to them that I slept with one of my dad's players when I showed up in the same dress I wore to the ball the morning after, so I left Asher a note with my number and headed home."

"Ugh, parents with the cockblock," Chloe mutters.

Addy shoots her a look before she turns to me. "Why didn't you wake him up?"

I reach up and tug at the messy bun my hair is currently in. "I tried. I don't know if it was the sex and whiskey or if he's just a heavy sleeper, but he was out."

"So how many hours before he called you?" Lauren asks.

I glance at my watch. "Four days and counting."

Addy winces. "Oh, babe. Maybe he didn't see your note." Her tone is hopeful.

"I don't know how he could have missed it. I stuck it under his phone. He presumably didn't leave his phone in the hotel room, right?"

"Maybe he was so upset and distracted that you were gone that he just…picked up his phone without looking at what was under it," Lauren suggests.

I lift a shoulder. "Maybe. But it sort of feels like the ball's in his court now, and I can't sit by the phone waiting for it to ring."

All three of my friends are quiet, and I know what they're thinking.

I wait for one of them to say it, and it's Chloe. "Then ask your dad for his number. You can't just leave it at one night, Desi."

"You know as well as I do that I can't ask my dad for Asher's number," I say.

"Then find him on social media," Addy suggests.

Chloe and Lauren agree it's a good idea, but I do not.

"No." My voice is firm as I shake my head. "No. If he wants to get in touch, he will."

"So you told him your dad is the new OC, then?" Chloe asks.

"I mean, not exactly," I admit. I tug on my bun again.

Chloe lets out a heavy sigh. "So you're telling me if he was a typical man who didn't spot the tiny detail like a note you left behind, he has no other way of getting in touch with you?"

I purse my lips.

Is she right?

Before I can answer, Lauren asks, "When are you going back to Vegas?"

I lift a shoulder. "No idea. I haven't made plans to return, and honestly, I feel a little burned right now. Maybe when the season starts."

"It's June, babe. The season starts in early September. You're telling me you're going to wait three to four months to visit your parents again?"

"I waited that long the first time to make it out there. Time flies when work keeps you busy, you know? And you know summer is our busiest time. I was shocked Angelica gave me this past weekend off. I can't take another one, especially not so soon."

"Who said it has to be a weekend? It's a short flight. Get your ass back out there," Chloe goads.

She's probably right, but the more someone tells me I should do something, the more I'm going to push back, and I blame my dad and the stubborn gene he bestowed upon his only daughter for that.

"We'll see," I finally say as a way to get them off my back.

I glance out the window at the darkened view of the ocean outside, my chest tight as I think about how it felt like so much more than a one-night stand.

It wasn't, and I remind myself of the truth.

I'm a sand-and-sunshine kind of girl at heart. This is home, and while my parents are in Vegas now, my first time to their new city taught me everything I need to know about it.

I'm not cut out for Vegas.

Chapter 14: Asher Nash

What's in Australia?

Minicamps are over, and the next thing on my calendar is training camp, which starts toward the end of July. Apart from a few engagements my publicist committed me to, I don't have a whole lot going on for the next month.

And I certainly don't want to spend it here in Vegas reminiscing about the woman who disappeared into thin air, nor do I want to spend it playing poker with my father every night.

I head into the training facility to talk to Lincoln on the Friday morning after the charity ball.

It's my last chance to attempt to find her, and if it doesn't pan out, then it was never meant to happen, and I need to get the fuck over it and move the fuck on.

His door is open, so I knock on his doorframe. When he glances up, his eyes focus on my shirt. He rolls his eyes.

"What?" I ask. I glance down at the neon lightning bolts.

"I'd invite you in, but I'm worried about electrocution."

"Then don't go out in a storm with metal in your hand, dickhead," I say.

He flattens his lips at me. "Cut that shit out. What do you want?"

I walk in and plop into the chair on the other side of his desk. "Two things."

He sighs. "One?"

"I want to take on a leadership role with the squad this year."

"Mentor the rookie tight ends, then," he suggests. "Our only formal leadership positions are captains, and those are snagged by people who've been around longer than you and who weren't suspended for a year."

"Thanks for the reminder," I say dryly.

He shrugs. "Truth is hard, bro. Lead by example."

"What about the resident bad boy who cleaned up his act?" I suggest half-jokingly.

"*Have* you cleaned it up, though?" he asks.

"I'm trying to. But that suspension, man." I shake my head. "It's following me. It's a shadow I can't kick."

"I'm not sure you'll ever fully kick it," he says, gentling his tone a bit. "At least not here in Vegas. Memories are short for the good things but long for the negative."

"Yeah, no shit."

"So work harder on positive press, then. Try to replace that shadow with a good one. Maybe move out of that place you're sharing with Dad," he suggests, and that thought hadn't occurred to me.

Maybe part of what's keeping that shadow hanging around is the fact that the guy who was my accomplice in the whole thing is still glued to my side, goading me toward the wrong choices. But he's my dad. It's easy to believe he wants the best for me, even if it isn't always true—even if sometimes he wants what's best for himself.

And it's not just that. I can't abandon him. He was there for me when I needed him, and maybe he needs *me* now.

"Did you have a second thing?" he asks.

"Oh, right. My extra ticket to the charity thing. Who ended up with it?" I ask the question casually even though my heart starts to race.

He shrugs. "No idea. Why?"

"Just curious," I lie.

"Sorry. I gave the ticket to Steve, and I don't know what happened to it after that."

Steve. I could go ask Steve, but that would be even weirder than sitting here asking my brother about it.

I need to let it go, and I think in order to do that, I need to get the fuck out of this place for a while.

"Anything else?" he asks, interrupting my thoughts.

I sigh as I make a snap decision. "I'm heading out for a few weeks. Is there anything I need to know while I'm gone?"

"Heading out for a few weeks?" he repeats. "Where are you going?"

Fuck if I know. Out of here. I need a distraction, and the only time I ever really feel distracted is when I'm traveling. "Australia."

It's the first place that comes to mind.

"Australia? What's in Australia?"

"Kangaroos, the Great Barrier Reef..." My lack of knowledge chooses that moment to show up. "Oh! The Outback."

"Like...the steakhouse?" he asks.

"Well, yeah. Outback Steakhouse is themed around Australia, isn't it?"

He shrugs. "I guess. How long will you be gone?"

"A month." The words are out before I can stop them, but I don't have any reason to sit here fixating on a fucking ghost.

"With who? Dad?"

"Fuck no. If anything, he's one of my motivations for leaving town for a while."

"Yeah," he mutters. "Can't really blame you for that. I don't think there's anything here you need to worry about. Try to stay in shape. Watch out for the crocodiles and be sure to hydrate."

"Yes, sir," I say, and I give him the salute.

"Travel safe, brochacho."

I nod as I stand. "Will do. Hi to Jolene and the kids. I'll bring a boomerang or some shit back for Jonah."

He chuckles, and I head for home, where I look up flights to Australia and book one leaving in the morning and returning in four weeks. I look up places to stay and find a gorgeous house near the beach, and it even has a pool.

It's not the first time I've ducked out of town at the last minute, and I'm certain it won't be the last.

I toss all my laundry into the machine that rarely gets used since I have a service that comes to do my laundry for me, and I add in a few of the soap pods to get it going.

"Are you doing laundry?" my dad asks when he walks in. He tilts his head toward the laundry room.

I nod. "I'm heading out of town in the morning and wanted to pack clean clothes."

He nods at my lightning shirt. "I see you scraped the bottom of the clothes barrel with today's choice. I always do that, too—wear whatever I'm not planning to pack the day before I leave for a trip. Where are you headed?"

I ignore the jab about my clothes. "Australia," I say nonchalantly, as if I've had this idea planned for months instead of minutes.

"Australia? Why is this the first you've mentioned it?"

I shrug. "Oh, didn't I mention it?"

"Who are you going with?"

I need to back slowly away from that question, or I'll somehow find him sitting on the airplane beside me.

"Dude, why all the questions? I'll be back in a month."

"You're leaving for an entire month, and you didn't think to clue your roommate in on that?" he asks.

"Oh, knock that shit off," I say. "You agreed when we moved in together that you weren't going to be standing over my every move."

"Fine, fine," he says, holding up his hands. "I'm going to miss my number one pal." He slugs my shoulder playfully.

"I'll miss you, too, Dad," I say.

Is my dad one of my best friends? Probably.

And to that end, I think I might need some new friends.

Or, at least, I need to form tighter bonds with some different people. Maybe the rookies Lincoln mentioned. If we could drop Austin Fucking Graham, I'd have a much tighter bond with the tight ends. Hell, I'd organize poker nights or strip club visits if it was the right combination of guys, but as it stands, we don't have the right chemistry for shit like that.

Graham is a dad now, though, and hopefully that changes his perspective on shit. I don't know if he's with the mother or not, but I know kids changed Lincoln, and I've seen it happen to other guys I've played with, too.

That's the kind of shit I'm not ready for, though. To be able to take off for a month to Australia for the hell of it because I want to—now *that* is the kind of lifestyle I want.

Having kids, being tied down…it's not for everybody.

Would having a woman at home be nice? Sure, it would. But maybe that's not for everybody, either. Just because my brothers all have that now doesn't mean I should.

For a minute, I might have fallen into some sort of trap thinking it was for me. I was wrong.

And as I step onto the plane that'll take me to Los Angeles before I board another one that'll travel seventeen hours toward Sydney, excitement steps in the place of whatever feelings I had after the charity ball.

Yeah…this is definitely the life for me.

Chapter 15: Asher Nash

Dialed In and Shutting Out

Lincoln wasn't wrong about hydration, though as a desert dweller now, I fared just fine in the Outback. And I learned that it wasn't the crocs that you have to watch out for as much as the snakes and spiders.

I made it back to the States without any Australian venom in my system—unless you count the Australian rum I consumed in rather copious amounts during my stay.

I also ate a fuck ton of Tim Tams, a delightful little treat, and went to the zoo where I had an encounter with a koala.

What I didn't do, however, was fuck my way through the country. In fact, I kept it entirely in my pants, and now that I'm back in Vegas and solidly centered in training camp, I haven't had sex since the night of the charity ball.

I've tugged myself to release plenty of times, but my fist is no replacement for the warm, soft, tight heaven of a woman's cunt. Specifically one with red hair, a gorgeous body, and the ability to call me out and make me laugh at the same time.

It's been a month and a half at this point. A sensible man might've moved on. Hell, a *normal* person should have moved on by now.

I've never been known for my sense or my normalcy.

I keep thinking that once the season starts, maybe I'll see her again. I keep holding out for that.

And also...I can't seem to find a woman who compares to her.

I met plenty of gorgeous women on my trip. I talked to some, even got as far as making out with one...but nothing more than that.

I couldn't seem to find my mojo. I just wasn't interested.

It's like this mystery woman showed up, stole a piece of me, and left with it. It sounds fucking ridiculous, doesn't it? That shit can't happen after one night. It can't.

And yet somehow, it did.

I don't even know who the fuck I am anymore. I thought I'd learn the answers in another country, but as it turns out, as incredible as my month there was...everything was exactly the same when I returned home, including my living situation. I rolled immediately from traveling into a new season, and where I lay my head at night is by far the least of my worries.

I didn't intend to run away from anything while I was gone, but that was essentially the effect of what I did. It didn't change anything, though.

And now we're in the middle of the second week of training camp at a vineyard in California, per the Vegas Aces tradition, and I'm throwing all my energy into leaving every other piece of me out on the field.

I'm proving I'm the best tight end to start this season, and I know I'm blowing all the other choices completely out of the water.

Even Austin Graham acknowledges it one night after a particularly grueling installation earlier in the day. "How'd you learn that play so quick?" he asks.

I roll my shoulders, which has the effect of looking like a shrug even though it's just from soreness. "I'm dialed in, I guess."

"Rub some of that shit off on the rest of us," he teases, and I offer a tight-lipped smile in return.

I think the truth is that nobody here would want the real reason I'm so dialed in.

It's my way of shutting everything else out.

But even though I'm focused and tearing it up at camp, that doesn't mean I've forgotten. It simply means I'm putting it on hold until a later date. But it'll still be there when I return...like it was when I got back from Australia.

Enough time has gone by that I can chalk it up to having been a dream.

Still, even if it *was* just a dream, I know what I want now, and I won't stop at anything short of what I want—what I deserve.

And I deserve a woman with long, red hair and green eyes that latch onto a piece of my soul.

Or, you know, something along those lines. I haven't been able to find anyone who compares, and to be honest, I'm not really looking.

Instead, I'm focusing.

Training camp is as horrendous as it always is, but running on the beach in Australia helped me stay in shape. We plow through our first three opponents in our exhibition games, easily sailing to our wins even with our second- and third-string players in.

Some guys make the team, and others don't. The final roster boasts only four tight ends, and I'm chosen as the starter.

Our offense has traditionally relied more heavily on receivers, but the new OC is a former tight end who wants to see our position get more play time. Coach Dixon has been a valuable asset to our team so far, and he and my brother have bonded over their shared ideals when it comes to play calling—namely, taking risks and surprising our opponents.

It's exactly the way I like to play, and the coaching staff is here to motivate us to reach new heights we've never stretched for before.

As a former tight end, Coach Dixon understands the intricacies that come with the position. What he doesn't seem to get is the fact that oftentimes, I read the play and switch up the route he calls. It's how I've always played, and none of my coaches have ever cared so long as it resulted in points.

I have to believe that he doesn't like it because it's a challenge to his authority as the play caller, but if I see an opening, I'm going to fucking take it whether he likes it or not.

It only happened once so far in a preseason game, and I caught hell for it during halftime.

He didn't care that I scored. He cared that I didn't run his route.

And I caught so much hell for it, in fact, that Lincoln actually pulled me aside before we ran back out to the field. "If you want to be a leader, it starts by listening to your coaches, bro. Let *us* take the risks. You run the plays."

"But I scored," I protested.

He gave me the kind of look that told me to shut the fuck up, and having grown up with three older brothers, let's just say I learned pretty quickly when to shut it down.

I was benched the rest of the game—not because I suck or because they were mad at me for running my own route, but because the coaches always bench the starters in preseason games to give us the best chance at staying healthy for the games that matter.

Our first game of the season is in Chicago, and we roll over the Bears to easily catch our first win. I scored at the end of the third thanks to the quick thinking of our quarterback, Miles Hudson. He was out most of the season I was out, too, but for different reasons. He tore his ACL, and I was suspended.

Still, we came back at the same time, and now we're starting what should be our third season together, but in reality, it's only our second.

He's young—only twenty-five now—but he's a hell of a player. He's quick on his feet and quick at reading plays, and he's also the kind of guy who I could see myself grabbing a beer with after a game.

But we don't.

Mostly because I jet out and don't make myself available. But I don't want to do that anymore. This season is about asserting my value on the Aces as more than just a guy who reliably grabs at least six points every game.

And that's why, after we win in Chicago and board our plane back home, I don't rush to be the first one on the plane. I don't sit in the back row with my AirPods firmly in my ears as I stare out the window so nobody makes eye contact.

Instead, I board somewhere in the middle of the group, and I end up across the aisle from Jaxon Bryant, our top running back. He's on the phone FaceTiming someone, and he hangs up before we take off. I give him his privacy, and when he's done, he glances across the aisle at me.

"What're you doing way up here? Don't you usually sit in the back?"

I chuckle. "Yeah. Just wanted to mix it up. Who was on the phone?"

"My wife. Sounds like our little girl gave her a rough time tonight during bath time, and the wife ended up soaked." He shrugs and laughs as he looks fondly down at his phone, and it feels like I can't escape everyone else's happy endings when I got nothing more than a first name and a hair color.

He turns his attention to his phone, and I slip my AirPods in, feeling more and more like I don't fit in anywhere anymore as I stare out the window at the darkness of night.

We win against the Giants at home in week two, and my dad's waiting at home when I get there.

"What was that fumble in the second?" he asks when I walk in the door.

When I say our relationship is complicated, well, it is. Sometimes he's my best friend and biggest cheerleader, and other times, this is the guy I come home to.

I blow out a breath, and that's when my phone pings me with a new text.

I glance at my watch first and see it's from my brother, Spencer.

Spencer: *You got any plans tomorrow?*

Since we won today, we have tomorrow and Tuesday off from having to go in for tedious meetings. All we have is a bit of homework to review some tape of next week's opponent and, of course, workouts.

Me: *Just a workout in the morning. Why?*

"I asked you a question," my dad says.

"It was a shitty throw and I didn't get a grip on it. Lay off, man. We won."

Spencer: *I need to take a trip to Temecula. Want to go?*

He's in San Diego, and I would guess Temecula is an hour or so from his place. But I can't help but wonder...why?

Me: *Temecula? What the fuck is in Temecula?*

Spencer: *Just have something I need to do and don't want to do alone.*

Spencer isn't the kind of guy who ever asks for help from anyone. I have no idea what's up, and I glance up at my dad, who's glaring at me over my shitty fumble.

I really don't want to sit here with dear old Dad when he's in this sort of state, and besides, family comes first.

Or my brothers do, anyway.

Me: *Name the time.*

Spencer: *My place at eleven?*

"Who are you talking to?" he asks.

"Noneya," I say, tossing one of his old lines right back at him. It's true, though. *Noneya* is short for *none of your business*, and if I tell him Spencer is asking me to fly to California to take a field trip to Temecula, he'll ask a million questions and I'll find myself booking a ticket for two.

Spencer called on me for help. He didn't call Dad.

He rolls his eyes. "Yeah, yeah, yeah."

I run a quick search for flights and find one that gets in at ten. Close enough. I book myself a ticket.

Me: *I'll be there.*

Maybe it'll even give me a chance to talk about my situation with someone who knows me but doesn't live in the same town as me.

Maybe he'll have some advice about how to move the fuck on since I'm still dwelling on her three months later.

Chapter 16: Asher Nash

Not For Long

It turns out my trip to see Spencer didn't solve any of my problems, but somehow it seemed to solve a bunch of his.

I'm still floundering around, lost in a daze, confused over what I really want out of this life.

It's Wednesday when I walk into Coach Dixon's office and slide into the chair across from him.

"Asher Nash," he says by way of greeting as he glances up at me.

"Coach Dixon," I say formally with a nod. I'm not sure what this meeting is about, but he's meeting with everyone on offense after the first two games. I'm sure I'll catch heat for the same fumble my dad already called me on, but I'd rather hear it from a coach than from my own father, I guess.

He taps a button on his computer, and we both see a play from our last game against the Giants pulled up on the television screen on the wall beside us.

"This play was executed perfectly," he says, nodding to a block I made that allowed Miles to throw to Tristan Higgins for a touchdown. "Look at that block." He draws something on the screen showing a route I could've taken, and honestly, it was my instinct to run it, but I knew I had to make the block instead. "I could see the fire in you that you wanted to run this one, but that block was critical, and because of that team effort instead of the individual heroics, we scored." He runs the play again without his drawings on the screen. "Beautiful," he murmurs at the end.

"Thanks, Coach." The play was designed for Tristan. He's fast as fuck, and I know my role along with my limitations. "It wasn't my drive to score on, and it was an incredible call."

He sits back in his chair. "I can't figure you out, Nash," he says. "Sometimes you take these risks that make me think you're one kind of player, and other times you run the play we call. Sometimes you take risks with fashion," he says, nodding toward my designer equestrian knight shirt, "and other times you're a bit more conservative. Tell me a little more about who Asher Nash is. Help me understand."

I press my lips together as I try to come up with an answer to that. "I, uh…" I lift both shoulders. "I'm the youngest of the Nash brothers, which is both a blessing and a curse." I nod down at my shirt. "I like wearing designer clothes mostly to get a rise out of my more traditional brothers. I thrive on adventure, and sometimes that includes taking risks."

He chuckles, and then he leans forward and rests his chin on his steepled fingers. "Talk to me about how it's a curse."

I blow out a breath. "I've lived in their shadows my entire life. It's hard to establish your own identity while still trying to meet the expectations the world lays on you from a young age. I was barely a teenager when Lincoln was drafted, and when both Grayson and Spencer followed, it was never even an option for me."

"You say that like you don't want to play," he says.

I shake my head. "It's not like that at all. I love this game. I love playing, and I have since high school. It's my entire life." So much so that I've pushed every other important thing off my radar altogether.

Not every player does that.

Many guys in the league have successful relationships, even marriages and families. But I've worked so hard to keep football at the center of my life that I haven't given anything else a fair chance.

"Why since high school?" he asks.

Oh. We're going there already.

I draw in a deep breath and bite the inside of my cheek before I lay out the confession. "It was all I had left after my best friend overdosed."

"Jesus, Asher. I'm so sorry. I had no idea."

I'm not sure why I keep talking, but I do. Just the way Coach Dixon is looking at me makes me feel like I can confide in him, I guess. "He was a running back, and we were really tight. I wasn't into experimenting with drugs since I knew I had a real shot at the league. He did, too, but he was a risk-taker. I guess that's when I started to take risks myself—just smarter ones, I guess. And I threw myself into football."

"But?" he prompts.

"But, also like my brothers, I don't know what else there is for me. Not For Long, right?" I say, repeating the mantra that we always say when talking about what the letters stand for in NFL. Players are lucky to get more than five years out of this career. I'm in my sixth year. I know I make the list as one of the lucky ones, but the peak for tight ends is ages twenty-five to twenty-seven. I spent one of my peak years suspended, and I'm still trying to dig my way back from that. I finally admit that to Coach. "I missed an entire year due to a stupid mistake, and I'm still trying to fix my reputation because of that."

"Tell me what happened. All I know is what I heard. I need it from the source," he says.

I clear my throat and divert my gaze out the window as his eyes seem to pin me to my seat. "My dad—the man who was there for me when I lost my best friend—asked me to place some bets for him. He was getting into some trouble with his gambling habits, so I did it. And then I got into some trouble, too. I asked Lincoln for help, and I took full responsibility for it." I turn my gaze back to Coach Dixon. "I shouldn't have done it. I knew it then, I know it now, and I paid the price. But paying the price doesn't fix my reputation, and even in the locker room, it doesn't feel like I have anyone's respect. They think I'm here because of my brother, that I got off easy by only getting one year for my sins." I hold up both hands a little helplessly.

I wasn't expecting to go quite that deep during this meeting, but I guess all the frustrations that have been brimming for the last year are coming to a head.

He presses his lips together and nods. He sits back in his chair, studying me. "I like you, Asher. I think you are one of the greatest assets we have on this team. You know, when we get you to run the plays we've designed for you consistently." He leans forward again. "Look, I'm new here, so this is a clean slate for me. Whatever happened in the past is in the past. I know you're here because you're a great player, not because of your brother. You know the best way to beat the locker room chatter is to prove them wrong."

I nod. I know he's right. "I'm trying."

"How?"

It's a fair question—one I'm not entirely sure I have the answer to. "Head down, focus on."

"That's important, but it's equally important to show up for your teammates outside of office hours. You catch my drift?"

I nod. He's right. I need to do more of the sitting in the middle of the plane thing. More joining them for a night at the bar. More leading by example to actually be the man with honesty and integrity that I want to be perceived as.

I admitted the truth when I placed those bets. Granted, I admitted it after I got into trouble and needed to borrow money from Lincoln, but I knew he'd have to go to the league with the information, and I did it anyway. I knew he'd have to prove he'd lead with honesty and integrity, and he did. I thought admitting it meant I was, too. But nobody took it that way, I guess.

"What about your dad? Are you still close with him?" he asks.

His innuendo is clear. My dad isn't the honest, trustworthy man who was there for his teammates, even if he was there for me when Jake died.

"Yes and no. I'm the closest to him out of the four brothers, but sometimes I think it has more to do with proximity."

"Proximity?" he repeats.

"We moved in together when my parents got divorced—the year I was suspended. He's hard on all four of us, most of all on Lincoln, but I think of the four of us, I was always closest to him. Probably because he focused so hard on my high school career after my brothers were out of the house. We had one-on-one time my brothers didn't get with him." I shrug. "It is what it is, though. When I get home after a game, the focus is never on what went well. It's always on whatever mistakes I made."

His brows draw together. "That must be hard. As a father myself, I take so much pride in the things my daughter accomplishes. I can't imagine what positives would come out of harping on the negative."

"I didn't know you had a daughter."

He chuckles. "I do. She's twenty-five and doesn't date football players, so don't get any ideas."

I laugh as I hold my hands up. "You have my word, sir. I respect the hell out of you, and I'd never dream of it."

He eyes me warily and shifts the subject. Clearly, his daughter is off-limits, and that's fine. I'm not interested anyway, even with that whole tempting, forbidden aspect. I can't be when my mind is still on a fucking one-night stand that happened three months ago.

I'll get over it. I'll move on at some point. But for now, I'm going to take Coach's advice and work on being the kind of player that commands the respect of my teammates.

It's my only option if I want to change the perception of me in the locker room.

Chapter 17: Desiree Dixon

Touchy-Touchied

"Come on, Desi. You missed the first home game because of a wedding. Can't you come to the second?" my mom asks.

I stare out my windshield as I try to push this conversation to the end. I thought I'd give my mom a quick call before I headed to Chloe and Lauren's apartment for our book club meeting tonight, but she's begging me to come visit, and I have a feeling she isn't going to let me hang up until I've committed to coming.

Truth be told, I've been avoiding Vegas.

I tried it once more in July before my dad took off for training camp at the extreme goading of my best friends, and I never ran into Asher.

I told myself that if it was meant to be, we'd run into each other again.

Well, we didn't, and it's time for me to move on.

Only…I haven't. Not exactly.

I've tried. Believe me, I've tried.

Chloe talked me into a dating app.

I went on three dates only to discover that the particular dating app I chose was a hookup app, and I wasn't interested enough in any of the three men to sleep with them five minutes after meeting them.

They didn't have the magic Asher and I had. I can't seem to recreate that no matter how hard I try, but it's been over three months at this point. I think I must be remembering it differently than how it really happened. I must be putting him on some sort of pedestal.

And I know if I go to the game and stand in the family area afterward, waiting for my father to walk out, and I watch Asher walk out and kiss some other woman waiting for him, it'll only break my heart.

I also know it'll reveal to him who my father is, and I have no idea what effect that'll have.

And that's why I've stayed away.

I want to see him again, but I want to do it in a way that doesn't make me look like I'm desperately chasing after him. Not when he hurt me by never calling me.

It might've only been one night, but the more time that passes, the more anger I feel. The more rage.

Why the hell didn't he call? Didn't he feel that connection the way I felt it?

"Yeah," I finally tell my mom over the phone. The truth is that I'm not really all that busy at work. The busy season of summer has come to an end, and I've been slowly backing away from projects as I've been taking the time to read up on creating my own business. "I suppose I can join you at the second game."

"For the whole weekend?" she asks hopefully.

"I actually do have an event on Saturday afternoon, but I can fly out afterward and stay through Thursday evening."

"We get you for five whole days?" she asks.

I laugh. "Unless I make friends there."

"Oh, yes! Steve and Barb's daughter. She's a couple years younger than you, and then there's Ellie Dalton, who is *such* a sweetheart, and she's a couple years older than you, I think." She's babbling, and wait a second...

"Did you just say Ellie?"

"Mm-hmm, yes. Why?"

"I met her at the charity ball. She was really nice," I say.

"Yes! That's her. She works with a lot of the players as a publicist. Oh! And Erin, who runs the charitable contributions along with Lily, the team owner's secretary. They were the two behind the charity ball, and I've heard murmurs that they want to outsource the planning next year." She says it as a hint, like I could get my hands in that pot, but she's always dreamed much bigger than reality. I already get the hint that she'd love nothing more than for me to move to Vegas and take on the charity ball as my first client when I open my own event planning business, but there are several issues with that.

One being that I'm not planning to move to Vegas.

Another being that all the research I've done about starting up my own business is based in San Diego...not Las Vegas.

"I'd love to meet all of them," I say, rather than giving into the big plans she's making for me.

"I'll tell Vicki to book your travel."

"Thanks, Mom. I need to go. The girls are waiting for me."

"I can't wait to see you, honey. Have fun, and tell the girls hi for me."

"I will. Love you." I end the call after she tells me she loves me, too, and I head up to Chloe and Lauren's third-floor apartment. Addy's already there, and all three women are waiting for me when Lauren opens the door.

"Finally," she scolds jokingly.

"Sorry. I was on the phone with my mom, and she wouldn't let me hang up until I committed to a visit." I roll my eyes.

"And?" Chloe prompts, her eyes lighting up.

The three of them have been up my ass about getting back to Vegas, and it's only made me push harder in the other direction, as one does.

I sigh. "And I'm going this weekend to attend the game with my mother, and I'll be staying a few days."

"Oh my God, oh my God, oh my God!" Chloe squeals as Addy claps her hands and Lauren says, "This is it!"

I roll my eyes at the three of them. "You are all way too much. He's not interested, and I don't know why you all think this means I'm going to see him again. I went in July, and he wasn't there, remember? He's moved on, I've moved on, it's fine." It's also a lie. I don't know if he's moved on, and I don't know if I have, either.

"I'm even more convinced this is happening," Chloe says as she shakes her head at me.

"Can we get to the book?" I ask, holding up my copy.

"Desi and Asher sitting in a tree," Lauren singsongs.

I purse my lips as that rage over him not calling me brims back to the surface. I don't want to take it out on them, but they've been teasing me for three months, and frankly, I'm sick of it.

I stand, and I head toward the door.

"Where are you going?" Addy asks.

"I'd rather go home than sit through this," I say.

"Don't be so dramatic," Lauren huffs.

"We'll stop," Addy promises. "Right, girls?" She elbows Chloe.

"Fine," Chloe mutters, and Lauren agrees, too.

I raise my brows and set my hand on my hip. "Not one more word about it, or I'm out. Okay?"

Chloe holds up her hands. "Touchy, touchy."

She's not wrong, and it's most likely because I have not been touchy-touchied in way too long.

I get through book club without any more teasing, and after the birthday party celebrating a family's seventy-five-year-old matriarch on Saturday, I head to the airport to catch my flight. I land in Vegas a little before ten at night, and I think about going out and doing something.

But I don't have friends here yet, mostly because I've been staunchly avoiding this town, so I head straight for Mom and Dad's mansion.

Mom is still awake when I get there, and Dad isn't at home since the entire team stays at a hotel the night before a game.

That means my dad is in the same hotel as Asher.

I try as hard as I can to push him out of my thoughts, but it's pretty damn hard when I'm *not* in the same town as him, never mind when he's only a few miles away.

She's ready for bed, so she heads up after she makes sure I'm settled and comfortable, and I take the opportunity to catch up on reading the next book we're talking about at book club.

I can't concentrate, though. It's easy to pretend like it was all some dream when I'm in a different state and over three hundred miles separate us. It's less easy to do that when I know we're laying our heads down in the same damn town.

Sleep eludes me, and we have the early game in the morning. I shower, curl my hair, and slip into the DALTON 5 jersey my dad left on my dresser for me. Jack Dalton isn't the quarterback of the Vegas Aces anymore, but he does own the team, and I think my dad wanted me to wear his jersey as a nod to his new boss. I pair it with a black sequined skirt, and I'm ready to go.

On the ride to the stadium, my mom tells me how she bought a pair of season tickets twelve rows up from the fifty-yard line, where she can see the whole field and keep an eye on my dad.

My heart races as I consider that.

I can't imagine how much she shelled out for the seats, but she always preferred to be in the center of the action versus up in the suites. It's how she met my dad, after all. *Her* dad was a huge college football fanatic, and she went with him to a game at his alma mater. My dad was a senior at the time, and he spotted her in the crowd from the field, ran over to the stands after the game, and got her number.

The rest is history.

I always sort of imagined something like that happening for me, too, but my dad would never allow it.

The closer we get to the stadium, the harder it hits me that I'm going to be in the same building as the man I haven't stopped thinking about since the charity ball. My heart isn't just racing now because of the location of our seats.

The truth is that if my dad spotted my mom from the field all those years ago, Asher could spot me here, too.

Will he be happy to see me? I have no idea, and I'm not quite sure how I'll feel, either.

My mom has been to this stadium a few times now, and as the car drops us at the front of the building, we head in with the fans. My heart beats faster as I walk through the metal detector. Still faster as my ticket is scanned and I enter the building.

We walk through the concourse toward our section, and the closer we get to our seats, the more nervous I become. By the time we locate the twelfth row, my heart is racing.

I glance down at the field. We're here early, but some of the players are out on the field warming up prior to the game. They're in the zone, and I scan for him, but I don't see him. It's hard to tell from up here, though, especially because the players aren't wearing their numbers ahead of the game. They're wearing joggers and Vegas Aces shirts or sweatshirts to keep their muscles warmed up.

"Are you okay, honey?" my mom asks.

I nod. "I could use some water," I croak. I push to a stand. "Need anything?"

"I'll take a water, too. And a bag of peanuts."

"Sure." I rush up the stairs toward the concourse, and I'm not sure how I'm going to talk myself into returning to my seat.

How the hell can I be *this* affected after *one night* with him?

And what the hell am I going to do after the game when I'll surely run into him?

Chapter 18: Asher Nash

Is That Something I Want

I'm dialed in again, focused, as rap music blares in my ears.

Or I'm faking like I am, anyway.

I can't seem to get in the right headspace. Everything feels like I'm looking in from the outside lately rather than participating, regardless of how much participating I'm actually doing.

It's sort of how I've felt my entire life, I guess.

I think a lot of it has to do with the fact that I'm the youngest. Nobody really ever knew what to make of me. I'm the unpredictable one. Spontaneous. Eccentric. Weird. A bad boy. A rule-breaker.

My brothers weren't like that. They followed the rules, got good grades, and worked hard. They weren't perfect. They got in trouble, had one-night stands, and broke hearts. But ultimately, they all ended up where they are now: happy, successful, and rich in many different ways.

I'm a hard worker, too, I guess, but I never really had to be. Things always came naturally to me. People say it's because my brothers paved the way for me. Maybe that's true.

I jog along the half of the field we have for our warm-ups, the light cardio getting my body ready for game time. I do some stretches, and then we have our position drills that Coach Bruce, our tight end coach, leads us through. Ben Olson, a former Vegas Aces tight end, is here today, too, and he's conferring with Coach Bruce while the four of us tight ends—Austin Graham, Justin Miller, Chase Morgan, and myself—run footwork drills.

I should be closer with these three men than I am, but there's a divide between us that's solely due to the fact that I'm starting every game this season and they are not.

In formations when we use two or three tight ends, they'll get playing time. But not as much as I will.

I don't need to be best friends with the people on this field, but having mutual respect would be nice.

It didn't feel like things were like this back in Indy where I started my career. I had friends there, but I still held back from getting too close. It's the nature of this business. People come and go, and watching all three of my brothers walk out the door when they each turned old enough to do it made me feel like everyone eventually leaves.

Even my parents split up when their boys were all grown, which only served as one more example of everyone leaving.

I suppose it's why I don't get too close to anybody.

My closest friends are probably my brothers, and that's only because we share blood.

Would I be friends with Lincoln if we met outside of our family? Probably not. He's serious and focused like I am when it comes to the game. He's a leader and probably the one of my brothers I'd most want to emulate…except he's married now and has a kid and a stepkid. We're in two different phases of life.

Would I be friends with Grayson if we met outside our family? Maybe. He's the life of the party, the charismatic guy everybody loves, but also the guy who doesn't really let anybody get too close. If I were deemed worthy of being let into his inner circle, maybe we'd be tight.

And what about Spencer? He's the logical, smart, responsible one. His hobby is building Lego sets, while my hobby is destroying them—much to his complete and total irritation when we were kids. But he's the one who called on me to accompany him to Temecula last week, and he's the one I confided in about my night with Des on that same trip. I was vague about it, opting not to get into the thick of it. I told him I'd met someone I only had one night with, but I left out the fact that it was over three months ago.

I didn't want to sound like a total loser, even if that pretty much sums me up.

We talked about how love isn't always logical, and I was easily able to talk him through his own problems by looking at what he was going through from an outside perspective.

He's scared of commitment. I don't want it. Grayson nearly walked away from the love of his life to avoid it. Lincoln waited around for the same woman for twenty years.

Honestly, each of these events just made me see how much our parents fucked us up.

I think for the hundredth time how I should move out of that place Dad and I are sharing, but truthfully, I'm not home all that much.

I glance up in the stands. Both my parents are here somewhere. I usually get my dad a single seat in the lower level, and he comes to every game he can so long as one of us buys him a ticket.

My mom usually sits in the owner's suite. With one of her sons coaching, one of her sons playing, and one of her sons recently retired from this team, she loves being here every chance she gets, even though she lives full time in New York.

I refocus on the field. The stands are filling as we warm up. I love the roar of the crowd, the sound of cheering, the deafening rumble when we score. I love seeing the faces of each of the sixty-five thousand fans who will fill these seats between now and kickoff.

I think about one more glance around the stadium. What if she's here?

Exactly. It's a colossal *what-if*, and I can't do it. I can't see her before a game.

But my gut tells me she's here.

I'm not sure *why*, but this strange feeling falls over me.

I can't look for her. It'll only steal my focus the way she stole a piece of me, and I can't afford that when I'm about to start the second home game of the season.

We head into the locker room, and my brother says a few words to motivate us. Travis Woods, one of our team captains this year, steps up and says some motivating shit, too, and then it's game time.

The starters are introduced, and we each run through the tunnel formed by our teammates as pyrotechnics explode on the field. I don't even hear the hype music over the roar of the crowd.

I take my place on the sidelines next to Travis, who's one of the starting wide receivers. He motions to somebody up in the suite, presumably his wife and kid, and I watch as Lincoln does something similar to his wife and kids.

I'm surrounded by these men who think of their women before they take the field for this game we're all so focused on, this game we all love so damn much…this game that has always come first.

I don't have that, and I never wanted it. But something feels like it's changing.

It's as I head off the field at the two-minute warning when I glance up at the scoreboard. We're up thirty-one to seventeen. We've got this in the bag. I don't even need to get back out on that field for the final snap, though I will.

My eyes edge from the scoreboard to the fans in front of me. They're all up on their feet now, yelling and screaming as we wrap up this win, and as my eyes move up the rows from beneath my helmet, that's when I see it.

Long, red hair swirling around shoulders.

She's yelling like all the fans are as they create a deafening cacophony of noise.

My eyes move to her face. Her green eyes are on me, and they sparkle brightly in that unique shade even from here.

My breath catches in my throat as I realize *it's her*.

She's here.

She can't know I'm looking at her from under my helmet, yet her mouth closes, and she freezes.

My eyes edge down a little lower, and it's all wrong. Totally wrong.

She's wearing a red Aces jersey with the number *five* on it.

It's missing the fucking eight.

She's here, and she's wearing the wrong man's number, and rage fills me at the realization.

But one thing is clear.

I need to find her after the game. It's time for the explanation she never gave me so I can finally put her out of my fucking head once and for all.

Chapter 19: Desiree Dixon

You Know the Rule

I freeze. Did he just spot me?

His head was turned in my direction, and I *swear* our eyes connected, but it was hard to tell with that helmet on.

It was like I could feel that shade of navy blue as it branded me in place. Holy hell, the chemistry is *heated* between us.

And I guess the next question is…what's he going to do about it?

What am *I* going to do about it?

I was hurt when he didn't call, but suddenly that hurt seems to fall to the wayside as I want to know *why* he never called.

An explanation is the least he can give me. It's not like this is the last time we'll run into each other. He's on my dad's team now, and by default, I have to cheer for my dad's team.

I'll be around, and if nothing else, it'd be nice to clear the air.

The game ends, and my mom and I give the stadium a minute to clear out before I follow her down toward the locker room. There's a family waiting area that's filled with wives and kids of the players and coaching staff as they wait for their loved ones to exit, and it's about a half hour after the game ends before the first player—the kicker—exits the locker room. He heads toward a woman waiting for him, and he bends down to kiss her before he takes her hand and they leave together.

More players walk out, some individually and others in bigger groups. The star players and some of the coaches have to talk to the media after the game, so my dad won't be out for a while. He drove here this morning, and my mom and I will go home with him, so we wait.

"It's Desi, right?" a voice to my right asks, and I glance over to find Ellie Dalton.

I lean in and give her a quick hug. "Yes! Ellie! So good to see you again. What are you doing here?"

"Well, many reasons." She laughs. "I work with a bunch of players here, my husband is a consultant to the coaching staff, and my brother-in-law owns the team. So I pretty much live here. Is this your first home game?"

I nod as I squeeze mom's arm. "Decided to tag along with my mom."

Ellie smiles. "Moms are the greatest, aren't they? Mine is at home with my kids right now, bless her heart."

I laugh along with her, but I have no idea what it's like to leave Mom home with the kids.

We make small talk until her husband walks out, and my dad comes shortly after that. "Good game, Dad," I say, slapping him a high-five, and he grabs me into a hug.

The quarterback exits behind my dad, which means the star players are coming out soon.

Asher is a star player.

He's going to come out soon, and he's going to see me, and…

Then what?

"Because my good luck charms were here." He hugs my mom next, and then he slings his arm around my shoulders. "Where to?"

Just as I open my mouth to answer, the door to the locker room opens, and Asher Nash walks out. He's wearing a silky shirt with pineapples all over it, and something about his fashion choices make him even more endearing. He doesn't seem to care what anyone thinks about him, whether it's that gold suit he wore to the ball or this pineapple shirt or any one of the dozens of wild patterns he's worn over the years in public.

It doesn't matter what he has on. He's always hot.

His eyes search the area where families are gathered, and he freezes when he spots me.

He can't be more than ten feet away from me, and all I can think about is how he had my tits pressed up against the hotel window as he shoved a finger into me from behind.

My entire body somehow freezes and heats at the exact same time.

Holy shit, the connection between us is *intense*.

A woman who looks like she's probably his mother walks over to him and gives him a hug, and I'm staring as my dad waits for my answer.

Asher is staring back at me.

Heat seems to be flying across the room between the two of us, and there's no way the people in here don't sense it. There's no way.

It's like time freezes as navy blue meets green across the room.

He's hotter than I remember. My memory didn't do him justice.

And it hurts all the more that he didn't bother using my number, that he could so easily write the two of us off when I *know* something big and important started that night.

That's when Ellie jumps in. "Oh, Coach Dixon, I was going to invite your daughter to come out with us. We're going to go to the Gridiron to grab a few drinks. Is it okay if we steal her?"

My head swings over to her and then to my dad.

My dad looks at me as if he's gauging whether I want to go or not. My eyes are bugging out of my head as Ellie just announced to the entire room that I'm Bill Dixon's daughter, and surely Asher heard that since he's within ten feet.

My heart races.

"If she wants to go, it's fine by me," Dad says to Ellie. He leans in toward me. "But you know the rule. No football players."

Right, Dad.

As if rules weren't made specifically to be broken.

He says the words loud enough that everyone around us hears them, and I know he's just trying to protect me.

It all stems back to Clayton Mack, the superstar wide receiver on the San Diego Storm. I'd watched him all through college, and we were the same age. So when the Storm held a family night at the stadium after he was drafted and we happened to be in the same place at the same time, I took my shot.

He asked me out.

We both fell hard and fast despite my father's warnings that he wanted better for me than a football player.

But as we became comfortable, I fell down his list of priorities until I felt like the only reason he was still with me was because my dad was a coach on the team.

He didn't exactly deny it. Things had fizzled out for him, and we were young at just twenty-two. He ended things, and I was heartbroken. And as my dad watched me cry over a football player, that was the moment when he made me swear I'd never date someone on his team again.

Ellie laughs. "I married one. Some of them really aren't so bad." She offers me a wink. "So you'll come out with us?"

Asher's eyes are still on me. How do I know this? Oh, only because mine edge over to him, and he's still watching me.

"Yeah, sure. I'd love to," I murmur.

I watch as Asher breaks away from the woman he's hugging as Luke walks over toward him.

They exchange words as my dad pulls my attention back to him, asking me what I thought of the game, and I'm too distracted to answer with anything coherent as I wonder what Asher and Luke are talking about.

Is he finding out where we're going so he can go, too?

What if he shows up?

Why did I come here? Do I *want* him to show up?

Of fucking course I want him to show up. I've hardly stopped thinking about our night together since it happened, and all I can do is hope that tonight I can finally get the answers I deserve.

I ride with Luke and Ellie to the Gridiron. Also in our car are Luke's sister, Kaylee, and her husband, former Aces star tight end and resident hot guy Ben Olson. Being in this car is sort of like stepping into a dream.

"Tell us everything we need to know about Desi Dixon," Kaylee says as we make our way over to the bar.

I laugh as I hold a hand to my forehead. "Oh, God. What do you want to know?"

I don't really want to get into the fact that my mom's a billionaire and I'm the sole heiress to her fortune. They may actually already know that about me if they bothered to do any research at all about their new OC.

"Where do you live? What do you do?" Kaylee asks.

"I'm a junior event planner in San Diego."

"You should come be a senior planner in Vegas," Ben suggests.

"Truthfully, I'd love to run my own event business someday. I always tell people I like to party, so I decided to make a living planning them," I admit.

Everyone laughs at that, though to me, it's just the truth.

"You would love Vegas," Ellie agrees. "There's a party pretty much every minute of every day somewhere around here, and most of them take some level of planning."

"What I'd really love to do is give back to my community. I've started looking into running my own business planning charity events," I say.

"Ooh, I know Erin wants help with the Wild Aces Charity Ball," Ellie says. "She's the director of charitable contributions for the Aces, and she already had a full plate when the ball was added. If she could outsource that, she could get her focus back into doing more community outreach with players."

"Jack was saying she's looking for an assistant," Luke pipes in from the driver's seat, referring to his brother and the team owner...and the guy whose jersey I'm currently wearing. "It's not the same as being a senior event planner running your own business, but if you want to get your foot in the door in Vegas, we know people."

I laugh. "That's really sweet of you, but I don't think I'm leaving San Diego."

"I don't blame you," Kaylee says. "We *love* San Diego. We're there all the time using Jack's beach house." She elbows her husband, and they both laugh.

"Why don't you want to move here?" Ellie asks.

I sigh. "I wasn't expecting my dad to move, to be honest. My life is there. My friends, my career." I lift a shoulder. "The Storm."

"The Storm," Ben snorts. "Look, we'll be your friends here, and we already practically got you the job at the Aces. We'll convert you to a fan, too."

I laugh as I hold up both hands. "I'm working on it. I always cheer for my dad. But if the Aces were playing the Storm…" I trail off and make a face that says how unsure I am of who I'd cheer for in that situation.

Everyone laughs as Luke parks at the bar, and we all hop out. Truth be told, I do feel like I fit in here. I don't know if I could sit with Ellie and Kaylee discussing the spicy scenes in whatever book I'm reading, but I could fly back to San Diego for book night, or we could do it over Zoom if we had to.

I'm not really considering moving here.

It's just a thought.

But as we walk into the Gridiron, I spot Asher Nash sitting at a table with a few of his teammates.

His heated eyes fall to me, and I'm filled with hope that maybe there's a chance.

Chapter 20: Asher Nash

Why the Fuck Does She Have to Be My Coach's
Daughter?

I had to come.

I had to talk to her.

I had to…have a drink.

"You're wearing pineapples on your shirt and drinking tequila?" Justin asks.

I know he's trying to make conversation, but I'm trying to make eye contact with someone across the bar.

"They say agave pairs well with pineapple," I mutter.

She seems focused on her conversation with Ellie Dalton, my publicist, and I wonder if I could covertly sneak Ellie a text to let her know I need a minute with the OC's daughter.

She's the fucking OC's daughter.

Of course she is.

That makes the fruit even more forbidden. It makes me want another taste, another thrust, another night.

Fuck, though. I can't. He's my new coach, and I'm doing everything I can to fix my reputation. Banging the coach's daughter isn't exactly part of that plan, particularly not when we bonded last week and I told him I'd never even think of going near his daughter.

Fuck.

It's been three long as fuck months, during which time I assumed the memory would fade. It hasn't. It's as if that night happened last night, and now that we're in the same room again…I can see the heat in her eyes. But there's something else—something that wasn't there before.

And I think it might be anger.

I need to talk to her. I need to get her alone. I need to find out why she bolted without so much as a goodbye. It's preyed on my confidence for months now, making me feel completely out of my usual zone. It's consumed me in a way that doesn't make any fucking sense, but now it does. It makes *so* much sense.

It's the universe fucking with me.

I try to focus on conversation with the men at my table, but it's useless. How can I focus when she's here, and I need answers?

"Dude, why'd you bother coming out if you're just going to sit there brooding?" Chase asks.

I'm sitting with the two tight ends who aren't total assholes, obviously not including Austin Graham, and a few guys from our O-line.

They're celebrating our win, and I should be, too.

I drain the tequila left in my glass, and my eyes have been on Des since she walked in the place. She ordered a drink. It's almost gone now.

I watch her walk across the bar and down the little hallway leading to the bathroom.

It's quiet there.

Private.

I've been down that hallway enough times to be quite familiar with it, and I'm not missing my chance to get her alone and ask the one question I need to ask.

"Fuck if I know," I admit to Chase. "Excuse me." I nod toward the end of the booth since I'm situated on the inside, and the two men beside me get up so I can get out.

When I walk into the hallway, I'm surprised to see her standing outside the ladies' room, leaning on the wall next to the door that leads into the break room.

Her head is tilted back as she looks up at the ceiling, and it's as if she's drawing in a deep breath.

Jesus Christ, she's beautiful with her long legs and her red hair, and the connection feels like it's still very much there. I didn't imagine it.

Her tits heave with her deep breath. She's so *different* from the women I've been with. She's a wild card, I think, and it feels as if I've met my match.

She senses motion by the doorway, and her head tilts down as her eyes fall to me. Her breath hitches as I take a step toward her.

"So you're Coach Dixon's daughter," I say flatly.

"And you're a player on his team."

I press my lips together and nod, and for the first time, I wonder if she knew that all along. We face off for a few intense seconds, and then I take a step toward her. She looks almost…scared.

"Why'd you leave?" I demand.

She looks confused. "Leave what?"

"The night of the charity ball. You left. You didn't say goodbye."

A light seems to snap into her eyes. "I tried to wake you. You wouldn't move."

"So you just left?"

She lifts a shoulder. "My mom texted me that my dad needed meds. She asked me to bring some home. I left my number."

Right. Her mom. Her *dad*.

My coach.

I push that aside for the moment as my brows pinch together. "You…left your number?"

"Right under your phone where you couldn't miss it."

I obviously did miss it. I take another step toward her. I can smell her from here—that coconutty, beachy scent that I remember so well.

"I was devastated you never called," she admits.

"Fuck," I mutter. "I never saw it."

"Oh," she says. Her eyes flick away from me for a second before returning to mine. "And if you had?"

That's one of the things I like about her. She's not afraid to ask the questions that leave her vulnerable, too. It makes me feel like we're in this together.

"That night, Des..." I trail off, not sure what to say, not sure what to *do*. I've never felt this unsure about myself before. Ever. "It was one of the best nights I've ever had," I finally admit. "And when I woke up and you were gone, I was devastated, too." It feels too raw, too real, too exposed to be admitting these things to her.

I take the final step toward her, closing the gap between us as I push my hips to hers, boxing her in against the wall.

Anybody could walk down this hallway. Anybody could see us here, and anybody could report back to her father what's going on.

I don't think I can make myself stop. I need to touch her. I need to kiss her. I need to fuck her.

She swallows, her eyes moving up to mine as heat passes between us.

I run my fingertips lightly along her jawline as my eyes search hers. "I want this, Des. I want *you* in a way I'm not sure I've ever wanted anyone before." I lean down and nip a kiss to her jaw where my fingers just were.

Her arms loop around my waist, and she pulls me tightly against her body. "I want you, too," she breathes.

I pull back to stare down at her, and the intensity between us is overwhelming. It feels so *right*. Why the fuck does she have to be my coach's daughter?

The thought snaps me back to reality. "Fuck," I mutter. "I can't, Des. I can't do this with the OC's daughter. No matter how much I want you, I can't be with you."

"Then we do it in secret," she suggests, and she rises up to her tiptoes to press soft kisses along my jawline. She trails them down my neck, and I tilt my head back, my neck cording as I stare up at the ceiling, as if the answer will be there. "Just one time, Asher," she begs. "Give me one more time, so I can see if whatever we shared that night is real or if it will always belong to that one night."

One night is a dangerous fucking game when the feelings between us are this strong.

It's just lust. Attraction. It can't be real feelings, not when it was only one night. Maybe I need to give in to prove that's true.

But the relief I felt when I saw her in the family waiting room earlier tells me it's not true at all.

And the stunned devastation that followed it when I heard Ellie's words that she's Coach Dixon's daughter tell me everything I need to know about my feelings for this woman.

They make no sense. They're overboard, overwhelming, out of control.

But that tracks. That's me. The baby of the family. Sometimes it feels like being the youngest—the baby—is my only identity.

Little Asher Nash, the adventurous, sometimes impulsive, sometimes petulant one. The one who sometimes bucks authority and has a wild streak and has an eccentric fashion sense but always manages to come out on top…until that one time he didn't.

And now I'm paying the ultimate price for that as I realize that in order to get back to the top in my career, I might have to sacrifice what has the potential to be the most important part of my personal life.

One taste. I can allow myself one taste, a final goodbye to the thing that never should've happened with the woman it never should've happened with in the first place.

I lean down and brush my lips to hers, and the mere brush isn't enough.

I press my mouth more fully to hers, and her mouth opens immediately to mine, plush and pliable. The urgency is intense as we make out in this tiny hallway, and anybody could walk down here at any moment.

Anybody.

Including teammates who don't want me to start over them. Including two of my brothers. Including *her father.*

It's that final thought that has me pulling back.

"I can't do this," I mutter, and I push back from the wall and walk out of the small hallway. I walk through the bar, not bothering to say goodbye to my teammates, and out the front door, and then I head for home.

Chapter 21: Desiree Dixon

Mansplaining Pro Baseball Teams

I stand in the hallway a little longer, the rejection raw and real as it pulses through me. Disappointment filters in, yet hope still remains.

I want you in a way I'm not sure I've ever wanted anyone before.

Those words play on repeat in my head. I'm not sure I'll ever get over them.

He wants me, and I want him…but we can't be together.

I should've known that's how he would respond when he found out who I was, and that's exactly why I didn't tell him the night we met. These football players form special relationships with their coaches, and while he didn't know my dad well back at the time of the charity ball, I'm willing to wager he does now.

I'll find out. I'll ask questions. I'll get the inside track from my dad.

I'm not sure if it'll matter given how adamant he is about the fact that he can't do this. But he was about to give in. He didn't forget me. I don't know that he was as obsessed as I was over the last three months, but the things he said to me tell me he's fighting a fight with himself over this whole thing.

But it's a fight he won't win.

Not when the pull between us is this strong and the temptation is this alluring.

I head out of the hallway and back toward Ellie, who's talking to a player. I glance over and spot Kaylee, who's making out with her husband.

I twist my lips as I realize these really aren't my friends—not yet. Not like the girls back home are.

It doesn't feel like there's a place for me here, and as hopeful as I was before I ran into Asher in that little hallway, I'm sort of feeling the opposite now.

Why would I move here when this isn't the place for me?

"What's wrong?" a voice beside me asks. I glance over and find Luke Dalton, and I offer a smile.

"Oh, nothing. I don't really know anybody here." I shrug.

"Well, then allow me to introduce you." He starts walking away without another word, and he expects me to follow him. I was using it as my excuse to get the hell out of here, but he's using it as his reason to keep me here.

We walk up to the table with a bunch of wide receivers and running backs, and Luke slings a friendly arm around my shoulders. "I'd like to introduce Coach Dixon's daughter, Desi. Desi, this is everyone." He turns to me. "What are you drinking?"

"Mexican mule."

"You got it," he says to me. He pushes the player at the end of the booth to indicate he should scoot in, and then he walks away toward the bar to get me that drink.

I wave awkwardly. "Hi, everyone."

The woman across the table from me grins. "Welcome to the crazy," she says. "I'm Victoria, and that's Tessa." She points to the woman on the other side of Tristan Higgins, the man next to me. "This is Mandy," she says, leaning around Travis Woods, who's sitting beside her, and pointing to the woman between him and Jaxon Bryant. "We like to drink vodka and talk about anything other than football. Specifically spicy books."

My ears perk up. "Spicy books?"

She nods. "Some call it smut, some call it trash, but it's neither of those things. We read stories about strong women finding themselves as they find love, and if there happens to be some hot sex in it, well, then our men get the added benefits of that." She elbows her husband, and I sort of feel like I walked into a conversation they were having before I got here. He grins and wiggles his eyebrows suggestively, and I can't help but laugh.

"The only people who call it trash are uninformed," I say. "Are you three in a book club?"

Victoria shakes her head. "No, we just trade the best books back and forth."

"Who called it trash?" I ask, narrowing my eyes at the men.

"Oh, nobody here. They all know better than that," she says with a laugh. "I actually own the cutest little bookstore not too far from here, and I heard a customer's husband say it the other day." She rolls her eyes. "He also started mansplaining to her about how there isn't a pro baseball team in the city the book took place in. Like, no shit, dude, it's freaking *fiction*."

"We were literally just talking about that at my book club back in San Diego!" I say. "I meet with my three best friends to talk about whatever book we're reading, but really it's an excuse to get together, eat, drink, and gossip."

Victoria leans forward. "How do I get an invite into this book club?"

I giggle, and we start talking about our favorite authors. Mandy pushes Travis out of the way so she can sit next to Victoria, and Tessa moves over her husband so she can be next to me.

And just like that, it sort of feels like I found some more friends here in Vegas—and maybe even a local book club.

But that's sort of the problem with making friends with players' wives. Nobody knows how long a player will stay on a team. Sure, these three have been around a long time, but one bad season, one bad injury, or even one personal moment that tells them it's time to stop playing, and they're no longer a part of this family.

It's such a weird phenomenon. These ladies are clearly all very close, but would they still be if one of their husbands was let out of his contract or traded?

They seem like they would be. But I'm in a different situation than they are. I'm not married to a player. I'm a coach's daughter, and sometimes being related to a coach isn't looked at as advantageous. And what's worse is that my dad is a *new* coach in town. He walked in, flipped everything upside down, and started training players on *his* plays, *his* playbook, when they were used to some other guy's stuff.

So despite being welcomed into this group tonight, I still have to question whether I'll be welcome as a permanent member of this group of friends. And even if I am, I'm coming in as not a third wheel, and not even a fourth or fifth…but as a seventh wheel. The numbers don't work out. I don't have a significant other for double dates.

All I have is a guy who claims he wants me but tells me he can't do this before he walks away from me.

The couples start to leave, and I take that as my cue. I bid goodbye to my new friends, which include Ellie and Kaylee, and I grab a Lyft back to my parents' place.

They're still awake when I walk in the front door, the two of them sitting on the couch watching a documentary about birds migrating, and I'm not a bird person. In fact, I'm sort of terrified of birds, and seeing them even on the television screen gives me a visceral reaction as I cover my eyes.

"Oh, sorry, honey," my mom says, and she presses the power button. "They're off. How was your night out? Did you make some friends? Are you moving here?"

I laugh. "Fun, yes, and no."

She snaps her finger in disappointment. "Shoot."

I twist my lips as I slide onto the recliner beside them. "Sorry. I did have fun, though. I made friends with some players' wives, and they like to read the same kinds of books that I do."

Truth be told, I've never admitted to my father what I read, but my mom definitely knows.

"Nonfiction books about knitting, right?" my dad says, and my mom and I both laugh.

"Right. Exactly," I confirm as I widen my eyes in horror and shake my head at my mom.

"Just like I read before bed each night." She winks at me.

"You don't need to tell me what you read, Mother," I scold.

She holds up both hands, and my dad wiggles his eyebrows suggestively.

"I do enjoy the books your mom reads."

"Oh, God," I mutter. "These are things I don't need to know about my parents."

"Who else was there?" my dad asks, changing the subject with a laugh.

"I mostly sat with Travis Woods, Tristan Higgins, and Jaxon Bryant," I say.

"Good. All three of them are married, so they'll stay away." He grins at me, but there's a sparkle in his eye that tells me he's kidding. Kind of. "Who else?"

"Some of the tight ends. I think it was Chase, Justin, and Asher," I say, careful not to give anything away when I say his name.

"Oh, good. Asher went."

"Why is that good?" I ask.

"Coach and player confidentiality, but between us, I think he's just trying extra hard to fix his reputation after his suspension, and I encouraged him to get to know his teammates a little more. Sounds like he's trying."

Is that why he was there? Or did he show up because he knew I was going?

I wanted to think it was the second thing, but since he didn't give me a chance to ask...I'm not sure if I'll ever really get the answer to that.

But now that I saw him again, and he whispered those words to me, and his mouth was on mine again, I'm more certain than ever that there's something between us that we can't ignore.

I just have to figure out how I'm going to get him to give in.

Chapter 22: Asher Nash

Can't Miss it When She Literally Places it in My Palm

We win out of town against the Cardinals, and the next weekend, we're back at home facing the Broncos.

Jack Dalton played for the Broncos for a number of years, so our coaching staff has pressed into us how very important this game is.

Every game is important, but our team owner has his pride on the line against the team that traded him to the Vegas Aces. Considering he owns the team now, it sounds like he made out okay in the end, but I'd still venture to guess he holds a bit of a grudge against them.

I've kept my head down and focused even more since I saw her at the Gridiron.

And still, she sneaks her way into my thoughts nearly constantly.

I haven't heard from her, though why would I? We still didn't exchange numbers. Instead, hers is on a piece of paper in a hotel suite that I never got. I wonder if whoever cleaned the room after we left it saw it. I wonder if it was thrown away. I wonder if the next guy got it and kept it.

I guess I left more than just her phone number in that room.

My sanity, for one thing.

I blow out a breath as I pump the power bar upward. Paul, one of our strength and conditioning coaches, is spotting me, and he pulls it back onto the rack. "Nice, Nash. Head over to squats."

I hate squats, but they're a vital part of the workout routine, and honestly, the burn I feel from doing them is a welcome reprieve from the burning that's been constant in my chest for the last week and a half.

I saw her. I kissed her. I let her go.

I walked away.

What a fucking idiot.

What fucking idiot just walks away?

I had to. I told Coach Dixon that I'd keep my hands off of her. Granted, that was long before I knew who the fuck she was, but I still said those words. I made that promise.

And as a man currently trying to live up to his promises…that one's a tough one to keep.

Thankfully, I haven't seen her since, though I know I'm not immune to seeing her. I likely didn't see her because we were on the road last week, but I'm willing to wager she'll be at our home game this weekend.

And then what?

It took every single ounce of my willpower to stay away the first time. I don't know if I can do that a second time.

I've jerked off about a hundred times, and none of it has been enough to alleviate the need I feel when I think of her.

That connection was still there, but I'm not sure knowing who she is made things any better. I think I was better off chasing a ghost than knowing the truth and being unable to do anything about it.

I finish my workouts and head home. I avoid alcohol, instead opting for water, but a beer to take the edge off doesn't sound horrible.

Sunday comes, and I have that same sensation like she's in the building.

I run out onto the field before the game for warm-ups, and as I'm stretching, I glance toward the seats I now know belong to Sue Dixon for the season.

And sure enough, she's sitting there next to her mom. She's holding a beer in her hand as she laughs at something her mom says, and when she pushes to a stand, I see the jersey she's wearing this week.

It isn't Nash 85.

Instead, it's Morgan 89.

I choke on something in the back of my throat. Is she fucking serious?

Rage colors my vision with a color redder than her goddamn hair.

I realize I have no ownership over her whatsoever. She can wear whoever's jersey she wants to. But she has to be doing this on purpose. To wear the number of a man who isn't even a starter but plays the same position I do...it's bullshit. It's acknowledging my rejection and making a move against me.

Well...check-fucking-mate.

I can sit back and pretend like it doesn't bother me, or I can...

I can...

What?

What the mother fuck am I going to do?

Walk up to the snack bar and buy her a beer before the game? I can't. I still don't even have her goddamn number to communicate to her that she shouldn't be wearing someone else's number when she's supposed to be wearing mine.

But I'm the one who closed that door. I'm the one who walked away.

And maybe I'm the one who can fix it.

"Nice stretch, Nash," Coach Dixon says as he walks by me. "Listen, I've made a few tweaks to our game plan, and we're going to start a two-tight-end formation, okay? Morgan will do the blocking, you'll do the receiving. Get your ass out there and catch some balls."

Fuck.

I nod my agreement, but it's a cold, hard reminder that I can't fuck this man's daughter. Not when he's giving me chances to show what I'm made of. Not when he's giving me chances to catch that goddamn ball when he knows that's my favorite part of this position. Not when he's opening the door for *me* to be the hero today.

Even though she's wearing *Morgan's* fucking jersey.

She'll live to regret that when I'm the one carrying the ball into the end zone.

She's on my mind the entire game, though I don't make eye contact with her. I do covertly sneak looks for her red hair, and she's watching the game intently every time—as she drinks her beer. What's so goddamn sexy about a woman with a beer in her hand?

I'm not sure, but when it's Desiree Dixon, I can't get enough.

I score in the first half, and I score again in the second.

Both times, after I celebrate with my team, I glance over at her. She's clapping and screaming and going wild as she hugs her mom.

I glance over at her when we score on the defensive side of the ball, too, and while there's similar clapping and jumping, the excitement was definitely more pronounced when it was *me* who scored.

Or maybe I'm seeing what I want to see.

After the game, I rush to get through my press conference. I don't want to miss seeing her again even if there's nothing I can do about it.

I head out into the family waiting room, and she's talking to Victoria Woods, Travis's wife. I walk by her on my way to see my mom, who's currently holding my niece, Josephine, and I accidentally-on-purpose bump into her shoulder.

She turns toward me with a glare as she grabs her shoulder.

"Oh, I'm sorry," I murmur. I'm not sorry.

The small bump of shoulder to shoulder caused an electrical current as strong as ever. I move to steady her, and as if she were waiting for me, she slips a piece of paper into my palm.

My brows knit together as my questioning eyes meet hers, and she nods a little. She averts her gaze toward the locker room door, and I hear Sue say, "Oh, there's Dad."

I glance down at the paper in my palm, and it has a phone number written on it.

I guess this time she isn't letting me walk away without her number.

I can't miss it when she literally places it in my palm.

But the question is…am I going to use it?

I don't know what the plan is for after the game, and I don't know if she's going out this time. We won again, and I should make an appearance to celebrate with my teammates. But I'm tired, and now I have her number, and I want to use it, but I still know I can't.

I glance back up at her, and when her eyes meet mine, I see the pleading there in them. She wants me to use that number.

I want to use it.

But I'm not sure if I can.

"Hey, man, you coming out with us?" Tristan asks me, slapping me on the shoulder.

While I don't feel like I've bonded with most of my teammates, there are a solid handful who have always made me feel included, and it's the true team leaders like Tristan and Travis and Jaxon. They've been around for a long time, and they're in the sort of leadership positions I aspire to be in.

But Travis wasn't always a starter for the Aces. He worked his ass off to get to where he is.

The same could be said for everyone in that locker room, I suppose. And yet I still have the stigma attached to me that I'm only here because of my last name.

I'm not sure how to break out of that, but fucking the OC's daughter probably isn't the way to do it.

I slip her number into my pocket as she takes off to greet her dad, and I tell Tristan I'll come out for a drink or two.

I'm sure she hears me. I hope she hears me. I hope we can find a quiet hallway to share another kiss in. But I also know that's all it can be.

I can't betray my coach like that…even if I want to rip that Morgan 89 jersey right off her shoulders, toss it to the floor, and run my tongue along her tits for the rest of the fucking night.

Chapter 23: Desiree Dixon

Game On, I Guess

I toss my head back and laugh at something Chase just said.

Was it really all that funny? No.

Am I playing a game after I saw Asher walk in? Yes, absolutely, I am.

He's going to pin me against the wall and give me a steamy kiss and then act like he's some goddamn hero for walking away? Well, that's a game, too, so…game on, I guess.

Ellie slides into the booth beside me. "So, Desi, have we talked you into moving to Vegas yet?"

I laugh. "Nobody has tried in the last five minutes."

"Enter Ellie. So I talked to Erin last week, and she is super excited to talk with you. She *really* wants to offload the charity ball for next year to someone with experience, and since you know football *and* attended this year's event, you're like the magical perfect fit."

I don't mention that I was so focused on Asher that I don't have a clear recollection of the rest of the ball.

I sigh. "Would it require me to be here in Vegas?"

She shrugs. "You can work that out with Erin. If you're *only* taking on the ball and you do it as a consultant, then I wouldn't think so."

"But my contract at my current job doesn't allow me to plan outside events," I say sullenly.

"So if you want in, you have two choices. Either A, run the ball through your current firm, or B, quit and move here. There are plenty of other events you could plan. Or better yet, start your own firm, and the Vegas Aces can be your first client." She raises her brows as if it's a great idea.

And maybe it is. Maybe I do want to move here.

I miss being close to my parents. I've formed some friendships here already, even though I've only visited a couple of times, and then there's the whole, you know, number eighty-five thing.

But maybe I don't want to move here. My eyes fall onto Asher, who's in the booth behind the one I'm in. His eyes are on me, and they flick away when we make eye contact.

He's going to fight this, and he's probably right to. I don't know if I have it in me to pull out the victory, anyway.

But as his eyes flick back to me, I see it there. He's close to giving up the fight.

I told him once, and I meant it—we can do this in secret. Nobody has to know.

It isn't ideal, but at least it would give us the space to explore, and if it turns into something more than lust and sex and the intense carnal connection we share, we'll deal with it then.

But why not have a little fun in the meantime?

I turn to Ellie. "I'll think about it. Promise."

She nods and holds up both hands. "No pressure, seriously. But I think we'd have a lot of fun taking this town together. And Victoria told me you read spicy books, and she's always passing books to me, too. We could start up a book club or something here."

I narrow my eyes at her. "Did Victoria tell you to say that to me?"

She shakes her head as her eyes widen innocently. "I swear, we haven't talked about it. Why?"

"Because I'm in a book club with my best friends back home. It's not just the book club, but the whole idea of leaving my friends behind, you know?"

"Is that the only thing keeping you there?" she asks.

I shake my head. "No. There's the beach and my job, too, and everything I've ever known since the day I was born."

"I get it. I grew up in Illinois, and moving seventeen hundred miles across the country was, well, terrifying. I was leaving my parents behind and trying something new, and you know what? I met my husband my first night in town, and it was like fate stepped in to push us together."

Fate. There's that damn word again, the same one Asher used when I showed up in the seat reserved for his date.

"Fate," I murmur. It's a nice idea and a cute word, even, but I'm not sure how much I believe in it. It's not as if my dad took this job so I'd get the chance to meet a player my father had no intention of introducing me to.

"I met Prince Charming and got the fairy tale. Maybe it'll happen for you, too."

I smirk. "Or not. I'm not really into fairy tales unless they're dirty ones."

She laughs. "Oh, that reminds me. Victoria told me about these dirty fairy tale retellings..." She grabs her phone and starts scrolling through her book app to show me.

Before she gets the chance, though, I back her up a step. "You said we'd take this town together. What did you mean by that?"

"I'm always helping out with various Aces events. Erin tends to be very player-focused, and I am, too, with my PR company, so we work fairly closely together on community outreach." She shrugs and sets her phone down. "So if you're here doing stuff for the team, I'm sure we'll end up on various projects together. And we'd have *so much fun.*"

I absolutely agree with her that we'd have a great time. I suppose now it's a matter of deciding if this is something I truly want or if I'm only considering it because it would greatly increase my chances of getting naked with Asher Nash again.

"Oh, shoot. My babysitter's calling. I need to take this, excuse me," she says, and she rushes out the front door.

Chase raises his eyebrows at me from across the table. "You're thinking of moving here?"

I shrug as I nod toward Ellie's retreating figure. "She's trying to convince me to, but I'm not really sure."

"You should."

"Why?" I pick up my now-empty drink and swirl the ice around the glass, and my eyes move up and to the side of Chase, focusing instead on Asher at the next table.

If it's not okay for me to be with Asher, it's not like it's okay for me to be with Chase for all the same reasons. This is nothing more than harmless flirting, and he's going to stay away like Asher claims he will. All the players will. It's a coach-player-respect thing, much to my dismay.

But the thing I know about Asher is that he's the wild card. Nobody ever knows what to expect out of him.

And that's why it's such a pleasant surprise when I'm waiting around the side of the building an hour later for my Lyft to take me home, and he saunters outside and moves in beside me.

It's dark out here, and we're alone—part of the reason why I moved to the side of the building when I knew his eyes were on me as I walked out.

Call it part of the game.

"You're flirting with Morgan now?" he asks. "Just so you know, he's a dog."

"Jealousy looks hot on you, Nash." I keep my gaze focused forward rather than glancing over at him, though it takes everything in my power to do it.

He moves so he's standing in front of me, filling my line of vision. His eyes are hot on mine before they flick down to my lips. "Goddammit," he mutters, and he boxes me in against the brick wall out here like he did inside the building the last time I was here. His hand moves to my hip. "You're making this so hard."

I run my hand along the front of his pants. "Mm, you're right. *Very* hard."

He shoves his hips against my hand, and he lowers his mouth to my neck. "I can't, Des. I can't do this, but I can't stop thinking about you." He thrusts his hips into my hand again as if to prove some point, and a thrill zips up my spine as a hot, aching need pulses between my thighs.

"One more night, Asher," I murmur. I duck my head so my lips catch his, and he kisses me for a beat before we're interrupted by headlights.

He jumps back, caught, and I let out a strained chuckle. "That'll be my ride. Unless…"

He quirks a brow. "Unless what?"

I lift a shoulder. "Unless you want to leave together."

He sighs, and it's a strangled, throaty sound of frustration. "You know I can't, but fuck, you're tempting me."

That's sort of the idea. "Your loss," I say with a shrug, and I walk over to the car waiting for me.

"You better not fucking wear another man's number again."

I laugh as I open the door and slide in. "Or what?" It's a clear challenge, and I slam the door shut before he gets the chance to answer.

And then I wait for him to use the number I slipped into his palm earlier tonight.

Chapter 24: Asher Nash

Or I'll Take It Off Myself

I stare at the number as I hold it in my hand and lean against my headboard later that same night.

What the fuck would I even say?

You got me all riled up and hot and horny and I need you to take care of it because jerking off in the shower isn't nearly enough to erase the memory of your sweet, tight cunt and gorgeous tits?

That seems somehow…aggressive.

Maybe she likes aggressive. Who knows? I don't because I haven't taken the time to get to know a damn thing about her.

But I have her number.

I could use it. I could get to know her. I could do that and still keep my promise to Coach. I think back to our conversation. All he said is she doesn't date football players, so I shouldn't get any ideas.

He never said we couldn't be friends.

You know…with or without benefits. Preferably with.

I don't know how much longer I can resist the temptation she keeps laying in front of me. She may only be twenty-five, but fuck if she doesn't know exactly what the hell she's doing. Showing up in a different jersey twice in a row?

Fuck that.

She better be wearing eighty-five the next time I see her in a jersey, or...

Or what?

She made a great point when she asked that very same question as she got into the car. What am I going to do about it if she shows up again, representing yet another one of my teammates?

As long as it isn't Graham, I can probably let it go.

Nah, fuck that. It better not be anyone.

As for what I'm going to do about it...I'm not sure yet.

I don't know why it bothers me so much, but it does. My number is part of my identity. It has been since peewee league. It doesn't have any special significance other than that was the jersey tossed to me when I was a kid, and like all three of my brothers, I held onto that number through my entire football career—with the exception of my freshman year of high school when eighty-five was taken by a senior.

It was my worst season to date even though I made varsity, so when he graduated and the number was free again, I took it back.

Is it sending the entirely wrong message to text her tonight after I saw her less than an hour ago?

Definitely, yes.

Do I care?

Nope. Not even a little.

So back to the question at hand—that little *or what* thing she brought up.

I type her number into a new message and draft a text.

Me: *Or I'll take it off myself.*

It's stupid, but before I can convince myself of that, I click the send button.

Her reply comes quickly.

Desiree: *Is that a threat or a promise?*

Jesus, I have my hands full with this one.

I have no idea when I'll see her again, but I hope to God it's soon.

Me: *Both.*

She doesn't reply, and I stare at my phone, willing the little text bubble to appear.

Eventually, I give up, tossing my phone beside me on the bed as I turn off the light.

I close my eyes as I wait for sleep to fall over me, but it's eluding me.

Can I go back on my promise to Coach now that I know she's his daughter? It's all kinds of wrong, but I'm not sure I can force myself to stay away…not when she keeps showing up. Not when she keeps tempting me with those eyes, that knowing smile, that sweet, sweet body.

And I have no idea when I'll see her again.

I blow out a breath and check my phone, and there's still no reply. It's also only been ten minutes since I last texted her.

I haven't tried very hard, but sleep seems pretty useless at this point. I head out to the kitchen to grab a beer and sit in front of the television to catch today's highlights on ESPN, but my plan is ruined when I see my dad already sitting on the couch watching some old western.

He barely acknowledges me when I walk into the room, and I really need to find a new living situation.

I have a hard time standing up to my dad, and it's probably because as much as he's been a dick to my brothers and me, he's also been a protector for the majority of my life.

He's the one who told me to *do it for Fitz* when Jacob Fitzgerald overdosed. He's the one who forced me up out of bed on the dark days and drove me to practice. He's the only one who was there. My brothers were grown and gone by then.

Plus, there's the fact that I get my athleticism from him—or the *him* of twenty years ago, anyway.

"What are you doing up?" he grunts when his show cuts to a commercial.

"Can't sleep," I admit.

"Why not? You thinking about something?" He doesn't mute the television, instead letting some infomercial about a medication blare all the possible side effects at us.

"Not the fumble from last week if that's what you're getting at," I say dryly.

He holds both hands up innocently. "You're the one bringing it up. Must be weighing on your mind if you're still thinking about it."

I roll my eyes and tip the bottle of beer to my lips, and he narrows his eyes at me.

"It's a woman, isn't it?"

I huff out a mirthless chuckle. "So what if it is?"

"I remember being twenty-eight and stupid," he admits. "Or younger and dumber, anyway."

My brows dip. Twenty-eight and stupid? I actually have two issues with that.

For one thing, he was married to my mom for nearly a decade back when he was twenty-eight. He better not have been doing stupid things by that point.

And for another…is he insinuating that I'm stupid?

Maybe my obsession with the coach's daughter is stupid. But I'm actively trying *not* to act on it.

I shouldn't have sent that text, and I regret it. Now she has my number, and who knows what she'll do with it.

I could block her…but I don't want to.

I want my phone to buzz with her reply.

I want to see her again.

I want to torture myself with her temptation because this is the strongest I've ever felt about a woman, and I'd rather live with the torture than never see her again.

I clear my throat. "Are you calling me stupid?"

"I'm saying it's best not to let a woman fuck up your future. You know that."

I press my lips together. "Yeah. You've made that clear our entire lives, but have you ever thought about what those words might mean to us beneath the surface?"

"You know I don't go much deeper than the surface, kid," he says, elbowing me in the ribs.

"Saying a woman will fuck up my future sounds the same as saying you regret having kids." I say the words point-blank, calling him out on his shit and standing up to him even though it's not in my nature to do so.

He's quiet, but he's the guy who always has a retort ready, and he's the guy who always gets the last word. "Regret is a funny thing, Asher, and the four of you turned out fine. I made sacrifices to ensure that would be the case."

He didn't deny it, and that hurts more than it should. I'm sure there's more to it than that. I have no idea what sacrifices he's talking about.

And I'm not sure I really care at this point, either.

I drain the rest of my beer and push to a stand as I make a vow to myself that I'll figure out some other living situation sooner rather than later. "Well, goodnight."

He grunts out some reply, but his show is back on, and I just chugged a beer, so it's not like I'm going to lay in bed and go right to sleep since I'll have to get up and piss in twenty minutes.

So instead of trying to sleep, I open up a browser and start to search for homes for sale nearby.

I save a few that look nice, though I'm not entirely sure I want to buy or rent. I'll probably finish my career out here in Vegas, and I love it here. Compared to Indy, the weather is gorgeous most of the year except for the hot months, and the scenery and nightlife are both incredible.

Most of my family is here, too, though I'm not sure that's a mark in the *pro* column.

It's just as I settle into bed for the second time that another text comes through.

Desiree: *Just wanted to let you know I'm no longer wearing number eighty-nine.*

Me: *What are you wearing?*

Desiree: *Nothing.*

I groan.

Me: *Prove it.*

Desiree: *I don't think so. What if I want to run for office someday? Can't have pics of my tits floating around.*

Me: *That's why you keep your face out of the shot.*

Desiree: *[smirk emoji] Sorry. In person only.*

Me: *The temptation is strong.*

Desiree: *Here's to hoping you give in next time.*

As it turns out, *next time* is sooner than I thought it would be.

We don't have practice Monday since we won, but I still stop by the practice facility for a workout, and it's as I'm working the ropes that she walks in with her dad, who appears to be giving her a tour of the Complex.

She's wearing fucking Austin Graham's number.

It's a dare.

And I never back down from a dare.

Chapter 25: Desiree Dixon

Is This an Interview

Oh. My. God.

Asher Nash on the ropes is truly a beautiful sight to behold.

All I can think of as I watch those strong, muscular forearms move up and down, slamming those ropes against the ground, is how he slammed into me that night we shared.

A snippet of his hand running along my thigh comes back to me. Those strong forearms holding himself up as he hovered over me.

My *God*, the need in me is strong right now.

He has to feel it too. He *has* to.

His eyes move to me, and he looks surprised. But when his eyes flick to my jersey and he sees me wearing Austin Graham's number, I *swear* the sound of the ropes slapping against the ground gets a little louder.

My dad's saying something about the state-of-the-art equipment in here, but all I can do is watch the man on the ropes. He's the only athlete working out in here—the only person in here, actually, except for one of the trainers in the corner doing something on a computer.

Our eyes meet, and he looks livid. He throws the ropes on the ground, offers me a glare, and turns away to walk toward some other machine, this one with a video screen in front of it.

"Have you met Asher?" my dad asks, and my ears perk up like a curious puppy.

I clear my throat, not sure what to say.

"Asher!" my dad calls over the music in here, and he turns back toward us with his brows raised. "This is my daughter, Desiree. I didn't think anyone would be around today, so I'm just giving her the tour."

"Hey," he says to me, and I offer a quick wave before he turns back to his video game workout thing.

"These guys are so focused in here, and I love to see it," my dad says to me. "That machine allows him to practice footwork in real time against an actual opponent. Technology is pretty incredible. Come on, let me show you the pools."

I follow him to the pool room, which has a hydrotherapy pool, a plunge pool, and some underwater treadmills. Eventually we head up toward the offices as I try to come up with some excuse as to why I need to get back down to the strength and conditioning room.

I'm coming up empty.

We wander the hallways that are like a freaking maze of offices, and my dad introduces me to a bunch of the executives here at the Aces. Then we stop outside the doorway marked *Erin McMahon, Director of Charitable Contributions*.

"Did Ellie Dalton put you up to this?" I ask, narrowing my eyes at my dad.

He laughs. "Maybe," he says, drawing out the word playfully.

I roll my eyes.

"Okay, fine. It was both Luke and Ellie. We had dinner with the coaching staff, and Luke was there. We talked about how much we miss having you close by." He tosses his arm around my shoulder and squeezes me in a little side hug, and I feel a little choked up at that.

I mean, really…is there anything keeping me in San Diego? Aside from my friends, which are important, of course, why *really* am I so hesitant to move?

Change is scary. But so is complacency, and I think I'm getting to the point where I'm staying because I'm comfortable. There's nothing saying I can't go back as often as I want. Hell, I could keep my apartment in San Diego so I don't have to uproot Addy, and I could split my time between both towns. But I can't do that while I'm working for Angelica.

"Erin, do you have a minute?" my dad asks as he stops in the doorway. I'm still behind him out of view.

"Come on in," Erin calls.

He steps in, and I walk in behind him.

"You must be Desiree," she says as she stands and smiles broadly at me.

"That's me," I say with a smile back. "And you must be Erin. I've heard amazing things about your work here."

"Doing my best, one charity event at a time."

"How was the Fostering Fletch event?" my dad asks her, and my brows pinch together nervously.

"Incredible," she says. "Brandon collected over a thousand articles of clothing plus enough supplies for the team to create five hundred hygiene kits. It was amazing."

"Fletch?" I ask.

"Brandon Fletcher, our backup quarterback," she clarifies. "His charity has really evolved over the last couple years, and he's working hard to make a positive impact on the community."

"That's amazing," I say, leaving out the fact that the reason it's such a good thing is because his reputation in the media isn't the best. He's been a backup most of his career except right before Jack Dalton was traded to the Aces, and he also has quite the reputation as a ladies' man, though I don't know much about him at all aside from the headlines. "What other events do you have going on?"

"I've helped twelve of the current players on the team launch various foundations, and they each hold one big event a year and some smaller events. I try to make it to as many as I can, but with a fifty-three-man roster plus other community outreach events for the Aces organization itself, I'm stretched pretty thin.

I hear you're potentially looking for work here in Vegas?" she asks, turning her full attention to me as she sits.

I shrug. "I'm considering it."

"If you'll excuse me," my dad says, and he bolts, leaving me alone with Erin.

She chuckles. "Talk to me about your experience."

"Is this an interview?" I ask, narrowing my eyes at her.

She lifts both shoulders innocently as she holds up her hands. "Just a director chatting with a coach's daughter."

I smile. "I've been working for one of the top event coordination firms in San Diego since I graduated from college with a degree in business management and a minor in marketing. We mainly specialize in weddings, parties, and that type of thing, but we've planned several charity functions as well. I hold the title of junior event planner with aspirations to learn from the best and someday launch my own firm."

"How long have you been there?"

"Three years."

She nods as she jots something down on a piece of paper in front of her. "You mentioned you want to learn from the best. Have you? Do you feel you're ready to level up from a junior planner?"

"Yes, I do. I feel a little stagnant where I am, to be honest. I'm ready for a new challenge."

"Have you considered consulting work?" she asks.

I nod. "I have, and if I were to leave San Diego, that's likely how I'd start. I've done a lot of research on starting my own company, and I think I'm in a great position to start slow and build."

"You're hired."

I laugh. "I thought this wasn't an interview."

"It wasn't. I was going to offer you the job either way, but I had to at least pretend like I was interviewing you. I've looked into your background, and it's impressive, Desiree. I would love the opportunity to work with you, and as you know, my first order of business would be handing over the Wild Aces Charity Ball. We already have the venue booked for the next three years, and much of the planning is already done, but given the size of the event, I just can't take it on for a third year. The auction items alone took up way too much of my team's time, let alone the raffles and everything else."

"Your team?" I ask.

"Well, it was really just Lily and me. Lily is Jack Dalton's assistant. We had help from Megan, Coach Nash's assistant, too, and of course Ellie and her crew, but they all have other responsibilities. I spoke with Jack, and he wants to build our charity division. He told me I can hire a new assistant as well as an event planner, and he's also dedicating a much larger budget to the ball next year because of its success, so more than likely you'll have enough to hire your own team."

Hire my own team? I don't even know anybody out here, which would sort of negate the whole idea of staying in San Diego and working remotely.

"It's a lot to think about," I admit. "Can I have a few days and get back to you?"

"Of course," she says, and she smiles warmly. "And just so you know, it wouldn't only be the charity ball. I also have the foundation events that our boys hold, things like that. It's a great opportunity to build your portfolio in Vegas, but I fully understand if you decide to pass on it. We'll have lines out the door for applicants if you decide not to take it, and I do need to get the position filled as soon as possible, so if you could let me know by Thursday, that would be great."

"Thanks, Erin," I say, and I stand to leave. "It was so lovely to meet you."

"And you. Whatever you decide, we're excited to have your family as part of this organization."

She smiles warmly, and I realize she's catering this position to me. She said Jack approved her hiring an event planner, and she's offering it to me as a consulting position. I wouldn't be employed by the Aces, but by myself, which is what I've dreamed of.

It's tempting, but I have to decide if leaving San Diego is right for me.

And now that my dad has ditched me to get back to work, it's time to wander around these hallways until I bump into Asher again.

Chapter 26: Asher Nash

One More Night

I take a shower after my workout, toss on a Vegas Aces tee that isn't really my style, and I decide to head up to my brother's office to see if he wants to grab lunch. And it's as I'm walking down the hallway that takes a turn toward the coaching offices that I spot her on the other end of the hall walking toward me.

Wavy red hair falling to the middle of her back, that fucking Graham jersey, and a skirt that makes her legs look two miles long.

Fuck.

She looks up, and her eyes meet mine. We both freeze, and it's as if time also freezes.

My brother is just around the corner. Her dad's office is a few doors down from that.

It's not like I can bend her over in this hallway and mark up that Graham jersey with my come, though I'm tempted to give it a try.

We both start moving toward each other, and we stop when we're close enough to talk. I nod toward the hallway to my right. "The coaching staff is down there if you're looking for your dad."

"I wasn't," she says, and her voice is all breathless and throaty like it was after I came in her mouth.

My cock stirs at the memory.

I glance around, and the small conference room beside us is empty. The lights are off. I duck inside, and she follows me in. I leave the lights off, but the room is bright anyway from the daylight streaming in through the windows.

We move away from the window in the doorway, and she leans against the wall as I shut the door.

I'm not sure why I shut the door. I glance at the table in here, and a flash of her laying naked on it while I taste her pussy passes through my mind.

"I was looking for you." She motions to her shirt. "You said you'd take it off."

I close my eyes and shake my head. "You know I can't. Least of all here."

"Then why'd you say it?"

"Because I want you, but I have to fight against that. I made a promise."

"Did you, though?" she asks. "Did you specifically say, *Coach, I promise not to fuck your daughter?*"

Hearing her talk like that makes me want to fuck her right here, right this very second, right there on that conference table.

"As I recall, you also made a promise to me," she says with a shrug.

When my brows knit together because I have no idea what she's getting at, she pulls out her phone. She scrolls for a second before she flashes it at me.

Her: *Is that a threat or a promise?*

Me: *Both.*

"So what's it gonna be, Nash? Keeping your promise to my dad or to me?"

"You know I can't do this, Des. No matter how much I want to. No matter how much I want *you.*" I sigh and rake a hand through my hair.

"One night, Asher. Just give me one night."

"Fuck," I mutter.

"I'll even let you rip this jersey off of me." She takes a step toward me, and her coconut hits my senses, though she's still too far away for me to reach out and grab onto her the way every instinct in my body is telling me to do. She lowers her voice to a whisper. "I'm not wearing anything under it."

Jesus, that's something I want to see with every fiber of my being.

I'm holding onto the last ounce of my control with every fiber of my being.

"What'll you wear home?" I ask, trying to keep some semblance of decorum with her father just around the corner.

"That's future Desi's problem. Present Des only cares about one thing."

"What's that?" My words are as big of a dare as her wearing this shirt here today is.

She takes another step toward me, and that does the trick. She's close enough to reach out and touch me, and she does. She runs her hand along the front of my running shorts, and she finds exactly what she's looking for.

Her breath hitches as she cups my cock in her palm, and as her eyes meet mine, hers are dilated and needy.

I shove my cock against her palm.

Fuck it.

Fuck promises.

Fuck all that shit about the right thing to do.

The right thing to do is *her*. The right thing is *us*.

And I need to fuck her like I need to breathe.

She backs up a step as I thrust my cock against her hand. She asked for it, and now she's going to get it.

I keep backing her up until she bumps into the wall and can't back up anymore. I box her in, pushing my hips to hers with her hand still on me.

Our eyes meet for one hot, intense moment, and then I lift my palm to her jawline as my mouth collides with hers.

She moans into me as she starts to pump me on the outside of my shorts, and fuck if I'm not going to come right here in the conference room. My tongue darts into her mouth, and I swirl my tongue around hers, my chest warming with the emotions I haven't allowed myself to feel since the last time we were in a room together.

She's begging. My cock is begging.

One night. She's offering one night, and I don't have the self-control to tell her no.

We'll never be able to keep it to one night. Not when the undercurrent between us is this powerful.

Maybe it'll prove me wrong, and we'll both determine it was lust all along.

I'm already well aware that I'm lying to myself by even allowing that thought into my stupid brain.

I back up and stare at her. Her lips are swollen from the brutal kiss I laid on her, and she's panting and needy…pretty much exactly like I am in this moment.

I clear my throat. "One night," I repeat.

She nods, and she snags her bottom lip between her teeth.

Fuck it.

"Fine. But it has to be the last time."

Her eyes light up at another lie I'm telling myself.

I press my lips to hers, and she moans into me…and I'm fucking done. I need to find somewhere to take her. Immediately.

I pull back, and her heated, green eyes gleam at me.

"Fuck," I mutter. "I have a meeting in a few minutes. Did you drive here?"

She shakes her head, and I glance at my watch.

"Make an excuse and meet me around the east side of the building at four," I demand.

She nods, and I kiss her one more time before I walk out of the conference room to the empty hall.

Chapter 27: Desiree Dixon

Reggae Music and the Backseat

I hang around with my dad until four, though truth be told, I'm a nervous wreck. My dad and I go out to lunch across the street at the Gridiron, which passes some of the time, and I have a margarita to calm my nerves.

I tell my dad I'm going out with some friends, and he's strategizing ahead of this week's game, so he nods absently as I head out. The plan was for me to work on some things for events back home while I was in his office today. I decided to stay all week since the Aces have back-to-back home games, and I'm working remotely. So far, it's going well...but not well enough to say I'd keep my job if I decided to move here.

And damn...that great meeting with Erin followed by that conference room kiss both seem like pretty big flashing neon signs telling me I should really spend a lot of time thinking hard about what I want out of my future. Or, more specifically, where I want that future to take place.

Vegas is looking pretty damn attractive at the moment.

I head down to the front doors, and I spot Asher as he climbs into the back of an SUV. He sees me and waves me in, and I'm not sure if we're being very covert, but I'm pretty sure my dad's view looked out on the other side of the building.

I don't know where we're going, and I don't care.

I'm trying not to get my hopes up *too* high, but the truth is that he wants this, I want this, and we're about to go…well, *somewhere* to do it.

Will he take me back to his place? I have no idea, though in truth, I'm dying to see where Asher Nash lives.

But the reality is that we promised this was only going to happen one more time.

I don't know if I can walk away knowing it's the last time. And with the way he was looking at me, I don't know if he can, either.

I rush over toward the SUV, and I peek into the backseat, where I find that there is a third row of seats in this car, and Asher is all the way in the back.

The driver apparently likes reggae music, and it's blaring.

Asher's hand is immediately on my knee when I take my seat beside him.

"To the Four Seasons?" the driver yells from the front over the music.

"Yeah," Asher yells back, and he leans over and puts his lips on my neck. "I haven't stopped thinking about what you taste like," he murmurs. He trails his lips up toward mine, and he pulls back. "Or what you feel like." His hand slides up from where it sits on my knee, and he keeps going when he gets to the bottom of my skirt.

My breath hitches as his hand moves up until his fingers brush the elastic edge of my panties.

"Jesus Christ, Des," he murmurs. "You have no idea how badly I need this. Need *you*."

I can't even form words, but the truth is that I need this, too.

And since I can't make myself sound coherent, I decide instead to show him.

We're far enough back that the driver won't know what's going on back here, especially not with the music blasting.

I reach over and take his face between my palms, and I press my lips to his. I push at the seam of his lips until he opens them, and our tongues swirl together in the back of this SUV as he slips his fingers beneath the band of my panties. I widen the position of my legs as he slides his finger into me, and he groans softly when he feels how wet I am.

"Fuck, baby," he groans, pulling back from my mouth for a second before he presses his lips to mine again.

I thrust against his hand as he finger fucks me back here, and that's when I decide to let go of where I'm holding his jaw between my hands.

I trail my hand down to his pants, and I run my hand along his rock-hard erection. It's as hard as it was a few hours ago before we parted ways, and I can't help but wonder if he's gotten any relief from it since we walked out of that conference room earlier.

He thrusts his hips toward my hand, and I reach into his pants and straight for his boxers.

He moans as I make a fist around him, and the sudden urge to taste him rockets through me. I pull back and glance up at him, and he looks as needy as I feel as I pump his cock with my fist.

Before he can stop me, I lean down and suck him into my mouth. His finger slips out of me as I shift to blow him. I realize I'm in the back of someone else's car, but I can't seem to stop myself from doing what I've wanted to do for nearly four months.

I want to ride him, too, but that'll come later. And so will I.

I suck him all the way to the back of my throat, and he rests his hands on the back of my head as I start to move him in and out of my mouth, my fist following along his shaft as I move. I stop to suck on the swollen head of his cock, and he thrusts his hips toward my mouth as I run my fist along his shaft some more.

He moves along with me, and I can tell he's getting close by his moans. The music is loud, but he's not exactly trying to hide it.

Something about that makes me suck harder, move faster, and give him everything I've got.

"I'm gonna come," he grunts, and I let the warning spur me on rather than slow down.

I'm here all week. I realize we both promised this would be the last time, but we both know it won't be.

If this ends up being nothing more than friends with benefits for a while, fine.

But I can't imagine that this is a two-and-done for us. Not when we exude this much heat when we're together.

"Now," he says, squeezing my shoulder, and I don't let up, signaling to him that I want this, I want *him*. I want him to give me every last drop.

"Fuck," he groans, and he holds my head still as he thrusts into my mouth. Hot jets of come stream out of him, and I swallow around the huge cock bumping into my throat.

As the thrusts slow, he lets up on his grip on my head, and I slowly pull back, swirling my tongue around the head one more time as I suck him clean.

I sit up, wiping the sides of my mouth with my fingertips in a ladylike way, and he hunches back into his seat as he tucks his cock back into his pants.

He rests his head back onto the seat, and then he turns his head in my direction without lifting it, as if the mere task of lifting his head is too much for him to bear right now.

He shakes his head a little, and I kind of love the fact that I left him speechless.

He looks exhausted, worn, and sated. A rather arrogant look crosses my face as I lean back into my own seat, but he's not letting me off so easily—not without getting *me* off, too.

He reaches back under my skirt and slips his finger right back inside me, and my body is warm, wet, and waiting for him. He shoves that finger up hard into me, hitting that place so few men before him have found before, and I twitch in my seat.

He leans over and drops his lips to my neck, and then I hear his voice, deep and hot, near my ear. "I want this pretty little pussy to come with my fingers first, then my mouth, then my cock."

The mere words are nearly enough to check the first one off the list. He continues to drive his finger in, and it's when he adds in a second one that I start to see stars.

"Oh, God," I moan, and I reach around him to hold onto his neck as my body gives into the pleasure he's giving me.

My legs snap together, and I bite down on his shoulder as I try my hardest to stay quiet. I fight through the orgasm as it rips through me, pulse after excruciating pulse of pleasure taking every last breath from me.

I'm panting when it finally passes through me, and he reaches up to touch his shoulder where I bit him.

In perfect timing, the car comes to a stop, and as I look out the window, I see we're stopped in front of Mandalay Bay, where the Four Seasons has four floors managed separately from the hotel.

"We're here," he says softly. "Ready for my mouth?"

I press my lips to his, and when I pull back, I nod—even though I'm not. I have no way to prepare myself, and my legs are shaky as I turn toward him. "Let's go."

His mouth tips up in a smile as I get out of the car first, barely able to stand, and he follows me. He bids our driver— who I can't seem to make eye contact with—goodbye, and we head inside. He must've already checked in on his phone because we bypass the front desk and head up to the thirty-ninth floor.

We walk into a corner suite with a panoramic view, and I'm sure it's lovely, but I don't even see it because his mouth is on me the second the door closes behind me.

He's kissing me like a starved man, like he needs this, needs *me*, like we didn't make each other come in the back of a car before we got here. He's kissing me as if he's making up for the time we lost over the last few months.

He's kissing me like he never wants to stop, and I'm kissing him back like I never want him to. He pulls back to say, "I've been tempted to slip my tongue between your thighs every time I've seen you." Every few words are punctuated with more kissing. "I can't fight it anymore."

God, I want him to. I want him to make me come with just his tongue.

"But first, the jersey," he says. He walks over to me and fists each side by the chest, and he rips it clean in half. It hangs on me like a jacket, and he pushes it off my arms before he leans down and runs his tongue along my tits, stopping to suck one of my nipples into his mouth.

He backs away abruptly. "Take off the rest of your clothes," he demands, and there's something wickedly hot about the way he says that to me, so hot that I scramble to do exactly what he's asking of me. I drop my skirt and underwear, and I kick off my shoes, too.

I lie back on the bed and wait for him to bury his face in my pussy, but he doesn't.

Instead, he gets naked, too.

He lies on his back beside me. "Crawl over me," he demands.

"What?" I ask, a little nervous to do what he's asking.

"You heard me."

I clear my throat as I sit up. "Crawl over you?"

"I'm going to suck on your cunt until you come, but I want you on top of my face. Now crawl over me and put your cunt on my mouth."

My eyes widen as my pussy throbs with need at the mere thought of sitting on his face.

I scramble onto my knees, but instead of rushing to get into position, I carefully straddle his waist first. He groans as I drag my pussy up his torso, the ridges of his abdomen awakening my clit as need bursts through me. He reaches up to grab my tits in his hands, and he squeezes them roughly before he eases up, only to pinch both my nipples. He tweaks them, rubbing his thumbs back and forth, and that throb of need intensifies at the feeling.

I slowly continue to drag my pussy up his body, and he continues his assault on my nipples as I move. Once I'm poised over his mouth, he lets go.

"Touch your tits for me," he says, and then his hands move to my hips, and he yanks me down over his mouth, his tongue moving immediately into my pussy.

"Oh fuck!" I yell out, the pleasure battering into me immediately as I continue to work my own nipples. Having two of my erogenous zones stimulated at the same time is fucking perfection, but when he brings one of his hands up so he can thumb my clit, I immediately fall apart.

I ride his face as my release whips through me, this one harder and stronger than the last one. I don't even realize how hard I'm pinching my own nipples as the pleasure rockets through me, and tomorrow I'll be achy and sore in the most delicious way.

But tonight…tonight's all about alleviating the ache that built months ago and has only gotten stronger with every passing day until tonight.

It's like he's some expert in the subject of my body, and I think it's because the two of us are so in sync. We fit. It's instinctual. I just came on the way here, and not twenty minutes later, I came again. That's *never* happened to me before, and I have to believe it's because there's something more at play here than an animalistic physical attraction.

He gently lifts me once my body starts to calm, and he lays me down beside him, wrapping an arm around my waist as he holds me close. One of his hands comes up to my breast, and I hear his voice soft and low near my ear.

"Fuck, Des," he mutters. "You're so fucking tempting. There's no way this is only happening twice and never again. No fucking way."

I couldn't agree more.

Chapter 28: Asher Nash

I Better Never See You Wearing Someone Else's Number Ever Again

I call room service and order a bottle of vodka along with some snacks. We need the sustenance since I've barely gotten started and I can tell her energy is already depleted.

That's what happens when you come as hard as she did. Twice.

I metaphorically brush my knuckles on my own shoulder, proud of that fact...and proud of the fact that my shoulder is aching where she bit it. She clamped down on that fucker, and it was hot as hell.

I'd love to take her again, but I need to get some food in her and maybe a little alcohol on top of my own recovery time.

She's dozing off on the bed, and I have no idea what her plans are for the rest of the night. I'm not sure if she can spend the night with me or if she's going to duck out on me again, and to that end, my voice breaks into her peaceful slumber.

"How long are you staying?"

She jolts as she opens her eyes. "Hmm?"

"In case you get the urge to sneak out again, or if I'm passed out cold like the night I drank whiskey, I need to know if I'm waking up alone or if you're staying the night with me."

She sits up, moving the pillows so they're perched behind her back. "Does it matter? You already said you can't do this," she says, motioning between the two of us.

"I can't. And neither can you. Rumor has it, your dad can be a little…"

"Psycho?" she fills in.

I laugh. "Your word, not mine. I was going to say overprotective."

"Rumor has it?"

I lift a shoulder. "Heard the last guy on the Storm who even looked at you was traded."

She rolls her eyes. "That's not true."

I walk over and move into place beside her on the bed. "Oh, really? So he'd be okay knowing you're naked in my hotel room right now?"

She twists her lips. "I mean, no. What dad would be? But the truth is that he doesn't usually let me get close enough for a player to get a look."

"I got a look today," he points out.

"And the night of the ball, you had no idea who I was."

"Fair point. Did you know who I was?" I ask. I've been wondering since the night we met.

"Of course I did. My dad's a coach, and you're a Nash. Even people who don't know a thing about football know who the Nashes are."

I blow out a breath. It's true. My family has gotten a lot of press over the years, some good, some not so good. "What you see in the media rarely paints the full picture."

"Is it true you live with your dad?"

I chuckle. "Yes, and that's also why I took you to a hotel and not my place."

"Aren't you like twenty-eight? Why do you live with your dad?"

"Yes, I am twenty-eight." I lift a shoulder. "He was going through a divorce, and I wasn't earning a salary the year I was suspended, so it worked out to share a place. But truth be told, I'm ready for my own place. I haven't had time to look since the season started. It's more of an offseason task, I guess. What about you? What's your place like?"

"I live with one of my best friends in San Diego."

"My brother just moved there," I say.

"Spencer?" she asks. When I nod, she says, "I'm excited to watch him play even if my dad isn't coaching there anymore. I was raised a Storm fan."

I lean in and softly bite her shoulder. "You better not be excited to watch him play."

She snickers as she pushes my face away. "Why not?"

"For one thing, he's a married man now."

"So I can't cheer for him?"

"No. You can't cheer for him because you'll be too busy cheering for me."

She rolls her eyes even though a smile plays at her lips.

I lean in to press a soft kiss to her lips before I lower my mouth toward her ear. "And I better never fucking see you wearing someone else's number ever again."

I pull back and give her a pointed look.

She raises her brow in a challenge, despite the shiver that tears through her. "Why not?"

I run my hand along her torso and stop to give one of her tits a squeeze. "Because you're mine, and I don't share."

Her eyes darken at my words. "Oh, I'm yours now?"

I shift until I'm hovering over her. I drop my lips to hers, and she wraps her hand around the back of my neck.

We're both naked, and our bodies are lined up perfectly. It takes every single ounce of my willpower not to slip inside her.

"That's right," I say, and I reach down between us and fist my cock. I slide it against her clit, and her eyes roll back. "Tell me you're mine," I demand.

"Oh, God, Asher, yes. I'm yours."

I dip inside her for a second, and it's soft and warm and so, so wet.

Fucking hell.

I could come just from that one little dip inside.

It's utter perfection.

A knock sounds at the door.

Our food. Our vodka. Shit we don't need nearly as much as we need each other. Shit I don't need nearly as much as I need to push inside that tight cunt again.

"Oh, God," she moans.

We haven't had the talk about the things we should talk about before I do that again, but I need to push in like I need my next breath.

"Do it," she goads.

She's back with that temptation again, and I can't resist her. So I don't.

I push into her, nothing between us as our bodies rock together in the ultimate pleasure.

She's so goddamn slick as I fuck her bare, and we move slowly together as if our bodies were made exactly for the other.

Her pussy is a vice over my cock, warm and wet, and she sucks me in with every thrust, the heat of her body overwhelming as I lean down and suck a tit between my lips. She moans as she arches her back to give me more space as I continue to move in and out of her perfect pussy.

I let go of my angle on her tit and lift myself back up to stare down at her. Heavy, hooded eyes meet mine.

The intimacy that passes between us in that moment is erotic and intense.

I've never felt anything like it, but it's like we're connecting on some other plane that isn't a part of this world.

Maybe it's forbidden, but it's also hot as fuck, and it's *right*. It's the lust, sure, but it's something else entirely, something I'm too terrified to acknowledge even though it's happening right before my very eyes.

It can't be. This is only our second time together. We hardly know each other. But the intensity is powerful, and I don't think either of us can fight against that.

My body gives way to the pleasure. My balls draw up as that familiar fire rips down my spine, but even in its familiarity, it's different. More intense, more erotic, more…everything. More Des.

"Fuck, baby, I'm gonna come."

"Not yet," she cries. "I'm so close. Wait for me."

"I can't," I grunt. "Your cunt is too perfect, Des."

"Oh, God!" she yells. "Fuck, Asher, give it all to me. Yes, yes, yes!" Her pussy tightens over me, and her body starts to writhe and thrash all around me.

It's too much, but I can't. I can't come inside her when I don't even know if she's on birth control, and my sex-starved brain can recognize that even in this haze.

My release hits me fast, and I pull out right at the last second. I fist my cock and reach down to her clit at the same time. I pump my palm up and down my cock, painting her lower stomach with my come as my orgasm rushes through me.

Once the pulses start to slow and the warm afterglow takes their place, I run the head of my cock through the mess I made as she fights her way through the end of her own climax. I dip my cock down against her clit, and she twists as she tries to clamp her legs shut, her body sensitive after a third intense climax.

I chuckle as I stop what I'm doing and move down to lay beside her, pulling her into my arms.

"Holy hell, Nash," she pants, grabbing a tissue off the nightstand to wipe off the mess I made on her. The strong scent of sex fills the air around us, but the quiet moments after we both raced toward the finish line are filled with a tenderness I wasn't expecting from *just one more night*.

"I agree," I murmur, and her breathing evens out as she loses her fight against consciousness from the intensity of it all.

Chapter 29: Desiree Dixon

A Girl's Got Needs, and I've Got a Vibrator

I wake with a start as my stomach growls, and I suddenly remember there's food outside the door that we never got.

It was just after he said the hottest words that have ever been spoken to me that the knock came.

I better never fucking see you wearing someone else's number ever again. You're mine, and I don't share.

I'm *his* now, I guess, and, in all honesty, that's exactly what I wanted to be.

I get it. Things could get awkward and weird. For now, we need to hide this. He's going to continue to fight against it.

And all that's fine so long as I find myself lying in his arms once again after he carries me toward the most intense climaxes of my life.

There's something different about sex with him—something powerful—and I can't give it up after two nights together. I can't walk away, and I already know he won't be able to, either.

Be that as it may, it's not like I want my dad to find out about us either—which means I also need to keep it from my mom as well.

Back to the food. We had intentions of getting it, but when he dipped his cock down inside me, I was lost.

I *am* lost. In him.

It's not like I've slept with a ton of guys or anything, but when I have, I've been safe. With Asher, though, this animal instinct washed over me that told me it was okay to be a little reckless with him. *He* is a little reckless, or at least all reports point that way, and I wanted to be that way, too. I wanted to feel every part of him. I wanted nothing between us.

It's a good thing he pulled out, though. I've never been great at consistency when it comes to birth control, which is why I'm not on the pill and opted instead for the shot. And I still have my partner wear a condom to be extra safe, and I know Asher has probably had more partners than the majority of guys I've slept with…but I also know he's a football player, and they have regular physicals, and if he knew it was risky, he wouldn't've pushed inside me.

There's a trust between us already, maybe because we've been in bed together once before and he wore a condom that time, or maybe it's because I'm the daughter of one of his coaches and he needs to be extra careful because of that.

I get up, and he groans when he feels me get out of bed. I use the bathroom first and pull on my skirt and the Vegas Aces shirt he wore here, and I open the door and find a cart of food and beverages waiting for us.

I pull it in. It's probably been sitting out there less than a half hour, but time is more of a theory than a reality when I'm with Asher.

He gets up and grabs his shorts when he sees what I'm doing, and I wheel the cart over to the table by the windows. The sky is starting to darken now, but we don't flip on any lights, opting instead to eat in the slowly darkening room lit only by the blinking lights of the Strip out the window.

He ordered appetizers and vodka, and he pours us each a drink while I dig hungrily into the sliders. He hands me a drink and holds up his glass, so I hold mine up to clink it to his, but I pause while I wait for him to say something.

"What are we toasting to?" I prompt.

"Sex?" he suggests, and I giggle.

"How about to reggae music and backseats?" I raise a challenging brow. I almost said to taking this past two nights, and even though I have a pretty strong suspicion we will, I don't think he's ready to acknowledge it yet.

"I mean, that's basically the same thing." He taps his glass to mine, and we each take a long, hard swig of the vodka mixed with Sprite.

"Do you think our driver knew what we were doing back there?" I ask.

"Oh, yeah. Totally."

I shouldn't ask questions I don't want an honest answer to.

I cover my eyes with my hand in embarrassment, and he laughs as he puffs his chest out a little. Why is that embarrassing as hell for the woman and a point of pride for the man? It's a reminder once again that maybe I want to be a little more like Asher.

To that end, I take another sip of my drink, shovel in another slider, and say, "Tell me more about Asher Nash. I've had, what, four orgasms by you now, and I feel like all I know about you is that you hate mushrooms."

"Five," he clarifies immediately. "Not that we're keeping track or anything."

I laugh. "Right. Plus the ones I've given myself thinking of you since the last time."

His eyes darken as he shifts a little in his chair. "You've touched yourself thinking about me?"

"It's been almost four months since the charity ball, and not a single man has held my interest enough to let him see me naked. So, yeah. A girl's got needs, and I've got a vibrator."

His jaw slackens at the mere thought. "To be clear, I've given myself plenty of secret handshakes over the last few months myself."

"Secret handshake?" I repeat with a laugh, dodging the real question I want to ask regarding whether he's been with other women since he was with me. "Is that what you call jerking off?"

"Oh, there's plenty more where that came from." He wiggles his eyebrows playfully, and I laugh. "But back to this vibrator business. Is that open for spectators?"

"Plural? No." I press my lips together.

He shakes his head and shoves his thumb into his chest. "Singular. Me."

"I thought this *had to be the last time*," I point out, tossing his own words right back at him as I throw air quotes around the end of my sentence.

"Right, that," he says dryly. "I guess I can make an exception. But just one more time."

"Mm-hmm," I say, nodding sarcastically. "I need two things before I'll agree to that." I chug down the rest of my vodka and tip the bottle over my glass, not bothering to add Sprite to it to dilute the alcohol content.

"Name them." He grabs the bottle and doesn't bother pouring it over his ice, instead tipping the bottle right to his lips.

"The time and place," I say.

"How long are you in town?" he asks.

"Through the game Sunday. I leave Sunday night."

He nods. "Then every day from now until Sunday that you are available."

I laugh. "I mean, I do need to spend a little bit of time with my family while I'm here."

He ignores my words. "Did you bring the vibrator with you, or do I need to provide the toys?"

"It's at home," I admit.

He narrows his eyes at me. "You were planning on this happening again, weren't you?"

"I was hoping." I lift a shoulder. "The night of the ball was one of the best nights of my life, Asher. And tonight, honestly, it's a close second."

He glances at the food on the table before his eyes lift to mine. "Feeling's mutual."

My chest warms.

He sets down the piece of fruit in his hand. "I don't want to fight against this, Des. You said you haven't been with anybody since the ball...and I haven't, either. I kissed one girl in

Australia, and I felt nothing. I tried, and it was *nothing*. With you, it's fucking explosions and electricity when we're in the same room together. I can't stop thinking about you."

He sighs, and my chest does a hell of a lot more than warm at his words. Until he continues forward before I get the chance to tell him that.

"But there are certain lines you don't cross in this business, and I'm crossing them. I'm running over them and leaving them in the rearview, and I have to be careful. I'm already on thin ice, and your dad is like the *one* fucking person who believes in me. I still get teased in the locker room about my suspension. People think I'm there because of my brother. Not Coach Dixon, though. I can't betray him, not when he believes I can be a leader like I want to be, and being here with you right now feels like a huge betrayal."

"Then we'll be careful. We'll get to know each other in secret, and nobody has to know."

"For now, yeah. Fine. But what happens down the road when this goes to a place neither of us can hide any longer?" His tone is both sincere and hopeful, and it gives me a great measure of joy that he's thinking that far ahead.

Or maybe, given how quickly our feelings are growing, it's not really all that far into the future.

"We'll cross that bridge when we get there," I say a little helplessly. It's not like me to respond that way. I'm a planner by trade, and I'm a planner in life. My backup plans have backup plans.

But sometimes in life we need to act off the cuff, and this feels like one of those times.

"I don't know if that's good enough." He twists his lips nearly apologetically, and I'm grateful for the near darkness in here since heat presses behind my eyes at his words.

But the truth is that I don't know if that's good enough, either.

I don't want to hide what I have with him. I don't want to leave in the middle of the night when I'm visiting my parents so they don't suspect anything. I don't want to act like a teenager when I'm an adult developing real feelings for somebody.

And yet I also get where he's coming from. His career is his life, and I'm not here to take away from that. If anything, I want to do whatever I can to support that.

I stand up and walk around the table, and I settle onto his lap. I loop my arms around his neck, and I lean forward and press a soft kiss to his lips as his arms come up around my waist.

He pulls back and leans his forehead to mine, his eyes closed as he draws in a deep breath.

"I can't stay away from you," he whispers.

"Then don't," I say softly, and he catches my lips with his again. We kiss slowly, languidly, tenderly there for a few minutes as we both try to process what's happening here between us.

And it's as he's kissing me in this hotel room that I think I make my decision about where my future is leading me.

Chapter 30: Asher Nash

I Don't Want to Go

We finish our snacks, and I head over to the bed, sated and full. I lay down and motion for her to come join me, and I wrap my arms around her as she rests her head on my chest.

"Tell me you're staying the night," I demand.

"You know I can't. If we're trying to keep this a secret, there will be far too many questions coming from my parents since I'm staying with them." She sighs as she draws little circles on my chest.

"They're overprotective," I say softly.

"My dad is, yes," she admits.

"Why?"

She glances up at me, pulling back a little. "Well, for one thing, a player on his team once broke my heart. And for another, he's told me I deserve more than a football player who travels half the season, whose life is dedicated to football instead of to me..." She shrugs as she trails off.

"Who was the player? I'll kill him." She chuckles, and before she answers, I add, "Plenty of guys make it work. Look at all three of my brothers. Two are married and still involved in the game, one is retired. But all three shifted their focus to the women in their lives when the right one came along." I'm staring at the ceiling as I speak from the heart, something I'm not sure I've ever really done before with a woman.

"That's what I've told him—or tried to. But I think he was the bad boy football player my mom's parents never approved of, and maybe my mom was more forgiving than she should've been." She's conjecturing, and I need to clarify something.

I clear my throat. "Not every football player is a cheater, Des—certainly not the Nash brothers, anyway. Our mom raised us with values and ethics, though the same can't be said for my father, who tends to be the crux of most of my issues."

"Is he a cheater? Is that why they got divorced?" she asks. She slaps her hand over her mouth. "Sorry. That might be overstepping."

I shake my head. "Not at all. I don't know if he cheated on her, but I think there were a lot of layers involved in their divorce, not the least of which involved the way our dad treated the four of his kids our entire lives. I think my mom might've stayed for the four of us, stayed out of complacency, stayed because she was comfortable. Probably a million different reasons. But it's over now, and having parents get divorced even when you're an adult can still have effects the kids never saw coming."

"Like what?" she asks.

"Just the whole idea of commitment. It fucked with all four of us, I think. None of us even thought about a future with a woman until our parents got divorced. It was like my dad brainwashed us into focusing totally on football and not our personal lives, and it's why Linc was thirty-six before he got married." I try to deflect a little, opting not to talk about how it made me fear commitment in general.

"What's your relationship like with your dad?" she asks.

I stare up at the ceiling some more. "Complicated."

"How?"

I shrug a little even though she's lying on my shoulder. "He was my hero when I was a kid. You know? In that stereotypical way dads are for kids. He was a pro football player, and that was pretty kickass, which I'm sure you can relate to."

She nods, and I realize for the first time that it's something we share in common. Most of the women who lay in a bed with me are only around for one night, and they don't understand a single damn thing about this life. But her dad lived it. He's *still* living it. She's been around it her entire life like I have.

Except I made it my career. She didn't.

"But then he retired, and he changed. He became obsessed with this bar he owned with his former friend, and he put everything into it. I don't know all the details about it, but I feel like his downfall stemmed from that. His pride took the wheel, and he lost a lot. Friends, family, money. It drained everything out of him, and it turned him into this bitter, selfish old man. Yet deep down, I know my hero is still in there." I find myself getting oddly emotional talking about my dad.

"Of course he is," she says softly. "What about your brothers? Are they close with him?"

"That's complicated, too," I admit. "None of them understand why I live with him, and sometimes I don't know why, either. Maybe to save him. He was there for me during some rough times in my life, and even if we butt heads now, I can't forget that. But living with him means I'm not as close to my mom as I used to be. She doesn't come around and stay with me. She'll go to Linc's to help out with the kids, or she'll go to Gray's to use his pool. I miss her."

I'm going much deeper than I thought I would with someone who's only supposed to be a two and done.

"What's it like having three brothers?" she asks.

"Do you have any siblings?" I ask before I answer.

She shakes her head.

"Sometimes it's the greatest thing in the world, and other times it's, well, the opposite of that. I always say Linc's the leader, which is obvious given his career choice. Grayson's the outgoing one, Spencer's the smart one, and then there's me. The youngest. The risk-taker. The wild one. I somehow fit in with all three of them, and at the same time, I don't fit in with any of them."

"I doubt that," she murmurs softly. "You seem so…"

I wait for her to fill in the blank, and my heart seems to pick up speed. The word feels like it'll hold a lot of weight, whatever it is, and I'm not sure why.

"Charming," she finally finishes. "Like you get along with everybody, but you also don't care what anybody thinks about you."

"I care what *you* think about me," I admit.

"And you fish for compliments when you don't need to." She pulls back off me and looks me in the eyes, simply to roll her eyes at me, and I grab her by the back of her neck and pull her down for a kiss.

She laughs as she resists, but eventually, she gives in and kisses me back.

"I never thought much about settling down until I saw them doing it. I never thought I wanted it. But then this gorgeous woman ordered a dirty martini, extra dirty, and I was immediately smitten." The words tumble out of my mouth before I can back up and stop them…before I can act like they aren't way over the top and too much too soon. I clear my throat as she stares down tenderly at me, and she runs a fingertip along my jaw. "I guess I never thought much about the future until I met you."

She leans down and presses a soft kiss to my lips. "And now?"

My eyes flick down to her lips. "And now I can't stop wondering when the next time I can get back inside you will be."

Her eyes widen a little at my words, and then I get my answer.

It's nearly an hour later when she sighs deeply. "I don't want to go…"

"But you have to?" I guess, and she nods.

"Yeah. My dad finding out about us would be bad for both of us."

I nod. I get what she's saying, and I get why she has to go…but still. "I don't want you to go," I admit.

"I don't even have a shirt to wear home since you ripped mine off me." She purses her lips at me.

"You can take mine," I suggest, and her eyes seem to light up a little at that. I can grab a shirt from a store downstairs. She moves to get up, and I playfully grab her and pull her back against my body. "When can I see you again?" I ask over her giggles. I pepper kisses to her neck.

"As soon as possible," she says.

"I have plans tomorrow night. Can you do Wednesday after practice?"

She nods. "Yeah, I think that should work."

"It's a date."

"A date? Like on your calendar, or a real one?"

I laugh. "How about a real one?"

"But we have to hide, and everyone in this town knows who you are." She twists in my arms so she's facing me, and I lean down and press another kiss to her mouth.

"Then I guess I better get planning." I have no idea exactly what to do, but I'm a creative guy. I'll come up with something.

She heads out, much to my disappointment, and I call down to the front desk to request a shirt from the gift shop. They send one up, and I head home myself. No sense in spending the night here when every place I turn just reminds me of her.

On my ride home, I look up some shit to do on Wednesday. We could go to a movie. We should probably avoid concerts and shows on the Strip since she's right, I could be recognized. There's a restaurant that's entirely dark inside, so that's a possibility. I could rent a space somewhere or do something after hours. We could drive out to the desert and stargaze.

All possibilities, and I'll make some decisions when my body isn't quite so depleted and I'm not so exhausted.

When I walk in the front door at one thirty, I'm expecting a quiet house. That's not what I get.

My dad is at the kitchen table with three other men around his age, and they're playing poker.

My dad isn't the friendliest, and I have no idea who these three men are. They're not former football players, at least not ones I recognize.

I sigh. I was kind of hoping I'd be able to quietly slip in and head to bed, but my dad's eyes lift to me when I pad by the table.

"Hey, here's our fifth!" he says. He stands and claps me on the shoulder like we're much closer than we are these days. "You want in?"

I shake my head, and it almost feels like he's the dude in his twenties and I'm the responsible adult. "Long night. I'm turning in."

"Ah, that's not the man I raised." He's taunting me.

"In fact, it is," I say dryly. I wave at the other men. "Hi. I'm Asher, his roommate."

"My youngest son," he says. "Tight end for the Aces." He says the words proudly, and I think it's less to do with my accomplishments and more to do with the fact that I'm following in his footsteps as a pro football player. "And these are my new poker buddies, Phil, Tom, and Herman."

Sounds like a lively bunch.

I nod at the three guests. "Nice meeting you." I can't help but wonder where he met them, but I don't care enough to find out tonight. "Have a good night."

It's a little after eleven the next morning when my dad walks into the kitchen and starts a coffee pod for himself. I'm considering heading into the gym near the Complex for a run and a swim when he says, "Where were you last night?"

I huff out a chuckle. "Noneya." As if I'd say a word to my dad about being with Desiree.

As if he can read my mind, he says, "Did you hear about Bill Dixon's wife?"

My brows dip as my chest races. Did something happen to Des's mom? "What about her?"

"She's a billionaire."

I heave out a breath, but my reaction to the mere thought that Desiree might be hurting over something going on in her family is startling, to say the least.

His words don't register for a second.

"She's a…what?"

He nods. "She owns Berkshire hotels. I guess her daughter's getting it down the road." He whistles through his teeth as my fucking claws come all the way out. "Can you imagine the fortune there? See what you can do." He wiggles his eyebrows suggestively, and I feel sick.

He has literally no idea that I spent most of the night with her. He has no idea that I find myself falling in deep with her as we start to get to know one another. He has no idea that I'm already addicted to her—to her eyes, her laugh, her scent, her cunt.

And I had literally no idea that she's the heiress to a hotel fortune.

It doesn't matter. It doesn't change anything. I don't care about her money any more than she cares about mine.

But it does give me a little insight into who she is…and the fact that she's being careful as we explore whatever this is between us.

Chapter 31: Desiree Dixon

Miss Too Busy for Book Club

I glance at my door, and I slip my earbuds in so nobody can hear the other end of the conversation. I talk barely above a whisper even though I'm sitting on my bed and my parents rarely frequent this side of the house, even more unlikely since I warned them I'm holding a video chat for book club with my best friends.

Addy, Lauren, and Chloe all appear on the screen, the three of them together at the apartment I share with Addy even though I'm not there.

"I miss you guys," I say when I see them, and I feel emotional seeing my three best friends together while I'm in Vegas.

It's a red flag where moving from there to here is concerned, anyway.

"Have you seen him again?" Lauren asks, cutting to the chase.

"Are we not discussing this week's book?" I ask, dodging her question.

"After we get the update," Chloe agrees. "Besides, it's Tuesday afternoon. Book club is for Wednesday, but since Miss Too Busy for Book Club can't meet tomorrow and has to cut it short tonight, we need the details first."

She has a point. Life gossip has to take precedence when we're short on time, but I'm attending a charity event this evening, and tomorrow during our normal book club time, I have a date.

With Asher.

"You guys, she's blushing. Look at our girl!" Lauren says.

"Leave her alone," Addy says, always the one to step in and defend her friends, even if it's just from teasing.

"It's okay." I draw in a breath. "I got a job offer."

"What?" all three of them gasp at the same time.

I nod. "The Vegas Aces want me to plan their annual charity ball for next year, and they have some other events lined up, too. And while I was at the training facility talking to the director of charity events, I ran into Asher. We went to a hotel, and, well…you know."

"Atta girl," Chloe praises.

"Define *you know*," Lauren says, narrowing her eyes.

"Uh, okay, so I blew him in the back of a rideshare, and then he banged me stupid at the hotel," I admit. I'm doing more than blushing now as the memory plows into me.

Addy's eyes are saucers, but Lauren and Chloe just stare at me dreamily.

"She is living her best life," Chloe murmurs.

"Vegas and Nash look *good* on you, girl," Lauren says.

"Are you going to take the job?" Addy asks.

I lift a shoulder. "When I'm with him, I think I want to give it a try. But he's skittish. I have to be careful since…well, you know."

"Since he plays for your dad?" Addy guesses.

I nod, and I leave it at that. I don't get into the private things he confessed to me—about his reputation in the locker room and how my dad believes in him. Or any of the other stuff we shared.

It was hard to say goodbye, but if we're going to continue seeing each other in secret, I had to. I have enough lies piling up where my parents are concerned. I really don't want to have to invent more by doing the walk of shame into their house in the morning and facing their questions.

I left his hotel room a little after one in the morning, and I crashed until after ten this morning.

My body is deliciously achy from the workout he gave me, and I'm physically exhausted. Mentally, though, and spiritually? I don't know if I've ever felt more in tune with what I want.

And what I want is Asher Nash. Any way I can get him. *All* the ways I can get him.

"Are you going to move there?" Chloe asks.

I sigh. "I'm not sure. If I do consulting, I was thinking I could split time between Vegas and home. But I'm not sure how realistic that is."

"Are you quitting your job?" Lauren asks.

I stare at my three best friends as I try to come up with the answer to that. "I don't know what to do."

"Start with the cons," Addy suggests, something we always do when we're trying to make a decision about anything, big or small.

"Leaving San Diego," I say. "Leaving you three. Book club."

"We'll make book club work, and you won't be leaving us. It just won't be as easy to grab drinks on a Friday night," Chloe says.

"She can never come out on Friday anyway since she's always got events," Lauren points out.

"True," Addy says. "And we can visit her in Vegas and hit up all the hot spots since she'll be a local, and then maybe she wouldn't have to work on Fridays so we could spend entire weekends together."

"Most events involving players during the season take place on Monday or Tuesday nights," I say. "Those are their days off. I'm actually attending one tonight, which is why I had to chat early."

"See?" Addy says. "So if you move to Vegas, there actually might be a better chance we could all go out together on a weekend because, in theory, you might not have to work."

I laugh. "And Addy, whatever happens, I'm not leaving you in the lurch for somewhere to live."

She waves a hand. "Don't worry about that. It's not a factor in your decision."

"Oh, move in with me!" Chloe says.

Addy's brows dip. "What?"

"We could carpool to work. It would be *so* fun!"

The two of them have their own side conversation for a beat before Addy says, "Wait, back to cons. What else?"

"We have to hide it," I say.

"For now," Lauren says.

"Yeah. Or maybe forever. At least until he's no longer playing for my dad." What if that's true? What if we can't tell my dad about us until Asher retires? What if we have to keep it a secret for years?

We haven't talked about his plans for the future at all. This is still way too new. It's still way too early to even be thinking about that, but the planner in me can't help but want to rush forward to the future.

"Anything else?" Lauren asks.

I twist my lips and shake my head.

"Not even his…you know, rather odd sense of fashion?" Chloe prompts.

I laugh. "No. I find his fashion rather endearing, if I'm being honest."

"You know next time we see her, she'll be wearing flamingoes or tigers or something, right?" Lauren says to the other two.

I make a mental note to get a shirt with flamingoes on it. Or, better yet, something matching for Asher and myself.

Except…we can't. We can't attend events together wearing matching obnoxious styles because we can't go public. If, you know, there was something to go public about. Which there isn't.

Not yet, anyway.

"Let's move onto pros, then," Addy suggests.

"Good in bed, hot as hell, big fat…" I clear my throat. "Paycheck," I finish weakly, but all three girls know I don't give a fuck about his paycheck given my own financial status. They do, however, know exactly where my innuendo was leading.

Lauren giggles.

"Okay, Desi, but those are all surface things. Are you really considering moving to Vegas over sex?" Addy asks.

I glance out my bedroom window as I think about the intense connection we share. It's vivid and bold and powerful, and I really, really want the chance to explore more of it.

I think about sitting in the hotel room with him last night as we made confessions over appetizers. We're still in the getting-to-know-you phase, but every new piece of information I unlock about him has my curiosity piqued more and more.

"It's more than sex," I admit. "I don't know exactly how much more, but there's something there. We bonded over our dads playing, and he's got his own paycheck, so I know he's not after my family's money." I shrug. "It's hard to find someone I trust these days, and he seems like one of the good ones."

"So a job and a man all in a few days?" Chloe asks.

I laugh.

"Take the job," Addy says.

"Take the job," Lauren agrees, and she says it like a chant. Chloe joins in, and then Addy does, too. "Take the job! Take the job! Take the job!"

I laugh and hold up both hands. "Okay, okay."

"You know you can always come back here if it doesn't work out," Addy says. "And none of us want you to go, but all of us want to see you soar."

Tears heat behind my eyes. "I know you do, and I love you."

"We love you more," Chloe says, and Addy wipes away some tears. It'll be the biggest change for her since we live together, but I feel the love, support, and encouragement from all three of them.

This doesn't have to change anything, and it'll be nice to be close to my parents again—even if I have to keep part of my motivation for doing this a secret from them.

It's worth exploring.

I know that for sure.

We hang up, and I guess I'll have some exciting news to share with my parents tonight.

Chapter 32: Desiree Dixon

I'm Fucking Addicted to You

"I have some news," I announce as I walk into the kitchen. My parents are all dressed up and waiting for me, and they're both elegant ahead of the SmartSports black-tie event tonight celebrating community partnerships and recognizing athletes and coaches.

I tuck my black handbag under my arm, and my mom smiles broadly.

"You look beautiful, darling girl," she says.

"Thank you. As do you."

She curtsies formally, and we both laugh. I love having an easygoing relationship with her, and it's going to be hard to keep the fact that I'm falling for Asher to myself since I tell her virtually everything.

"What's the news?" my dad asks.

I draw in a deep breath. "I've decided to take Erin's offer. I'm going to be moving to Vegas."

"Oh!" My mom squeals, and she holds a hand up to her mouth before she rushes over to pull me into a hug. "Oh, I'm so happy!"

I hear the emotion in her voice, and I chide her. "Don't cry, Mom. You'll mess up your gorgeous makeup."

She laughs as she pulls back, and she wipes her eyes. "You're right." She fans her face as she pulls it together, and my dad hugs me next.

He kisses the top of my head. "I'm so proud of you, Desi. You're a superstar, and you're going to blow Vegas away."

I preen under his praise, and I have to admit, I'm excited to see what the future holds for me here in Vegas.

The car arrives to take us to tonight's event, and I can't help but wish I had a date tonight. I wish Asher could rest his hand on my knee, and we could walk arm-in-arm up to the bar, and we could dance and laugh the night away together.

It's only the beginning for us, and someday I think my dad will understand. Just maybe not while Asher's working to fix his reputation while earning the respect of everyone in his locker room—coaching staff included.

I feel like I've met everyone on the Vegas Aces staff at this point, and when my dad starts talking to Steve and my mom and Barb get to talking, I excuse myself to the bar.

"Dirty martini," I order.

Just then, a voice behind me adds, "Extra dirty."

I spin around and find myself face-to-face with Asher Nash in a red and black camouflage suit, looking like an absolute *snack*.

What are you doing here? seems like a stupid question since this event is celebrating athletes in the community. I knew he had an event tonight, but I didn't know it was the same one I'd be attending.

"Make it two," he says, and he shoots me a wink as he runs a hand through his hair.

"Filthy," I murmur.

"I wasn't expecting to see you here," he says quietly as the bartender turns away to make our drinks. "But I'm glad."

I smile. "So am I."

"Jesus, you look hot in that dress," he murmurs as he looks away from me, trying to make it look from afar like we're not even having a conversation.

"Even hotter out of it." I raise a challenging brow.

His eyes return to me, heated as always. "Show me."

"Right here?" I tuck some of my hair behind my ear, and he groans a little. Something about my hair seems to do it for him.

He glances around the room as if he's looking for a place for us to go. "The patio?" he suggests.

"I haven't been out there yet."

"There are also some executive meeting rooms near the bathrooms that looked like they weren't in use."

"You scoped the place out?" I ask.

He chuckles. "No, my brother pointed them out to me, actually. He was teasing me, but joke's on him." He pauses. "Shit," he mumbles under his breath.

I'm about to ask him why he cursed when I spot Miles Hudson sauntering over.

"Nash," he says, clapping Asher on the back. "What are you having?"

"Two dirty martinis, extra dirty," the bartender says, and I realize the innuendo as Asher's eyes widen a bit.

"Oh, those are mine," I say smoothly, and I pick them both up and head off in the direction of my parents, chugging down one on the way.

Why does it suddenly feel like this is going to be a long night?

And how many of these events can I do where I'm secretly seeing Asher and we pretend we don't even know each other?

It's going to get harder before it gets easier, that's for sure.

After my second dirty martini, I head to the restroom. It's quiet in this hallway as we're the only event on a Tuesday evening in this huge events center, and when I exit the bathroom, I spot a lone figure standing in the hallway leaning against the wall and apparently waiting for me.

He pushes off the wall with his heel and stalks down the hall toward me, a little menacing, a little aggressive, and very, very hot.

He stops short of me, and he reaches out and lightly grips my throat. He guides me back until I bump into the wall, and his lips move immediately to mine.

I wrap my arms around him, knowing full well that anyone could walk down this hallway at any time, and maybe the secrecy of it all is part of what makes it so hot with him.

I tend to think that has nothing to do with it at all, though.

He bucks his hips against me, and I can feel how needy he is. How much he wants this…wants *me*.

"Christ, Des," he murmurs as he pulls away from my mouth. "I can't stay away from you." His lips find my neck, and he kisses his way back up to my mouth before he pulls back. "I'm fucking addicted to you."

My only response is to move my hungry mouth back to his.

"We can't do this out here," he says, some semblance of responsibility falling back over him, which is lucky because mine up and left the premises.

He thrusts his hips to mine again, and then he grabs my hand and leads me to those executive meeting rooms he mentioned earlier.

He tries the first door, and it's locked. The second, however, is open.

He looks both ways before he slips inside one, yanking me in behind him, and he has me pressed against the wall with his mouth on mine and his hand fumbling with the bottom of my dress in a near instant. He shoves my panties aside and slides a finger into me, and I whimper at the feel of his hands back on my body as I grip onto his upper arms, my head rolling back and my eyes closing as I bite my lip to try to move the sensation somewhere else on my body so I don't start to come too soon.

I don't want to. I want to live in this moment a little longer.

His mouth is still on mine, and he groans as he feels how wet I am. Without any sort of warning whatsoever, he drops to his knees, tosses my leg over his shoulder, and yanks my panties harder to the side before he dives face first into my pussy.

He moans as he tastes me, and I lean back against the wall as I wrap my hands around his head, pulling him into me as I ride his face. God, he feels good. His scruff tickles my thighs as he sucks on my clit, lighting the fuse that's about to lead to the explosion of fireworks.

It doesn't take long. That man can use the hell out of his mouth, and as he slides his long finger back inside me, I detonate into a million tiny pieces. The one knee I'm balancing on nearly buckles as I start to come, and I hold onto his head as my leg that's tossed over his shoulder clings onto him. He stays right where he is as he guides me through an intense, brutal release, and when the tremors of pleasure start to fade into warmth, he finally gently lowers my leg from his shoulder and straightens to a stand, careful to continue holding me up.

Once he's fully at a stand, he reaches behind my knees and pulls me literally into his arms, carrying me over to the conference table and depositing me on the end of it. He reaches under my dress, bunching it up around my waist, and slides my panties down my legs. "Don't need these," he mutters, tossing them to the floor, and then he fumbles with his belt buckle.

He pulls out that gorgeous cock of his, stroking it a few times before he gazes at my darkened eyes. "How has it only been twenty-four hours since the last time I fucked you? It feels like it's been forever."

He leans over me, and his mouth collides with mine before I get a chance to agree.

It's a messy kiss, the first signal that he's falling apart with need. He pulls back, yanks me down toward the end of the table, and grips his cock, sliding it through me and jerking it against my sensitive clit a few times.

I moan at the feel of him, my eyes hot on him as I watch his handsome face. He's looking down at the spot where our bodies are about to join, his dark lashes fanned out high on those strong cheekbones.

He exudes this animal magnetism, this charm, and to know that I'm the one who caught his attention makes me feel self-assured and proud as fuck.

He pushes into me, and his eyes flick up to mine. "Fuck, yes, Des. You're so hot and tight for me."

He clenches his jaw but parts his lips as a hot determination passes through his eyes, and he growls as he starts to move inside me with nothing between us for the second time.

He leans forward and tucks some of my hair behind my ear, a tender caress in an otherwise carnal act. He drives into me harder and harder, picking up the pace like he needs to cross the finish line in order to breathe again. He leans all the way down and kisses my neck before stretching to find my mouth.

He grunts and groans as his tongue batters mine, the tang of my own pussy still on his tongue, and I inexplicably feel my second release building.

He'll return to the ballroom where tonight's event is taking place and talk to other players—maybe even his coaches—with my scent hot on his tongue. It's all sorts of forbidden and wrong, and the mere thought pushes me into a pulsing, quaking climax.

My body clenches tightly over his as I start to come. "That's my good girl," he grunts. "Come all over my cock. Squeeze it harder, baby."

God, his words are hot as I come all over him, my body fighting to thrash as his body holds me still. He pushes up off of me and hammers into me a few times, bracing himself by placing his hands on my tits where my dress is still in place.

"Oh fuck, I'm coming. Fuck, fuck, fuck," he says over and over as he lets go inside me this time, not bothering to pull out.

I feel a sense of heat as he continues pumping into me, his semen jetting into me. I moan at the feel of it. There's something insanely hot about knowing I did this to him.

He slows his thrusts before he stops, holding still inside me a few beats, and then he reaches beside us to a box of tissues I hadn't noticed. He pulls out of me, careful to catch anything that slips out of me with the tissue before he discards it in the trash. I sit up, and he tucks himself back into his slacks then helps slip my panties back on.

I stand to shift them back into place, and then I collapse into one of the chairs around the table, completely spent and not sure how the hell I'm supposed to walk back to the ballroom as if I didn't just get the hell railed out of me in executive meeting room B.

Chapter 33: Asher Nash

I Swear We Sanitize

I'm not sure how those words slipped out, but they did.

I can't stay away from you.

I'm fucking addicted to you.

Hell, I may as well have said *I'm obsessed with you.*

They're all true statements, but it's a little early to be saying any of them to her...mostly because it's fucking scary as hell to admit.

It's scary to *feel* the way I feel.

It's not something I've ever felt before, so I'm not exactly sure what to do with it all. My instinct is to run, but when her bright green eyes fall on me, I feel instantly calm, like this is right.

But at the same time, she's the one making me want to run. It doesn't make any sense.

"You ready to head back out there?" I ask.

She lifts a shoulder lazily. "We probably should, but honestly, I don't know if I'm physically capable of walking yet."

"Because I just impaled you with my huge cock?"

She laughs. "Something like that. More that my legs are a little shaky from the back-to-back orgasms, but your huge cock had something to do with that."

My mouth tips up in a half smile. "Can I get you anything?"

She shakes her head. "You head out. I'll be right behind you. We shouldn't walk in together anyway."

"Good call." I bend down to kiss her one last time, and then I sigh as my eyes meet hers. "Well, see you around."

She nods as she averts her gaze to the floor, and it suddenly feels a little heavy in here. We're at the precipice of whatever this is, and there's nothing wrong with taking it slow and keeping quiet about it.

Though, to be fair, we're not exactly taking it slow.

I carefully check out in the hallway and find that the coast is clear, so I bolt back to the ballroom. I'm not sure how long she sits in the meeting room, but my eyes keep edging to the door as I watch for her.

I've just finished a conversation with one of the SmartSports executives when my brother Grayson walks up to me and flicks my ear. "Nice suit, motherfucker."

I glance down at the suit I chose for this event, a deep maroon and black camouflage pattern. "Thanks." I know he's teasing me, but I pretend he's complimenting me. "How's the cookie business?"

He and his wife opened a bakery earlier this year, and by all accounts, it's thriving. "Oh, I've had my share of cookies today." His wolfish grin makes me think he's not talking about actual cookies, and I'm about to tell him I just snacked on my own sweet cookie when I realize I can't even tell him.

I can't tell any of my brothers. I can't risk anyone in my family finding out and blowing my cover with Desiree's father.

"What's going on with you?" Grayson asks.

I can hardly admit the truth. "I need to get the hell out of that house with Dad."

"Dude, come stay with Ava and me a while…if you don't mind middle of the day cookie eating on my kitchen counter." He shrugs and offers another of those wolfish grins.

I grimace. "Things you don't need to know about your big brother," I mutter, and he laughs.

"I'm mostly joking. We're usually at the bakery in the middle of the day."

I wrinkle my nose. "Do you fuck on the counters at the bakery?"

"Only after hours, and I swear we sanitize." He shrugs.

"Remind me to go to that other bakery around the corner."

He chuckles, and then he tilts his head at me. "You sure everything's okay? It's just Dad?"

I nod. "Just Dad. But you know how it is. In season, it's hard finding a new place to live when you have so much other shit to focus on. So I'll probably tough it out for now."

"Yeah, but if it's that bad…"

I nod. "I've gotten a hotel a few nights, to be honest."

"So you're covering his rent *and* paying for a hotel? Dude, that's not right. What if the four of us chip in on new a place for him so you don't feel like you need to take the brunt of it?" he suggests. "And I can take the lead on finding it since you three are busy."

Relief filters through me. "You'd do that?"

He nods, and he mock slugs me in the shoulder again. "Of course I would, man. As long as you promise never to wear the purple velour tracksuit again."

I twist my lips and shake my head. "Damn. We were *so close* to having a deal, but no can do, brochacho. It's my favorite."

He laughs, and that's when I see a vision with red hair walk through the doorway.

She brushes right past me on her way to the bar without so much as a second glance, and it feels a little worse than it should.

But in twenty-four hours, she'll be all mine.

Chapter 34: Asher Nash

What the Hell is Goat Yoga

The next twenty-four hours getting to our date are brutal.

Practice is intense, and after some locker room drama involving a very focused veteran player and a rookie who was mouthing off combined with one of our linebackers working his ass off to take me down during practice, I know I should spend the night resting and recuperating—at least, that's what Coach Dixon told me to do during our heart-to-heart.

But I can't because I have a plan. One that involves the daughter of the very man who told me that, and guilt racks me because of it.

I push that guilt away. I don't have a choice, not when I'm addicted to her.

As much as I want to take her to a hotel somewhere and spend the night worshiping her body, I also want to take her on a real date. I think the last time I took a girl on what I'd consider an actual *date*, I was eighteen and showing up to her house with a wrist corsage before I took her to prom.

Is that right? It's been *ten years* since I've taken a woman on a date?

I've been with plenty of women, some more than once or twice, but none that I felt like I needed to *date*. So what makes this one different?

I guess that's the million-dollar question that I don't have the answer to.

When the Lyft carrying her pulls into the parking lot of the grocery store I told her to meet me at, my chest thumps like it always does when I'm around her.

I'm listening to my playlist curated today of songs by all my favorite bands just to see what she says. It's eclectic, but then, that's usually a pretty good word to describe my tastes in most things in life.

The car drops her near the store's entrance, and she glances around the parking lot before she spots my...wait for it...*red* Ford F-350 parked halfway down one of the rows. She walks toward me wearing a sexy as fuck sundress and a pair of Converse on her feet, a sweater draped over her forearm, and her purse slung across her body. She looks somehow cute and hot all at the same time, and my cock strains against my jeans as I watch her walk toward me.

Why are sundresses my kryptonite?

I'm not going to start this date with sex, but I can't guarantee it won't end that way.

She slips into the passenger seat of my truck, and I lean over the console, reach around the back of her neck, and pull her to me for a quick kiss. I lean my forehead to hers and take a deep breath, and for as much as the last twenty-four hours have felt chaotic, everything feels peaceful when she's beside me.

I pull back and catch her eyes, and she looks as smitten as I feel. Her lips curl into a smile as she turns to look out the windshield as she buckles her seatbelt.

"What's the plan?" she asks.

I shift the truck into drive. "You'll see."

We head out of the parking lot and toward the highway, and soon we're cruising toward our destination. It's about a forty-minute drive, and I figured it would be a good time to get to know a little more about each other.

"What's life like in San Diego?" I ask.

She huffs out a small laugh. "It seems like everything's in flux since my parents moved here, if I'm being honest. I live near the beach with one of my best friends, and I've never lived in a different town than my mom and dad."

"Even in college?"

"Even in college," she confirms.

"Do you miss having them close?" I ask.

"Yes and no. I like the freedom, but I miss weekly dinners on Tuesday nights, you know?"

"Yeah. My parents moved to Vegas just before they got divorced, and it was nice having them both around. Truth be told, I miss my mom." I stare out the windshield as I say words I've never actually voiced out loud to another person.

"Where is she?"

"New York. She had this dream of owning a farm with goats on it, and my brothers and I helped make that dream come true. My dad tried to sell it, and I think that was the end of the road for my mom. It's her pride and joy."

"Not her four boys?" she teases.

"I guess we're up there on the list somewhere—behind the goats, maybe." I laugh when I say it with affection, but it feels similar to what a lot of adults are like when they become empty nesters. They get pets, and those pets become their pride and joy. My mom happens to own a bunch of them, and they're her babies now that her human babies are all grown up.

"What does one do with a goat farm?" she asks.

"My mom does all sorts of stuff. Soaps, mostly, but also goat yoga."

"What the hell is goat yoga?"

I glance over at her with a grin. "You really don't know?"

She shakes her head.

"Well, I'm not spoiling any surprises, but I will definitely take you there someday." The words slip out before I get the chance to think them through or stop them. I don't know if we're there yet. I clear my throat as I weakly amend that previous statement. "I'm sure we can figure out somewhere local we can go and still maintain privacy."

She snags her bottom lip between her teeth, and she looks like she wants to say something. My chest tightens as nerves climb up my back.

"What's wrong?" I ask, not bothering to keep the alarm out of my tone.

"I was going to wait until tomorrow to tell you this, but…" She pauses, and her eyes stay focused out the windshield. "Erin McMahon offered me a job planning next year's Wild Aces ball, and I decided to take it."

Those nerves climbing up my spine seem to explode through my whole body. "You're taking a job with the Aces?"

She nods.

"So…you're moving to Vegas?" I clarify. Why does the thought send me into a panic?

Oh…I can think of a reason or two. Building trust with my teammates. Being there for them even when I don't have to be. Being a leader in the locker room. Staying true to my word with my coaches.

I'm supposed to be at home resting up ahead of practice tomorrow, and instead, I'm driving across town to take this woman on a date.

How much more will I do that when she *lives here*?

"I am," she says carefully. "Is, uh…is that okay?"

"Of course. It's incredible news, Des." I say the words, but the thought pulses a fear in me anyway. How will this change things between us?

"And I'll be looking for a place because I don't want to live with my parents—" She freezes for a beat. "Oh. Sorry. I mean, well, you know what I mean. So we won't have to sneak around at hotels or find unlocked conference rooms or whatever."

"Right," I murmur, keeping my focus on the road. "That's great."

"Are you sure?" she asks, and she sounds nervous.

"Yes. Of course I'm sure. I can't wait. And you won't leave me at one in the morning to get back to your parents' house. We can spend the entire night together."

She nods, and an awkward silence falls over the car. I should be excited about this. I should be happy. And I am, but I'm also anxious about what this means and how we're going to handle it all moving forward.

It's good news. This is great news. I'm falling in love with this woman, and she just unlocked the way for us to find more time to be together.

So why the hell is it making me want to run?

Chapter 35: Desiree Dixon

It's Okay, Buddy

Maybe I shouldn't have told him. Something shifted when I said I'm moving here, and I'm not sure if he's excited about it or not.

He fell quiet when he's normally not. He just invited me to his mom's goat farm and then backtracked.

I think he's getting in his own head, and I'm not sure what to do about it.

We pull onto a fairly deserted road as the sun dips behind the mountains, but the scenery is pretty and still lit as we drive in the desert toward what I'm guessing is Lake Mead. I discover I'm right when he pulls into a parking lot that's probably filled with cars on the weekends but is empty right now, and we hop out of the truck and head toward the dock.

He grabs my hand, and we walk down the narrow cement walkway toward the slips where the boats are parked. I don't know much about boats, but they look mostly like sport boats and fishing boats to me.

"You're quiet," I say as we stop and look out over the water as the skies continue to darken. "I feel like something changed when I told you I'm moving here, and now we're stuck out here with all this awkwardness."

He turns toward me and pulls me into him, and I rest my head on his chest, feeling comforted in his strong arms. He draws in a deep breath. "Something did change, Des. This is big, and it's exciting. But it's also scary."

I nod against him. "I agree. But why's it scary for you?"

He shakes his head and clears his throat. "I had a heart-to-heart with your dad after practice today."

He lets go of me and wanders over to the next row of boats, and I walk a few paces behind him.

"What did you talk about?" I ask carefully.

He turns toward me. "Not us. I wouldn't do that to you."

A bit of relief filters through me at that.

He clears his throat and heaves out a sigh. "Austin Graham was a starter before my brother took over as head coach. He brought me over and started me over Graham, and Graham holds a grudge because of it. He's been giving me shit about every single mistake I make. Then Terry Lawrence fucking laid me out at practice today, and I saw him laughing with Graham on the sidelines, and it felt like my entire team was against me." He hangs his head a little at the end.

"I'm sure they're not," I say quietly as I loop my arm around his waist and step onto my tiptoes to press a kiss to his cheek.

"I'm working my ass off to be a leader, and it feels like your dad is the only one who sees it. He's becoming one of my only allies on the team. He's more than a coach to me already, and it's only been a few months. And I feel like I'm betraying him with you, but I can't stay away, Des. And on top of that, this is all so new, you know? You and me, I mean. I don't want to fuck it up, yet it feels inevitable."

I look up at him as I shoulder the weight of all that heavy stuff, setting the thoughts about my dad aside for now as I focus on the two of us. "Why?"

He lifts a shoulder. "I don't know how to do this, and the example set before me is two adults who were married forty years and ultimately split." He lets out a heavy sigh as he keeps his gaze focused out over the water. "I guess I've learned that nothing lasts forever."

"So it's not worth trying?" I ask.

"That. That right there," he mutters more to himself than to me. "Your ability to call me out on my shit is something nobody has ever done. My brothers, maybe. But my parents?" He flattens his lips and shakes his head. "Nope. They let me get away with murder because they were too tired from my older brothers to bother with me. And that's how I've lived my life. I've never had to answer to anybody, and I *want* to answer to you. But we had this space, this bumper with you in another city, and I've got my career, and your dad is involved in mine, and you've got yours, and those feel like they're merging together when we hardly know each other, yet I want to know every single part of you." He lets go of me to rub his temples. "It's fucking confusing, that's all."

"Hey," I say with a small chuckle as I rub his back a little. "Hey. Deep breath. It's okay, buddy. We've got this."

He laughs. "Buddy?"

I lift a shoulder. "It slipped out."

"I kind of like it, buddy." He raises a brow.

"Did you really just call me buddy?"

"I did. And now I'm going to kiss you." He does, and it's a sweeter kiss than the passionate, soul-crushing ones we've shared before. It feels good, like the foundation of friendship is forming, and as long as we keep open lines of communication, I think we're going to be okay.

He runs back to the truck to grab a basket of food he packed for us, and we sit at the edge of the dock as we eat and look out over the water for a while. He tells me more about living with his dad, and I tell him all about Addy, Chloe, and Lauren. He tells me his closest friends are probably his brothers and that he's not as close with his teammates as he wishes he was because of his suspension and his beliefs about nothing lasting forever.

It's the first time I really think about what that must be like. New faces come, old faces go, and that's really the only guarantee from season to season.

I want to stick around a while. I want to show him that not everything has to end.

But I can only hold his hand if he'll let me. If he decides to let his fear win, we might be over before we even really get a chance to get off the ground.

"And it's not just my parents' divorce or teammates leaving," he says, his voice low. "I lost my best friend when I was in high school."

"Oh, Asher. I'm so sorry." It feels like he wants to say more, so I encourage it. "You mentioned that your dad was there for you during a rough period in your life. Is that what you meant?"

"Yeah. His name was Jacob Fitzgerald. We called him Fitz, and we were at a party. We drank a little, and someone offered him ecstasy. We found out too late that it was laced with heroin and cocaine. Sometimes I can't stop seeing him passed out cold before someone called nine-one-one." He shudders a little, and I reach over and grab his hand.

"I can't imagine how hard that must have been," I say softly, and he lays his hand over mine.

"When it first happened, I wanted to stay in bed and be miserable, but my dad would come in my room and force me to get up and face the day. *Do it for Fitz*, he'd tell me. So I did. I got up, and I worked hard, and I never forgot that one stupid mistake could end it all." He shakes his head with regret. "Fitz was adventurous. He got me into rock climbing and parkour and all kinds of weird shit. He's the reason I take risks today. And I want to do something to honor his memory, but I have no idea what."

Hmm…I'm accepting a job with the charitable contribution division of the Vegas Aces, and I'm an event planner.

An idea starts to take shape before he even takes another breath to say more words.

"What about a foundation raising awareness for the dangers of drug use for teens?" I suggest.

Do it for Fitz runs through my head. DIFF—like make a DIFFerence. What if we ran an event where we made a difference by saying who we're doing it for?

It's a sketch of an idea right now, but that's how all great ideas begin.

"I can work on a proposal if you want," I say. It'll give me a reason to work closely with him, which sounds pretty damn good to me right about now.

"I'd love that. Thank you," he says softly.

We finish the picnic he brought for us, and it feels like we've turned yet another corner together.

Chapter 36: Asher Nash

You're in Love with Someone in the Locker Room

"I didn't picture you as the romantic type, but tonight has been amazing," she says as we climb back into my truck after the picnic on the pier.

I narrow my eyes at her. "You didn't picture me as romantic? What *did* you picture me as?"

"A sex god," she deadpans, and I laugh…but then I recline my seat.

"Hop on, baby."

Her eyes widen a little as she glances around us only to see exactly what I see.

We're in a dark, abandoned parking lot after hours at a pier. Even if someone else was around, we're not parked under any of the lights, so they'd really have to be staring into the truck to see anything at all.

I unzip my jeans and pull my cock out, and it's hard and ready as ever for her as I stroke it up and down a few times. The friction feels fantastic after I've been fending off my erection the entire night. "Mouth or cunt?" I ask.

"Oh my God, Asher," she murmurs.

"Say that again, but moan it while you're riding me." I stroke it a little more as I slide my head to the side and look at her.

"Unless you want to watch me jerk off until I come all over my hand."

"Kind of," she says, raising a brow.

"Touch yourself," I demand. "Tit for tat."

"You want my tit?" she asks, and I laugh.

"Always. Preferably in my mouth."

"I think I can arrange that." She reaches under her dress and slides her panties down her legs, abandoning them on the floor of my truck, and then she climbs over the console and onto my lap.

I fist my cock as I wait for her to lower herself over me, and I let go as she does, seating herself all the way down on top of me. I'm enveloped by a tight, velvety warmth that I could sink into for the rest of my life.

She reaches into the top of her dress and pulls one of her tits out, lowering her body down until she has it poised over my mouth. I grab onto her ass with one hand and her tit with the other as she starts to ride me, bracing herself with one hand on the car window and the other on my upper arm.

Christ, this is hot. I've had car sex before, but never with someone I've had such deep, intoxicating feelings for.

Never with someone I'm falling for.

Fuck, is that what this is? It has to be.

The feeling like I never want to stop fucking her, never want to stop being with her, never want to stop laughing with her.

I flick my tongue over her tight nipple, and she lets out a loud moan, so I do it more. I explore every dip and curve of her breast, massaging it as I hold it in my mouth, and fuck, I'm not going to last long.

I can't take it. I'm overwhelmed by her, and my body betrays me as I feel my impending orgasm rushing toward me.

"Oh fuck, fuck, fuck," I growl around her tit, and I pull back to look up at her. She's a fucking vision with that red hair moving all around her as she writhes over me, her eyes closed and her neck corded as she slides up and down my cock, her moans gaining in volume to let me know how much she loves it when we fuck.

God, I love it, too.

I think I love *her.*

The thought pushes me into my release as jets of come launch from me into her. She moans as I shove up into her, fighting my way through the pleasure, and then she falls apart, her body convulsing as I feel her cunt clamp onto me like a vise.

I stare at her as she comes, the intense connection we share bonding us even closer through this act of intimacy after a night of conversation that drew us closer in other ways.

Her tits are pushed out, her eyes are squeezed shut, and she's biting her lip as she comes, bracing herself with one hand still on the car window, the other on my shoulder now, where fingernails dig in.

Jesus, she might be the sexiest woman I've ever laid eyes on. I can't get enough as my eyes drink in the vision in front of me.

Her eyes open lazily once her body calms, and she catches me staring at her. Her lips curl up into a smile, and she takes my jaw between her palms and presses her lips softly to mine, a tender kiss after an intense act between us.

I draw in a deep breath that's shakier than I'm expecting it to be as the emotions bear down hard on me.

I'm in deep.

Way too deep. It's too soon to feel this way.

She lifts off of me, and I don't have any tissues to catch the come that drips out of her and onto my jeans. She settles into her seat and pulls her panties back on, and we sit in silence for a few seconds before she clears her throat. "Are there bathrooms here?"

I shrug. "I've never been here before, but we can go check."

"You've never been here before?" she asks, and she studies me.

I shake my head.

"Why'd you take me here?"

"I was trying to come up with somewhere deserted instead of another date in a hotel room. I didn't want you to think all I'm good for is sex."

She laughs. "Trust me, Asher. I don't think that at all."

We both get out of the car and explore for some bathrooms. She heads in when we find one, and I wait outside for her, staring at the water as I try to process what I'm feeling.

It was only supposed to be sex. A good time. I wasn't supposed to feel so much for her, especially not when she's my coach's daughter.

I shouldn't. I can't. It's wrong.

When I'm with her, everything is perfect. It's right. But the second we're apart—even if it's for three seconds while she runs to the bathroom—I start to get in my head about it.

We blast music on the way home, both of us singing all the words to everything from Jelly Roll to Doja Cat to Justin Timberlake and beyond, and the ways we're so similar continue to amaze me.

And having the music blaring allows me to focus on the songs rather than on the confusion swirling around my head.

As we get closer, I turn down the music. "We're about ten minutes out. Are you sure I can't drop you off at home?"

She shakes her head. "I don't think it's safe. Especially not in this bright-ass red truck." She giggles, and I can't help a laugh, too.

"Touché. I'll get another car that isn't as obvious so we can sneak around together." What the fuck did I just say? Do I *mean* that?

The scary reality of it is that I think I do.

We wait until her ride pulls up out front, and she gives me a quick kiss before she smiles at me and gets out of my truck. "Bye," she says, and she shuts the door and walks to the car.

I watch her the whole way, my eyes never leaving the car carrying her away from me until it rounds the corner out of my sight.

I lean my head back on the headrest as I blow out a heavy sigh.

I feel like I need to talk to someone about all this shit, but the question is…who?

I can't talk to Lincoln since he's too close to the big picture. But that doesn't necessarily rule out Grayson, who's close enough to know the major players but far enough removed to keep anything I say to him to himself.

I dial up his number right there in the parking lot before I lose my nerve.

It's not like I can go home and call him with my dad right the fuck there all the time.

"Asheph, what's going on?" he answers, blending my first and middle names—Asher Joseph—together into one.

"Graychael," I say formally, mashing up Grayson Michael, and he laughs. "You find a place for Dad yet?"

"Ah, fuck. I knew I was supposed to be doing something."

Oh. Right.

"Kidding, broski. Ava found a great place centrally located between the three of us, a two-bedroom condo with a pool and clubhouse and all that jazz. We could likely close on it by the end of the month. I talked it over with Av, and we're fine with buying it outright if you, Spence, and Linc want to split the monthly association fee. The other two are good with it if you are."

"If you think we can really get him to move when I'm the one who's technically crashing with him."

"You are, but you're also footing the bill each month, right?" he asks.

"Yeah, I am now," I say. "We said it made sense since I was out a paycheck an entire year thanks to him, but let's be honest. It never made much sense."

"No, it didn't. You two can be a lot together when you're getting along, but when you aren't? Forget it," he says.

"We're fine. I just, you know…" I trail off as I try to shift the topic over to the *real* reason I called.

"Wanna bring girls by without his prying eye?"

"Something like that," I say dryly. "More specifically, one girl, if I'm being honest."

"What?" he gasps with a huge dose of dramatics for my effect. "There's a girl?"

"It's complicated."

"Aren't they all?" he mutters. "What's complicating it?"

"No one can know."

"I won't tell," he promises.

I shake my head even though he can't see me. "No, that's not what I mean. I wasn't swearing you to secrecy. What I mean is that no one can know we're seeing each other."

"Why not?" he asks. Just as I open my mouth to tell him it's complicated, he says, "And don't give me the *it's complicated* bullshit answer. I'm your brother, and I know you called to talk this out, so get on with it."

I sigh, debating how honest to be with him, and then I decide to lay it on the line. "You know how things were in the locker room for me last season coming off the suspension since you were there. We both took heat for being the coach's brothers."

"Oh, shit," he breathes. "You're in love with someone in the locker room? Ash, I swear, I had no idea—"

"No, dude! What the fuck?"

"Sorry. I really thought that's where you were going. Sometimes you throw us for a loop."

I heave out a breath. "I'm working on my reputation in the locker room. That's all I'm saying. I'm trying to be a leader. And our new OC, Coach Dixon, he's been incredible. He believes in me. He's taken me under his wing, and he's helped point out places where I can step up. He's...he's great."

"So you're in love with him?" he guesses.

"Jesus Christ, Grayson, no! His daughter. I'm in love with his daughter." My eyes widen as soon as the words are out. It's the first time I've spoken them aloud. I guess there's no going back now.

He's silent on the other end of the line, so I add more as I run my hand along my jaw.

"Fuck, I don't know if it's really love or just strong feelings, but it's definitely something. And I can't betray him like that." I think about adding more since he's still silent, but I give it a moment before I say, "Say something."

"Damn, Ash. Sounds like you've really gotten yourself into a jam."

"Thanks, that's helpful," I say dryly.

"No, I'm trying to figure out what to say. I'm trying to do the big brother thing and come up with the right advice, and I'm just…I'm at a loss, I think," he says quietly. "Are you sure you can't be honest with him?"

"No. She doesn't want him to know any more than I do. He's a bit overprotective of her, and he even mentioned her to me once and told me not to get any ideas. The thing is…" I trail off.

"The thing is?" he prompts me.

"I fucked her before I knew she was his daughter."

"Bam! There it is. How'd you meet her?"

"The night of the Wild Aces ball. She was a last-minute addition, and I gave my spare ticket to Lincoln. I guess he gave it to Coach Dix, and she ended up in the seat beside me. We had a fun night, and I assumed it wouldn't lead to anything more when she was gone when I woke up, but then she was in the family area after a game, and I learned who she was."

"The redhead?" He lets out a low whistle. "Damn, dude. And you think it's love?"

"I don't know," I mumble a bit uncomfortably.

"You've got three choices, then," he says.

"What are they?" I ask, trying to keep the begging out of my voice as I hope he has the answers I'm looking for.

"You can continue to sneak around and betray the OC, you can be honest with him, or you can end it with her."

"What else you got? Is there some hidden choice I haven't thought about?" I wonder aloud, not really liking any of those options whatsoever.

"Afraid not, brochacho." He sighs. "I'll be honest, man. The sneaking around bullshit is tough. Ava and I did it for a little while, and I wouldn't wish it on you, little bro. Be proud of who you're with, or don't be with them." He says it like it's so simple, so easy, when it's just not.

Of course I'm proud to be with her. She's amazing, and she's fun and smart and sexy.

But maybe it's better to end it now before we fall deeper and deeper into something we can't get out of.

"You think I should end it with her?" I ask softly, the thought alone causing a hollow feeling in my chest.

"I didn't say that, man. I think you should do whatever is right for you, and if that's ending it with her so you don't feel like you're betraying Bill Dixon, then that's what you should do. If it really is love, then be honest with him. You didn't know who she was when you met, so it's not like you went into it with the intention of betraying him. Maybe he'll understand."

"He won't. Maybe he's taken me under his wing, but that doesn't mean he wants me porking his daughter," I point out.

"No dad would ever want any dude porking his daughter," he argues. "But maybe he'll surprise you."

Maybe he will. Or maybe he'll take it out on me by punishing me on the field. Maybe he'll decide he doesn't want tight ends to have the role they do now, or he'll be harder on me in practice, or he'll backtrack in his vow to help me become the leader he sees in me. Maybe he won't see that leader in me at all anymore, and it'll spell the ultimate end of my career.

And maybe Grayson's right, and none of that will happen, and I'll be surprised as he welcomes me into his family with open arms.

But the slim chance of that happening might not be worth the risk when my own career and reputation are on the line.

Chapter 37: Asher Nash

Complicated Dinosaurs

I walk into the house, and my dad is in the family room watching another western. I swear, the guy doesn't do anything except gamble, watch westerns, and sponge off his kids.

I wait for a commercial, and then I walk into the family room and stand in front of the television.

He makes a little flip of his hand motion to indicate that I should step aside, but I stand firmly where I am.

"I have news," I announce.

He raises both brows.

"Grayson, Lincoln, Spencer, and I are all chipping in on getting you a new place."

He sinks back a bit as if I just dealt a physical blow.

"Gray thinks it can be ready by the end of the month," I continue. "He's going to buy you the place, and Linc, Spence, and I will split your monthly fees."

"What about utilities?"

Those are his first words since I walked into the room. I literally just told him we're buying him a house and taking care of one of his monthly expenses, and he has the nerve to ask that question.

Is it any wonder why I don't want to live with him anymore?

"We'll figure it out," I finally say dryly.

"You're kicking me out of my own house?"

"Dude, I'm twenty-eight, and I'm still living with my dad. Would *you* have wanted to live with *your* dad when you were my age?"

"No, but to be fair, my dad was an asshole."

The thought that the apple didn't fall far strikes through my brain, and it pulses a new fear that I've never once thought about before.

What if it's a generational thing?

What if I'm destined for the same fate—to being an asshole to my kids the way my father is to the four of us? I don't remember him being like this until I was an adult, but the truth is, maybe I was too blind to see it.

If it's a cycle, I'll break it, because the last thing I want is to turn out anything like him.

"Look, Asher, I like living with you. We have fun together, don't we? I know you just got started on a new season, and I'm sure that's where this is stemming from. Don't make me uproot my entire life because you're in flux right now."

Is he right? I'm back to the question at hand, and that's whether I want to settle here in Vegas. It's part of why we live together anyway. I'm in the third year of a three-year contract, and while I know my brother will fight for me to stay here if this is where I want to be, there are absolutely no guarantees.

Is Vegas where I want to end up?

I don't think it's something I need to decide right now. I can always rent, and that's probably what makes the most sense.

But I do know one thing for certain. I don't want to live with my dad anymore.

"You're right," I finally say, and he grins as he nods at my acknowledgment that he's right.

His face falls, however, on my next statement.

"I don't want to uproot your whole life, so you stay here. I'll move out." I press my lips together and nod my head resolutely, and then I walk out of the room and head upstairs to start packing.

I don't have any clue where I'm going to go, but it feels right to get the fuck out of here.

Practice the next day is brutal—likely because I didn't rest up the way I should have. I'm off my game, and Coach Dixon walks over to the tight ends before practice is over. "Coach Bruce, I'd like a word in my office with you and Asher after practice."

With Coach Bruce and *me*? I must've fucked up in practice more than I realized.

This is two days in a row that Coach Dixon wants to see me in his office. We had a quick meeting yesterday with a nice heart-to-heart about Terry Lawrence beating the shit out of me, so I can't imagine what today might be about.

Coach Bruce is already in the office when I walk in after my shower. I sort of wish for the first time that I would've brought more reserved clothes to slip into after practice, but in my defense, I'm hardly ever called into a superior's office after practice.

And today, it's dinosaurs.

"What the hell are you wearing?" Coach Bruce asks.

"Dinosaurs, obviously," Coach Dixon says.

I laugh, though Coach Dixon is one of the few people who doesn't mock my sense of style. His daughter, too, come to think of it.

If anything, I think she likes it. I think she likes *me*.

Fuck, this is complicated.

"Before you both start in on me, I wanted to say that I'm sorry I was awful at practice today. I'm just—"

Exhausted after the sex in my truck last night?

It's not like I can say that.

Coach Dixon holds up a hand before I can continue, thankfully.

"Did you have a bit of an off day today? Yes. You also had some good catches. And your footwork drills were phenomenal. It's to be expected after what Terry put you through yesterday, and Andy is talking with him today," he says, referring to the defensive coordinator. "I called you both in because I wanted to talk about what's been going on in the locker room. Hopefully the Terry situation will fix itself, but I wanted to talk to you about Xavier Thomas mouthing off to Jaxon Bryant."

"To me?" I ask, pointing at my own chest.

He nods. "We have a rookie fullback acting superior to a veteran running back, and you fall somewhere right in the middle. In terms of leadership, I think you might be the right person to tackle this…no pun intended. And I wanted Bruce in here so he's aware of what's going on."

My brows crinkle. "What do you want me to do?"

"I talked with Coach Nash, and we decided to institute a more formal mentoring program. And Bruce, I'd like you to keep an eye out for other pairs that might be able to take advantage of this new resource."

Coach Bruce nods.

"What exactly will this entail?" I ask.

"I'm so glad you asked. I want it to be whatever you want it to be. I want the focus to be guidance on events taking place off the field. I want you to build this program."

"Me?" I ask, pointing to my own chest.

He nods. "You want a leadership role? Prove that you're a leader. Get a basic outline for what you're thinking on my desk by next Wednesday."

My jaw slackens. "You…you trust me with that?"

He nods. "I do. Your brother does. Coach Andy does, too. Don't let us down."

"I promise I won't," I say.

This feels big, and it feels good.

Coach Bruce stays behind to talk with Coach Dixon, and I head home, already brainstorming some ideas on the way.

And when I get home, my dad is at the kitchen table playing poker with that same group of friends. I bypass them and head upstairs to my bedroom to get some more work done, but when the smell of cigars wafts up from downstairs, I've had more than enough.

I pack a suitcase with the essentials plus clothes for the next few days, and I sneak out the front door before my dad can stop me.

I drive to Grayson's place, and I call him on the way.

"Brochacho!" he answers.

"Hey. Can I stay with you for a few days?"

"Of course, but may I ask why?"

"I have some work to do, and Dad's in the kitchen playing poker and smoking cigars."

"Did you tell him about the place we found?" he asks, not sounding surprised in the least by our dad's actions.

"I did, and it went over like a lead balloon. So new plan. We find *me* a place to live, and we let him stay."

"Jesus, man," he mutters. "Why are we so dedicated to appeasing him?"

"I don't know," I admit, and the truth is, I hate it. But I do have an inkling as to why we do it. "Because he's our dad, and he instilled this forced sense of loyalty to family."

"Worked out for you since I'm letting you crash with me for a few days," he says.

I laugh. "Maybe you can help me with my new project, too. You know, since you have all that free time after retiring."

He snorts. "I'm still at the bakery, for what it's worth. I think I have *less* free time now than I did when I was playing."

"Bring me home some cookies."

"Will do. You know the code, so let yourself in. We should be home in a couple hours." He pauses, and then he asks, "What's the new project?"

"Coach Dixon asked me to head up a new one-on-one mentorship program with rookies. He wants an outline on his desk next week."

"That's incredible, Ash. What are you thinking?"

I launch into all the ideas that have been brewing in my head since Coach asked me to do this. Life in the league, building relationships with teammates, managing time commitments, commitment to the game, dealing with fame while staying grounded, even avoiding temptation while knowing what to look for when it comes to personal relationships.

He tells me he's on board to help me, and I'm excited about this new opportunity as well as the trust Coach is giving me by handing it over to me.

I get to work at Grayson's kitchen table as soon as I walk through the doors. I'm focused on the task at hand, breaking only to order dinner and eating it once it arrives while I work.

I shut everything else out, but when a text comes through from Desiree shortly before I know I need to head to bed, I can't ignore it.

I do, however, stare at it for a long, long time.

Desiree: *Hope you had a good day. Just wanted to let you know I'm thinking about you.*

I contemplate what to say in reply.

I've never done this. I've never been in a relationship, and I don't know how to handle myself.

I want to choose her with everything in me, but Coach Dixon just gave me this new responsibility, and I feel torn.

I can't lie to him when he's putting trust in me. I can't let him down when he's giving me the chance I've been looking for in the locker room.

Football first. It's how I was raised, and I can't see any other way out of it.

I think my only option is to start pulling back.

The mere thought of pulling back all the way sends a deep pang of despair through my stomach. I don't want to cut off contact with her, but I also don't know how to keep seeing her and maintain my coach's trust in me.

I'd love to explore where this could go because I've never met anyone like her. I don't know that anyone exists like her that could fulfill me in the sort of way she has in the short time we've known each other, but I don't know that I have it in me to continue betraying someone who is intent on giving me his trust.

And so I keep my reply simple for now so I can focus on everything else until I can come to some conclusion about what to do.

Me: *Practice was brutal. I have some things I need to take care of, so I probably won't be able to meet up before you head back.*

I hit send and wish I felt some relief after sending that message, but all I feel is sadness.

Chapter 38: Desiree Dixon

The Right Man for the Job

I sensed it last night after I told him I was moving to Vegas. Maybe I shouldn't have told him. Maybe he thinks my entire decision hinges on what's happening between the two of us, but in truth, there's more to it than that.

I wouldn't move my entire life to a new city solely because of a man, but my parents are there, and I already have a job offer. It feels like all the pieces fell into place at the right time, and that's what drove my decision, not the great sex with the football player.

But I think I've scared him off at this point. I hope that's not the case, but he's pulling back, and I'm not really sure what I'm supposed to do about that. The reply to my text was a very clear brush-off, which hurts more than it should since we never promised each other anything.

It hurts because it feels like history is repeating itself. It was the first step to Clay breaking my heart three years ago, and here we go again.

But this is different. Asher and I…we were never really dating. We didn't fall in love.

We had a few good nights together, and the sex was great, and we were starting to form a foundation, but that's it. We didn't get that first layer of cement strong enough to build on top of it, I guess.

Maybe I'm making too big of a deal out of this. He does have intense practices and a game on Sunday. I grew up around this life, so I know what his schedule is like. I try to cling to that rather than to disappointment. Maybe I should take him at his word rather than feeling like I'm dropping off his priority list.

It's just my past coming back to haunt me. It has nothing to do with Asher.

Except…it feels an awful lot like the same thing.

In the morning, I head to the Complex to meet with Erin. I haven't told Angelica that I'm leaving yet, but I get the process moving to secure my position with the Aces. The offices are fairly quiet when I arrive, which is another reminder that both players and coaches are busy as they prepare for Sunday's matchup.

After I meet with HR, I head down to my dad's office to say hi. I stop outside the open door when I hear voices, and I recognize one of the voices as Asher's.

"I know you said you wanted an outline by Wednesday, but I got it done last night."

I hear some papers rustling around and a long pause, followed by my dad's voice. "Holy shit, Asher. This is fantastic." More page flipping, and then my dad says, "I knew I picked the right man for this job."

I have no idea what they're talking about, but I also feel like it's probably not my business even though the office door is open. I turn and weave through the maze of hallways to let myself out as I think about how Asher is the right man for *my* job, too.

That conversation made it clear that my dad and Asher have become close, and I wonder if that is pulsing even more of a hesitation in Asher regarding the two of us. He must feel torn between his obligation to my dad and his feelings for me, if they are even a fraction as intense as the feelings that I'm having for him.

I can't let this go, but I also don't know how to save it. I don't know how to fight against his history when it comes to how he feels about relationships.

He has openly admitted he's never had a serious relationship, and it scares me that his instinct is going to be to run, especially after our talk about commitment and how he felt about his parents' divorce.

He is committed to football. That's where his first allegiance has been for his entire career, his entire *life*, second only maybe to the Nash family.

I do not fall into either one of those camps, and it's scary to think that I might end up disappointed—or worse, heartbroken.

My mom and I go out for dinner a little later in the evening, but my dad doesn't join us since he's working long hours drafting up the game plan for this weekend.

After we order and our wine is served, my mom says, "So you signed the paperwork with the Aces today?"

I nod. "I'm so excited for the opportunity."

"You know you have to be an Aces fan now, right?"

I laugh. I'm a big fan of the tight end already, though I refrain from mentioning that. Instead, I shoot her a wink. "Unless they're playing the Storm."

She laughs. "Are you sure you don't want a position with Berkshire?"

I press my lips together and shake my head. "The people you chose to run it are doing a fabulous job, Mom. I appreciate the offer, as always, but I'm not interested."

"What about event planning for the hotel group? There's plenty to do there."

"I know, but you know how I feel about it."

"Mm," she hums as she presses her lips together in disapproval before she takes a sip of her wine.

"I know I'm a disappointment," I say quietly.

"Oh, honey, no. That's not at all what I think. I'm very proud of you, even more so because you're strong and stubborn and willing to do things your own way. You remind me of myself in that way."

I raise my brows. "You do things your own way?"

"My mom and dad never approved of your father, but I married him anyway." She shrugs. "They drafted up an airtight prenup, but I knew we'd never need it."

"I think that's really sweet. Did you want a part in Berkshire?" I ask.

"Yes and no." She lifts a shoulder. "I took on a bigger role than I probably should have, but I grew up around it. You didn't. You grew up around football, and now that's where your life is leading you."

"I know Dad is solidly against me ending up with a football player, but what do you think?"

She narrows her eyes at me. "Why? Do you have one in mind?"

I clear my throat as I do everything in my power not to give myself away. Thank goodness the lighting in here is dim because I can't control the heat rushing to my cheeks. "No," I lie.

"I think you have to be willing to brace yourself for certain things. Like with Clayton," she says softly. "It's hard. If you go into it expecting his full attention, you'll end up sorely disappointed. But if you go in managing your expectations knowing you *can't* be his top priority because he has an entire locker room depending on him, you'll be okay."

"Is that what you did?" I ask.

She nods. "We talked at length about what he wanted out of his future before we ever talked about a future together. I knew he wanted to play until his body couldn't take it anymore, and then he wanted to coach. And I was fine with him being a position coach, but I knew he dreamed bigger."

"Do you think he wants to be a head coach someday?" I ask.

She shakes her head. "He always wanted to be an offensive coordinator. I think he'll stay here as long as he's welcome, and then he'll retire." She takes another sip of wine. "You're awfully inquisitive tonight."

"Just curious since I'm going to be working with the same team," I say, forcing nonchalance into my tone.

She nods as she presses her lips together, and I'm pretty sure she buys my answer. "Have you spoken with Angelica?"

I shake my head. "Not yet. I need to do it in person, so probably Monday."

"Always a tough balance," she laments, and I nod. "When are you moving here?"

"My official start date with the Aces is November first, so I only have two weeks. I won't have an office there, so I'll be working from home."

"Home with Dad and me?" she asks with hope. "Or are you getting your own place?"

"You know how much I love staying with you, but I think I'd like a place of my own. Since it's remote, I can take my time."

She nods. "Of course. I'll have Joyce get in touch. She's the realtor we used when we moved."

We chat about the best areas to live in and around Vegas, and then our food arrives.

"So how's Dad adjusting to his new role?" I ask.

"He's totally in his element and loving every second. He decided that every year, he quietly wants to take a player sort of under his wing and help that player be the best version of himself."

"Oh?" I ask. "Who did he pick this year?"

"Asher Nash."

I nearly choke on my salmon, but I manage to pull it together. "What's he doing with Asher?"

"He saw a hole in the mentorship program, so he's having Asher devise a whole program and implement it with one of the struggling rookies. I think it's an incredible idea."

Aha! So *that* was the project they were talking about. "Totally incredible," I agree.

And it makes so much sense that he'd be cautious about being with me if he's getting closer with my dad.

Still, despite both knowing and understanding all that, the call that comes Saturday night when players are staying at a hotel ahead of game day catches me completely off guard.

I spot his name on my screen, and a smile lights up my entire face as I answer. "Hey, stranger."

"Hey," he says softly. I haven't heard his voice since Wednesday night when we had our Lake Mead date.

"It's good to hear your voice."

"Yours, too. And before I lose my nerve, I need to tell you something."

Alarm bells ring out in my head. "What?"

He blows out a breath. "I'm, uh…going through some things with my dad, with your dad. It's all getting overwhelming and complicated, and I think it's probably for the best if we cut this off before we get too serious. Maybe we can revisit after the season. My contract will be up, and I'll be potentially facing free agency. If I go somewhere else, even better. But I can't keep doing this behind your dad's back. It's wrong even though it's so goddamn right."

He's babbling, but even if he wasn't, I'm not sure exactly what I'd say.

I felt it coming, but it still takes me by surprise. It's still a blow.

It still breaks my heart.

I'm silent as I look up at the ceiling to try to ward off the tears, and my chest feels like it's cracking in half.

"Say something," he whispers.

"I don't know what you want me to say."

"Say we can try again when the time is right." His tone is desperate, and I wish I could promise that, but I can't. I can't wait around forever until he decides to be strong enough to take me on.

"I can't guarantee that," I say flatly.

He blows out a breath, and an awkward silence falls over the line.

"I get it. You shouldn't wait around for me. You're amazing, Des, and I want you to have everything you deserve."

But what if what I deserve is you?

I want to ask the question, but I don't. I can't—not when it leaves me open to the vulnerability of his answer.

"Thanks," I mutter instead. "I need to go. Good luck tomorrow."

I cut the call before he can respond, and then I cry myself to sleep.

Chapter 39: Asher Nash

When the Right Thing Feels So Wrong

I play like shit.

I *feel* like shit.

I almost call in sick ahead of the game, but I don't. I can't. I've never missed a game due to illness or anything other than suspension, and I'm not about to start now.

We lose against the Bills, and while it's always a team effort, I can't deny I had a fairly big part in the loss. A pass that should've been an easy catch for me was intercepted for a pick-six, and we lost by one touchdown.

Instead of heading back to Gray's place after the game, I head back to the house I share with my dad. I'm not sure why other than the fact that I don't feel like being around a happy couple who's very much in love, and my brother and Ava are disgustingly happy.

I've never felt so alone.

I know I'll catch shit from my dad for the pick-six, but it's better than watching Grayson make out with his wife.

When I walk into the house, my dad isn't around. I feel a sense of relief as I head toward the pantry and grab a bottle of tequila.

And that's when he saunters in. "Hitting the hard stuff after a game? I guess I won't bring up the mistakes tonight."

"That'd be much appreciated," I say dryly, and he chuckles.

"What's going on, son?" he asks, clapping me on the shoulder as I tip the bottle to my lips.

I blow out a long breath after I swallow a mouthful. I guess that for as much as I've written my dad off lately, he might be the sounding board I need…as long as I don't get too detailed, it can't hurt to get his perspective. Maybe he's an asshole half the time, but the other half of the time, he isn't.

"I ended it with someone I started to care deeply for, and it hurts."

"Oh. I had no idea," he says.

I take another sip of tequila. "Because I didn't let you in on it."

"Why is that?"

"Because you ran to the media with shit about Lincoln, and you killed our trust in you."

"I didn't run to the media. I talked to a friend in the media about the history between two families at odds. I've apologized profusely," he says defensively.

"You were trying to ruin a family twenty years after you already ruined yourself," I say dryly.

He sighs heavily. "Call it what you want, but that's not true. It's in the past, and why are we talking about this right now?"

"I know you lost everything when you lost the bar. I know you blame Lincoln for all of it. And I know you're trying to mend your relationship with him. But I'll be honest, Dad. You haven't been the same since you and Mom ended things, and you haven't made me feel like I can come to you when I'm going through something."

"Is that why you ran away to Grayson's for the last few days?" he asks. He takes the tequila from my palm and helps himself to a sip.

"You bet your ass it's why. I had something I was working on, and I needed a quiet space to do it in. You had your friends over for poker night, and you were smoking here, and…" I trail off and shrug. "I had to get away for a while."

"I'm sorry. You should've said something."

"I'm saying it now. It's why I'm moving out, Dad."

He claps a hand on my shoulder. "You don't have to do that. I know you wanted me out, and I'll figure something out. I know you don't want to know this about your old man, but I've been where you are. I've done the thing where I had to end it with someone I cared deeply for. Sometimes in life, we have to make choices that aren't what we want, even if they're right."

"Yeah," I murmur, and I realize how I don't really know a damn thing about this man. He was with my mom since they were in high school, so how could he have been where I am?

He said something not so long ago about being twenty-eight and dumb. Is this related to that?

I have no idea, and I don't have the energy to find out. I take the bottle of tequila back, and I take another sip.

"So what are you going to do?" he asks.

"About?"

"The girl."

"Oh." I shrug. "Nothing, I guess. It's over now. It was good while it lasted, and I'll have to chalk it up to that."

He nods. "You could do that. Or you could really think about what you want out of your future. I know I pushed hard to make football the center of your life…but look where it got me. I'm an old man now with no wife, kids who hate me, and no job. I lost the respect of the league I loved so goddamn much, all in the name of doing what I thought was right for the people I cared about most. Don't end up like me."

"Your kids don't hate you, Dad," I say softly.

He presses his lips together and raises his brows. It's the one part I commented on, but it's not the biggest part of what he said.

He's right about pushing hard to make football our priority, and he's right that I don't want to end up like him.

Am I putting football before her? I'm loyal to my team, and her dad is a part of that. I'm putting respect first. Loyalty and honor.

It's the right thing, isn't it?

So why does it feel so goddamn wrong?

I want to call her. I want to hear her voice. I want to reverse the damage I've done.

But I don't.

Instead, I rely on football to carry me through the weeks without her.

I force my focus on the field instead of searching out red hair in the stands during our home games. I wait until I'm the last player in the locker room so I can leave without running into her.

I get to know Xavier Thomas. I touch base with him daily, and we take an extra half hour after practice almost every day to talk. Sometimes it's about respect in the locker room, sometimes it's about mindset, sometimes it's about how to make better decisions. Coming from someone who's made some pretty shitty decisions, it feels like I'm getting through to the kid.

And when Jaxon Bryant comes up to me after practice and thanks me for all my work with Xavier, I know I'm doing something right. I know I'm leaving the kind of impression I intended to in the locker room.

But as the weeks seem to fly by, one thing is certain.

I'm in love with her. Hopelessly, endlessly, and pitifully.

But at this point, I don't even know if she'd want to take me back.

When the plane lands in Vegas on a Sunday evening after our game in Jacksonville, it's officially the start of our bye week.

I spend the week at a quiet retreat in the mountains of Vegas by myself to reset, and when Sunday rolls around, I know how I want to spend the rest of my time off.

I finally gather up the courage to get in touch.

Me: *I miss you. I'm sorry for running scared, but I need to see you. Are you around?*

And then I wait for an answer that doesn't come until morning.

Chapter 40: Desiree Dixon

He Kind of Has it Coming

I stare at my phone as I lay in bed. I have no idea how to respond, and maybe I would if I didn't have the worst stomach flu in the history of the stomach flu attacking my body right now.

I toss my phone on my nightstand and beg for sleep to wash over me, but it doesn't. Instead, my stomach rolls, and I get up and slowly drag myself over to the bathroom to try to heave, but there's nothing left in the well.

I slide down the bathroom wall and hope for sleep to hit me there, but it doesn't.

I'm still in San Diego even though I started my position with the Aces over a month ago. Angelica talked me into changing my contract to a consultant rather than leaving altogether, and since the Aces are allowing me to work from home anyway, I didn't see the point in uprooting my life when I wanted to do everything in my power to avoid Asher Nash.

Erin is cool with me commuting to town when I have big events, but my parents don't really seem to get why I changed my mind.

It's fine. They don't need to. I've told them I haven't found the right place yet, and I've left it at that.

I spent a little time planning the foundation for Asher, but since he ended things, I put that project on the backburner.

I force myself to my feet, and I head to the kitchen to get some water. I take tiny sips as I head back to my bedroom, and then I toss and turn as I wait for sleep that never comes.

When morning dawns, I don't feel much better, but I suppose I should reply to Asher.

Me: *I'm actually not around. I'm in San Diego.*

I leave it at that, but he doesn't let me get away with it.

My phone rings a few seconds after I send the text, and I blow out a breath. He knows I'm here since I just texted him, so it's not like I can ignore him.

"Hi," I answer.

"Hey. You're in San Diego...like for the day?" he asks.

"No. I never moved to Vegas. I still live here."

"So you didn't take the job with the Aces?" He sounds surprised by that.

"I did. I'm working remotely."

"Oh. Will you move here when it gets closer to the charity ball?"

"I don't know yet. Is there a reason why you called?" I ask, and I know I sound like a bitch, but, well, he kind of has it coming.

"Are you okay?" he asks. "You sound...strange."

My voice is scratchy from spending the last two days vomiting, but I'm not about to admit that to him. "It's probably because you haven't heard my voice in two months, but yes, I'm fine."

I hear Addy yell from the other room. "Are you talking to me?" At the same time, Asher says, "Look, Des...I'm sorry. Please give me another chance."

I don't respond to Addy since I have to address Asher. "I'll still need to hide it from my dad, and you still won't be comfortable with that."

"*Do* we have to hide it, though?" he asks.

Addy appears at my door, but her voice enters before she does. "You feeling any better?" She's dressed and ready for work.

I point to the phone when she comes into view.

"Oh!" she says. "Sorry. Can I get you anything before I head to school?"

I shake my head and mouth *thanks*.

"Why's she asking if you're feeling better?" Asher asks. "Are you sick?"

I blow out a breath. "It's the stomach flu," I mutter. "I'll be fine."

"Where are you?" he demands.

"I'm at my apartment in San Diego," I say dryly.

"Text me the address. I'm on my way."

"Stop it, Asher," I say. "It's a little stomach bug, and I don't want you to get it." You know, besides the fact that I don't want him to see me at my absolute worst when it's been a month and a half since the last time I saw him.

"Text me the address," he grits out, and then he hangs up the phone.

I'm too stubborn to listen to him, so I don't text him a damn thing. Instead, I close my eyes and try for more rest, but Addy shows up at my door.

"I didn't leave yet. Who was that?"

"Asher."

Her eyes widen. "Asher? What did he say?"

"That he misses me and wants to see me, but honestly, hearing from him made me feel even worse."

"Then let me take the day off so I can take care of you," she says.

"Don't be silly. Your students are depending on you, and I'll be fine. It sort of comes and goes anyway, but I'm just really tired and need some rest."

"Can I ask you a question?" she asks.

I nod, not moving to a position for a chat.

"How long have you been feeling like this?"

I lift a shoulder. "A few days. A week maybe."

"Does the stomach flu last that long?" she wonders aloud.

"No idea, but this one is."

"Is, uh…is there any chance you might be pregnant?"

I sit straight up at the question as my eyes widen. The sudden shift in my position pulses nausea in my stomach.

"Oh, shit," I mutter. "Shit," I say a little louder. "I was on the shot, and I had to cancel my appointment when I went to Vegas, and I can't remember if I ever rescheduled."

I grab my phone and look through my calendar, and it takes me a minute to realize my last shot was in July.

It's December now. I'm supposed to go every twelve weeks, and I missed the one scheduled in early October.

We had sex in mid-October…but that would be too soon, wouldn't it?

These thoughts are swirling around my mind as Addy stares intently at me. "Well?"

"I think there might be a tiny chance."

She closes her eyes, and then she says, "Stay here."

She heads out into the family room as I try everything in my power not to freak out. She returns a minute later. "Okay, I called in. My lesson was already sitting out for the day, so it's easy peasy for a substitute anyway. Do you have any pregnancy tests?" She's being so calm and rational, and I feel like…well, like I'm going to throw up again.

"No, do you?" My voice is a tad hysterical.

"No. I'll go get some. Do you need anything else?"

I shake my head, though some water sounds good right about now. And a banana. And a peanut butter and jelly sandwich. And some Doritos.

Peanut butter and jelly? I haven't had one of those since I was in middle school.

Holy fuck. What if I'm pregnant?

Chapter 41: Asher Nash

I Can't Let You in

A flight to San Diego leaves in ninety minutes, so I rush to the airport with nothing more than my phone and my wallet. I purchase the ticket while I'm in line for security, and I'm boarding a plane a few minutes later.

This wasn't on my bingo card for today, but here I am.

I reserve a rental car before the plane takes off, and I spend the flight putting in an Instacart order I can pick up not too far from the airport when I land.

She still hasn't texted me with her address, but one thing at a time. Maybe the text will be waiting for me when I land.

It isn't. I call her again, but she doesn't pick up.

And then I take a selfie of me on the plane and text it to her.

Me: *Just landed in San Diego. I need that address.*

If she doesn't respond, maybe I'll pay Spencer a visit. Maybe I will anyway since I'm in town on a one-way ticket.

But, thankfully, shortly after I've picked up the groceries, she texts me the address. She's actually not terribly far from my brother.

I click the map and let my phone guide me to her place, and I stare up at the skyscraper she lives in. She's close to the water, and I'm sure she has some top-notch views from her place.

A doorman opens the door to the lobby, and he asks me where I'm headed.

"Desiree Dixon," I say. I glance at my phone. "Apartment 2503."

"Your name?" he asks.

"Asher Nash."

He narrows his eyes at me. He rounds the desk, and the narrowed eyes deepen into a glare. "Mm, yes. You *are* one of the Nash brothers, but I'm afraid I can't let you into my building."

Why the fuck not?

It's what I want to say, but I keep the words in my head rather than blurting them.

Did she tell him not to let me up? It would figure since she didn't seem too excited to send me her address. But I've come bearing gifts—not light gifts, by the way, currently held up in the large box the grocery store gave me to carry all this shit inside.

"Oh, uh…can you ask her again?" I ask politely.

He grins. "Ah, kid, I'm just messing with you." He presses the button to call the elevator. "I'm a big fan of the Storm, and your brother is killing it this season out there. Had to rib you a little, anyway." The elevator doors open. "Go on up, and, hey, take it easy on my Storm when you play here next weekend, yeah?"

I offer a laugh. "No promises."

"I didn't think so, but it was worth a shot."

His laughter follows me up the elevator, and I land on the twenty-fifth floor.

I make my way to apartment 2503, and I knock lightly on the door. It takes a minute, but eventually the door opens, and I find Desiree.

She's wearing a sweatsuit, and her red hair is tied up on top of her head in one of those messy knot things women do that are so goddamn hot. Her face is pale. She isn't wearing any makeup, and circles darken the pigment beneath her eyes, but she's still as gorgeous as I've ever seen her.

I feel a sense of relief that we're in the same room together again.

242

"Hi," she says.

I gesture to the box I'm holding in my hands. "I brought you some things to help you feel better."

"No thanks," she says, and she moves to shut the door.

"Des, please," I beg.

Her eyes lift to mine, and she looks angry even through the illness she's dealing with.

I don't blame her. I broke up with her because I got scared. I realize now how fucking stupid that was.

I'm here to right that wrong. I'm here to try to fix things.

I'm here to get her back, and it starts by taking care of her. "I'm sorry. I never should've walked away, and I will do anything to prove that to you."

"What changed?" she asks, still holding the door partially closed.

"Nothing. I guess when I had time away from the game, from the locker room, from my teammates, from…well, everyone, something snapped. I had time to think it through and realize how wrong I was to walk away." I hear the begging in my own tone, but I don't care. I'm not leaving without laying it all on the line.

She studies me for a long time before she finally sighs and relents a bit, walking away from the door so she's not blocking my way in. It's as good as an invitation, and I walk in and kick the door shut behind me.

I follow her toward the kitchen, and I set the box on the counter. She peers into it and finds all sorts of supplies, from cans of soup to crackers and vegetables to Powerade. Some of the good stuff is hidden underneath the blanket I picked up, but she picks up a little electronic slot machine game I added to my list at the last minute and raises her brows.

"To remind you of home," I say, meaning Vegas.

She gestures to the view out her window. "I *am* home."

"You lay on the couch, and let me take care of you," I demand.

She purses her lips but holds onto the slot game and heads over to the couch. I fumble around the kitchen and find a pot to make the soup in, and I find a bowl and a spoon while it heats. I bring the blanket over to her, and I show her the spa set I picked up.

"For after the soup, and you can go in and relax by yourself. I promise I won't peek…unless you want me to."

She cracks a small smile at that, but it's short-lived. There's thick tension in the air between us, and I'm not sure how to break it.

"I'm sorry," I say softly. "I will do whatever it takes to make it up to you."

She raises her brows, but she doesn't say anything.

"Are you feeling any better?" I ask.

She presses her lips together, and then she starts to cry.

I know she was concerned about spreading germs to me, but fuck that. She's crying, she feels like shit, and I'm not about to just sit by doing nothing. I slide onto the cushion beside her and wrap my arms around her as the quiet tears turn into body-racking sobs. I'm not exactly sure what to do here, but eventually she leans into my chest and cries there a while. She sucks in deep breaths as she starts to calm.

"Where's a box of tissues?" I ask, and she nods toward what I assume is one of the bedrooms.

I get up and head that way, and this must be her bedroom. I don't allow myself the time to take stock of what it looks like in here, and instead I search around for that box.

I don't see it, so I walk into the connecting bathroom. There it is on the counter, and I make my way over toward it when I spot something on the counter.

A shudder races through me as it takes a minute for what I'm looking at to register.

I stare down at it, and it's when I pick it up that I hear a whispered, "Oh, shit," from the doorway.

My head whips up, and my eyes meet hers. "You're pregnant?"

Chapter 42: Desiree Dixon

Shaking the Pee Stick

A shudder races through me. I've barely had time to register for myself that this is my new reality. I certainly wasn't ready to share it with the guy who walked out on me because he's scared of my father.

I clear my throat as I study him carefully. "Well, the good news is that it turns out it's not the stomach flu after all." I'm trying to make the air in here feel a little lighter, but I can't help wondering whether that really is the good news after all.

He stares across the small space at me, his jaw slightly slackened and his face pale as he moves to sit on the edge of my tub.

"I…uh," he begins. "I don't know what to say."

I sit beside him. "Join the club." I suck in a breath and lightly pat my stomach. "This is yours, by the way. I haven't been with anybody…"

He nods and presses his lips together. "Neither have I."

My brows dip together. "Really?"

He shakes his head. "How could I when all I could think about was you?"

My face softens at his words, but I can't just let him off the hook. "Then why'd it take you so damn long to get in touch with me?"

He sighs. "I was scared, Des. I *am* scared. And this?" He shakes the stick, and I want to tell him that I actually peed on it if he'd like to set it down, but it seems like the wrong moment. He sighs. "This is fucking terrifying."

I nod my agreement. I'm only twenty-five. I'm not ready to start a family, least of all with someone who's already a proven flight risk.

Yet it's our reality, and we're going to be connected together regardless of whether we give this another try. Still, I give him the out.

"I haven't had time to digest it. I just took the test about an hour ago." I clear my throat. "But if you don't want—"

He silences me when his head whips in my direction, and a fire roars to life behind his eyes. "Stop right there," he warns a little menacingly. "We have a lot to figure out, but I'm not going anywhere."

I let out a sigh of relief at that. I'm scared to do this at all, but the thought of having to go through it alone is another level of fear.

"Have you thought about going to see your doctor?" he asks. I shake my head.

"Call now," he demands. "See if you can get in today."

"I don't know how this works," I admit.

"I do. Well, sort of. My sister-in-law has a kid, so I witnessed a bit of the process through them. And they'd be open to any questions we have."

"Your sister-in-law…as in the coach's wife?" I ask, pointing out the obvious flaw in his plan without saying a word.

"Oh," he says a little dejectedly. "Yeah. But don't you think we'll *have* to tell your dad eventually?"

"Eventually, yes. We'll find the right time to do it, but I don't think the middle of the season is that time, do you?" I ask.

He blows out a breath. "It depends how far along you are, Des. You might start showing soon, and then what? Your dad will have questions about who did this to you."

He has a point. The last time we had sex was mid-October, which would put me close to the two-month mark. And if I'm already two months along and didn't even know it, I wonder what sort of damage I've done. I haven't been drinking or partying much because I haven't felt like it. In truth, I've mostly felt sick and exhausted.

He's right, though. I should get to the doctor to get everything checked out.

The mere thought of making the call is terrifying.

"What can I do?" he asks softly.

I stare at the floor a long time before I clear my throat. "Call the doctor."

He stands without saying a word and walks into the other room. I follow him, and he glances around until he spots my phone. He picks it up and carries it to me. "Unlock it and tell me the name of your doctor."

I do both, and he dials a moment later.

It's a small act that feels like it lifts some of the weight off my shoulders.

"I'm calling to make an appointment for one of your patients, Desiree Dixon," he begins. I listen to his end of the conversation, and he nods at me to sit down. He turns off the burner on the stove where the soup is bubbling, and he moves around the kitchen as he talks on the phone, locating the bowls and spoons and carrying my lunch over to the kitchen table.

"Thanks, we'll see you then." He hangs up the call, and he turns to me. "We have an appointment today at three, so eat your soup, and then we'll go."

I stare at him as I try to reconcile Asher, the guy who wears dinosaur shirts and can make me see stars with his tongue, with this man who's taking control and making sure I know he's not going anywhere.

The thought pulses heat behind my eyes, and the chicken soup he made me isn't just for my upset stomach. It feels like it's also for my very soul.

We arrive at the doctor, and after a full exam, we find out I'm about seven weeks along and the baby is growing on schedule.

The baby.

It's been a mere few hours, and the thought that there's an actual *baby* forming inside me hasn't really hit me yet. The thought of the word *baby* didn't even come into my brain until I heard it at the doctor.

Pregnant, sure. I'm pregnant. Okay, fine. But what happens at the *end* of that pregnancy?

Then I have a *baby*. Then I'm a *mom*.

I'm not ready to be a mom. I always sort of thought, sure, someday down the road, and it was easy to kick that can down the road hard and fast.

I never thought it would be *now*.

I schedule some follow-up appointments, and we sit in the car in the parking lot in total silence. Not even the radio is on as we both stare straight ahead at the cars racing by us on the street on the other side of the parking lot.

I think we're both feeling a sense of whiplash.

I know I am, anyway.

"Congratulations," he finally says softly.

I grunt a little. "I could say the same to you."

He reaches over and takes my hand in his. "I know this is scary, Des, but you won't be alone."

Tears fill my eyes at his words—not at how sweet the sentiment is, but at the fear of what comes next.

It's nice he's saying I won't be alone for the pregnancy, but how can I not dread the idea of a future when the baby is here and we're still not a guarantee? I realize nothing is a guarantee, but he's already proven he'll run when things get too scary. How do I know he won't run again?

I don't. And even if he doesn't, I think about my own father's warnings when it came to life in the league and being with a football player. He wasn't around for half the year when I was a baby. Was my mom alone and scared? It's not something we've ever talked about.

My own heart has already been broken by this man once, and I'm not sure I can walk into all the risk of Asher Nash when there's a baby involved.

Chapter 43: Asher Nash

I Love You

She's quiet all the way back to the apartment, and her roommate is there when we get back. The roommate eyes me carefully.

"You're Asher," she says.

I nod.

"I'm Addy." She sticks her hand out. "I've heard so much about you. It's nice to finally meet you."

I shake her hand. "And you."

"You okay, Desi?" she asks.

Des twists her lips and nods, and I stand helplessly as I'm not sure what Addy knows and doesn't know.

"We went to the doctor. I'm seven weeks," Desiree says.

Addy rushes over and gives her friend a hug. The friend seems like a good one as she rubs her back and murmurs how everything's going to be okay. "I'll, uh, give you two some time," she says, and she walks down a different hallway, presumably toward her bedroom.

"Do you want to sit outside?" I ask, nodding to her balcony so we can have some privacy. There are a few things I want to say to her.

She nods, and I follow her out. We each take a seat and stare out over the water, and I'm not even sure where to begin.

"I came here today to beg you to take me back," I say quietly.

"And now?" she asks.

I lift a shoulder. "Now it feels even more like we belong together. Like this happened to draw us back into each other's lives."

She presses her lips together. "A baby doesn't fix things, Asher. If anything, there are even more complications to consider now."

"I realize that, and I know it won't be easy. But I would love it if you considered moving to Vegas. I'm stuck there at least until the end of the season, or else I'd move here to be closer to you. And on the plus side, in Vegas, you'll be closer to your parents."

Her jaw slackens a little as she looks over at me. "You'd move here? Just like that?"

"I'm struggling here, Des. I want to do what's right for you, and for us…and for the baby, and if that means San Diego, then it means San Diego." I leave out the fact that she was planning to move to Vegas anyway.

She hasn't really said *why* she didn't go through with her plan to move there, other than the fact that Erin allowed her to work remotely. I can't help but get the sense that she didn't come because she didn't want to run into me.

And I don't blame her for that. When I walked away, I stayed in the locker room longer than I needed to after games in order to avoid her, too. I threw myself into workouts and managing relationships with my teammates, and I worked on becoming the leader I wanted to be—the leader her dad believed I could be.

Because I knew how much it would hurt if I didn't—if I saw her standing outside the locker room and knew I wouldn't be able to take her to a hotel or go on a date to a lake or find some other way to get a secret meeting with her.

Because I stayed away, I'm finally breaking into the place I wanted to be in when it came to my teammates. The veterans love the mentorship program, and they credit me with bridging the gap between the rookies and the vets. And I have Coach

Dixon to thank for that—you know, the man whose daughter I apparently knocked up.

But the leadership and the accolades…none of it means a damn thing if I don't have this woman to share it with.

"I'll think about it," she finally says. "I guess I have a whole lot to think about."

"Like trying again with me?"

She sighs. "One flight to San Diego because you got a bug up your ass that you miss me, and suddenly I'm supposed to drop everything and come running back to you?"

I shake my head. "No, Des. I didn't get a bug up my ass. I've missed you from the second I last saw you. I didn't see any other way out, but maybe it's time for us to be honest with your dad. Maybe it won't be so bad after all."

She's quiet as she stares out over the water. "I don't want to say a word to him until I have a little more faith in you and me."

"Does that mean you'll give this a try with me?" There's way too much hope in my desperate voice, but I can't help it.

She glances over at me before her eyes return to the water, and I'm trying to be patient, but nerves tackle my spine. "I'm not sure how I stayed away as long as I did," she admits, and my face breaks out into a grin as I jump to my feet.

My heart feels full as I hold out a hand to lift her up with me, and she settles into my chest before I can kiss her.

"I'm scared, Asher. I'm scared you're going to leave again after you get me to fall even harder for you. I'm scared I won't be able to pick up the pieces next time."

I press a kiss to the top of her head, basking in the coconut smell that feels like home. "I know what it's like to be with you, and I know what it's like to be without you. I never want to put myself through that pain again."

She draws in a deep breath before she pulls back, and I stare down into the face of the woman I love.

I haven't said the words to her because I wasn't sure or because I was scared or any one of a million other reasons, but I'm going to say exactly what I feel right now.

"I love you, Desiree Dixon."

The words feel unfamiliar and scary coming off my tongue. I've never said them before to a woman.

She tips her head back to look up at me, and I see the fire back in her eyes. She doesn't say it back, instead opting to show me by pressing her lips to mine, and my senses kick to life between the scent of her coconut and the feel of her lips back on mine, right where they belong.

This feels good.

It feels right.

And it also feels like something is missing.

I get that she's skittish after I left, but I can't help the feeling clawing at me that she didn't say it back.

I try to chalk it up to her being scared, but I intend to prove to her that she has nothing to fear.

To that end, I make some tea for her, and she settles into bed with a book after I tell her I need to make a call. I head back out to the balcony as a mix of emotions plows into me.

I pull up my dad's contact and stare at it as I realize that the baby inside her stomach might be standing on a balcony someday pulling up a contact labeled *Dad*, but that child will be calling *me*.

It's a heady realization as I stand out here on the balcony by myself, and it pulses this strange new feeling of protectiveness and possessiveness over the woman inside carrying that child.

I realize too, for maybe the first time in my life, that maybe I need to cut my dad a little slack. He's done the best he could with us, presumably, and I'm not always very forgiving of him. None of us are.

Little do I know that he's about to prove once again why that's the case.

Chapter 44: Asher Nash

Tanner and Miller

"**H**ey, I know we had plans to go out for my birthday, but I'm going to have to cancel," I say once he answers.

"Why?"

I debate how honest to be, though my instinct is to tell him the truth—especially given the thoughts I literally just had about being too hard on him.

I clear my throat. "I, uh…I'm having a kid. Well, I'm not, but a woman is, and I'm staying with her for a few days since we just found out."

He's quiet on the other end of the line.

"Say something," I say.

"Asher, Asher, Asher. My wild one." He heaves out a breath. "You want my advice? Pay her off to keep quiet, and send monthly checks the way I do with the twins."

"With the twins?" I repeat, my heartrate picking up speed.

"Tanner and Miller," he says nonchalantly. "I send checks every month to their mother, have since the day they were born, and nobody has to know I'm involved."

"Excuse the fuck out of me?" I say, my chest tightening as he lays this truth bomb on me so freely, so casually. "You have twin boys you've never told us about?"

He sighs. "I went through a midlife crisis thirty years ago, okay?"

"No, not *okay*," I say, mocking his tone. "What the fuck are you even talking about?"

"I'm not getting into this with you," he says firmly. "I made a lot of mistakes in my life, and clearly slipping this to you is one of them."

He hangs up, and I stare at the phone as I try to process what he said to me.

I have twin half-brothers?

How old are they? *Where* are they? Who's their mom?

Does Mom know?

I have a million questions but exactly zero answers other than two names: Tanner and Miller.

My instinct is to call Lincoln with this, but I feel like I should do a little research first. I just…don't even know where to start.

I'm getting hit with all sorts of unexpected things today, and I suddenly feel the need to sit.

I slide onto the chair I was sitting in earlier when Des said she'd try this again with me as I ponder my dad's advice to pay her off.

That's not me. I could never do something like that, and the mere thought of it kills me.

My heart hammers as panic seems to travel like a poison through my veins. I don't even realize I'm clenching my hands into fists until I feel the sweat sliding on my palms and my stomach knots.

What the fuck else has my father been hiding from me all these years? Because that's a pretty fucking big one.

Fuck research. I dial up Lincoln.

"Bro, it's my week off, what the hell do you want?" he answers, and he sounds sleepy, as if he were taking a nap.

I clear my throat as I try to figure out what the hell I'm going to say, and then the words blurt right out of my mouth. "I just learned Dad had twin boys with another woman thirty years ago."

Silence greets me on the other side of the line, but eventually he says, "What?"

"Tanner and Miller," I say, repeating the names I committed to memory.

"With who?"

"I have no idea," I admit.

"How'd you find out?"

I guess I didn't think this through because if I answer that question, I'll have to admit the truth I wasn't ready to admit to him.

I blow out a breath and skirt around it as best I can. "I told him I got someone pregnant, and he told me I should just pay her off to keep quiet the way he does with the twins."

"Wait a minute," he says. "Fuck, I'm half-asleep, and you're laying all this shit on me. *You* got someone pregnant?"

"Yeah."

"Who?"

"Fuck off." I'm being childish, but I'm not ready to tell him, and it's a simple turn of phrase that tells him that.

"Do you, uh…need anything? Can I help?"

"I've got it under control," I admit, and for the first time…I feel like I do. My instinct wasn't to run away. My instinct is to work it out with Des so we can work together to be good parents to the baby we created.

Am I scared? Yes. Will I fake like I'm not for her sake? Abso-fucking-lutely.

To be honest, hearing she's having our baby is less of a shock than hearing my dad has a secret family.

"With the number of curveballs you throw at us, I swear to God, I'm surprised you didn't pick up baseball instead of football," he mutters. "You've got it under control?"

"Yes."

"You," he repeats, disbelief evident in his tone.

"I said yes," I repeat, feeling a little tired of being treated like I'm incapable of life because I'm the youngest. "You do realize I turn twenty-nine in two days, don't you? I'm not a kid anymore. I got this. Now back to the other thing."

"Right, the twin brothers." He clears his throat. "Let me see if Grayson or Spencer know anything. You said thirty years ago?"

"Yeah, that's what he indicated."

"Hm," he murmurs. "That would make them about the same age as you."

"Weird," I say, not really sure how else to respond to that fact. So he was sleeping around while Mom was pregnant with me? Great. Everything I ever wanted to know about my parents.

"Yeah. I wonder if Mom knows."

"Want me to ask?"

"That's up to you," he says. "If she doesn't, do you really want to be the one to tell her?"

He makes a good point, but if she does know, maybe she can point us in the right direction to track them down or find out more.

When I head back inside to check on Desiree, I find her asleep in her bed. I stare down at her for a few beats. Her red hair isn't in the messy bun anymore but makes a halo around her, and I commit the beautiful, peaceful sight in front of me to memory.

It won't always be peaceful. She's fiery, and I can see plenty of fireworks in our future. But right now, it is, and I'll cherish that for as long as I can.

I leave her to rest, and I head back out to the kitchen to grab a drink before I make the call to my mother. I find Addy at the counter holding onto a stack of papers.

"Mind if I help myself to some water?" I ask.

She shakes her head, and she sets her papers down as she watches me. "Can I ask you a question?"

I grab a glass out of the cabinet where I spotted them earlier when I made the soup, and I turn to face her. "Shoot."

"What are you doing here?"

I snag my lip between my teeth. "I came to see Des."

"Desi's my best friend," she says quietly. "And her dad always warned her about football players, especially after everything with her ex, but that girl is a stubborn one."

I chuckle at her assessment. "So I've learned."

"What are your intentions with her?"

"I suppose since she doesn't want her father to know about us, you're grilling me instead?" I tease.

"Look, I have a lot of papers to grade tonight," she says, nodding to the stack. "I have little time to spare. I was here for her when you broke it off with her the first time, and I need to know you're not going to choose her dad or football or anything else at all over her again." She raises a pointed brow, and I get the very real sense that she doesn't like me.

I suppose I haven't given her a reason to.

I'm an offensive player through and through, though, so I don't jump to the defense even though she's trying to put me there. "I won't. I realize the only person I need to promise that to is her, but I made the wrong decision the first time. I threw myself into work while we were apart, and I reached lofty goals I didn't expect to reach. But at the end of the day…none of it meant a damn thing when I didn't get to share it with her." I press my lips together, and when I glance up and my eyes meet Addy's, she looks a little misty.

"Atta boy," she says, and for the first time, her lips tip up in a small smile. If she's half as tough on her students as she is on me, well, they're pretty damn lucky to have her.

"What grade do you teach?" I ask.

"Seventh."

I think back to seventh grade. I was a little shit, that's for damn sure. "Thank you for what you're doing for them."

She preens a little, and I think maybe I've got the best friend on my side.

I fill my water glass, and then I excuse myself back to the balcony to give my mother a call.

"Asher Joseph, *whyyyy* do you make your mother go weeks and weeks without a call?"

I laugh. "Because you text me nearly every day?"

"Still, I like to hear your voice."

"I'll start sending you voice memos," I say dryly.

"What's new, baby boy?" she asks.

I blow out a breath.

"Uh oh, that was a heavy one. What'd you do?"

"Why do you think it's me?" I ask.

"Because I know my boys, and whenever you let out a heavy sigh like that, I know darn well something's on your mind."

"Fine," I mutter, acknowledging that she knows me pretty damn well. "I, uh…I'm gonna be a dad."

Shocked silence greets me on the other side, and then a gasp. "I'm gonna be a grammy again?" She sounds slightly choked up.

"Confirmed," I say.

"Who's the girl, and when can I meet her?"

"I'm not saying a word, and I have no idea," I say, answering both her questions.

"Why and why?"

"We're sort of seeing each other in secret for now for, uh…reasons. Once she's ready to go public, we'll go public," I say.

"Ooh, is it someone I know? Like someone famous?"

"No, Mother."

"I mean, when Lincoln told me they were having a baby, I got a video call. I don't even get to see your cute face while you tell me this amazing news. Are you going to marry her? Tell me you're going to marry her!"

I knew I shouldn't have led with the fact that I impregnated a woman. "I have no idea, Mom. I just found out today, and it's…complicated. But to be perfectly honest, it's not why I called."

"Oh," she says, and she sounds disappointed.

"I called Dad to tell him I had to cancel dinner with him on my birthday because I'll be out of town—"

"With the girl?" she interrupts.

"Yes."

"You're spending your birthday with her?" She sounds far too excited.

"I'm planning on it, but I'll have to call in sick to practice." She makes an *eep* sound, and I continue. "Anyway, when I blurted out that I got a girl pregnant, he told me to pay her off…the way he did thirty years ago."

She's silent.

"Mom?"

"He told you," she says flatly.

"He did," I confirm.

"Okay, hit me with your questions."

"My first was whether you knew, which, obviously, you do," I say.

"Yes. But I didn't find out because he was honest with me," she admits. "I found out because when the boys were fifteen or sixteen, their mom called him, and I happened to be there. I guess they had some talent when it came to football, and she was hoping Dad would help give them a nudge since the four of you boys were all on track for the NFL."

"Not because of Dad," I protest.

"No, not because of Dad. Because you were each talented, too. But those genes didn't come from me, honey," she says softly.

"So what do we do?" I ask, and I hear the desperation in my own voice.

"What do you want to do?"

"I don't know," I admit.

"You can leave it as it was, or you can go meet them. Your call."

"You have their information?" I ask.

"I do," she says carefully.

"Do they know who their father is?"

She clears her throat. "No, they don't. It's why your father paid off their mother."

"So they're not even Nashes?"

"I mean, technically they are, but they go by their stepfather's last name."

"Which is…" I prompt.

"Banks."

"Tanner and Miller Banks," I say, and it dawns on me as I repeat the last name. "Holy shit, Tanner and Miller *Banks*? As in the twins from Arizona that the NFL started looking at when they were freshmen in high school?"

She clears her throat. "Yep. That's them. Your half-brothers."

Whoa. I did *not* see that one coming.

Chapter 45: Desiree Dixon

Comfort Food

Asher looks like he's seen a ghost when I wake up and pad into the living room. He's sitting on the couch, staring at his phone.

"You okay?" I ask.

He nods as he glances up at me. "Yeah. I, uh, found out some news…" He trails off, leaving it at that.

"Is everything okay?"

He glances back at his phone and then at me again. "I'm not sure."

"Want to talk about it?" I plop down beside him.

"I do, but not yet. I need to figure out a few things, and I need to head over to see my brother."

"Okay," I say instead of voicing the anxieties in my head.

"You can come with. He's not far from here, and he has the day off."

"No, it's fine," I say softly. "I'm tired anyway. Go see your brother."

He glances over at Addy, who's at the counter grading papers, and then he angles his head toward the balcony as if to ask if we can have this conversation in private. I nod and follow him out there.

"What's going on?" I ask.

He clears his throat. "Long story short, I just talked to my dad and found out I have twin half-brothers none of us ever knew about."

My jaw drops open. "What?" I breathe.

He nods as he walks over to the railing and looks out over the view. "My dad apparently had an affair thirty years ago, and my twin half-brothers are also pro football players." He turns back toward me. "They're phenomenal athletes…I've heard of them. I know them. Fuck, I've played against them. I've *met* them. I just…" He shakes his head as words fail him.

"What are you going to do?" I ask.

He grips onto his hair with both hands before he lets it go, and it sticks up. "I don't know. I'm going to start by talking to my brothers and seeing what they want to do, and I guess we'll devise a plan together."

"Yes, of course. Go. Be with your brothers, and call me if I can do anything."

He nods, and then he takes a few steps to close the gap between us. "I'll never be far, okay?" He drops his lips down to mine, and I feel the familiar warmth and comfort I've always felt in his arms. It's safe here, and I'm protected from the craziness of our lives and the world surrounding us.

"You need to go," I say.

"I know. But I don't want to."

I rise to my tiptoes to press another kiss to his lips. "I'll be right here."

His eyes soften, and I know he knows I don't just mean physically.

At least I hope he knows it.

He leaves, and I walk back into the kitchen to find Addy collecting her papers into a pile. "Done," she announces proudly.

"Well done."

"I texted Chloe and Lauren. They're bringing dinner over. I figured you can tell them if you're ready, or you don't have to, but either way, some comfort food sounded good."

"It does sound good," I agree. "What are they bringing?"

"Your favorites. Mac and cheese, chicken fingers, and fries."

My lips tip up into a broad smile. "You three really are the best."

She shoots me a wink as she slides her papers into her backpack. "Don't you forget it."

Chloe and Lauren arrive an hour later, and we sit at our usual spots at the table as we start to dish out the food.

I feel a little better than I have, and maybe it's because I finally know the reason I've been feeling so horribly lately—combined with the two-hour nap and the fact that Asher and I are going to give this another try.

"So what calls for comfort food?" Chloe asks as she digs into her macaroni.

Addy looks at me to take the floor, though I assume she'd take it back and make something up if I needed her to.

These three women are my best friends. We're the Fearless Four, and if I'm going to live up to that title, I should probably stop living scared and start acting like the badass I know I am.

"Asher and I are back together," I begin.

Chloe and Lauren both gasp.

"This calls for champagne, not chicken fingers," Lauren complains, and I laugh.

"Well, I can't have any for the next seven or eight months," I say, and I wait for them to piece it together.

They both turn to stare at me.

"Wait a minute," Chloe says, narrowing her eyes at me before she jumps to any conclusions. "Why not?"

I clear my throat, and silence fills the air as they wait for my announcement. "I'm seven weeks pregnant."

More gasps fill the air, and then Chloe jumps up and rushes over to hug me. "Oh my God, congratulations!" She turns to Addy. "This is congratulations, right?"

Addy chuckles as she shrugs. "I think so."

"Yes," I say. "It's a surprise, but I've had a few hours to get used to the idea, and I can actually see myself doing this."

"Of course you can do this," Lauren says, and she rounds the table to give me a warm hug, too. "And then you can tell us all about what it's like and we can learn the dos and don'ts from you."

I laugh. "Thanks. Always happy to be the guinea pig."

"It's Asher's?" Lauren asks, and I nod.

"Is it a girl or a boy?" Chloe asks.

"I won't find out for a while yet," I say. I read through the paperwork, and it looks like I can do an optional blood test at ten weeks, or more traditionally and more accurately, I can wait for twenty weeks.

"But do you, like, *know* already? Mother's instinct?" Lauren presses, leaning in as if she's asking me to tell a secret.

"First hunch is a girl, but I guess we'll see."

"Let's talk names," Addy says.

"My vote is for Chloe," Chloe says, and we all laugh.

"There's only one Chloe," I say dryly. "I haven't thought about names."

"Yeah, but haven't you ever picked them out before and held onto them your entire life?" Lauren asks.

My brows dip. "No. Have you?"

She nods, and then she pretends to zip her lips. "But I'm not telling you, or you'll steal them."

"I will not!" I promise.

She sighs. "Fine. David if it's a boy, Isabelle if it's a girl."

"I love both, and I promise not to take either," I say.

"What are you going to do? Live here with Addy?" Chloe asks.

I shrug. "This is all very, very new. I literally heard from Asher this morning, was convinced by Addy to take a pregnancy test, and then he showed up when he heard I wasn't feeling well and took me to the doctor before he left. It's been a whirlwind, and I haven't really thought about what comes next—aside from, you know, food."

"Then I won't ask if you think you'll be moving to Vegas to be closer to your family and the baby daddy," Lauren says. She grabs another chicken finger out of the box.

In all likelihood, that's what makes the most sense.

But I'm also dreading the conversation I'll have to have with my parents. I'll tell them I'm moving there, and they'll want to know why I changed my mind, and meanwhile I'll be growing a baby and unable to hide the bump, and then they'll want to know who the father is, and I'll need to admit who it is because we can't hide out forever, and...

It's complicated. Asher and I getting back together is complicated enough, but we're adding a baby into the mix, too.

And I have less than eight months to prepare for an entirely new reality.

Chapter 46: Asher Nash

Two More Brochachos

Istare at Grayson and Lincoln on the screen as we hold a video chat at Spencer's place. This might be a strange situation, but it's exactly the sort of brotherly bonding our parents raised us to have.

Which is why it's so goddamn weird that our dad had an entire other family that he never told us about. That he chose us and wrote off his other two kids.

Two more brochachos in the Nash mix.

Are there more?

Maybe. Who knows…and who knows whether we'll ever learn the truth?

Would he have told me the truth if I hadn't gotten someone pregnant? I doubt it, but maybe he would have. It's part of the unspoken bond of closeness we shared—at least I thought it was. Now I feel more than a little betrayed by the man.

"Brochachos," I say in greeting, and they both grin at me.

"I hear congratulations are in order," Grayson says to me.

I lift my glass of whiskey, and Spencer does, too. Grayson and Lincoln do the same on the other side of the screen.

"To surviving each other," Grayson quips, and Spencer and I touch glasses before we each take a sip.

"So what's the plan?" Spencer asks, directing his question to Lincoln.

It makes sense. Lincoln's the oldest, and he's the natural leader.

But Lincoln nods toward me. "This is Asher's gig."

I twist my lips as my three brothers turn their attention to me. It's a rare sight, if I'm being honest. I was always sort of brushed aside. I was the one getting in the way. I was the baby, and now they're looking at me in earnest as they wait for me to take the stage.

I clear my throat as I try to step up into the shoes Lincoln just left out for me. "I think we should meet them. I think they deserve to know who their father is…who their brothers are."

"Was there some reason Dad didn't want them to know?" Spencer asks, trying to look at it from all angles like he always does.

"I don't have a solid answer to that, to be honest," I say. "I think he didn't want to fuck with the balance of the four of us and Mom. Mom didn't even find out until the twins were teenagers."

"What did she say?" Grayson asks.

"She knew about them because their mom tracked down Dad when they started showing real talent in football. She wanted him to help them break in, and somehow Mom got wind of it. I think that might be when things started to crumble for Mom and Dad, but she didn't say as much." I shrug. "She said they've never known who their father was."

"So they don't have the last name Nash?" Grayson asks.

I shake my head. "Banks. Tanner and Miller Banks."

All three of my brothers have recognition in their eyes at the name—just like I did.

They both play for the Cardinals now, and the Cards are at home this weekend.

"I think we should go to Arizona and introduce ourselves to our brothers," I say.

"I'm in," Lincoln says.

"I'm down," Grayson says.

"Depends when," Spencer says. "I don't want to miss out, but I need to be at practice Wednesday since I play you assholes next weekend."

Our bye week is over, and we have practice on Wednesday, too—my birthday, and I'm planning to *call in sick* so I can spend the day with my pregnant secret girlfriend.

Is that what she is? My girlfriend?

I think she's somehow *more* than that, but we haven't defined it.

"Let's go now," I suggest. "It's a short enough flight."

He nods. "And I have tomorrow off."

"So do we. Let's do it," I say. They all look at me like I'm a little crazy, and maybe I am. I'm the one who's spontaneous, who will hop a flight with no baggage, who will leave at the drop of a hat.

It's not their style—any of them.

I've strived my entire life to be more of a leader like Lincoln, to be outgoing and fun like Grayson, to be smart and responsible like Spencer. But I'm not them.

I'm Asher, and maybe it's time these three be a little more impulsive like me.

"Let's do it," Lincoln echoes, and Spencer and Grayson agree.

I guess that means we're off to meet our long-lost twin brothers.

Now there's a sentence I never thought I'd say.

Lincoln says he'll get in touch with the head coach in Arizona, and he texts our group chat to let us know that the coach called in Tanner and Miller, and they'll be there waiting for us. I feel bad that we're ambushing them with this news, but the four of us don't want to go another day without knowing our family.

Spencer and I land a little before eight, and Lincoln and Grayson are already at the airport waiting for us. The team sent a car service to greet us, and we're taken straight to the team's practice facility.

The second I walk in, I'm distracted by the twin boys who share so many of my own characteristics.

Blue eyes. Dark hair. Height. Athleticism. There's some unspoken characteristic about both of them that immediately tells me we're related to them. They look quite similar, but I can still tell one is more of a combination between Lincoln and Spencer, and the other is a mix of Grayson and me. These two are very well known around the league. Tanner is an incredible quarterback, and I know he's the taller one. The other one has ridiculous leg muscles, and that's Miller, the running back.

The coach is there, too, and Lincoln looks at me to take the floor. We haven't really discussed *how* we're going to broach this topic, but now we're here, and this is where the negative impacts of being spontaneous start to step in.

I think about nodding to him—about letting him take the lead here. But Lincoln is a coach, and there's a careful line he can't cross when it comes to coaches talking to players from other teams outside of the appropriate times.

This was my idea, and it's me who initiated all of this. The responsibility to drop the truth falls squarely on me.

I think about Desiree, and somehow the image of her face in my mind calms and centers me.

"Hi." I draw in a deep breath. "I'm Asher," I begin a little awkwardly. They know I'm Asher, and I don't know how to just blurt out that we know who their father is. "And you may already know Lincoln, Grayson, and Spencer." I point to each of my brothers.

What the fuck do I say here?

"We, uh…" I glance at Grayson, and he nods encouragingly. "Would you like to maybe go to dinner with us so we can talk?"

"Talk about what?" Tanner asks. He's definitely a *take-control-of-the-situation* kind of guy, a trait that translates well to his role on the field.

"It's kind of…well, we found out some news earlier today, and we wanted to share it with you, but I'm not quite sure how to say it," I admit.

Tanner glances at Miller before he looks back at me. "Just say it. You came all this way, and this is intense."

I have no idea what they know and what they don't know, and he told me to just say it, so I do. "I found out earlier today who your biological father is."

The twins look at each other and have some sort of secret conversation with their eyes before they both turn back silently toward me.

"You *what?*" Tanner asks.

I clear my throat. "It's Eddie Nash. You're our half-brothers."

Their eyes widen as they both stand a bit dumbfounded at the news. Miller backs up and sits on a chair, and Tanner takes a step toward us. "I'm sorry. What did you just say?"

"We're your brothers," I say softly, as if a softer voice will soften the shock.

It doesn't.

Neither of them says a word, and Lincoln nods to me as if to tell me to keep talking.

"I know this is a shock, and I'm sure you have a lot of questions," I continue. "So do I, to be honest. We've gone our whole lives not knowing about you, and all four of us agreed we don't want to let another moment pass with the six of us in the dark. Our brotherhood is everything to us, and you are a part of that. But we also understand and respect however you want to handle this news going forward."

The four of us wait with bated breath for a reaction, and finally Tanner glances back at Miller.

"I think we need a minute to let this sink in," Tanner says.

"Can I talk to the two of you in my office?" their coach finally says, piping into the conversation.

They glance at each other before they follow him into his office, and they shut the door in privacy.

I look to Lincoln to take the lead, but even he seems to be at a loss for words.

"I see the resemblance," Spencer finally says.

"Between each other?" Grayson asks. "They're twins, dipshit."

Spencer rolls his eyes and huffs out a breath. "To us, you idiot."

He's not wrong, though both Lincoln and I laugh at the ridiculousness of their conversation. The twins have blue eyes and dark hair like Spencer, Grayson, and me. Lincoln's the odd man out with slightly lighter hair and darker eyes like Mom, where the rest of us have a stronger resemblance to Dad. And so do the twins.

I shake my head. I discovered my twin brothers on the same day I found out I'm going to be a father.

I still can't believe it. Any of it.

"Want me to find a place for dinner?" Lincoln asks while we wait for the twins to come back.

He's met with nods of agreement from the rest of us, and the twins emerge from the office with the coach a few minutes later.

Tanner clears his throat and nods toward his brother. "Miller and I—well, we both feel a little…shocked, I think. We'd love the chance to get to know our brothers, but we're not quite ready to go public with any of this."

"We won't tell a soul until you're ready," Lincoln says.

Tanner nods. "We appreciate that."

"I made reservations at Culinary Dropout for six. You two in?" Lincoln asks.

They glance at each other and nod at the same time.

"We'd like that," Tanner says.

A quick beat of awkwardness follows, but good ol' Grayson smashes it with his next question. "What's the key to telling you two apart? Because you look exactly the same to me."

All six of us laugh at that.

"I've got about three inches on Miller," Tanner says.

"And I'm the better-looking one," Miller adds, and it's the first time we've heard him speak—a reminder to always watch out for the quiet ones.

We get another laugh out of that.

"When did you find out about this?" Tanner asks.

"Earlier today, actually," I say. "I, uh, found out some news, told my dad, and he sort of let it slip."

"Twenty-nine years, and this was his first slip?" Miller asks.

I glance at my brothers, and they're nodding along with me.

"He had to know this would come out eventually," I admit.

What other secrets has he been keeping?

We head toward the restaurant, and on the way, I text Desiree.

Me: *Just wanted to update you. I met the twins, and we're on our way to dinner with them now. I'm in Arizona. Probably spending the night here, but should be back tomorrow. You feeling okay?*

Desiree: *Better now that I heard from you. Be safe. I hope you get what you need out of meeting them. I'll be here waiting for you to return.*

My heart feels full as I read her words. We might still be on shaky ground, but somehow it feels like everything's going to be okay.

Someday.

I learned a hard truth today, and it's going to change the entire dynamic of my family.

Anxiety pierces into my guts as I wonder how the news about Desiree and me is going to change the dynamic of *her* family, too.

Chapter 47: Desiree Dixon

Make a DIFFerence with Asher Nash

I flesh out some final ideas, and then I spend some time looking at places in Vegas. It's a search I gave up a while ago, but I really do think it makes the most sense.

All the places I liked two months ago have sold, but a new crop of houses are on the market. I bookmark a few I like, and I figure I'll visit soon to choose the place that's the best fit for me.

Addy and I had a long talk about our living arrangements, and she's going to move in with Chloe and Lauren. It's the best-case scenario even though I don't want to give up this apartment or my life here in San Diego.

I have to, though. I'm considering it the first of the many sacrifices I'll make as a mother, just like my own mother has done for me. And to that end, I want to make sure this little muffin in my oven has every chance in the world to be around her grandparents.

And by grandparents, I mean *my* parents. Asher doesn't talk very highly of his own father, and his mom is long-distance.

The thought pulses the ever-present fear about telling my parents about this. I love Asher, but we *just* got back together like twelve seconds ago. I need time to let this grow and develop before I'm ready to tell my dad, and I doubt Asher wants to make the admission mid-season when there's so much on the line.

No, it's better to let the season play out. That buys me a month or two, anyway, but by then, I'll be showing, and it's not like I really want to keep this a secret from my mom for that long.

I'll tell them after Christmas. I'll leave the father's name out of it for now, and we'll keep seeing each other in secret so we can figure out whether there's really a future for us or if he's sticking around because of the baby.

Though if fate put me in that chair beside him at the charity ball, then I think fate also put him in my apartment the same day I found out I was pregnant.

Fate keeps stepping in to push us together, and maybe I'm starting to believe in the cheesiness of it all a little.

By the time he arrives back at my place on Tuesday afternoon, he's carrying a duffel bag of new clothes and toiletries he must've picked up in Arizona, and I have the proposal ready to present to him. I give him a quick kiss when I open the door to greet him, and then I pull him in.

"How did it go?" I ask a little tentatively.

"It was good. Or as good as it could be given the circumstances." He shrugs.

"What's the next step?" I study him as I try to find some clue as to how he's feeling about it, but he's a little guarded.

"I mean, it's not like they're going to change their last names and their entire lives to be part of the Nash family, but at the same time, I can almost see it happening down the road. For as much as my dad fell from grace, there's a history and a legacy with our last name, and I can't imagine they wouldn't want to be a part of that."

"Who would've thought, two more Nash Brothers for the ladies to watch out for?" I tease.

He chuckles. "We didn't get into that kind of talk, but since they're the same age as me and I'm the one who found out about our relationship, I think I can see myself forming a bond with them. Especially after the mentorship program I've been working on with Coach Dix…uh—your dad." He gets a little awkward at the end, something that's very unlike him.

"I knew you were working on a project with him. You two have gotten close, haven't you?" I ask.

He sighs. "Yeah, we have. And it throws more than a wrench into what we have, but to me, it's worth whatever price I have to pay. But I need to know before we take this any further whether it's worth it to you, too."

My brows pull together. "What do you mean?"

"I mean, what if your dad doesn't approve? What if he writes me off, or he writes *you* off? Is that something you can handle?" he asks.

I'm surprised by his question since he seemed to be all for telling my dad yesterday. I didn't consider the thought that my dad might be mad at *me* for going after a football player when he expressly told me not to. I guess I mainly pushed the whole idea out of my head, thinking we had plenty of time down the road to worry about it.

And we do, but the time is getting shorter and shorter by the day.

I want him to be with me through the pregnancy, but I also want to wait until the season is over. We can do both…right?

We were planning to see each other in secret anyway. We can figure out a way to make it work.

"I, uh…I don't know," I answer honestly, and then I shift the subject. "I have something for you."

I spent most of the day today working on this project, and I'm excited to share it with him. It was exactly the distraction I needed, and I realize only now that I haven't felt nauseous at all today.

I'm bouncing up and down on the balls of my feet as I hand him the paperwork I finished about an hour ago.

His brows crinkle together. "What's all this?"

"The proposal for your foundation." There's a bit of tentativeness in my tone, along with a bit of pride.

He reads aloud from the paperwork.

"The mission of Make a DIFFerence with Asher Nash is to inspire adolescents to make healthy life choices by educating them on the dangers of drug use and honoring the memory of Jacob Fitzgerald, who tragically lost his life at the age of seventeen to drugs."

He glances up at me, and I see the emotion in his eyes as he looks back down at the paper to continue reading.

"Make a DIFFerence will host an annual 5K run in which all participants will declare who they're running for. Asher is Doing It For Fitz, or DIFF. Who are you doing it for? The event will end with a fun zone full of activities and games focused on healthy choices, vendors who will educate and inform, local food vendors, live music, and an awards ceremony for the top runners and contributors. Fundraising will come in the form of registration fees, donations, sponsorships, and merchandise sales. The funds raised will support the Make a DIFFerence with Asher Nash Foundation to award scholarships to students either affected by or pursuing careers in addiction treatment and prevention. The DIFF5K will promote awareness, education, community, and support in the fight against drugs."

He stops reading and sets the paper down on the table, and he's silent as he looks out the window over the view of the ocean that I'm already starting to miss even though I haven't left it yet.

"Say something," I whisper.

He closes his eyes and shakes his head a little, and they're a little foggy when he opens them. He keeps his attention trained out the window. "You couldn't have known this, but Fitz was a runner. He *loved* running, and he was always begging me to participate in every 5K, 10K, and marathon that came to town. He was adventurous. He made me go rock climbing with him, whitewater rafting, biking, hiking, you name it. But running was his passion." His eyes move toward me, and he sets his hand on top of the papers with my proposal. "This is perfect, Des. It's incredible, and I couldn't have even tried to put into words what you created here."

My eyes fill with tears at his earnest approval. "Yeah?" I ask softly.

He nods, and he blinks a little as he takes a step toward me. He reaches around my waist and hauls me into him. "Yeah." He lowers his lips to mine. "Thank you," he murmurs, his voice raspy and deep, and I sink into him as he kisses me softly in the kitchen.

Our kiss turns a little more passionate, a little more urgent. It's bonding us again in a way that's stronger than we were before, all through the simple task of doing a job I told him I would do for him.

But there's a depth to this kiss that's new and different. It's as if this kiss is a physical manifestation of the love he feels for me, and it's on some level beyond hot. It's an inferno as we reconnect in this way after way too long apart.

There's no hesitation from either of us even though I felt a little hesitant yesterday.

I've had time to sit with his words. I've had time to feel the love he has for me. He checked in when he didn't have to. He's back already. He's tending to my needs—and he was even before he found out I'm carrying his baby. He came all the way to San Diego on his week off just to buy me soup when he heard I wasn't feeling well.

If that doesn't scream that he's really in this with me, I'm not sure what else would convince me.

He lifts me up into his arms, and he doesn't stop kissing me as he carries me through my apartment and toward my bedroom. The papers are abandoned on the table, but we'll get back to them.

For now, though, we have some making up for lost time to do.

He gently sets me down on the bed, and he climbs so he's hovering over me, careful not to press his body weight onto me.

He kisses me like that for a while, and I feel the passion in him—a new fire ignited because there's a bond growing inside me that will forever tie us together. As I told him, a baby won't solve our problems. We'll field complications, and we'll have differing ideas, and it won't be easy. But if we're holding hands through it and communicating instead of running scared, then I think there might be a chance for us.

He shifts to move in beside me, and he pulls back from our kiss. He sets his hand on my stomach, and then his eyes meet mine.

"Is this okay?" he asks quietly.

I shrug. "I think so, but I've never been pregnant before, so I have no idea."

"I do remember Lincoln saying pregnancy sex is the best sex, so I think we're safe there. I just meant are you okay with doing this, or do you need more time? Do you feel okay, or do you still feel sick?"

My eyes soften as my chest bursts with love for this man. It's the sweetest sentiment I could possibly imagine in the moment when surely he's ready for this reunion as much as I am.

"Oh, yeah. I'm definitely okay for sex, cowboy," I say.

"Cowboy?" he repeats, and I giggle as I think back to our first night together when I called him that.

"If you'd like, I can ride you like a cowgirl," I suggest.

"Now that is a deal I will definitely take you up on."

"And Asher?" I ask, and his heated eyes move to mine as the corner of my mouth tips up in a wicked smile. "There's no need to be gentle."

He smirks at me but then races to peel my shirt off and then my bra, and he does all the work as he strips me out of my sweatpants and panties, too. I'm lying naked on the bed, and he spends some time worshipping my body, sucking my tits between his lips as I writhe and moan beneath him at his touch, his mouth, his heat. He peppers kisses from the middle of my chest to my neck and back down. He moves past my tits on his quest down my body, and he leaves a trail of kisses on my stomach and to my pubic bone before he sinks lower, getting off the bed and kneeling on the floor as he adjusts my legs over his shoulders.

And then he dives right in.

I thread my fingers into his hair as he works to alleviate the ache that I've felt for him since he left me. All the vibrators in the world are no comparison for this man's talented mouth. He licks my clit as he slides one of his glorious fingers into my pussy, and I clutch the sheets as my hips start to move in time with his mouth. He reaches up with one arm to tweak my nipple between his thumb and forefinger just as he slides in a second finger, and it's all the best sensations crashing into each other at one time.

It's too much for my body that hasn't had a workout like this in months, and I claw at my sheets as my climax plows into me. He keeps pace with me despite my thrashing as my legs clamp around his ears and I ride out pulse after pulse of sweet, hot pleasure.

As my body starts to come down, he pulls his fingers out but kisses my clit a few more times, and then he rocks back onto his knees and stares up at me.

"Fuck, Des, I'm never going two months without tasting this sweet cunt again."

I raise my brows pointedly—or I try to, anyway, but I'm a little hazy after that orgasm, so I probably look like a clown. "You better not," I warn.

He chuckles, and then he pushes to a stand and starts to take off his clothes. He lays on the bed beside me, and he glances over at me as he motions for me to hop on. "I believe you mentioned cowgirl?"

I laugh as I revel in the fact that somehow he can turn this erotic moment light and fun. It's one of his many charms.

"I said that before you wrecked me with that orgasm." I turn into his side and toss an arm over his abdomen.

"Close, but a little lower," he teases, pushing my arm down toward his cock.

"Someone's getting a little desperate."

"It's been two months, Des. All I've thought about is you."

I sit up and move to straddle him. "Who am I to deny you a second longer?"

He fists his cock as I move into place, and I align myself with his body. He pushes into me, and I set my hands on his chest for balance. He groans as I sit all the way down on him, and I pull upward and shift my hips as I start to ride him.

God, he feels good. He *looks* good as he takes in the pleasure, his eyes heated as he stares at me with heavy lids. Sex with him was always incredible, but there's something different about this time, and I know exactly what it is.

It's the L word.

It lays heavily between us, spoken by one and not the other, and though I feel it, I'm scared to say it. But as I move over him and our bodies reconnect in the language they know best, I know without a doubt that I feel it too.

I didn't start to feel better until he showed up to take care of me.

I was dragging through my daily tasks, forcing myself to get out of bed each morning.

I thought I could chalk it up to just being sick and exhausted, but the truth is, I think it was something much darker than that.

I was missing the piece of myself that he holds in his hands, and as our bodies rock together in pure, carnal pleasure, I feel like I have that piece of myself back again. It's not just the sex or just the pleasure, but it's the feeling like I'm connected to this man in a way that I've never felt connected to anyone before. He's my life, and he's my future, and now that we're back where we belong, it feels like my world has shifted back to the way it was always meant to be.

He growls as he starts to come, and the feeling of his heat spreading inside me is too much for me to bear. I slide right into my second orgasm, something only he has ever been able to gift me, and we moan together through the intense release.

It's only when I climb off him and slide into the place in his arms where I'm most comfortable that he says, "That was one hell of an early birthday present."

"It's your birthday?"

He nods. "Tomorrow is."

"And you're turning twenty-nine?" I ask.

He nods.

"And at what age can I trade you in for a younger model?"

He chuckles. "You don't have that option. Sorry." He shrugs playfully.

"That's good because I don't want it, and for the record, you don't get it once I hit my next decade, either."

"Deal," he says, holding out his hand so we can shake on it. I don't know if I've ever made a deal while still naked and totally wrung out from what a man just did to my body, but here we are. "What are your birthday plans?" I ask sleepily.

"Well, I'm supposed to be at practice, but I'm calling in sick. I canceled my original plan to go out to dinner with my dad when I found out he fathered my twin half-brothers. I went to meet them, and then I decided life's too short to fuck around, so I'm back here to spend my birthday with you."

I yawn and close my eyes as I lean into him. "I didn't get you anything."

He sets his hand on my stomach, and he leans down and kisses the top of my head. "That's okay. I have everything I'll ever need right here."

A wave of love crests through my chest at his words. I wish we could stop time and live in this moment a little longer. I know it won't always be as perfect as this feels, but there's an awful lot we need to figure out as we plow ahead into the future.

Chapter 48: Desiree Dixon

I Have Some News

We spend Asher's birthday at my apartment. We pack a little to start the process of moving me out of here, we look up houses in Vegas, we order food from my favorite places, we laugh, and we get naked. A lot. Lots of naked time when Addy is at work, and again when Addy is starting to bring some of her stuff over to Chloe and Lauren's place.

Asher has to head home for practice when he should've been there today, but he'll be back in town this weekend since the Aces are playing the Storm. My mom will be in town, but she's staying at the home they didn't sell when they moved to Vegas so they'd always have their home here in San Diego.

And then next week, I'll be moving to Vegas.

It's still a little surreal, and I still haven't told my parents.

Maybe I'll get up the nerve this weekend, but I have a feeling they're going to have about a million questions, and I'm not sure I'm prepared to answer any of them.

Because the charity ball is getting closer. Because I need to be in town to manage the auction items.

Because I want to be close to my baby daddy, and oh, by the way, I'm pregnant.

Yeah...I'm not ready for that.

Christmas is less than three weeks away, so I do a little online shopping from the comfort of home, I watch the Aces roll over the Storm at the Storm's home stadium, and I head out to dinner on Sunday night after the game with both my parents.

"I have some news," I say, clearing my throat after we're seated.

A shudder runs through me.

I have multiple pieces of news, but the thought of telling them the biggest one brings back a brand-new bout of nausea.

I'm not ready for that.

They're both staring at me as those thoughts run rampant through my mind.

"Is everything okay?" my dad asks, and God, it feels so *wrong* to keep such a *big* thing from them.

"Everything's fine," I say with a smile that I have to force. Is it fine? Will it ever really be fine again, or was Asher right about my father potentially writing me off for going against his wishes?

He wouldn't do that. I know football is his life, but I'm his world…like my own baby will be for me.

But then there's people in the world like Eddie Nash who abandon their kids and pay off their mother, and, oh my God, is *Asher* going to be like that? Does the apple fall far from the tree?

I can't imagine a world where he would be, but for a minute there, I couldn't imagine a world where he'd walk away from me…and then he did.

"Are *you* okay?" my mom asks, studying me.

"I'm getting over a stomach bug," I say a little weakly.

"Still? I thought you were quiet at the game. Is that why?" she asks.

I nod. "Yeah, I think so."

"What's the news?" my dad asks.

"I decided to move to Vegas after all," I blurt.

My mom gasps, and the server chooses that moment to take our drink order. I skip over the alcohol as my parents order champagne to celebrate, but they don't question my choice because of the stomach bug thing.

"Oh, I'm so thrilled!" my mom gushes.

"What made you change your mind?" my dad asks.

I lift a shoulder. "We're six months out from the charity ball, and I need to be closer to manage the auction items and help Erin with some other tasks." I wonder if I can talk her into giving me Asher's foundation as one of my first tasks aside from the ball.

I wonder if I can talk to Ellie and admit the truth. She represents him, and as one of her clients, maybe she'd have some ideas to help us manage our relationship.

I make a mental note to ask Asher his opinion on that.

I need to stop saying his name in my head while I'm sitting at the table with my parents before it slips out of my mouth.

"What other tasks for Erin?" my dad asks.

"Oh, I don't know. She mentioned some different player foundations and things like that." I keep my tone schooled so as not to raise any suspicion, and I think it works.

"Will you still work for Angelica?" my mom asks.

"I've actually thought a lot about that, and I think I'm going to part ways with her when I move." I haven't told her that yet, and I also haven't mentioned that I'm moving. But I have so few tasks with her these days that I'm sure it won't come as a shock.

"Where are you looking to live?" my dad asks. "We know the good areas now if you need any help."

"I think I'd like to be close to the Complex," I say.

We chat about where I should live all through dinner, and the next weekend, I find myself pulling into my parents' driveway in Vegas with my California plates on my Mercedes.

I gifted Addy with the furniture and a contact who will help her sell it if she chooses to, and my parents paid for a moving company to move the rest of my stuff here.

And that's it. I cried when I said goodbye to my friends, and then I drove by myself to Vegas on a Saturday so I could attend tomorrow's home game.

It's all a bit surreal to me as I get out of the front seat and draw in a deep breath of dry desert air. This is home now.

Well, *this* is home for the next few days until I settle on a place of my own, and on Monday I'll be touring potential new homes with my mom and her realtor, Joyce.

It's getting harder and harder to keep this secret from her, though. And to be honest, I don't *want* to keep it from her.

But I can't tell her and expect her to keep it from my dad, and I'm not ready for him to know yet.

Still, I have questions. Lots of them. The kind you want to ask your mom as you go through something she went through about twenty-six years ago.

I'm ten weeks pregnant when Christmas comes, and as we open gifts by the fireplace, even though it's in the seventies outside, I count my blessings.

But later, when my dad pours eggnog and adds the traditional brandy to it, a drink we've laughed over annually since I turned twenty-one—or nineteen, if nobody's counting—I freeze.

It slipped my mind that he'd want to share a glass with me, and I'm not sure how to decline. I don't have the stomach bug anymore. I've been eating like a horse all day.

I hand my glass to my mom as if I'm passing it over, and my dad moves to pour a third.

I can fake it, or I can fess up.

I hold up a hand. "I, uh…I don't want any," I say.

My dad's brows furrow. "It's tradition, Desi-Doo."

"I know…I just, uh—"

They both look at me expectantly, and the longer the pause is drawn out, the longer I fight with myself over what to say next, the more they start piecing it together.

"Wait a minute," my mom says, narrowing her eyes at me. "You didn't have a drink when we went to dinner after the Storm game. You said you had a stomach bug…"

I glance over at her with guilt in my eyes.

"Oh my God," she murmurs, her hands moving to her mouth.

"What? What's going on?" my dad asks, and I'm reminded of the keys he can't find when they're right there in his hand.

"Are you?" my mom asks.

"Is she what?" my dad asks.

I close my eyes and nod my head. "Yes," I whisper.

My mom screams. Legit. She screams.

"What the hell is going on?" my dad asks, still clueless.

"She's having a baby, Bill," my mom says, and she rushes toward me to hug me.

"She's having a *what*?" my dad thunders, but my mom ignores him as she squeezes me.

"How are you feeling? Are you okay? When is she coming? Who's the—"

"Mom!" I interrupt before she gets that last question out. I draw in a breath as I pull out of our hug and hold my mom at arm's length. "I'm ten weeks and due in July. I feel mostly good, but it's true I thought I had a stomach bug when this all started. And I'm not quite ready to answer any more questions. I wasn't planning to tell you yet. It's still so early."

"Oh, I'm going to be a grandma!" my mom squeals, and I'm happy she's so excited. It makes *me* feel excited, too.

On the other hand, my dad sounds pretty damn angry.

"Who is the father?" my dad asks thickly. "Who did this to you?"

"Nobody *did this* to me, Dad," I say quietly.

"Then why won't you tell us who it is?"

I draw in a breath. "It's complicated."

"Screw complicated, he got you pregnant and isn't even around. I'll find out who it is, and he will pay for leaving you," he hisses.

"Dad, that's not what happened," I say, my tone full of desperation. "It's not like he ditched me. We're taking things slow, that's all." I need to protect Asher. I'm so scared he's going to run again, and if I tell my dad without giving him a warning, that'll be his out. I wouldn't blame him for taking it.

I need to get over this fear. He promised me he wasn't going to leave again, especially not now that I'm pregnant, but trying to move on from him was harder than I expected it to be.

Maybe because I was carrying a part of him all along that I didn't even know about until three weeks ago.

I can't go through it again.

"Having a baby with another person is not taking things slow," he says, his jaw clenched.

"I realize that, but like I said…it's complicated. Can we just enjoy the rest of our day celebrating Christmas together for the last time as a family of three?" I've been thinking about it all day. Next Christmas, if all goes well, I'll have a five-month-old. And Asher…will he still be in the picture?

I can't imagine not having him by my side a year from now, but we have a whole hell of a lot to get through before we get to that point.

Admitting the truth. Having a baby. Who knows what else is in the cards for us?

All I know is that right now, I can't tell my dad the truth. I need to let Asher finish out the season as he finds his footing with my dad.

My dad, the man who was always the most important man in my life.

My dad…the man who quietly sets down his full glass of eggnog and brandy and walks out of the room without another word as he processes the announcement I just dropped on him.

Chapter 49: Desiree Dixon

We'll Know a Year From Now

I head out to my car and sit in the driver's seat for a minute knowing full well it's too dangerous to make this call inside the house. While I know they respect me and my privacy, I also know they want answers that I'm not ready to give them yet.

I dial his number, and he's quick to answer.

"Hey."

"Hey." I blow out a breath.

"You okay?"

"Yeah. Did you have a good Christmas?"

"I did. But I also kept thinking how different next year's Christmas will look. And I kept wishing you were with me today."

"So did I, and I have to tell you something." I pause and wait for him to ask me what before I continue. "My dad and I always share eggnog with brandy the night of Christmas. It's been a tradition since before my twenty-first birthday. Anyway, tonight when he pushed the glass over to me, I couldn't take it, and, well, my mom put two and two together."

"You told them?" He sounds surprised, but there's a hint of excitement there, as if he's ready for the world to know we're together—including my parents.

"I admitted to what but not to who. I couldn't blindside you like that, not when we agreed it's not the right time."

He's quiet, and then he says, "I gotta admit, Des, I think we should tell them. We're going to have to tell him eventually, so let's get it over with instead of having it hanging over us."

"No." My voice is firm. "I get it, Asher, and I would've loved to have spent today with you too. But it's just another month and a half until the season is over."

"I guess," he says quietly, and I get the sense he's holding something back.

He'll say it when the time is right.

I hope.

He has practice and an away game, so our conversations over the next few days are brief. I can't seem to find a house I want to buy, but I look at a few with my mom and her realtor.

The Aces lose to the Eagles in Philadelphia the next weekend, and I can't help but think it's because my dad is off his game. I know I can't blame myself for a team effort, but the last game of the regular season is at home next weekend, and the Aces have already secured their spot in the playoffs, so Asher is taking it easy since he won't have as much playing time to make sure he's ready for the upcoming games that matter.

New Year's Eve is on a Tuesday night, and since neither one of us is able to be with the other at home, Asher gets a hotel room for the two of us.

I don't tell my parents where I'm going, but I do tell them I won't be home until morning. They shoot each other a look that tells me they have an idea of who I might be meeting up with, and I wouldn't be surprised if they sent someone after me to snoop and figure out who the father is.

My mom has asked me a couple times who he is, and I've remained silent—but it's been hard.

Before our night together, he sends me a text.

Asher: *First food that comes to mind when you read this text.*

Me: *Mac and cheese and pizza. Sorry, can't pick one.*

He texts me where to meet him along with the digital room key and room number, and I head to the hotel with my overnight bag.

This is the first time I've ever been in Vegas and gotten to spend the night with him. We only had a few nights together at my apartment in San Diego, and I'm excited that I get the whole night without having to leave early to get home so my parents won't question where I was.

And maybe they'll question me anyway, but it's New Year's Eve. For all they know, I'm going out with a group of friends and staying out all night.

When I walk into the suite he booked for us, I see that he thought of everything. Two champagne flutes sit on the table beside a bottle of sparkling cider. Pizza and mac and cheese are waiting for me on the table, and there's even little confetti party poppers and silly hats for us to put on as we bring in the new year. I chose a dress with fireworks on it, and it's the perfect complement to his hot pink button-down shirt with *Happy New Year* written all over it.

He pulls me into his arms and holds me for a few seconds before he presses his lips to mine. "I missed you," he says. He leans his forehead to mine.

"I missed you too." Life feels a little empty without him around, and it feels so much fuller when we're together.

I think I realized it on Christmas when he told me he was thinking about how different it would've been if we'd spent the day together. By all accounts, his brothers are a lot of fun, and his mom's a sweetheart. I've heard mixed reviews about his dad, so I already know I'll be tiptoeing around him when we eventually meet, but he's told me stories about his sisters-in-law, and I can imagine growing closer with them as the two of us start our own family together. I've always wanted a sister, and I can't wait for the day when I fit into his family and have three of them.

It sounds so magical, and I wish it felt more within reach than it does.

He tips the bottle of sparkling cider over the two flutes and hands me one. "To all the memories of this past year and all of the joys in the one ahead."

My eyes fill with tears as I reminisce on the past year. The first six months of it, I didn't even know who this man was apart from watching him during football games, and then, like a whirlwind, June and the second half of the year were filled with him.

The second half of the year was filled with falling in love, getting my heart broken, and him mending it back together. And now, as I grow this baby, it's filled with thoughts of the future and how no matter what happens, our lives are about to change.

It's a scary thought, but it's also starting to sink in. It's starting to feel exciting and right. And it's as if he can read my thoughts as he asks, "How different will our lives be one year from now?"

"Some things will change, but I think some things might not."

"What won't change?"

The more I think about it, the less of an answer I have for that question. His third year on his contract is up in a month and a half, so his future with the game is unknown. We'll have a baby. My parents will know who the father is. I'll be part of the Nash family—not in name, obviously, since it's not like he's proposed marriage and we're not there yet even though we're having a baby together, but the child we share will have his last name and the child will be half me.

I guess I can't define that yet...but we'll know a year from now.

Chapter 50: Asher Nash

The Secret Woman

I'm trying to be everything she needs, but I'm starting to wonder why she's so dead set against telling her parents. She says it's to protect me, but sometimes it feels like it's because she isn't sure she wants to be with me.

I'm certain it's just me projecting. I'm positive it's because of my reputation and the repercussions of getting suspended for a year. But it's still in the back of my mind.

Does she think I'm not good enough for her? For our baby? Or is it *me* who thinks that?

Maybe I need to hear her tell me the words back. Maybe I need the reassurance that she sees the same future I see.

But I'm not sure I'm getting that reassurance, and I think it's because she's scared I'm going to run again. I'm not sure what I can do to convince her that I'm not going anywhere. I'm new to this commitment thing, and I fucked it up once already. I won't fuck it up again.

There's way too much on the line to risk it.

We ring in the new year naked, and I hold her in my arms as we sleep until well after the sun rises.

I could get used to this.

Where I've always run from commitment in the past, when it's just the two of us in the quiet of morning in a hotel room, I think I want to run *toward* it. For the first time in my life, when I think about the future, it's not just me.

It's a frightening realization, but it also feels right.

Except we can't fully explore what life would be like together if we have to keep seeing each other in secret.

I'd love to have her as my date at the next event on my schedule. I'd love to take her to listen to live music in the park or to see a show on the Strip or to go out to dinner together.

But we can't do any of those things if she won't admit the truth to her parents.

I guess we'll continue doing this her way because the alternative isn't an option.

I've been staying with Grayson since we found out about the twins. I haven't found the right words for my father, so I've been avoiding him.

He *has* to be curious as to what I did with the information about his twin sons. As far as I know, none of my brothers have told him anything, but I don't know if the twins got in touch with him.

We have a home game this weekend, our last one of the season, and then we get a bye during Wild Card Weekend since we've secured our spot in the playoffs. That bye is supposed to be used for recovery and preparation for the intensity of the next game, but I plan to spend the entire week with Des—or as much of it as I can, anyway.

I'm on my way down to the locker room ahead of practice on Friday ahead of our final home game this weekend when my father turns the corner from the hallway the coaches use to access the locker room.

"What are you doing here?" I grunt.

A few players pass by us on their way into the locker room, and there's really nothing I want to do *less* right now than have a confrontation with Dad just outside the locker room. I've worked my ass off to earn some respect in this place, and now they'll see me as the little kid getting yelled at by his dad outside the locker room.

"Came to see why you've been avoiding me like the plague," he admits.

"How'd you get in?"

Lincoln chooses that moment to walk by, and he widens his eyes at me as if to say *good luck with him.*

I need it.

"I'm the head coach's father," he says, slugging my brother on the arm as he crosses between us to get to the locker room. "How do you think I got in?"

Lincoln grunts and disappears into the locker room.

I press my lips together. "I guess I don't have much to say to you right now."

"No? Not even about meeting your half-brothers?"

I sigh as I shake my head. I really, *really* don't want to do this here, and it's not like he's keeping his voice down. Anyone and everyone walking these hallways could hear him, and does he really want my teammates gossiping about my half-brothers? I know Lincoln wouldn't want it.

"Nope. Not even about that," I say dryly. "If you'll excuse me, I need to get to practice." I turn to walk into the locker room, but he stops me.

"Wait," he says. "What about the secret woman you knocked up? Your mom said she's nearly three months along. Who is it?" He leans in a little as if I'll whisper it to him, but before I get the chance to tell him to shove off, Coach Dixon rounds the corner.

He freezes when he sees me standing there talking to my dad, and I'm *positive* he heard what my dad just said.

He couldn't've known who my dad was talking to until he rounded the corner, but he definitely heard.

And he definitely pieced it together the moment his eyes landed on me.

"Secret woman you knocked up?" Coach Dixon asks, and the recognition turns icy as he pins me to my spot. "My office, Nash. Now." He spins on his heel to retreat back toward his office, and he fully expects me to follow him.

Fuck.

"What the fuck have you done?" I hiss at my father, who looks absolutely clueless that he just revealed his daughter's baby daddy to the one person we weren't ready to tell.

And then I take off to follow Coach and face the music.

Chapter 51: Asher Nash

This Isn't Going Well

My heart thunders in my chest as I approach his office, and the second I step through the door, he turns on me.

"Tell me I'm wrong," Coach Dixon hisses. "Tell me this isn't what I think."

I draw in a deep breath. I wish she was here. I wish we could do this together. She's going to be livid that she didn't get to be part of this conversation, but I can't lie to him. Not when he's been so goddamn good to me this season. Not when I've already been lying. I can't add another one on top of the pile when he already knows.

I close my eyes and admit the truth. "You're not wrong."

"*You?*" he demands. "*You* got my little girl pregnant?"

I press my lips together. "It's not what you think, Coach."

"Don't you fucking *Coach* me right now, Nash. I can't believe you'd betray me like this."

I shake my head. "It's not a betrayal. We met before I knew she was your daughter. Before I even knew you *had* a daughter."

"She had to have known who you were," he points out.

I don't know how to answer that without making it worse for her, but he doesn't let me get words in anyway.

"And eventually you did know, but you kept seeing her anyway."

"I tried to stop it," I say, holding up both hands. "I told her I couldn't lie to you, and I walked away."

"What the fuck did you just say to me? That you *walked away* from my pregnant daughter?"

Jesus. This isn't going well.

"No!" I say, and I tug on my hair as I try to get this situation under control. "It was before I knew, and I came crawling back to her because I'm in love with her, and then I found out she's pregnant."

He bites down on his lip as if he's trying to control his own emotions, and he runs a hand through his hair. "Get out of my office."

I stare at him. He's the one who made me walk in here, and now he's demanding I leave. I know he's angry, but I don't have anything else to lose by being honest with him.

"I'm not going anywhere."

He leans toward me menacingly. "I said *get out.*"

I shake my head and hold up both hands. "I will leave if it's what you want. I meant I'm not leaving your daughter. I'm doing everything I can to be what she needs, sir. I'm sorry this is how you found out, but I can assure you, I won't do anything to hurt her."

His brows practically lift off his face. "You won't do anything to hurt her? You just admitted you abandoned her once. You think that didn't hurt her?" He shakes his head and turns away from me. "Because of *you*, she's been lying to *me* for months. I need you to leave."

I blow out a breath. "This doesn't change who I am, Coach. It doesn't change the man you believed in."

He turns around to face me. He nods a little as he stares at me. "You're right. It proves that you were exactly who they said you were all along."

It's a clean shot to my heart, and he knows it. It's shoving the knife in and twisting it around for good measure.

It hurts more than it should, but I've gotten closer to this man than I have to my own father. I get why he feels betrayed, but maybe in time he'll understand. I *need* him to understand. I respect the hell out of him as my coach.

His voice is quiet as he says his next words. "Do the right thing, Asher. Either quit playing or leave her alone. You can't have both. Now get to practice."

I turn and leave, granting his request, somehow not surprised at all that my father is the one who fucked this whole thing up for me. He didn't even know who the woman was, and he still managed to ruin everything.

I head to the locker room, and my dad is long gone. That's a blessing, at least.

I walk in right in the middle of my brother's motivational speech about how we're about to play the last game of the season and blah blah blah.

I can't focus on anything. I'm late, and everyone is staring at me as they wonder why, and it's also clear that Coach Dixon isn't here since he usually says a few words after Lincoln does.

Coach Dixon doesn't show up until we're out on the field, which tells me he stayed in his office for one of two reasons. Either he was cooling down after learning what he just learned, or he had a phone call or two to make. Maybe both.

I need to talk to Desiree, but I can't. Not while I'm here at practice, and especially not while all eyes are on me.

Rumors travel quickly, and there had to be at least one or two players out in that hallway when Dixon yelled at me to get to his office. Everyone saw that we were both late to practice.

But nobody knows why, and I'm not close enough to anybody here for them to actually confront me about it.

Except my brother.

"We need to talk," Lincoln demands as he makes the rounds during practice.

Just fucking great. I guess the secret's about to be out now, but clearly Lincoln wants to know why his OC demanded to talk to his star tight end right before practice.

I'm dreading that conversation. I'm dreading the end of practice, and at the same time, I can't make it go by fast enough so I can get to my phone and explain to Des what's going on.

I run drills with the tight ends, doing my absolute best to remain focused, and Desiree's father walks over to Coach Bruce toward the end of our drills.

"Extra leg drills for Nash," he barks at Coach Bruce.

He knows what he's doing.

It's going to be a late night for me, and he's not even giving me the chance to give Desiree a fair warning about what's to come for her—if he hasn't already told her that he knows.

He's setting us up to fail, and there's not a goddamn thing I can do about it.

Chapter 52: Desiree Dixon

Picking Out Paintings

"What do you think about this one?" my mom asks, flashing her phone at me to show me a painting she wants to buy me for the baby's room once I figure out what house I want to buy. We're standing in her kitchen, and I tilt my head as I study the painting.

I think part of the reason why I can't find a place is because I keep thinking about what the future holds. I can't move into a house where I can't picture Asher, me, and our baby, but there are so many uncertainties right now.

It's easier to stay with my parents for now.

Truth be told, the painting she's showing me is a little gaudy. We have completely different styles, I guess, and I'm trying to figure out a diplomatic way of saying that when I see an incoming call on her phone. "Oh, Dad's calling."

Her brows push together as she looks at me with a bit of worry. "He should be at practice. Why would he be calling me?"

She scrambles to pick up the call. "Bill?"

I hear his voice as plain as day through her phone in the silence of the house.

"Are you with Desiree?" he asks.

Her eyes edge to me. "Yes. Why?"

"Ask her about Asher Nash," he says, and his voice may be a bit tinny and muffled through the wrong side of the phone speaker, but I can still hear the anger in his voice.

Oh, shit.

He knows.

How does he know?

And why on earth would Asher tell him the truth without me there?

"I need to get to practice," he says, and the anger is still there through the gruffness.

"Wait! What's going on, Bill?" my mom asks.

"Just ask her." He ends the call, and she slowly lowers the phone as I close my eyes and brace myself.

"He said to ask you about Ash—" she begins, but I shake my head a little and cut her off.

"He's the father," I say quietly.

Her jaw drops. "The…"

"Father," I finish, resting a protective hand over my stomach that's starting to feel bloated but not quite showing yet. "And I have no idea how or why dad found out, but it seems as though he did."

"Oh, Desi," she says, and she pulls me into a hug as I start to cry.

"I wanted to wait until the end of the season," I blubber. "I didn't want to distract Dad with this news, and I don't want him to be hard on Asher because of it."

"He won't be. He's fair and impartial," she assures me, and yes, while I would typically agree with that, he's also never been in a situation like this before.

I can't imagine he's going to remain that way knowing a man he trusted was the one who was sneaking around banging his daughter.

I don't say that to my mom, obviously.

"What is this with him?" she asks. "If you want to talk about it."

I wander over to the kitchen table and pull out one of the chairs as I blow out a breath and sit. "I hated keeping it from you, but I hope you can see now why I had to."

"Of course I do. You could've told me. I wouldn't have said anything to Dad," she gently scolds as she slides into the chair next to me and sets her hand over mine.

"I know, but I didn't want to put you in that position." I sigh. "I think I'm in love with him, Mom."

Her lips tip up as her eyes soften. "And Asher?"

"He's said the words to me. I was too scared to say them back. It's…well, it's a long story."

"Start at the beginning," she suggests.

And so I do.

I tell her about the charity ball and how I ended up in the seat that was supposed to be for his date, and how we didn't see each other for months after that. I leave out the hot sex, but I tell her about how he tried to stay away out of respect for my dad, but we couldn't fight against our connection. I tell her about how we got closer and closer until one day he walked away and left me devastated, but then he came back the same day I found out I was having his baby, and he vowed to be here for both of us. "And that's when he told me he loves me. We agreed we'd see each other in secret until the end of the season."

"I can see why you'd be scared, but if there's one thing I've learned in this life, it's that you shouldn't let the moment pass you by." Her voice is soft.

"What made you learn that?" I ask more out of curiosity than out of nosiness. I lean my elbows on the table despite the manners ingrained in me since birth.

She sighs softly. "It wasn't always easy with your dad. He asked for my number when I was in the stands. You know that part of the story. But he wasn't a commitment kind of guy, and I think that's why he was scared for you to be with a football player. He thinks they're all like him, but even *he* changed his life around when he found the woman he was meant to be with." She reaches over and squeezes my hand. "And I have no doubt that Asher will do the same for you. Asher came back to you all on his own. Your dad…" She shakes her head a little as she trails off. "Well, let's say he wasn't as smart back then as he is now." She winks at me. "And I take all the credit for being the one to fix that."

I laugh. "What happened?"

"Oh, he ran scared, and I had to exercise extreme patience with him. I very nearly gave up and walked away. But it all worked out in the end."

"What fixed it?"

She clears her throat. "Another man proposed to me."

My jaw drops. "Who?"

She laughs. "Jerry O'Callahan."

"Jerry O'Callahan?" I breathe as I repeat the name of the Director of Operations for Berkshire.

"My parents *loved* him. They wanted me to end up with him. He came from old money, and he was a businessman. But he didn't give me butterflies the way your dad did. I wasn't in love with him, and I very nearly accepted his proposal. But eventually your dad got off his butt and figured out he was about to lose me to another man."

"And that's how you learned not to let the moment pass you by?"

She presses her lips together and nods. "Basically, yes. Or…your dad learned it, anyway." She lifts a shoulder. "And now look where we are. Thirty years later, and it's been a pretty darn good run for us so far."

I consider that. They're ten years shy of Asher's parents' length of marriage. Where will they be in another decade?

They're still as in love now as they ever were. I can't imagine a future where they decide to part ways, and I don't think Asher would've been able to say the same a decade ago about his own parents.

But our parents' paths aren't our paths. This is our story to write, and I think my mom is right.

Even though I'm a little confused and hurt that Asher told my dad without me there, I still trust that there's some explanation as to why. And I trust that as soon as he's able to, he'll clue me in on what that is.

In the meantime, I'll look for paintings with my mom that I can hang up in my baby's bedroom.

Chapter 53: Asher Nash

A Few Hurdles

It's late when I finally leave the Complex, and I call her from my car before I back out of my space.

"Hey," she answers softly.

I don't realize how nervous I am until the words come trembling out of my mouth. "Can I come over?"

I have no idea what she knows or doesn't know, and I certainly don't want to go home and face my dad right now after he's the one who fucked me over. I don't particularly want to go to Coach Dixon's house, either, but I do need to talk to Des.

"Yes. I'll text you the address."

I breathe out a sigh of relief.

Fifteen minutes later, I'm pulling into her driveway.

She's standing at the door waiting for me, and she's all I can see.

She's perfect, and she's mine.

But there are a few hurdles we'll have to jump over if I'm going to be able to keep calling her that.

Like the hurdle pulling into the driveway behind me honking his horn.

Apparently I'm in his way.

I sigh as I back out of the driveway and park along the street, and he races past me and into his garage.

"You told him?" she hisses at me as I approach the front door. He walks in through some other entrance, and I hear him yelling her name.

"Desiree Joy!"

"I didn't intend to. He pieced it together."

"How?"

He appears behind her. "Asher Nash? You're kidding me, right?"

I spot the guilt in her eyes before she spins around to talk to him. "Well, now that we're all here, I guess it's a good as time as any to tell you that Asher's the father." Her voice is bright—too bright. Fake. She sets her hand on her stomach, and I stand beside her totally awkwardly as her parents stare at me.

Her dad knows me, obviously, but I haven't really spoken with her mom. I'm not sure we've actually formally ever met.

"Hi," I say stupidly. "I'm Asher." I reach out a hand to shake hers, and to be totally transparent, I'm glad I'm wearing a Vegas Aces sweatshirt and not a silk shirt covered in T-rexes.

"I know who you are," she says, and she pushes my hand out of the way and pulls me into a hug. "And you can call me Sue. Or Grandma, since that'll be my next title."

It feels good here in this hug. It's warm. Welcoming.

But as I pull back, I spot her father glaring at me, and the warmth evaporates right out of the air.

"What are you doing here?" he barks.

"Daddy, leave him alone," Desiree says, crossing her arms.

I reach over and squeeze her shoulder gently. "Thank you for defending me, but he's angry, and I don't blame him."

"You're goddamn right I'm angry," he hisses. "At both of you. I told you no football players, and you're doing...doing..." His eyes flash down to her stomach as he fumbles for the right words. "Doing *who knows what* with a player on my own team!"

"Bill, calm down," Sue says as Des leans into me a little.

"Asher and I need to talk, so if you'll excuse us," Desiree says, and she reaches for my hand and starts to walk toward a staircase.

"Oh, I don't think so. If you two want to talk, you're not going up to your bedroom. I can see what happened the last time you two did that." He nods toward her stomach meaningfully, and I think I might actually throw up.

"Dad!" Desiree yells at the same time her mom yells, "Bill!"

Des glances at her mom, and she purses her lips before she turns toward her dad. "Dad, I'm twenty-five years old. I'm an adult, and I know you tend to forget that and still see me as a five-year-old, but I'm not. I'm having a baby of my own, and I love you to pieces, but I will not stand here and be treated like a child."

He presses his lips together as he glares at the two of us.

"It's okay, you two," Sue says to us. "I know you need to talk, and I'm sure you'd like some privacy. Go ahead. I'll make sure Bill stays down here."

Desiree exhales roughly, mutters a quick *thanks* to her mom, and pulls me along with her. I'm not quite sure where to look because I don't really want to make eye contact with Coach Dixon right now, so I keep my eyes trained in front of me as Desiree climbs the stairs—a mistake I realize too late since it probably looks like I'm checking out her ass.

It doesn't matter. Coach already hates me, and I've already betrayed his trust. He assumes we're heading upstairs to bang when all I want to do is explain how he found out in the first place.

I follow her down a hallway and into her bedroom, and I glance around. It's her bedroom at her parents' house, so it's not really *her* room, and I wonder how much of the décor in here was her design and how much of it was her mom.

As I take stock of what's in here, it doesn't feel like Desiree. It's all white and cold, where she's warm and inviting. Her place in San Diego had more blues and browns, now that I think about it.

She settles onto her bed and leans back on her pillows, and I turn and face her.

"You wanted to talk, so talk," she says.

"Are you mad?" I ask.

She lifts a shoulder. "Do I have a reason to be?"

I sigh. "No. I was heading into the locker room for practice, and my dad was standing outside the door. I guess he'd been talking with Lincoln." I shrug. "Anyway, I told him to leave, and he asked me about the secret woman I knocked up that's three months along. Your dad walked around the corner and overheard the question, pieced two and two together, and told me to get in his office."

Her brows knit together. "The guy can't find his fucking car keys, but he pieces *that* together?" she mutters.

"Apparently so. He was understandably furious, and he yelled at me a bit, made me feel like a worthless piece of shit, and then gave me extra drills at practice to really hit that point home."

She pats the bed beside her, and I walk over and sit. She sets her hand over mine and rubs back and forth. "I'm so sorry he did that. I'll talk to him."

I shake my head. "I don't think it'll help, Des. He's not mad we kept it from him. He's mad it's *me*."

"I thought you two were getting close, though. Why would he be so angry?"

I frown as I look down at the ground. "For the very reason I feared from the get-go. He gave me a chance. He said he's new and it's a clean slate for him, that the sins of my past didn't matter. When it came to the locker room, anyway. I guess when it comes to his daughter, he's going to hold all of that against me."

"He can't hold it against you forever," she points out.

"Can't he? Or will he do whatever he can to drive me out of here so I can't be close to you?" I'm being vulnerable as I speak my greatest fears to her.

She blows out a breath as she considers that. "Then we don't let him."

"But how do we stop him?"

She doesn't have an answer for that. Instead, she sighs as she sets her hand on her stomach, and I set my hand over hers. I lean down as I pull her hand out of the way, and I push her shirt up and lean over to press a kiss to her stomach. I turn my face so my ear is up against her, and I listen for our baby in there.

It's not the first time I've realized we're having a baby, but it's the first time I've done this. "Hey, there. You in there?"

Desiree chuckles.

"I'm your dad." As the words fall from my lips, an unfamiliar heat presses behind my eyes, and this strange wave seems to pulse through my chest.

It feels like I'm finally figuring out who the fuck I am.

It feels like my entire life, I've worked my ass off to find my place. First it was in my own goddamn family as I tried so hard to be as incredible as my three older brothers, and then it was on every team I've ever been a part of as I was looked at as the youngest of the Nash brothers, and then it was here at the Aces as I tried to overcome the reputation that I made for myself before I ever even got to complete a whole season. It was through the ridiculous fashion choices I made as I tried to assert my own identity. It was in sleeping with a variety of women as I tried to fill some void that they never would've been able to fill.

They couldn't. None of them had that ability. How could they when it belongs solely to the woman beside me now?

How could it when it feels like the reason I was put on this earth was to find Desiree and have children with her?

I thought commitment wasn't for me. I thought kids weren't for me. I thought my entire life had to be football, and there was nothing else for me.

How very wrong I was.

Because this right here?

This is everything. This is where I was always meant to be, and I won't always be perfect, but I will work my ass off to be the best man I can be to Desiree and the best father I can be to our child—or maybe even our children if we're lucky enough to have more.

I think I finally found my place. The back of my throat is clogged with emotion, so I don't say those words to Desiree.

I will. Someday. Or at least, that's my plan.

First, we have to overcome the hurdle labeled with her father's name.

Chapter 54: Asher Nash

Good Score, Kiddo

Her parents must've gone up to bed because they're not downstairs when I head out. As much as I want to spend the night holding Desiree in my arms, I wouldn't feel right doing that in her father's house.

I think about inviting her home with me, but first I need to confront my own father.

She kisses me goodbye at the door, and I hate saying goodbye. We make a promise we'll see each other soon. Tomorrow night we'll stay in a hotel ahead of our final home game on Sunday, so it won't be tomorrow. Maybe Sunday, and then I have an entire week off. I plan to worship her body during that week, that's for damn sure.

Laying on a bed with her and kissing her naked stomach didn't do me any favors in that department. I'm turned on, but I force the neediness away as I head home. I'm not really in any rush to get there, and it makes me realize what I want.

I want to live with Desiree.

I want to make a home with her. I want to make a *life* with her.

Her dad gave me something to chew on earlier in his office when he said I should either quit playing or leave her alone. But maybe he was wrong.

Maybe I *can* have both.

She's here in Vegas now, and she's here because of me—in part, anyway. He doesn't know that.

Presumably, he also doesn't know that she stayed away as long as she did because of me. He doesn't *need* to know that one.

I pull into the driveway of the house I've shared with my dad for the last two and a half years. I can't believe I've been in Vegas that long, and I'm not sure what's next.

I'm not sure if the Aces will keep me or if Coach Dixon will be lobbying to get rid of me. He's a damn good coach, and he would want the best players on his team, so I doubt he'd *really* try to get rid of me. But he doesn't seem to like me very much right now, and I'm not sure what I can do to change his mind about that.

I'm also a little nervous he'll change Desiree's mind about me in the process.

She loves her father, and they're close. I asked her once what she'd do if he chose to write her off, and she didn't think it would come to that.

But I saw how he was last night when I came over. I can wish and hope all I want that Sue will be able to get him on our side, but wishes and hopes can end up being pretty damn empty compared to reality.

That's the cynic in me speaking—the side I inherited from Eddie Nash, next on the list of people to confront tonight.

He's watching his western when I walk in, and he doesn't pause the show until I'm standing in front of him.

"What did Coach want to talk to you about?" he grunts.

"Jesus, you're clueless," I mutter.

"Excuse me?" he asks, putting the recliner of his chair down but not standing. "What did you just say to me?"

"The woman I got pregnant is his daughter."

His eyes light up at that, and not because of anything less than a nefarious reason. "Oh, she's the billionaire heiress, isn't she? Good score, kid."

"Good score? *Good score?* That's what you have to say to me?"

"Sure. You'll both be set for life. Not a bad way to do it. Wish I'd thought of it, to be honest. Your Grandma and Grandpa Roberts were decently well-off, but they had four kids to split their money between, and most of that, as you know, went to the bar." He shrugs. "I tried. I failed. But look at you, doing the Lord's work."

"Are you fucking kidding me? You think I got her pregnant on purpose to take a shot at her fortune?" I ask.

"Well...yeah. Didn't you?"

I stare at him, totally dumbfounded that he would *ever* think that of me.

He thinks I'm like him...and that tells me he doesn't know a damn thing about me.

I walk out of the room totally disgusted that he'd make that insinuation, and when I get to my bedroom, I start to pack in earnest.

I haven't asked her yet.

I don't know where we'll go.

But I know I can't stay here any longer.

My phone starts to ring, and I glance at the clock. It's after ten, and my first thought is, *what if something's wrong with the baby?*

It's just Lincoln calling, so that fear is immediately alleviated as another one steps into its place.

"What's going on, Brochacho?" I answer brightly.

"Don't Brochacho me," he hisses. "I told you we needed to talk."

"Coach Dixon gave me extra leg drills, and you weren't in your office when I stopped by. What can I do for you?" My tone is light.

His is not.

"Desiree Dixon?" he demands.

I exhale a long, heavy breath. "You know?"

"Yes, I know. Don't you know the unwritten rule about staying away from any family members of coaches or teammates?" he demands.

"Teammates? No, I was actually unaware of that one. Guess I should call Hodges back in Indy and apologize for putting it in his sister."

"Jesus, Asher," he mutters. "When the fuck were you planning on growing up? Because this is out of control."

"Actually, my eldest brother, I'm not out of control. For once in my life, I think I might actually be *in* control."

"By impregnating your coach's daughter?" he demands.

"Look, it's not like that, okay? I love her. I want to spend my life with her."

Silence greets me on the other side, and I let it play out. I wait for him to make the next move.

Predictably, he does. "Dixon was pissed, Asher. How are you going to handle that?"

"As a professional," I say. "My personal life has nothing to do with the kind of player I am. I'll remain focused and prioritize the way every guy chained up by a woman and kids on every team does."

He's quiet a beat as he considers that. "Well, holy shit. First you handled the twins, and now this? I think…yep, I think my little brother might actually be growing up." He sniffles in jest, and I can't help a small laugh.

"Thank you for finally acknowledging it. I mean, you *are* pushing forty over there."

"Fuck off with that nonsense. You're only as old as you feel."

"Oh yeah?" I ask. "How old do you feel?"

"Fifty," he deadpans.

I laugh. "Well, old man, I'll be looking to you for advice with how to do this whole dad thing."

"You've already got the cheesy shirts down, but dad gear really leans more toward Hawaiian than toward random animals and colorful patterns."

"I'll keep that in mind," I say dryly. "Thanks for the first tip."

"I've got another one for you," he says, and I wait for it. "The first year is all about the mom, and it takes a minute to find your footing. But once you do, Asher, I really believe you're going to be an incredible dad."

"Thanks, Linc."

"Now get some rest and study some tape because Dixon won't be going light on you tomorrow," he says.

"Yeah, I had a feeling," I admit.

We hang up, and then I grab my tablet to study some film like a good, focused player. When I finish that, I start a search for new houses.

Ones with lots of bedrooms and plenty of space to grow.

There might be hurdles in our way, but knowing a life with Desiree is on the other side is enough motivation for me to start leaping over them now so I can leave them in the rearview with our future fully ahead of us.

Chapter 55: Desiree Dixon

Exactly How Drunk is He?

The Vegas Aces win their last home game, and I notice that Asher doesn't get as much playing time as usual. It's common for teams to rest their starters a bit during games that really don't affect the outcome of the season, but in the back of my mind, I wonder whether my dad is playing Austin Graham over Asher out of anger.

Logically. I know that's not why, but it still eats at me.

After the game, I don't hang around the family waiting area for my dad *or* for Asher. I don't want to make things weird when players need to focus on what comes next, and that's the playoff game in two weeks—not on what may or may not be going on between a player, a coach, and the coach's daughter.

Instead, my mom and I wait in the car for my dad. Asher calls me as I'm on my way home with my parents.

"Are you coming out tonight?" he asks.

Oh…I guess before players focus, they celebrate.

I'm trying to be discreet in the backseat as my dad navigates toward home, but it's hard to be quiet when his background is a bar blaring with sound.

"I wasn't planning on it," I admit.

"What?"

"No!" I yell.

My mom turns around, startled at my yelling, and I yell into the phone, "I'll text you!" I hang up and draft the message.

Me: *I wasn't planning to go out. I'm heading home.*

Asher: *Why?*

Me: *I figured we don't need the rumor mill working overtime.*

I watch as he drafts a slightly longer message, and when it comes through, I can't help but think he's making a solid point.

Asher: *We don't, but I want to celebrate with you. Do we really have anything to hide now that your parents know?*

Me: *I guess I can be your designated driver since I can't drink. Give me a half hour. Are you at the Gridiron?*

Asher: *I am. See you then.*

Me: *Can't wait to make our debut.*

I'm nervous as we pull into the driveway, and I bid my parents goodnight and mention that I might go out with some friends. I head up to my room to freshen up. I'm wearing a Vegas Aces tee paired with a sequined skirt, and while my outfit isn't really what I'd typically wear to a bar, it's comfortable with my changing body.

My heart pounds as I navigate over toward the Gridiron, not sure what I'm walking into yet knowing that Asher will be there with me every step of the way. Except, you know, the part where I have to walk in by myself and hunt him down in the crowd.

With that in mind, I shoot him a text.

Me: *I'm here.*

He's waiting in front of the bar for me as I walk up, and relief filters through me. He grabs me into his arms and leans his forehead to mine, and I smell whiskey on his breath. A thrill races through me as it reminds me of the night we met.

"You ready for this?" he asks.

"Nope," I admit, and he chuckles then lowers his lips to mine.

A voice interrupts our kiss. "Whoa! Nash and the OC's daughter?"

We jump apart as if we've been caught, which we have…but we're not hiding anymore.

This is weird.

We both turn to face Travis Woods as he walks out with his arm around Victoria, whose eyes are wide.

"Ooh, the coach's daughter in a secret romance with the star tight end. I swear we just got a new release like this in the store," Victoria says. "We should totally read it for our first book club!"

Asher clears his throat as I blush wildly.

"It's not a secret...anymore." He glances at me, and I think we're at the point where I can read his silent question. I nod at him, and he tosses his arm around me. "We're having a baby."

Oh, shit. My nod was to encourage him to tell them about us. I didn't realize he was going to tell them, well, everything. Maybe we're not at the reading each other's silent questions stage quite yet, but word is out now.

"Oh my God!" Victoria squeals. "Congratulations!" She rushes toward me for a hug, and while we've hung out a few times, I didn't realize we were that close.

But I guess we are.

I was quickly accepted into this group as the coach's daughter, and then as a contracted employee with the charities division. But it looks like my role here is about to shift to a WAG—which means wives and girlfriends of players—and Victoria is the first to welcome me into that inner circle.

Victoria and I squeal for a bit, and she offers me a shoulder to cry on for everything pregnancy-related—something I could really use from a friend since none of my close friends have been through it yet.

I thought I was too different from a lot of these women when I first met them to become friends with them. I think there's some things that might bond us together yet.

"Congrats, you two. Come on, Hartley," Travis says as he grabs his wife's ass.

She rolls her eyes playfully, and they say a hurried goodbye as they take off.

I move to start heading inside, but Asher stops me with his hand on my arm. "Where do you think you're going?"

"Inside?" I say as more of a question than an answer.

"I want to take you somewhere. Or, rather, I guess I want you to take me somewhere since you drove."

"Where are you taking me?" I ask.

"You'll see." He shoots me a sly look, and while I've never really been one for surprises, I have to admit, he's got me curious.

He tells me where to turn, navigating me to whatever destination he has in mind through the dark streets of Vegas at night. We pull into a neighborhood, and he directs me to pull into a driveway.

The house is dark, so it's not like he's taking me here for some party or something. "Where are we?" I ask. "Is this some secret sex club?"

He laughs. "No." He gets out of the car and starts walking toward the front door, where he types in a code and opens the door.

"Asher, what the hell are you doing? Are we allowed to be in here?" There's a slight hint of panic in my voice. Why is he taking me to some deserted house at night?

"It's fine," he says gently, and he walks inside and holds his hand out to me.

I wonder exactly how drunk he is as he walks into someone else's house. He flips on some lights, and I find that the house is totally empty. No furniture in the rooms, no pictures on the walls. It looks like a brand-new home that no one's ever lived in.

He holds up both hands to indicate the house around us. "Well, what do you think?"

I twist my lips and shrug. "I think maybe you've lost your mind or had too much whiskey."

"Neither of those." He walks further into the house as he waits for me to figure out what the hell he's doing. "Follow me." He starts on a path to another room. I find myself in the kitchen that looks like it stepped right out of a gourmet magazine. He flips on the outdoor lights, and we peek into a beautiful desert oasis complete with a pool and plenty of shade structures around a built-in barbecue.

We look into the family room and a guest bedroom on the first floor along with two office spaces before he starts climbing the stairs.

"Asher, what are we doing here?"

"You'll see," he says.

We walk into a primary suite that's three times the size of my rather luxurious bedroom back in San Diego, and I think I'm starting to figure out what we're doing here, but I don't want to make any assumptions.

He leads me through the bedroom and out onto a balcony. The view is absolutely breathtaking as I see the Complex and the entirety of the Vegas Strip from here. It's distant enough that we can't hear the sounds but close enough that we can see the lights that indicate the excitement and action in the distance.

I set my hands on the railing as I look out over the view, and I feel him as he moves in behind me. He sets his hands on the railing on either side of mine, and his lips move to my neck. Thrill races down my spine at his proximity, and I feel his hard cock as he settles in behind me.

His lips move to my ear. "Hell of a view, isn't it?"

"It's lovely, but you still haven't told me why we're here."

His hands move from the railing, and he wraps his arms around me, his hands moving to my stomach. "When I first walked into this house, I thought it was way too big. It is. It's ridiculous. But I kept thinking about this place. It's so close to the Complex. It's close to your parents. It's close to the airport. It's big enough to grow. It has a pool where I can watch you skinny dip, and it's got this balcony where I can bend you over the railing and fuck you until you can't see straight."

His words pulse a needy ache squarely between my legs. I push my hips back toward him, and he groans a little as he thrusts back toward me.

"I never knew what I wanted out of my future. I wasn't sure if I should try to be like my brothers, or if I should just focus on football, or if I should keep being wild, adventurous Asher. And then I met you, and it was like my entire existence clicked into place. I fell for you hard and fast, and every second of that time pushed me closer and closer to knowing what I want. And now that we're having a baby together, it feels like the future I was never sure about is crystal clear."

He spins me around, and his lips move to mine for a soft kiss. "I love you, Des, and I want you to move in here with me. I want to raise our baby together, and I want to build our future together. No more secrets. No more lies. No more sneaking around. Just you and me and this baby, and whatever other babies we're blessed enough to have. I don't want to be the wild, eccentric one anymore. I want to be the best husband, the best dad, the best *version* of myself I can be, and the only way I can do that is with you by my side. Will you move in here with me?"

Tears pinch behind my eyes at his words. I feel the genuine, heartfelt emotions behind his words, and it's suddenly everything I want, too. It feels like he's committed to making sure this will work between us, and suddenly that fear that he's going to run again is wiped away.

And that's why I'm finally ready to say the words I've felt for a very long time. "I love you, Asher, and nothing would make me happier than to start building our life together right here."

"Good. Because I put in an offer." His lips collide with mine, and I wonder how many times we'll stand out on this balcony kissing like this. I wonder how many times in our future we'll talk out here, or fight out here, or laugh out here.

I wonder how many times we'll have sex out here.

As his fingertips inch down and grasp the hem of my skirt, I can't help but think this will count as the first time.

He slowly pulls my skirt up, and it feels so much like our first night together at that hotel room after the charity ball. Those feelings of lust and attraction are still there as strong as ever, but now we have emotions and feelings behind them to back them up. There's a future ahead of us that we're galloping toward together, and it's so, so beautiful.

He breaks our kiss and spins me back around, and he slips my panties to the side and pushes a finger into me. I tighten my grip on the railing as I grind my hips over his hand and at the same time against his cock pressing into my backside.

He moans quietly next to my ear as his lips drop to my shoulder. "Fuck, that's a wet pussy," he groans softly, and I grind down harder onto his hand.

"Fuck me, Asher," I moan, and he fingers me another few seconds before he pulls his fingers out. He reaches up for the top of my underwear and drags them down my legs, and as I step out of them, I hear the hiss of his zipper.

A moment later, I feel the cool breeze of night on my ass as he lifts my skirt, and I bend slightly over the railing to give him access. I feel him as he moves in behind me, and when he thrusts into me, I see literal stars as I look out over the Strip.

"Oh, fuck, Des," he mutters as he starts to move. "This sweet pussy was made for me."

I couldn't agree more.

He slows down as if he wants to prolong the moment, but I need friction.

"Faster," I cry out, my voice begging, and he gives me what I want like he always does.

I push back against him, thrust for thrust, and it's pure heaven as he fucks me on what will be our balcony soon enough.

He reaches around me to thumb my clit, and I'm gripping the railing so tightly my knuckles must be white. It feels so good—too good—but I'm not ready for it to be over. Not yet.

"Tell me how much you love it when I fuck you," he hisses near my ear, and I nearly pass out from how hot he sounds.

"I love it," I pant. "I love it so much. I love *you* so much."

My words seem to trip him into his own release. "Fuck!" he groans as he pushes in as hard and fast as he can, which drives me straight into my climax.

He continues to rub my clit as we come together in the peace of night here on the balcony of our new house, and once our bodies both start to come down from the thrill and transition into the warmth of the afterglow, he presses his lips to the curve between my neck and my shoulder.

He slips out of me and pulls my skirt back into place, and I turn around and reach for his neck to pull his lips down to mine as the future feels like it's just within our grasp.

Chapter 56: Asher Nash

My Past Mistakes Are Continuing to Haunt Me

Somehow I blink, and the bye week ahead of the playoffs is at an end. We closed on the house, but we haven't officially moved in yet. Desiree agreed to start ordering furniture and filling the place with everything we'll need, but it'll just be a little easier to move in once the season is officially over.

For now, I have practices to attend and film to study to make sure I'm ready for every opponent we'll face in the coming weeks.

Desiree is busy, too. Between furnishing our home and meeting with different utility providers, finding a date and planning our 5K along with the Wild Aces Charity Ball, she has plenty to keep her busy. She also mentioned something about book club, and she has started going to Victoria's bookstore every Wednesday. She's settling in and making a life here, and she's creating her own identity separate from me even though it's tied up with me.

And I think that's part of what creates a successful foundation. We each have our own things, our own passions and our own interests, but we're putting each other as the top priority.

We plow over the Ravens in the divisional championship, giving us a week to prepare for the conference championship next weekend against the Bills.

If we come out victorious in that matchup, we'll have a week off before we head to the big game—the one with all the marbles.

It's the game I've never gotten to play, the one we all strive for every season.

My focus is exactly where it needs to be as I spend late nights and early mornings in the locker room rather than going home to face my dad and all the weird shit we're going through as a family.

I hang out in our meeting rooms to watch projections of game footage on the big screens. Sometimes teammates join me, which just offers another perspective as we study together, take notes, and know what to watch for in the coming game.

I mostly communicate with Des via text message over the next week. She ducks out to San Diego to visit her friends, but she keeps me updated on the planning progress of the first 5K event for my new foundation, which is coming along nicely.

I give my agent a call on Thursday morning before practice.

"Asher Nash. Good to hear from you, man. You all set for the Bills?" Jake answers. He's been with me for many years, and he also represents my brother, Spencer.

"As prepared as I can be," I admit.

"What can I do for you? Must be important if you're calling me this week."

"It is." I draw in a deep breath and let it out slowly. "Word will get out soon enough anyway, but I'm going to be a dad."

"Holy shit, man. Congratulations."

"With that comes more responsibility, and with this being the last year of my contract, I'm worried. I haven't heard any talk about next season, and in the meantime, I want as many sponsorship opportunities as you can find for me."

"I get that, man. You know it's been a tough road since the scandal," he says apologetically. "But if you can get someone other than your brother on the coaching staff to speak on your behalf, I think you'd have a better chance at drumming up some opportunities. Maybe the OC?"

I clench my jaw. "Yeah, probably not the OC."

"Why not?" he asks.

"The woman I got pregnant is his daughter."

"Oh, Jesus, Asher," he mutters. "What the fuck were you thinking?" Before I can answer, he says, "Doesn't matter. Damage is done. Have you spoken with your publicist?"

"No. I figured I'd check in with you first." To be honest, I wasn't planning to call her yet. She and Desiree have become friendly, and I don't know what sort of wrench this whole secret might throw into their friendship.

"Have her call me after you two talk, and we'll get a plan together for you," Jake says.

"Thanks, man." I really hadn't considered the potential consequences of knocking up a coach's daughter immediately coming off a suspension and rebuilding my reputation in terms of how it could affect opportunities off the field. I only thought about how it would affect me *on* the field.

Now I'm concerned my plan for packing away extra finances might not work out the way I was hoping.

And it's not just that.

Another insecurity plows straight into me.

If I can't handle the finances, how am I going to handle being a father? A partner? Maybe even a husband?

It feels like my past mistakes are continuing to haunt me as they put pressure on the present. I might not be able to get the types of big-money deals that would provide a secure future for my family because I was an idiot nearly two years ago.

Truth be told, I'm getting anxious. I have some money in the bank, but I haven't been smart about it. I haven't invested or saved much, and I lost a lot when I was suspended—including all my sponsorships, which is where a lot of players make big money.

And I just took what I did have sitting in the bank and sunk it into the house.

I don't have any sort of savings for my kid's future, and I don't plan to rely on someone else's family money to pay the way. That's not me.

It is, however, my father.

As I pass through the kitchen to grab breakfast before I head to the Complex, my luck has run out. My dad sits at the kitchen table with his bowl of cereal, and he drops the spoon on the table with a clatter when he sees me.

"There he is," he says. "The baby daddy of the billionaire."

I close my eyes and draw in a breath as I wait for patience. "You really going to start in on me on a day like today when I'm trying to prepare for the Bills?"

He holds both hands up innocently. "Sorry, sorry. It must be nice to know you don't have to worry about those things."

"Are you fucking kidding me? I just got off the phone with my agent to figure out how to get more sponsorships, but nobody wants me because my dad fucked me over two years ago."

"Oh, we're back on that train?" he asks, and he rolls his eyes.

"You're goddamn right we are," I hiss. "We never got off it. Look, if I were more like you, I'd be happy to breeze through life and let her handle the finances. But I'm nothing like you, and I thank God for that every day." I turn to let those be my parting words, but he jabs right back.

"You're a hell of a lot more like me than you care to admit. You wouldn't've knocked up the billionaire if you weren't."

I turn around, my jaw clenched. "Her money has nothing to do with my feelings for her."

"No? Kind of strange that you never found *love* until you met her." He says *love* with a heavy dose of sarcasm.

"I'm not going to stand here and defend myself to someone who wouldn't know love if it fucked him in the mouth." I leave *that* as my parting shot as I walk to the garage.

I call Des on my way to the Complex, and she picks up right away.

"Hey, stranger! How are things at the Complex?" Her voice is bright, and I can tell even over the phone that she's having a good time with her friends.

"I'm on my way there now. To be honest, your dad is giving me hell physically, and my dad is handling the emotional side."

"Oh, Asher," she says, and the sympathy in her tone nearly breaks me. I wish she was here. I wish we were together. I don't want to wait potentially three more weeks to move in with her even though I don't want the season to end prematurely. "I'm so sorry. What can I do?"

"Nothing," I mutter. I don't want to lay all this on her and bring her down, so I fake my way through it. "It's just nice to hear your voice."

"Yours, too," she says.

"I have a question for you."

"Hm?" she hums.

"I spoke with my agent this morning, and he thinks I need to tell my publicist about, uh…about us."

"Your publicist? Isn't that Ellie?" she asks.

"It is. And that's why I wanted to run it by you first." I turn into the parking lot at the Complex and pull into my usual spot, and I sit idly as we talk.

"Oh. That's really thoughtful of you. I appreciate that. Um…I guess people are going to start finding out, so that's okay."

"She won't tell anyone. I just wanted to make sure you were prepared for me to tell her." I watch as a black BMW pulls into the parking lot, and her dad steps out of the car. I sink down a little into my seat, not prepared to face him just yet.

He doesn't even look in my direction.

"Oh, that reminds me. I actually need to call her today to talk about the 5K, so I'll tell her. And I'll tell her to get in touch with you, too."

"You sure?" I ask, though, to be honest, it feels like a weight off me.

"Positive. Go get 'em at practice, cowboy."

"You only ever call me that when I'm about to be inside you." My voice is a little raspy, but she can't just lay a line like that on me and expect me not to have an instant erection.

She laughs. "Well, I'm coming home tomorrow, so there's always that possibility. Bye."

I cut the call and stare at my phone, drawing in a fortifying breath before I get out of the car to face the music at practice today.

Chapter 57: Desiree Dixon

Someone I Want You to Meet

"Come on, come on, come on," I mutter under my breath as I watch Nick Dawson as he takes a step, plants his foot, and swings his leg to kick the ball through the uprights. My folded hands are under my chin as I say a silent prayer for it to go where it's supposed to go.

It goes wide to the right.

The Aces lose the conference championship to the Bills at home.

Poor Nick Dawson. I can't imagine the weight he's feeling right now even though it's a team effort. It's not his fault, but he'll feel like it is.

I feel horrible for the entire team. They played their hardest, but in the end, they came up short. They couldn't seem to find a rhythm, even here at home—even when it seemed so damn easy all season.

It's the fucking conference championship game that killed their season last year, too. Two years in a row, they got to the game before the big one, and now...

The season is over.

I watch as the Bills players rush out onto the field in celebration. I glance up at the rafters where the black and red confetti was waiting to fall.

Instead, it'll be saved for next year, I guess. I'm not really sure what they do with confetti when the home team loses, but they're not releasing it onto the field for the visitors.

"Oh, no," my mom says beside me, and it's almost like a hushed silence falls over the crowd.

I look through the players on the sidelines for eighty-five, and when I spot him, he's facing me.

He takes off his helmet, and though he looks disappointed, his eyes find mine.

Something passes between us in that moment, and it's not disappointment. It's not even the heat I usually feel when he looks over at me.

It's excitement.

For as much as neither of us wanted to see the season end like this, we still get to take a step in the next direction.

This offseason will hold a lot of weight for us. Before next season officially begins, we'll be parents. We'll be moving into a house together. The future we've talked about and fretted over and prepared for will be in our hands.

I'm wearing a jersey with his last name and number on it, and his eyes flick down to my chest in approval—of my tits or of what my shirt says, I'm not sure. Probably both, knowing him.

My mom and I head over to the family area after the game. It's somber down here tonight as we wait for our players and coaches to exit the locker room. Nobody's talking, and there isn't the usual buzz as we all think about the men we love in that locker room. They'll be disappointed in the way their season came to an end, even though there's no shame in being one of the top four teams in the entire league.

They never see it that way. I've been around the game long enough to know that much.

The first of the players emerge, and they leave quietly with their families. It feels like a funeral back here, to be honest, and my hormones can't take it.

I let out a deep sigh, and some more players exit.

Ellie comes over and gives me a somber hug with a little bit of enthusiasm as she quietly congratulates me on the news in person for the first time since I told her.

It's nearly an hour after the game by the time Asher walks out before my dad does, and he looks around the room and spots me.

His lips tip up in a smile as he turns to the older woman running toward him for a hug. After he hugs her, he takes her arm and escorts her across the room.

"There's someone I want you to meet," he says quietly to me. "Mom, this is Desiree. Des, my mom."

"It's lovely to meet you, Mrs.—" I begin as I stick my hand out to shake hers.

She shakes her head instead and walks straight past my hand to pull me into a warm hug. "Call me Missy. And it's wonderful to finally meet the woman who my boy can't stop smiling about."

I catch Asher's eye over his mom's shoulder, and he mouths *sorry* to me. I grin.

Missy introduces herself to my mom, and I walk into Asher's open arms.

"I'm sorry about the game," I say softly.

I feel his lips on the top of my head. "Me too." He leans down closer to my ear and says quietly, just for me, "But to be honest with you, I've been ready for what comes next for months now."

My smile widens into a grin as I back up. "Me too."

He leans down to drop his lips to mine, and I'm positive his teammates are watching. I'm certain gossip will run rampant around the locker room tomorrow during exit interviews.

But I can't find it in me to really care anymore.

I hear a throat clear, and I break apart from Asher with a healthy dose of guilt. The man doing the throat clearing certainly cares.

His brows are raised and his lips are pursed, and I'd swear if I didn't know better that he sucked on a lemon before he left the locker room.

"Oh, Bill, lighten up," my mom says, elbowing him. She hugs him and murmurs something to him—surely something about how she's sorry about the loss or something along those lines.

I hate the tension between the two most important men in my life. I'm not quite sure what to do about it. I've gone easy on my dad because he was focused on the playoffs, and I'll give him another night or two since they just lost.

But the reality is that I'm moving out of his house and into one with Asher. The reality is that I'm having Asher's baby.

Bill Dixon is my dad, and he always will be. If he chooses to write himself out of my story because he doesn't like that we kept our relationship from him, that's on him.

I can't pretend any longer that I'm not head over heels for the man whose arm is slung over my shoulder.

An older man with many similarities to Asher saunters over to us next. We haven't had the pleasure, but from the slick way he punches Asher's arm to the slightly sleazy smirk on his face, I know exactly who he is.

I get the feeling if he wanted me to meet his mom, he *doesn't* want me to meet his dad.

Asher clears his throat. "This is my dad, Eddie."

"Hi," I say with a small wave. "I'm Desiree."

"I know exactly who you are," he says. "And I'd love to take you two kids to dinner one night." He turns to Asher. "Tough loss, kid. I'll see you back at home."

Asher raises his brows and nods, essentially brushing his dad off. What the hell is with our dads? His is a sleazeball, and mine's being all overly protective and completely out of line.

This isn't the time to address any of it, so I simply offer him a smile. "Dinner sounds nice."

"Great. Tomorrow night." He walks away before I can protest, and knowing what I know about his dad, I have a feeling he's someone I need to watch out for.

"You ready?" Asher asks.

I glance up at him with a question in my eyes.

"Some of the guys are going out," he clarifies. "Do you want to come?"

I look at my dad, who looks like he's about ready to take my mom and me home as usual, and in the split second I have to make a decision, I realize my dad has my mom. Asher needs me more than he does.

"I'd love to," I say to Asher, and then I turn to my parents. "I'll probably be late."

My dad looks angry, but he doesn't say a word. I chalk it up as a win. It's one of the first instances where I get the chance to assert my independence, and since I'm going to be a mom in about a little over six months, it's about damn time I stop letting him call the shots.

We head to the Gridiron for an hour or so before Asher asks me if I'm ready to go.

"Go where?" I ask.

"Home," he says, his eyes twinkling.

I narrow my eyes at him. "Where?" I repeat.

"Our home."

My lips tip up into a smile. "I'd love to."

On the way *home*, a word that puts warmth into my chest every time I merely think about the house Asher bought for us, we chat about what we have going on in the coming weeks.

"What do you usually do in the offseason?" I ask.

He chuckles as he glances out the window of the backseat we're sitting in together. "Usually I do whatever the hell I want. Last year, I went to Australia for a month. The year before, I took a trip to Costa Rica. Sometimes I travel, sometimes I spend time hiking or biking or finding some adventure. But this offseason, I have Ellie filling up my calendar with appearances."

"How are the sponsorships coming along?" I ask.

He lifts a shoulder. "Not great. I have a couple of offers, but nothing worth the effort. But appearances? Every nightclub in Vegas is thrilled to invite Asher Nash to party for a few hours. My social calendar is full."

"Do you like doing them?" I ask, wrinkling my nose at the thought of him out partying every night of the week.

"Not really." He lifts a shoulder. "It's an hour or two of fake smiles for photos and pretending like I'm having a good time with people I don't know."

"Then why are you doing them?"

He glances at me, and it's hard to read his eyes in the dark backseat of an Uber. "Because I have a baby on the way, and it's extra cash in the bank."

My chest tightens at his words. There's something so sweet about the sentiment that heat pinches behind my eyes.

"You don't have to do that. We'll be fine."

He leans over toward me and presses his lips to my cheek. "Yes, I do."

The sentiment feels so honest and sweet. So perfect, just like everything seems to feel when it's just the two of us.

I just wish my dad could see it, too.

Chapter 58: Desiree Dixon

Good Thing He's Got You

I wake before he does in our new bed in our new home together. I'm snuggled into his side, and his arm is tossed around my waist.

I can't wait to wake up every morning exactly like this…especially if we get to have the kind of night that knocks us both out the way last night did after we got here and had sex in our new bed for the first time.

None of my stuff is here, so I can't take a shower, brush my teeth, apply makeup, or change my clothes, but soon enough, I'll be able to do all those things. The thought sends a thrill of excitement through me.

It's crazy how quickly priorities can change. I went from wanting to find a friend with benefits in Vegas to moving in with a football player whose baby I'm having.

I snuggle more closely into him as he sleeps quietly beside me, and I listen to his breathing as I watch the rise and fall of his chest. It's as I lay here, still in the quiet of morning, that I feel something in my stomach. It's a flutter—barely a whisper—but it's something, and it fills my heart in a way I wasn't expecting.

I've been sick, and I've been tired and moody and achy. But this is the first time I've felt movement in there. I may have seen the baby on the screen at my ultrasound appointment, but this is different. It's a signal to me that there really is a baby, and I move my hand down protectively over my stomach to let her know I'm right here.

I don't feel that same movement with my hand. Just inside. But soon enough, she'll be kicking, and I'll wake Asher to press his hand there to feel it, too. And he'll look at me and smile warmly, his eyes crinkling at the corners with the pure joy that we're both feeling these days.

I can't wait for those sweet little moments with him.

This wasn't something I was ever sure I wanted, but now that I'm on the path toward it, it's something I don't think I could ever live without.

Eventually he wakes, and he leans over and presses a kiss to the top of my head. "Morning," he grunts.

"Good morning. I need to go home and shower, but do you want to go out for breakfast?" I ask.

"I would love nothing more. Except, you know, not having to leave here and just having breakfast downstairs."

I chuckle. "Okay, then let's order in."

He grabs his phone and places an order, and we lay together in bed while we wait for it to arrive. We eat at the brand-new kitchen table that was just delivered a couple days ago. We agree to move in over the next few days, but no matter what items we have or don't have here, we agree we'll sleep together here going forward.

Asher has to get to the Complex for his exit interview this morning, and I'm curious what will go on in that interview. I know my dad will be there, and I wish Asher some extra luck before we part ways.

And then I wait nervously to hear from him. I'm nervous about dinner with his dad, nervous about moving, nervous about the baby…nervous about life in general right now, I guess, so I dig into work.

I pack my essentials into a suitcase and haul it down to my car, and then I pack a few boxes worth of clothes. My mom is out at a spa day, and I'm careful not to lift anything that might be heavy.

After all that, I check on the auction items for the charity ball, and I make some final arrangements for Asher's 5K. We've chosen a date in mid-April, so I have three months to finalize plans and another two months before the charity ball.

I think I'm in good shape, and I realize it's nearly time for dinner by the time I get a text from Asher.

Asher: *Can I pick you up in an hour for dinner?*

I check the clock and realize I've worked most of the day away. My stomach seems to awaken at the thought, too, with a loud growl.

Me: *Yes, I'll be ready.*

I change clothes and brace myself for dinner with Eddie Nash.

On the way there, Asher says, "Ellie booked me an appearance at a nightclub tonight if you want to come."

I have a feeling dinner is going to take a lot out of me, and my feet feel swollen and tired after standing and packing for a few hours this afternoon. "Let's see how I feel after dinner," I say. I don't want him to have to go alone, especially if he doesn't like doing them, but I also have to put my own health and that of the baby first.

We get to the restaurant, some steakhouse Eddie chose, and he's already sitting at a table when we arrive. The hostess brings us to his table, where he's enjoying a glass of what appears to be whiskey.

He holds it up as Asher slides out the chair across from his father for me and takes one in between us.

Asher immediately stares down at the menu, and his father is eyeing me.

I glance through the menu and decide on a chicken dish, and I set it down and glance up at Eddie.

"So how did you meet my son?" he asks.

"We met at the charity ball," Asher says absently.

His brows shoot up. "You've known her since last June?"

I nod. "And now I'm planning this year's event. Funny how it comes full circle." I offer a tight smile.

"You're planning it?" he asks.

I nod. "I'm an event planner, and the Aces have contracted me for their charity event. I'm also working on the first annual 5K for Asher's new charity."

"What's this?" Eddie asks.

"It's the Make a DIFFerence with Asher Nash Foundation," Asher says. "We're hosting a charity run to promote the fight against drug abuse, specifically in adolescents." He clears his throat. "I'm doing it for Fitz."

Eddie seems to soften a bit at that. "That's great, Asher. I'm proud of you."

Asher sits up a bit at his words, and I get the sense he doesn't say that too often. But from Asher's account, Eddie was the one who picked Asher up after he lost his friend.

"Thanks," he mumbles.

"How was your exit interview?" Eddie asks. "Any word on next year?"

Asher shrugs. "It was fine."

"You don't want to talk about it?" Eddie presses.

Asher glances at me and twists his lips. "We went over this year's accomplishments on the field and off. We talked about the 5K."

"Did they mention a contract?" he asks.

Asher shakes his head. "Not yet."

"You'll hear something before free agency. Linc won't make you go through that," he says.

Asher nods, and he glances at his watch as he reads a text that just came through. "Can you excuse me a minute?" He stands and leaves me alone with his dad, and my eyes edge over to him as that nervousness from earlier is back in full force.

"Good thing he's got you," Eddie says, jamming his thumb in my direction as he nods toward his son's retreating figure. He shakes his head a little.

"Me?" I ask.

"Sure. He doesn't have to worry about that big money contract."

I clear my throat uncomfortably. "He's never...I mean, we haven't really talked finances."

"You should. You're having his baby," he points out, and I want to believe he's just trying to be sensible, but my gut tells me he's insinuating something far more sinister. "But it's always easier for the *haves* not to be concerned about it. I've been both—a *have* and a *have not*—and I remember the good old days well. It's what I want for my sons, anyway."

I snag my top lip between my teeth as a means not to cry. I hate that he's making it seem like the only reason Asher is with me is for my money.

He didn't know who I was when we got together, but I also don't know how to handle myself around his father.

I clear my throat and take a sip of water to keep myself busy. Where the hell did Asher run off to? Why did he think leaving me alone with his father was a solid plan?

I'm hurt by his dad's words, but I refuse to let him see that. Instead, I rush to Asher's defense. "He's a hard worker who would never rely on someone else's means."

"Then I fear I didn't teach him a damn thing," he mutters.

The server comes by with a basket of bread, and I set my focus on that while I wait for Asher's return. But I feel awkward through the rest of the meal. My answers are short and stilted, and Asher picks up the check at the end even though his father invited us to this meal.

The man is something else, that's for sure.

"I hate to eat and run, but I have an appearance to get to," Asher says. "Are you coming with me?"

"I think I'll just head home," I say quietly. He gives me a long look to ensure I'm okay, but I'm not.

I sort of wish he'd duck out on his appearance. I know that's silly. He made a commitment, and he needs to follow through on it.

But it marks the first time I feel like he's prioritizing something else over me. I know he will when it comes to football, and I know that's what my dad *didn't* want for me.

He had his exit interview today, and we haven't even talked about it. We haven't talked about the possibility of him moving into free agency, where he could be picked up by any team in the league. We haven't talked about how many more years he wants to play before he retires.

We haven't talked about an awful lot of important stuff, yet I'm having his baby. These are things I need to know, but they're things I won't get the answers to tonight since he's off to make a few extra bucks to prove his dad wrong.

Chapter 59: Asher Nash

Let's Be Late

I feel like I've been out every night this week…because I have.

I'm exhausted. It's late nights at clubs and bars and early mornings meeting with my teammates to continue offseason workouts at a gym near the Complex. I'm trying to prove that the team needs me for my leadership skills by showing up even when I don't have to.

That's what Coach Dixon told me to do, right?

Except by showing up for them, I feel like I'm failing Desiree.

I'm being pulled in two opposite directions, and the worst part is that either way, I potentially upset her father, my coach. If I'm not there for my teammates, I'm not a leader. If I'm not there for his daughter, I'm a disappointment.

I can't win.

Speaking of not winning, it's only been a week since the offseason officially started for me, and I'm being pulled so hard in those two directions that I already feel like I could snap.

It doesn't get better in the following weeks.

In early April, we attend the twenty-week appointment where we decide we want to be surprised when the baby comes. It doesn't matter if it's a boy or a girl, though Des is convinced it's a girl. All that matters is that the baby is healthy, and so far, he or she is growing right on track.

Lincoln fights to keep me with the Aces despite the OC's protests, and I'm granted a two-year extension worth twenty-eight million before the March deadline. I gladly sign on the dotted line, feeling a load of relief when it comes to finances, and that's the moment I decide to stop having Ellie line up new appearances for me as I finish out the commitments I've already made.

Before I know it, I wake up on the morning of the first event for my foundation. Desiree has been working tirelessly to ensure every last detail is taken care of, and she's already out of bed and working on details for the day by the time my alarm wakes me up. It was another late night last night, and I really should've canceled the appearance since I knew I had to be up early today.

I pull on my running shorts and the T-shirt promoting today's event, and I head down to the kitchen where I find Desiree mixing up a couple of protein shakes for us.

"Thanks," I say when she hands mine over, and I bend down for a quick good morning kiss. "What can I do?"

"Nothing. It's all set." She chugs down her shake, and then she follows it up with a banana. She sets her hand over her stomach that's swelling with my baby, and my chest warms. She's wearing a custom-made maternity shirt with *Make a DIFFerence* on the back and *I'm doing it for Asher* on the front.

Each runner will get a similar shirt—not maternity, obviously—and the front will say *I'm doing it for [blank]*. Runners will get a set of markers to fill in the blanks.

"How are you feeling?" I ask.

"My back's a little tight, but overall, I feel okay." She puts one of her hands on her lower back to massage it, and I set my shake down and bat her hand out of the way to massage her lower back for her. I've had enough of these in the training room that I know just how to dig into muscles to give them a little relief.

She leans her head back while I work my magic, and she lets out a soft moan.

"That noise is how you got into this situation in the first place," I say low and raspy into her ear.

She laughs. "You're right, and we don't have time for that this morning. We need to get out the door."

"Let's go."

We head toward the local park she reserved for the event, and vendors are already starting to arrive and set up. Erin gave her two interns to work with, and they're already there checking in the vendors and getting tables set up.

The bounce houses arrive. The cornhole and croquet tournaments are set up. The deejay starts spinning tunes. The course is marked off by the police department. The food trucks and specialty drink trucks pull in.

The Nash family is here to support me, with Lincoln, Grayson, and Spencer all donating hefty sums. My mom is helping pass out T-shirts while my dad is talking to one of the food truck owners, and all three of my brothers and their wives will be running in the event today.

We invited Tanner and Miller, but they couldn't make it this weekend. It's probably for the best since I don't really want today's event to be overshadowed by the twins being around their birth father for the first time publicly. As far as I know, they still haven't met, and word hasn't hit the media yet, either.

I'm sure it won't be long.

We're ready to roll.

I'm nervous, but as runners and their families start to arrive and I greet guests and sign autographs, I discover there is absolutely no reason to be.

Desiree thought of everything, from educational vendors to raffle baskets to games with prizes.

The event is a huge success, and between corporate sponsorships, raffles, donations, and entry fees, we raise just over seventy-five thousand dollars.

Seventy-five thousand dollars.

I'm in awe of this woman.

A week later, our team drafts a new crop of players. OTAs start at the end of May again, and a new season is about to get underway. Desiree becomes hotter and hotter to me as I watch our baby grow in her stomach, and I spend as much time with her as I possibly can, tending to her every need as the house I bought starts to really feel like a home.

She's busy planning for the charity ball, and when the week of the ball is upon us, I'm stuck at mandatory minicamp all week as she puts every last detail into place—including the dress she'll wear to the ball as she chairs it at thirty-five weeks pregnant.

She walks into our kitchen wearing a formal dress with leaves on it—very different from the leaves of last year, but this year she's absolutely glowing.

"You're gorgeous, Des," I say softly.

A small smile lifts her lips, and then she sets a hand on her side. "Oh! That was a big kick right to the ribs. Come here."

I walk over and set my hand on her stomach, and I feel a movement. It's a little jab coming from her stomach, and it's something I never thought I'd care about…but it might just be the most exhilarating feeling in the world.

My eyes meet hers, and her small smile widens. "Can you believe it's the anniversary of the night we met?"

"Who would've thought a year ago that we'd be going to this ball tonight where we are now?" I ask. "You're planning the entire thing, we're going together, we're living together and totally in love and having a baby in just a few weeks?"

"Well, some things didn't change."

I narrow my eyes at her. "Such as?"

"I booked us the biggest suite at the hotel for afterward. Except this time, I packed an overnight bag."

"I'm going to fuck that dress right off of you," I say, and I pull her into my arms.

"Up against the window?"

"Whatever way you want it," I promise, and I lower my lips to hers.

She pulls back abruptly. "Okay, enough of that. You know I have to get to the ball early, and if you keep kissing me, we'll end up late."

"Then let's be late," I groan, and she laughs.

"As hot as you are in that suit, I can't be late tonight." She looks me up and down with a bit of regret that we didn't budget time to fuck before we headed out, and then she sighs. "Damn, you look good."

I glance down at my navy suit with a bright red tie. I guess my fashion choices have calmed a bit over the last few months, but the bright red still feels like me. And I open my jacket and flash the stitching on the inside lining at her.

I put it in the event planner.

Just underneath the words is a silhouette of a pregnant woman.

She giggles and shakes her head.

I shrug. "If I didn't make some sort of bold fashion statement, my brothers would never let me live it down."

"Just don't let my dad see that."

"Fair point. I'll keep it on and only flash it at anyone with the last name Nash."

"Speaking of, what's the latest on the half-brothers situation?" She walks over toward the fridge to grab a bottle of water.

"I talked to Spencer last week, and things are going well with OTAs in San Diego."

"I can't believe both of them were traded to the same team," she says as she moves toward the pantry to grab some snacks to stuff into her purse. "What are the chances?"

I nod. "Now there's three Nashes on the Storm and three who either are or were formerly part of the Aces."

"So weird. How's Spencer doing with it?" she asks. She walks back toward the counter where I'm standing. "You ready to go?"

I nod. "He's actually doing great with it. He's excited to work with both of them, and I think San Diego is going to be the team to beat this year with all that talent in one place." We head out toward the garage and climb into my truck as I'm talking.

"Are they changing their last names?"

I shake my head as I fire up the truck. "No idea. I haven't talked to them much since we found out. Between hitting the offseason, moving in with you, the foundation event, and all the appearances, I've been swamped."

She reaches over and touches my arm. "You should make an effort, Asher. They're family."

"I know. You're right. I keep thinking I've got my own thing going on, but I still make time for Lincoln, Grayson, and Spencer. And everyone will be there tonight, so I'll put in the effort."

"Whatever I can do to help, you know I'm right here."

My eyes soften as I glance over at her. "I know you are."

"Except Monday through Thursday. Don't forget, I'm going to San Diego."

I narrow my eyes at her. "I did forget, and remind me why you think it's a good idea to travel this late in your pregnancy?"

She sighs and rolls her eyes. "I'm only thirty-five weeks. My doctor said it's totally safe up to thirty-six, and even then I'd be fine, but they'd just prefer to keep me close to home." She lifts a shoulder. "And I miss the girls. We're going to have three days of sleepovers and books and chocolate, and then I'll be back before you know it."

"I'll miss you," I say, my chest tightening as I reach over and grab her hand.

"I'll miss you, too. But we have tonight and tomorrow."

I grimace. "Not tomorrow night. It's my last nightclub appearance."

"Again?" she asks, and I sense a bit of accusation in her tone.

"I promise to make it up to you."

"Cancel it," she demands. "Stay home with me tomorrow. We don't have that many more nights before the baby gets here, and then who knows how our lives will be turned upside down?"

She's right. And if this will make her know that she's my top priority, then I'll do it.

Chapter 60: Asher Nash

What's Beneath the Leaves This Time

Desiree perfected every last detail for the ball. She had a team helping her put it together, and I did what I could over the last few weeks, but this wonderland tonight is one hundred percent thanks to her hard work.

I'm blown away, and it seems like everyone else here tonight is, too.

Jolene is standing by the entry, greeting guests and interviewing them for the podcast she hosts with my brother. Grayson and Ava are over by the bar, chatting with Spencer and Grace, and the Nash family is out in full force tonight, including Tanner and Miller, who are heading together toward the bar.

My dad is across the room.

I'm fairly certain this is the first time my dad will be in the same room as his two sons, and I wish it would happen any night but tonight. I want everything to go well for Des, and I don't want to be distracted by my family.

But that's what my dad seems to do, even when he doesn't mean to.

"What are you drinking?" I ask Desiree as she talks with Jolene.

"Sprite would be great," she says, and she turns back to my sister-in-law.

I head toward the bar, and I spot Ellie on my way. I pull her aside. "Can you cancel tomorrow night?"

Her brows dip. "Are you sure?"

I get her hesitation. She's been amazing about finding me different opportunities, and I hate to cancel given how hard I've worked to rebuild my reputation.

But it's taking its toll on Desiree, and I can't allow that anymore—especially not as we close in on the final weeks of her pregnancy. I don't want to miss a single moment with her.

"Positive," I tell her, and she smiles at me as if she thinks I'm making the right choice.

I know I am.

I head toward the bar and greet my brothers—the three standing there, anyway. It still sounds so strange to me that there are two more in the mix. Spencer, Tanner, and Miller aren't part of the Vegas Aces organization, but they're family, and that's enough to get them a golden ticket in.

I missed the greetings between my brothers and half-brothers in my detour to talk to Ellie, but I walk up to them just as I hear Tanner say to Grayson, "We heard Eddie's here."

Grayson nods across the room. "He's over there. You know, the tall guy that looks like an older, out of shape, not as attractive version if you mixed the five of us together, not counting Linc since he favors Mom."

The twins both look over at our dad. Of course they know who he is. They're pro football players, and Eddie Nash is a legend.

"I need to sit," Desiree says, walking up beside me with her hand on her stomach.

"Can someone order her a Sprite? And a whiskey for me, please," I say to my brothers as I walk her over toward one of the tables nearby.

I sit with her, and Grayson delivers our drinks a minute later. "You doing okay?" he asks Des, and she nods.

"I'll be doing better when the night is over." She smiles, and Ava sneaks her some little miniature cake things that she baked for the event.

Grace sits with her a while, too, and it's like Des just fits in with the family. She's met my sisters-in-law a few times now, and each time they seem to grow closer. I'm pretty sure Grace and Des are on a regular texting basis now, and they share the San Diego link since Grace now lives there full time with my brother.

I don't get to see what's going on with Tanner and Miller, though I'm sure someone will fill me in later.

We eventually move to the table we're assigned to and sit through most of the event. Desiree only gets up when she has to, and I stick by her side just in case she needs anything. She may be the main planner for the event, but the event is hosted by the chairpeople—including Lincoln, Erin, Jack and Luke Dalton, Travis Woods, and Ben Olson.

We dance a bit, and someone is always stopping by to sit with us, from my mom to my brothers to their wives to my teammates. I don't even get to flirt with her about seeing what's beneath the leaves this time because someone is always with us.

Her parents are across the room and spend most of their time with the general manager, but her mom swings by to check on her every now and again.

She's doing amazingly well for being thirty-five weeks pregnant, and as the night draws to a close, we dance once more before we head up to our hotel room.

"Don't go to San Diego," I beg of her.

"Don't go to your appearance tomorrow night," she shoots back.

"I told Ellie to cancel it."

Her head whips over to me. "You did?"

I nod, and her eyes soften.

She wanders over to the window, and I move in behind her, my cock hard as I anticipate what comes next.

If she's up to it.

If not…it'll be a long, cold shower, I guess.

I thrust my hips against her ass, and she moans as she pushes her ass back against me.

I pull her hair to one side and drag my lips along her neck.

"I've been waiting to get this body naked all night," I murmur. I reach down and grip the fabric of her dress, and she shivers a little. "I need to see what's beneath the leaves."

She chuckles at my reference to a year ago, but then she moans again as I pepper kisses along her warm skin.

My brother was right about one thing: pregnancy sex is fucking incredible.

Her body is changing, and it's mind-blowingly remarkable. Knowing that she's growing our baby and the things she's putting her body through to do it makes me feel ways that are completely unexpected.

I'm in total awe of her, and the way it affects me takes me by surprise every single time the wave of emotion plows into my chest.

My love for her seems to grow exponentially and inexplicably by the day, and every moment we spend together verifies to me that I want to spend every other moment I possibly can with her.

It's as if I fall in love with her more every day, and just when I think I can't possibly love her more than I already do, I fall a little harder.

I pull the fabric up still more until I'm able to lift it over her head and deposit it on the floor beside us. I slide her panties down her legs, and I unhook the bra holding her engorged tits hostage.

She's naked, and she's beautiful.

"Press those gorgeous tits against the window," I say, and she tries, but her stomach gets in the way. I rest my hands over her belly, and she sighs contentedly. I raise one hand to her tit and lower the other one until I'm pushing a finger into her, and she moans as she leans back into me.

"Fuck, Des. Your body is perfect, and your pussy is soaked."

"I was waiting all night for this," she admits, her voice raspy with need.

Last time we were here, I remember sliding a finger into her and not giving her friction. I was playing with her. Seeing how far I could push her and how much it would take to get her to climax. It was supposed to just be one night, and fuck, look at us now, staring at the edge of forever.

I give her friction this time. I don't want to make her stand too long, but the easiest position these days is doggy style or her on top.

So rather than make her wait, I finger her for a few hot beats as she rides my hand, and then I pull my finger out, unbuckle my belt, and say, "Palms on the window."

It forces her to bend forward a little and stick her ass out toward me, and I slide right into that hot, wet cunt.

She groans with need as I start to move inside her, and I know I won't last long tonight. She always feels good, like her body was made for mine, and maybe it was.

I pick up the pace, my body slamming into hers as she claws at the window, our moans and grunts filling the air with the sound of our bodies slapping together.

I feel my balls tighten. "Oh fuck, fuck, fuck," I growl. "I'm about to come."

"Me too," she cries, and I lean forward to brush my fingers along her clit as my body explodes into hers. My hands move haphazardly along her slick cunt as jet after jet of hot come fills her completely, and she cries my name over and over while we ride through the hot climax together.

Once our bodies hit the peak and start to come back down, I pull out of her and lead her over to the bed. She sits on the edge while I grab a washcloth to help her clean up, and then we climb into bed together. She leans over for a kiss goodnight, but rather than just a quick kiss, her lips linger on mine. I open my mouth to hers as urgency takes over, and we kiss a while just like that before she pulls back.

"I love you," she says.

"I love you, too. Tonight was incredible, Des, and it's all because of you."

Her eyes soften even in the dark, and my heart feels full.

We wake in the morning after a successful event, and I order breakfast in bed. We spend the day laughing together, and we spend the night wrapped together as I press my hand to her stomach.

She's right. We won't get many more nights with just the two of us, and I'm grateful I canceled the appearance for this moment in time together.

And even though I canceled my appearance, she decides not to cancel her trip to visit her friends, which gives us even fewer nights together before the baby arrives.

Chapter 61: Desiree Dixon

Myers Briggs

These three days away from each other will do us some good, I think. Being pregnant comes with a whole host of pressures, and doing it away from my three best girlfriends as I adjust to a whole new life—one my father wholeheartedly still disapproves of—has been harder than I thought it would be.

Which is why I burst into tears as I stand on their front porch when they open the door.

"Oh my God, what's wrong?" Chloe asks as she throws open the door.

"I miss you three so much!" I wail as all three women somehow toss their arms around me at the same time.

They took time off work—well, Lauren did. Chloe and Addy are on summer break, and it feels so, so good to be back here with my best friends.

"How's everything with Asher?" Addy asks once I've stopped sobbing and Lauren has hauled my suitcase into Addy's room, where I'll be sleeping for the next couple of nights.

"It's good," I say. "I mean, my dad hates us together, and I have no idea what the future is going to be for us, but other than that, things are great." I force a fake smile.

The three women stare at me with their jaws slightly slackened.

"Whoa, whoa, whoa," Lauren says, holding up a hand. "Back the truck up and start at the beginning."

We walk into the family room, and I sit on the couch, where I recount the latest details about my father's disapproval of the father of my baby.

I set my hand on my stomach as I feel a deep shot to the ribs. "Ugh," I gasp. They look at me in alarm. "I'm fine." I rub my ribs where the baby just kicked.

I feel another big kick, but this one feels different.

I gasp again, and while the kick is normally a quick jab, this starts with a jab but feels like a tight, dull ache that seems to put pressure on my back.

That's new.

I haven't felt that one before.

I gasp again, and my friends stare at me.

"Are you having a contraction?" Lauren asks.

My brows dip together. "No! No way. I'm only thirty-five weeks. It's too early for contractions."

"Maybe those Myers Briggs ones?" Chloe suggests.

"Do you mean Braxton Hicks?" Lauren asks her, and I want to laugh at the two of them, but I can't. I'm nervous now that Lauren mentioned contractions. Is that what that was?

The pain seems to pass after thirty seconds or so, and I draw in a deep breath. "Anyway, so my dad still hasn't given us his blessing. He actively tried to get Asher traded, but the head coach is his brother, and he fought for Asher to stay. I guess my dad and Asher got close during the season, and my dad felt like it was a huge betrayal that we were sleeping together in secret the whole time."

Addy wrinkles her nose. "I can't imagine my dad knowing I slept with anybody."

I lift a shoulder. "Get knocked up and everyone will know."

"Ew!" Chloe makes a face. "Imagine being pregnant in front of a classroom of middle schoolers. They're old enough to know and immature enough to gossip about it."

"I'd sooner quit," Addy says. "Aside from that, how are things with you and Asher?"

I sigh in total contentment. Well, as content as one can be at thirty-five weeks pregnant. "Blissful. He's attentive and sweet, and he's really stepped up. I feel like we're ready for this."

We shift topics to what everyone else has been up to. I feel another sharp jab that turns into a pressure ache in my back again. I gasp as the laughter falls from my lips, and my friends stare at me.

"Babe, that was only nine minutes since the last time you made that face," Lauren says. "I have a new mom client who told me all about labor and contractions, and I think we need to take you to the hospital."

"Stop it," I scold, even though the pressure is still there. "It's not labor. You're being ridiculous." I suck in a deep breath. I just got here. I'm just settling in from traveling. It's the stress of traveling, of being away from Asher. Right? That has to be it.

Except nine minutes later, it hits again.

"Let's go," Lauren says. "We're taking you in just to get checked out."

I nod a little nervously. "Okay."

I text Asher on the way just to keep him in the loop.

Me: *I made it to San Diego safe and sound. I love you.*

His reply is immediate.

Asher: *I love you, too. How are you feeling?*

Me: *Totally fine, but my friends are worried about the kicks I keep getting from the baby, so they're taking me to get checked out.*

I watch as Asher types out a reply.

Asher: ...

Before it comes through, however, my phone starts to ring.

"Hi," I answer a little weakly.

"What do you mean they're making you get checked out?" he roars.

"We're on our way to the doctor."

"The doctor? Just a regular doctor?" he asks.

I clear my throat. "The hospital."

"Are you really okay?" he demands.

"I don't know," I admit. "It might be contractions, so we're getting me checked just to rule it out."

"I'm on my way."

"Asher, no, it's fine. I'll be fine. It's just a sharp pain every nine min—"

"I'm on my way," he hisses again, and then he cuts the call.

And somehow…I feel a big measure of relief that he's coming.

I love my friends, and it's great being here with them. But there's nothing like the arms of Asher to make me feel safe, warm, and secure.

We arrive at the hospital before I get a chance to call my mom to let her know what's going on. I'm sure it's nothing—probably just Braxton Hicks like Chloe suggested, so there's no need to worry her.

Except I'm not admitted into the emergency room, and instead I'm sent straight to labor and delivery.

A nurse attaches some belts around me to monitor the baby, and then she does a quick exam. "You're four centimeters dilated and in active labor. How far along are you?"

"Thirty-five weeks."

She nods. "Preterm," she murmurs. "Ideally, we'd want the baby in there a little longer, but we'll run some tests to make sure the baby isn't in any distress. The doctor will be in shortly to discuss the best course of action. Is the father involved?"

I nod. "He's on his way from Vegas. I'm in town visiting friends."

"Those are the women who brought you in?" she asks.

"Yes."

"They're good friends." She studies the screens that are monitoring the baby.

"The best. And Asher—the father—he told me not to travel, but I thought I'd be safe." I feel tears welling behind my eyes. It'll be at least a couple hours before Asher can get here. What if I have the baby before then? What if he misses it all because I had to visit my friends one more time? Why did I think this was a good idea?

I'm scared, and I'm alone. "Can they come back here?" I ask.

"Only one nonrelative at a time," she says apologetically.

"Addy," I say immediately.

"Give me two seconds, and I'll go get her." She returns a moment later with Addy and also with the doctor. Addy rushes over and holds my hand as we watch the doctor glance at the screen and look over at me.

The doctor does a quick pelvic check, and then she says, "We have some good news, Ms. Dixon. There are no signs of infection, and the baby's heart rate is stable. We don't have any concerns with your health right now, so I think that while it's a little earlier than we'd ideally like, we're safe to proceed with the delivery. We'll let things progress naturally and see how it goes."

Addy glances at her watch, and she excuses herself. Less than a minute later, my mom and dad appear in the doorway.

I burst into tears.

"What are you doing here?" I ask as they rush over to me. My dad stands beside me a bit awkwardly, and my mom sets her hand on my stomach as I brush away the tears.

"We'll get to that in a minute. How are you?" she asks.

"I'm okay. Scared, but okay. Asher's on his way…" I glance over at my dad, and he nods.

"I know." His voice is flat and serious, and I can't get a read on what he's thinking.

"He called us," my mom says.

"He did?" I sniffle.

She nods. "We were here in San Diego. Dad had a rare few days off, so we flew out to visit with our friends here. Lucky break."

"Asher called you?"

She nods, her eyes getting a little misty. "He called your father."

My chest squeezes at that.

The contractions are still about seven to eight minutes apart, but I haven't dilated past four centimeters—which is good since it gives Asher time to arrive.

It's over an hour after my parents arrive when Asher appears in the doorway.

They excuse themselves as I burst into tears yet again. What a freaking emotional roller coaster.

He stands in the doorway after they leave, and he stares across the small space at me. He rushes across the room and drops his lips to mine, his hand moving on top of my stomach.

I feel safe again. I feel like I can do this.

Without him, I was scared. Even when my parents got here, I was still scared.

But Asher's here now, and he always knows how to make everything okay.

It's what I've come to rely on.

And that's what tells me the one thing that's become very clear to me over the last few months. No matter what happens over the next couple days…this is the man I'm meant to spend the rest of my life with.

Chapter 62: Asher Nash

She's About to Be a Mother

"**A**sher, honey, I don't know how to thank you for calling us." Desiree's mom pulls me into a tight hug.

We're still waiting for the action to really get started. She's dilated six centimeters now, and contractions are starting to come a little more frequently at six minutes, but the doctor says we still have lots of time.

She can't eat anything, but I can, and I am a growing boy. Or I'm an athlete who has fairly strict dietary concerns even in the offseason.

Addy is in with her now, and I'm about to grab a bite to eat with Coach Dixon and Sue.

"Before we go down, can I talk to both of you?" Nerves climb through my chest as I make myself say the words.

"Of course. Anything," Sue says as Coach continues to narrow his eyes at me.

"Look, Coach, I'm sorry we kept this from you. We both knew how you'd feel about the two of us together before we had a chance to give it a real shot. But I've known your daughter now for the better part of a year. We're about to have a baby together. I know it's not what you want, but I'm not going anywhere. Like it or not, I'll be a part of your family for the rest of my life. I'll always be there for Des and the baby, and I want nothing more than to marry her and to spend the rest of my life with her. I may not be good enough for her, but I'll sure as hell try every single day to be. I love her more than I've ever loved anyone in my life, and I'm begging you for your blessing before I go in there and ask her to marry me." The words come out rushed and nervous and *genuine*.

He studies me and then glances at his wife.

She gives him an encouraging smile. "You know how I feel about it." She raises her brows pointedly. "Bill, she's about to be a mother. Let her be happy. Let her go."

He draws in a deep breath, and he presses his lips together before he answers my question. "I always knew she was going to end up with somebody like you." He shakes his head a little. "It's why I warned her off players. But you, Asher Nash...I think you're her other half in pretty much every way. It pains me to admit it because I always wanted better for her than I was able to give her mother. I've gotten to know you pretty well over the last year, and I think that's why it hurt that you didn't feel like you could tell me that you were seeing her. But to know that you'd still reach out to us to make sure we knew when she was going through something despite the way I've treated you...well, it means the world to me. And seeing you drop everything to get to her in her time of need tells me exactly the kind of husband and father you'll be for her and my grandchild. I know that she's getting better with you than what I was able to give because I don't know that I would've been able to do that knowing how much Sue's dad hated me."

I glance over at Desiree's mom, and she brushes away a tear on her cheek.

"I hope you don't hate me, sir."

"I don't," he says, shaking his head. "Far from it. And that's why of course I'll give you my blessing."

Relief filters through me at his words, and I can't help when I leap at him and pull him into a hug. "Thank you," I murmur, overcome with emotion.

"Don't let her down."

"You have my word," I promise.

We head down to get food, and once we're sitting with plates in front of us, Sue asks, "So when are you going to do it?"

"I hadn't really thought about it, but I suppose I'd like to do it right away. It's sort of feels like the final piece of the puzzle to make our family complete once the baby's here."

She clasps her hands together. "I think that might be the sweetest thing I've ever heard."

We finish our dinner and head back up to Desiree.

"How's progress?" I ask as soon as I walk in. I head over to her and press my lips to hers as I set my hand to her stomach.

"Moving along," she says. "The doctor says I'm at eight centimeters now."

"What does that mean?"

She shrugs. "I guess it means we're getting closer."

She's not wrong. It's not long before the doctor comes in and lets her know it's time to start pushing.

Her parents leave the room so it's just the two of us, the doctor, and two nurses. The nurse shows me how to hold one of her legs up as she holds the other leg, and when the next contraction hits, Des has to push.

Her red hair flies around her shoulders with each heave of her body, and I've never felt more in awe of another human being in my entire life. She literally grew our baby in there over the last thirty-five weeks, and now she's pushing it out of her body and into the world. What a fucking phenomenon.

She pushes with everything she has, but it's not quite enough.

After an hour of pushing, I can tell she's starting to get tired, but she's not about to give up now.

"Okay, the next one's starting," the nurse says as she watches the screen.

"Give it everything you've got, Desiree," the doctor says.

I grab onto her leg with one arm and grab her hand with the other. She squeezes the shit out of my hand as she pushes with all her might, and a moment later, the baby slips from her with a loud cry.

A loud cry.

That's a good thing.

The anxiety that has filled my chest all day knowing that he or she is coming early seems to ease a little at that cry, and the nurse's next words leave me with this feeling of pride and love and wonder that fills me to my very soul.

"It's a boy."

The nurse hands me scissors to cut the umbilical cord, and I watch as they take the baby for just a moment to examine him and clean him up.

His lungs are definitely working based on the little cries he's producing as he's introduced to this strange and wonderful world.

"He looks healthy," the nurse says as she sets the baby on Desiree's chest, and I'm looking at her as she looks down at our son. *Our son.* Tears stream down her face, and emotion clogs the back of my throat as I look at the two people I love most in the entire universe.

I don't even know his name yet, and I love him more than I ever knew I could love another person.

"Do we have a name yet, Mom and Dad?" one of the nurses asks in the periphery, and hearing someone call me *Dad* for the first time is a bit of a shock.

We haven't discussed *boy* names. She seemed so sure it was a girl that we only tossed around girl names. She liked Miley, and I liked Cassie. But boy names?

I have no idea.

She glances up at me, and I see the light in her eyes. "Jacob?" she asks softly.

My chest aches at the tribute to my best friend. I think about how much more Jake was than his final moments, about how he was adventurous and fun, always up to meet a new challenge, always laughing, always smiling.

That's what I want for my boy.

I can see this kid being my little best friend as we go on adventures together. We'll go to parks, and he'll ride on my shoulders as we hike up mountains, and we'll travel and see the world as a family.

"Are you sure?" I ask.

She nods.

"What about William for the middle name?" I ask.

"After my dad?" she asks, brushing a tear away.

I nod.

"Jacob William Nash," she repeats, looking down at our boy.

He has a light dusting of dark hair on his head, and I think he'll look a lot like me. Maybe someday down the line, we'll have a little girl who will have gorgeous red hair like her mother, and I'll keep her inside until she's thirty-five because if she's anything at all like her mother, I'm in big, big trouble.

"It's perfect," we say at the same time.

We spend the first hour of Jake's life as a quiet family of three. He lays on her chest, and the two of us gaze at him in wonder as he starts to calm. He falls asleep, and I press my lips to his forehead.

I can't believe he's mine.

I can't believe *she* is mine.

The nurse takes the baby and shows me how to swaddle him—which I immediately forget—and hands him to me. I stare down at him before I hand him to his mom, and I can't believe we're parents now.

These are the two people I will prioritize and love and adore and sacrifice everything for…for the rest of my life.

"Marry me," I whisper softly, brushing my lips across her temple.

Her eyes lift from the baby up to mine. Her brows are a little furrowed, and her eyes are rimmed in red and watery as the tears continue to fall.

She's never looked more beautiful. She nods as her eyes connect with mine. "Yes."

I lean down, and my lips collide with hers just as they'll do thousands of times to come. She'll hold our son and maybe another one or a daughter down the road if we're so lucky, and we'll kiss and remember this moment right now. I feel like I'm at the peak of love, on the precipice of emotions, and yet I also know there's so much more to come, that I'll fall more in love with her every single day just as I have since the night we met despite the trials and tribulations we've faced.

I pull back and lean my forehead to hers as this new sensation of joy bursts through me.

We revel in this feeling for a few minutes, and then she whispers, "I need a cheeseburger."

I bark out a laugh so loud that I almost wake the baby. He jerks in his sleep but doesn't wake, and I let out a breath.

I'll need to get a handle on my volume, I guess.

The nurse puts in a call to the cafeteria, and before the food comes up, I ask her if she wants me to call her parents in. She nods, and I turn to walk out to get them.

"Wait," she says.

I back up and move in beside her.

"Do you think it's okay to tell them that I just agreed to marry you? That was genuine, right? Not, like, out of emotions in the moment?" She's fretting, and I try to come up with the right words that will ease her fears.

Only one thing comes to mind. "I asked your parents for their blessing earlier today."

Her jaw slackens. "You did? So...this was planned?"

I chuckle. "I didn't really have a plan for where or when, and I don't have a ring to give you, but I will. I know I want to spend my life with you. So I asked, and I got the blessing. From both of them."

"Both of them?" she repeats. "Oh, Asher." She bursts into tears again, and somehow, I know, I just *know*, that life is going to be full of these wonderful emotions together.

For the rest of our lives.

Chapter 63: Desiree Dixon

A Minivan with Ninjas Painted on the Side

I glance up as Asher walks into the private room we were moved to after recovery with my mom and dad, and all three of them are smiling. I wonder what I'm missing and what they're smiling about.

My dad and Asher are walking into a room together. *Smiling.*

A deep and pure happiness seems to fill me at a time when I already thought I was at the peak of happiness.

Somehow, this life just keeps getting better and better.

"Hey, Grandma and Grandpa," I murmur with a smile. The baby is swaddled—something the nurse did since I'm still learning what that even means—and he's sleeping, but I got a look at his eyes before, and they're Asher blue.

He's perfect.

Both the baby and the baby's daddy.

Asher dropped everything to travel over three hundred miles to be by my side even when we didn't know if I was actually in labor, and the thought that I'm not a priority to him is long cast aside. I know he'd do anything for me, including calling my parents to ensure I wasn't alone here when he knew how upset my dad was with him. Including finding some way to patch things up with my dad—a story I *still* haven't heard, but one I'm sure they'll fill me in on someday.

My dad stares at the baby in my arms, and my mom clasps her hands in front of her and pulls them up to her chest.

"Would you like to hold him?" I ask them.

"Ooh, me first," my mom begs, and I laugh.

"Wash your hands first, please," the nurse says, and my mom complies with the request before she walks over toward me. The nurse ducks out to give us more space, though Asher somehow talked them into giving me what has to be the biggest room in this place.

Asher moves in beside me on the far side from the door, and my dad stands at the foot of the bed while my mom washes at the sink by the door.

"What's his name?" my dad asks, and I wait for my mom to walk back over as I stare down at him.

"Meet Jacob William Nash," I say, handing him carefully over to my mom as if he'll break.

"Jacob William?" my dad repeats. "William?"

I look up at him and nod, and the big, tough football coach looks like he's about to cry.

God, just the thought of it makes *me* cry. These hormones are no joke. I thought I'd go back to normal now that the baby is out, but I guess not.

I look at my mom, who looks so happy and content as she holds the baby, and the thought that my parents would ever not be okay with *whoever* I ended up with is the furthest thought from my mind.

My dad was upset, and I get that. Two people who are important to him kept something big from him, and he threw a tantrum. If anyone ever wondered where my stubborn streak came from, well, it's pretty easy to see it now.

My mom coos quietly to Jake, and Asher leans down and brushes his lips to my temple.

The doctor said it will be six to eight weeks before I can have sex, and I am *not* looking forward to that.

I mean…I'm not exactly horny mere hours after delivering a baby, but fuck, Asher looks hot as a daddy. Seeing him as he holds our newborn would've made my ovaries explode if they weren't currently recovering from a pretty damn big explosion.

My dad washes his hands next, and he awkwardly takes the baby from my mom. My mom slings her arm around my dad's waist as they smile lovingly down at their grandchild, and my dad looks up at Asher before his eyes move to me.

"You did good, kids."

I grin, and Asher chuckles.

"Oh, and Dad?" I say. He glances up at me, and I smile. "Thanks for giving Asher your blessing. I said yes."

"Oh!" my mom squeal-gasps, and I laugh as she lets go of my dad to rush over to the bed to grab me gently up into a tight hug.

I only stay in the hospital for forty-eight hours after delivery, and as it turns out, we were lucky that the baby was the son of a football player since he was a big baby. He had developed perfectly despite the preterm scare, and he's ready to go home with us when I'm discharged.

He's too little to fly, so Asher rents a minivan, and after a tearful goodbye with Addy, Chloe, and Lauren, I sit in the backseat and stare at the sleeping baby for the better part of the five-hour drive back home.

"This thing's pretty fucking sweet," Asher tells me at one point about the minivan, and I can't help a laugh. It would be exactly Asher's style to get a souped-up minivan to tool around town in, if I'm being perfectly honest. And knowing him, it would probably have ninjas or tigers painted on the side just to really irritate the shit out of his brothers.

We walk into the house with Jake in his car carrier and find a surprise party waiting for us—a quiet one, anyway, filled with my future in-laws here to give us gifts and meet the newest Nash. They all whisper, "Surprise!" when we walk in, and Missy rushes up to us first.

"Congratulations, my sweet girl," she says to me with a huge hug. "On everything. The baby, the engagement, just all of it."

"Thank you," I say softly with a smile, and she looks down into the carrier I'm holding at her grandson.

"Oh my goodness, he's absolutely perfect!"

"He is," I agree with zero modesty.

He wakes up, and he's ready to meet everyone—after he eats first, of course—and it's a big Nash family party with Lincoln, Grayson, and Spencer, along with their wives, Lincoln's stepson and daughter, Missy, and even Tanner and Miller.

The only one *not* here is Eddie, and it isn't until after Grace heads up the cleaning crew so we don't have to lift a finger and then everyone leaves that I ask Asher about it.

"My guess is he didn't want to face the entire family with our half-brothers here. The charity ball was one thing. He could escape there. Here? Nowhere to go." He shrugs, and he pulls his phone out of his pocket. "But he did text me with an apology. He claims he had to work, but last I checked, he didn't even have a job." He shrugs. "We haven't spoken much since I moved out."

"Hm," I murmur with a shrug, and then I get back to my new favorite activity in the world—holding the baby and staring down at his precious little face.

"I need to run a quick errand. Will you still be awake when I get home?"

I laugh. "Me or the baby?"

"You. I know he'll still be sleeping since he's only awake for a total of about six hours a day."

I laugh. "And collectively, those hours are all at night when we want to sleep."

"Exactly."

It's our first night at home with the baby, and it'll definitely be an adjustment. We were able to get some rest at the hospital when the nurses took the baby out to give us a break, but we won't have that at home.

Asher leans over and kisses me. "Be right back."

"We'll be here." I say it in a cooing voice like I'm talking to the baby.

"Need anything while I'm out?" he asks.

"Just your quick return since we'll miss you while you're gone."

He grins. "You got it."

He's only gone about an hour, and I must doze off with the baby in his bassinet right next to me as I lay on the couch because I didn't realize he was back until I feel the couch dip beside me.

"Sorry. I didn't mean to wake you."

"It's okay. I could use some dinner. Where'd you go?"

"I picked up dinner. Scallops and mushroom soup."

I smile as I sit up and stretch, and I wince a little at the sharp pain below deck. It's sort of like a bruise every time I sit after pushing a baby with a head the size of a watermelon out of there.

I pad over to the kitchen table, where I find mac and cheese, chicken fingers, fries, and chicken noodle soup. I glance over at my future husband. "You got all this for me?"

"Addy told me it's your comfort food meal, and I added in the chicken soup since I made you some the day your stomach flu turned out to be Jake."

I giggle. "That's really sweet."

He moves in behind me, and he wraps his arms around me. "Get used to being taken care of because I plan to do it for the rest of my life."

I spin in his arms and lift to my tiptoes to press a kiss to his lips. "I love you."

He smiles down at me, and then he lets go of me without saying it back. Instead, he bends down and kneels on one knee. "I love you, too. And the first time I asked, it wasn't in the traditional way, so I wanted to ask you again." He reaches into his pocket and pulls out a ring. "Desiree Joy Dixon, will you marry me?"

My lips tip up. I'm in sweatpants and a T-shirt stained with breastmilk, and my hair is piled in a messy bun on top of my head. I'm exhausted and could use a shower, and we won't be able to seal this promise with sex for another six to eight weeks. And somehow, it's perfect. "Yes."

He slips the ring onto my finger as he grins at me, and I can't help but stare at him as he pushes to a stand. His dark blue eyes are heated on me, and those full lips are tipped up into a smile. He hasn't shaved in a few days, and his scruff somehow makes him even hotter, and he's wearing a T-shirt that proclaims he's the best dad ever.

I never believed in fate until she deposited me directly into the chair right beside the tight end I always dreamed of. And that was just the start of our happily ever after.

Epilogue: Desiree Dixon

The Universal Invitation

A Month Later

"Jakey Jakey, eggs and bac-ey," I singsong, and Asher laughs.

"I don't think bac-ey is a word," he points out.

"But it rhymes with Jakey, and it's what I want for breakfast."

Jake is a month old today, and it's also the last Wednesday we have with Daddy before training camp starts.

Oh, and for the record...Asher *loves* it when I call him *Daddy*.

Somehow hearing him call me Mommy is pretty damn satisfying, too, but just not in the sexual sense with which he likes his own moniker. Except we're still waiting on the doctor's green light, and it's been a month filled with hand jobs, blow jobs, and the best oral sex of my life as he worships my pussy with his mouth.

Somehow, about a week after I delivered the baby, I was suddenly *ready* for all the things, but to avoid the risk of infection, we're listening to the doctor's orders.

It's hard, though. And so is Asher. Constantly.

He'll be at training camp by the time I can have sex, and then we'll be apart for a couple of weeks as he goes to California to train with the team.

I'm not looking forward to two weeks away from him. Two weeks alone with the baby. Two weeks on my own.

Well...sort of. My mom is going to stay here with me for those two weeks since Dad will be gone, too, and it'll give her lots of time to bond with the baby. Missy is also coming out and staying with us, and Addy is still on summer break and is coming, too. So, it'll be slumber parties with my bestie, my mom, and my future mother-in-law as we all gaze at Jake.

I'll miss the hell out of Asher, and I know he's devastated to miss two entire weeks with the baby, but I'm focusing on how much fun the girl time will be.

I feel the love and support of the Nash family as Jolene, Ava, and Grace all text or call me daily to check on me. Jolene has been a fountain of information when it comes to babies since Josephine is two years and three months old...and Jolene is pregnant again.

She hasn't told anyone except me yet—well, and her husband—and it only slipped out when we were chatting about the joys of pregnancy. I'm fairly certain I can keep a secret, but it's going to be hard to hold that one in with Missy here.

I lift the baby into my arms as he squirms a little, and I sit on the couch to feed him while Asher gets some bacon into the oven.

"Grace said Spencer's getting close with the twins," I say absently from the couch.

"Spencer told me that, too," he says. I hear him slide the pan into the oven, which means just twenty minutes until hot, fresh, delicious bacon. "He said exactly what I suspected when I met them. Tanner is a mix of Grayson and Lincoln, and Miller is a mix of Spence and me."

"I can't imagine a mix of Spencer and you. Logical and wild? They don't go together."

He chuckles as he walks over and sits next to me. "More the fact that it's the quiet ones you have to watch out for."

"Tanner is going to kill it out there," I say. Tanner Banks is one hell of a quarterback. He led his previous team to a championship and to six winning seasons, but after butting heads with a new head coach, he was actively seeking a trade.

It was a blockbuster deal that also included Miller, and now he'll be leading Spencer—the brother he didn't even know he was related to—as well as his twin brother as the team's new quarterback.

It'll be fun watching them this season, and even more fun knowing that someday they'll be my brothers-in-law, too. As a San Diego Storm fan, I can't help but be thrilled that the team acquired the type of talent the Banks brothers have.

The baby finishes eating, and I lift him to burp him. I cradle him in my arms, and I know he won't always be big enough for me to do this, so I'm soaking in every sweet moment I have with him.

I can't help but think about the future. Will he turn out to be a football player like his daddy and both his grandfathers? Or will he turn away from football as a way to stubbornly set his own path? Who knows where time will lead him, but I'm excited to be a part of every single second of it.

He's sleeping, and the bacon is ready, so I join Asher in the kitchen as he pulls the steaming tray out of the oven.

I moan as I take a bite, and he visibly shifts in his chair with each of my moans.

"You need to stop that. You're tempting me again."

I laugh a little, and then I moan again, just for good measure.

We each have a few pieces, and then he glances at me and raises his brows as he nods upstairs. It's the universal invitation for sexy time, and my eyes light up as I nod.

We carry Jake's bassinet into his room, where he'll be next to a monitor in case we need to listen for him, and then we head toward our bedroom down the hall.

We steal these moments when we can, and that tells me we'll always make time for each other. I love that even after a year of knowing each other, I still can't get enough of him. I can't wait to make him my husband, and we decided we're going to wait until the season is over. The end of February is the perfect time for us, and I've started looking at venues. It'll obviously have to be the event of the season given my profession, and I think I want a destination wedding, but I haven't decided for sure just yet.

The second we're in our room and Asher closes the door behind us, his mouth finds mine. He kisses me like his life depends on it, and these are the moments I'll think of when I'm missing him next week. He holds me close, our bodies melding together as he kisses me, one of my hands resting on his chest as the other moves around his neck.

He thrusts his hips toward me, and I moan into him.

He pulls back abruptly. "Get naked, and then lay on your back on the bed."

I scramble to do exactly as he says, and he gets naked, too. A moment later, he's moving over me, lavishing my tits with his mouth, sucking as he takes some of the milk that's already filling in even though I just fed Jake.

"Mm," he moans as he keeps sucking. He lifts up from me to look me in the eye. "Why is breastmilk so fucking hot?" He ducks his head back down and sucks some more, and I feel his cock as it moves between my legs.

God, what I wouldn't give for him to rail the hell out of me right now. I'm nearly desperate for it, but it'll still be at least two and a half weeks before we're able to.

He lets go of my breast and lifts off me, and then he turns around, lines up his cock with my mouth, and teases my lips with it as he balances on his hands and bends his head down to my pussy.

He slides his tongue into me before he pulls back and sucks on my clit, and at the same time, he moves his hips so he's fucking my mouth. I bring my hands up to fist his cock as he moves over me, and he moans at the feel.

We pleasure each other like this for a few glorious moments, and then he pulls out of my mouth and lays down, urging me to shift over him so he can get a better taste of my pussy.

"Mm," he hums onto my clit as I slide my lips down his shaft, and as nice as it was laying on my back, the sensation this way is even better. I ride his face as I suck his dick, and hearing his grunts of pleasure at the same time I'm being pleasured is too much for my needy body to handle.

I burst into an orgasm, and it rocks my body, taking me completely by storm as I thrash around. My wild movements push him into his own release as he pumps up into my mouth, and I feel the hot release of his come as I suck.

I swallow around him, draining him of every last drop as my body starts to calm down, and I lick him clean once his cock stops pulsing into my mouth. I collapse beside him, and I'm pretty sure we both fall into a pleasure-induced hazy nap that's very much needed after a month of only getting sleep in two-to-three-hour windows.

I wake with a start about an hour later, and he's sleeping soundly beside me. I head into the shower, and when I emerge, I find my future husband clothed in the bedroom, holding our baby, who appears to be wearing a clean outfit and diaper.

Something about this tough, strong, athletic tight end of mine as a daddy just does it for me. I'm ready to go again as I look at him looking down at our boy, and I could see having ten more kids with him just to watch him hold a baby like this again and again and again.

I can't wait to continue tempting my tight end for the rest of my life.

Bonus Epilogue: Desiree Dixon

Marrying the Tight End

Seven Months Later

We have a lot to celebrate.

Today I'm sliding a ring on Asher's finger, and in a few months, the ring he won a few weeks ago in this year's Super Bowl game will be ready for him to slide onto a different finger.

This year, he went from no rings to having two of them. Big year for Asher Nash.

It's been an emotional and exciting few weeks in both the Dixon and the Nash households, and today we'll stand in front of our families and our closest friends as we join those households into one family.

Addy, Chloe, and Lauren are standing up with me, along with Grace, Ava, and Jolene.

On the other side of the aisle, Asher's best man is his brother Spencer—the first of his brothers that he ever spoke to about our relationship, long before he knew who my dad was.

Also standing up with him are Lincoln, Grayson, Tanner, and Miller along with—believe it or not—Austin Graham.

It shocked me as much as it shocked anybody, but the two of them bonded over fatherhood and football, and once Austin was able to check his ego and do what was best for the Aces, the team managed to find the winning combination they were looking for.

I suspect my dad might've had a little something to do with it, too, though it's not something we've ever really talked about.

Asher and Austin also bonded over the fact that they're both getting married this offseason. All it took was the right women to whip these tight ends into shape.

We talked about having my dad officiate today since he plays such an integral part in both our lives, but we decided we wanted my dad to focus on being the father of the bride. I wanted him to be the one to walk me down the aisle and to take his seat next to my mom, where she stood in the front row holding Jake, who's now eight months old and crawling everywhere.

Instead, we asked Luke Dalton to officiate. He and Ellie were some of my first friends even before I decided to move out here, and Ellie has been an amazing mom friend to me. In fact, I drop Jake off at her house almost daily so I can get some work done since she practically runs a daycare out of her house between her kids and her nieces and nephews, who are all associated with the Aces in different capacities.

Victoria, Tessa, and Mandy have become close friends here in Vegas, and we get together every Wednesday at Victoria's bookstore for book club—even streaming in Addy, Chloe, and Lauren. It's one of my favorite nights of the week because I get a little girl time, and when I get home, I get to walk in the house and see Asher doing his daddy thing with our sweet boy. It melts my heart every single time.

I walk out of the bridal room into a luxurious suite, where my bridesmaids are gathered and waiting for me.

"Oh, Desiree," my mom says, clasping her hands in front of her mouth as she starts to cry. "You are the most beautiful bride I've ever seen."

I walk over and pull her close to me for a tight hug. "Don't cry, Mom. You'll ruin your makeup, and you'll make me cry and ruin mine too."

She laughs, and we cling to each other for a while.

She pulls back and studies me as she holds onto my upper arms. "I'm so proud of you, honey. You're strong and smart and independent and stubborn and the best mommy to my sweet grandson that I ever could've imagined."

I wipe the corners of my eyes. "I knew you were going to make me cry."

"I'm sorry," she sobs, and my dad comes over and puts his arm around her to guide her away.

"You are a beautiful bride," Addy says, and she hands Jake over to me. He makes some little noises that sound an awful lot like *ma-ma-ma-ma*. He does it all the time despite his dad saying *da-da-da-da* to him constantly, and I know soon enough he'll be talking up a storm.

"And this place," Chloe says, holding her hands out to indicate the bridal suite. "This is incredible, Desi."

When I asked Asher where he wanted to get married and where he wanted to spend the first few weeks of the off-season, the answer was the same: Santorini, Greece. But given that we wanted a destination wedding and didn't want to make our entire crew travel nearly seven thousand miles and over twenty-four hours across the world, we ended up at a Berkshire resort in Oahu, Hawaii—a mere six-hour flight to paradise. We basically took over the villas, and we'll be walking down the beach in a few minutes to join together as husband and wife.

We'll stay here two weeks, and then we're taking off to Fiji for two weeks. We haven't decided where we'll go from there, but four weeks away with an eight-month-old is going to be an adventure regardless. And the man I'm about to marry loves nothing more than a grand adventure.

The wedding planner—Angelica, my former boss—appears in the doorway. "It's time." She smiles warmly at me. "You're gorgeous, Desi."

I look down at the elegant beach bridal gown I chose. It's traditional white lace, an A-line, V-neck, backless dress with leaf appliques on tulle as a throwback to the night we met.

My hair is curled in loose waves down my back, the front and sides secured loosely back with a matching leaf clip with pearls.

We thought of every detail today, and hearing that it's time—it's *finally* time—gives me a feeling of joy rather than the anxiety I've dealt with when helping so many brides in the past.

"I'm ready." I smile broadly, and my bridesmaids each hug me before they line up. Angelica leads my mom out first, and she's escorted to her seat. She returns for the bridesmaids, and then it's just my dad and me in the bridal suite as we wait with excitement to walk down the aisle.

"My little Desi-Doo is all grown up," he says softly, his eyes falling to me. "I'm so happy for you, sweetheart."

I rush into his arms. "Thank you, Dad." I sniffle as he hugs me, and then I pull back and brush at the corners of my eyes again.

"He's a good man, and I've already warned him that he'll have to deal with me if he ever hurts you. But he's one of us now, too, and I love him like a son. So…take good care of him, okay?"

My lips tip up. "For the rest of my life."

Angelica appears in the doorway with the signal, and I slip my arm through my dad's elbow. We walk out to where our guests are gathered, and the scene before me takes my breath away. It's scenic with the ocean behind the archway where we'll be married, but I can't see any of that beauty because my eyes have zeroed in on the man I'm about to marry.

In four months, we'll have known each other two entire years, and he still takes my breath away.

Today he's wearing khaki pants and a white linen shirt with a stripe of golden leaves down each side, a throwback to the night we met just like my dress is—something we never discussed when I told him he could pick out whatever he wanted as long as Angelica approved of it.

His brothers sure teased the hell out of him about what he was going to make them wear, but we went with traditional beach wedding attire in white button-down shirts and khaki pants.

I think back to that first night when I slipped into the chair beside him, ate that cheese puff, and then looked around me. He was there smiling at me, and he was right back then. As cheesy as it sounded to me, it was fate. It's what led us here today, where we were always supposed to end up, and I feel like our entire future is as wide and vast as the ocean sprawling in front of me.

My dad stops at the end of the aisle and sets my hand in Asher's.

"Take good care of her," he says to Asher with a hug, and my God, the waterworks are in full effect today.

"For the rest of my life," he vows—the same words I just said to my dad.

Asher's eyes move to me, and I swear he gets a little misty.

My dad moves to sit, and before Luke starts talking, Asher leans into me and presses his lips to my cheek. "You're the most stunning bride who has ever walked down an aisle, and I'm so lucky that you're mine."

"I love you. And you look hot as hell." I wink at him, and he chuckles.

Luke welcomes the guests and says a few words about his own wedding in Hawaii several years ago, and then he performs the ceremony. Twenty minutes later, our guests are clapping as we walk up the aisle and into the tent where we'll party for the next few hours.

Before they're dismissed, though, and before the rest of the bridal party follows us down the aisle, there's a split second where it's just the two of us.

He pulls me into his arms and presses his lips to mine. "Congratulations, Mrs. Nash."

Whoa. The words send an unexpectedly searing ache right between my legs.

Holy shit. I'm a *wife* now.

And I need my husband to fuck me.

He must see the lust in my eyes because he laughs, but then we're no longer alone as our bridal party rushes toward us with hugs and cheers.

We've done it in secret plenty of times. Surely we can escape for a few minutes to our villa to alleviate this ache…right?

We're pulled in opposite directions as we greet our guests. We kept the guest list fairly small, but with Asher's large family and our network of friends, we still ended up with a hundred fifty guests even after paring down the list.

Just before dinner is served, though, I see my chance. People are mingling and moving toward the bar, Jake is content with my mom, and Asher is walking toward me.

I lean into him. "Take me to the room. Now."

He pulls back and looks at me. "Yeah?"

I nod. "Definitely. Now, before someone else pulls one of us away."

He grabs my hand, and we both laugh as we run toward our villa, not caring who sees us as we rush to take a minute—or five—alone even in the midst of this party in our honor.

It's one of the things I love most about my tight end. He'll always put me first, always make me a priority, and always, always, *always* make me see stars as he drives me to pleasure.

And he will.

For the rest of our lives.

THE END

Acknowledgments

Thank you first as always to my husband! Thanks for inventing hours for me to write, for supporting me, and for being the best dad to our sweet babies. I love having you as part of my team, and I love the family we've created together.

Thank you Valentine PR for your incredible work on the launch of this series and this book.

Thank you to Valentine Grinstead, Diane Holtry, Christine Yates, Billie DeSchalit, and Serena Cracchiolo for beta and proofreading. I value your insight and comments so much.

Thank you to Renee McCleary for all you do.

Thank you to my ARC Team for loving this sports world that is so real to us. Thank you to the members of the Vegas Aces Spoiler Room and Team LS, and all the influencers and bloggers for reading, reviewing, posting, and sharing.

And finally, thank YOU for reading. I can't wait to bring more football and more Nash family! I'm so excited for what's coming next!

Cheers until next season!

xoxo,

Lisa Suzanne

About the Author

Lisa Suzanne is an Amazon Top Ten Bestselling author of swoon-worthy superstar heroes, emotional roller coasters, and all the angst. She resides in Arizona with her husband and two kids. When she's not chasing her kids, she can be found working on her latest romance book or watching reruns of *Friends*.

Also by Lisa Suzanne

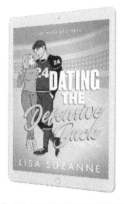

DATING THE DEFENSIVE BACK
(The Nash Brothers #1)

WEDDING THE WIDE RECEIVER
(The Nash Brothers #2)

FIND MORE AT AUTHORLISASUZANNE.COM/BOOKS

Made in the USA
Coppell, TX
31 October 2024